SPIRIT

OF THE

FOX

SPIRIT

OF THE

F*a novel*OX

MATTHEW O'CONNELL

**STATION
SQUARE**
≡ **MEDIA** ≡
New York, New York

SPIRIT OF THE FOX

Published by Station Square Media
115 East 23rd Street, 3rd Floor
New York, NY 10001

Editorial: Write to Sell Your Book, LLC
Cover Design: Kathi Dunn
Interior Design: Vinnie Kinsella
Post Production Management: Janet Spencer King

Printed in the United States of America for Worldwide Distribution.

ISBN: 978-0-9966693-6-8

Electronic editions:
Mobi ISBN: 978-0-9966693-7-5
Epub ISBN: 978-0-9966693-8-2

First Edition
10 9 8 7 6 5 4 3 2

To Mari, my constant companion on this amazing journey.

PROLOGUE

Wherever she looked it seemed like there was nothing but hostile faces. Neighbors who had turned against her family. Their faces were a distorted blur of hatred and anger flickering on a backdrop of black smoke and orange-red flames. They looked like demons. They were taunting her family, yelling horrible things about her and her mother. She huddled close to her mother, who pleaded and begged with the people who used to be their friends but who long ago had turned against her and her family. Her mother sobbed and sheltered her and her younger brother the best she could against a sea of hostility. She held tightly onto both her brother's and her mother's hands. Her father carried an enormous canvas bag on his shoulders. It contained all the essentials they could take from their house before the neighbors set it ablaze. He had a look of both resignation and defiance. Resignation about the inevitability of having to leave their home and their village mixed with a defiance that would over time grow into vengeance.

They slowly made their way out of town while the jeering mob followed them and hurled invectives at them, vile, hurtful words that stung like the acrid smoke from the burning remains of their home. She was confused and frightened. Her little brother was crying, and so was her mother. She tried to be strong, like her father. Gradually, as they came into the fields that surrounded the village, along the dirt paths that led to the rice fields and then to the forest, the sounds of the villagers died down, and they were left with the sound of their own feet, marching steadily on the dusty path. She had no idea where they were headed but was confident that her father had a plan and would deliver them somewhere safe where they could start their life again. The past year, and especially the past three months, had been a literal hell on earth. Anywhere must be better than Izumo. At least, that's what she hoped.

CHAPTER 1

TOKYO
JUNE

Meiko and her father, David, knelt on the floor of their small, swelteringly hot Tokyo apartment, gradually working their way through the cardboard boxes filled with assorted items they felt were essential for their year in Japan. David had taken a visiting scholar position at the prestigious Waseda University. Meiko had finished her undergraduate degree in psychology at UC Santa Barbara two months earlier and decided to take a year off before starting graduate school. She wasn't sure what she wanted to study and hoped this year would give her some inspiration.

David had warned her that their apartment was going to be small and not to pack anything unnecessary, especially since they would likely accumulate more things as they shopped around the seemingly endless shops, boutiques, and department stores of Tokyo.

"Meiko, seriously, I don't know what you're going to do with all of these clothes you packed," said David, shaking his head.

"I was hoping that you would go the minimalist route and I could borrow some space in your closet," Meiko responded with a playful smile.

"Have you seen my closet? I don't know how I'm going to fit the things that I brought with me, let alone the fall, winter, and spring lines from Nordstrom that you seem to have packed. By the way, have you even seen your closet? It's smaller than mine."

Meiko nodded. "Don't worry, Dad. We'll find a way to make it work. I think we're going to have to pick up some dressers to fit some of these clothes into anyway. It'll all fit. Trust me."

David looked at his daughter in playful disbelief. "Why is it when you say, 'trust me,' I get the feeling that somewhere along the line I am going to be ceding most of my precious storage space over to you?"

Meiko laughed. "I'm a girl. You don't need as many clothes as I do. Besides, remember that you're smart, while I'm smart *and* organized. I already have a plan to make this work."

"That's exactly what I'm afraid of," grunted David, continuing to pull things out of the cardboard boxes and suitcases, stopping occasionally to wipe away the sweat that dripped from his forehead, while the small fan in the corner of the room valiantly blew warm air around the apartment. "By the way, are you saying I'm stupid or disorganized?"

Meiko laughed. "You have to admit, Dad, that your office typically looks like a tornado ran through it."

"OK, that's fair. Really brings home what a true genius I must be to overcome such a handicap."

"Indeed," agreed Meiko, digging farther into the box next to her. She pulled out a rectangular object that looked sort of like a thin book wrapped in white packing paper. As she unwrapped it, her face pinched into a grimace. *You're complaining about me overpacking and you brought this photo?*

"Really, Dad? You packed this?" She held a wooden picture frame with a photo of her mother, Chieko, and father standing behind an eight-year-old Meiko, who was wearing a tennis outfit and proudly holding a silver trophy.

David took the photo from Meiko's hand and looked at it longingly. He was silent for a moment as a warm smile broke across his face, which contrasted with the sadness of his eyes.

"Your mother and I were so proud of you when you won this junior tennis tournament. You worked so hard and beat that girl from Del Mar who was ranked, like, number five in the entire state." He laughed. "It's sort of crazy when you think about ranking eight-year-olds in anything, but we were very proud of you, and you were so happy."

Meiko's grimace evaporated, and her features softened. "Lisa Wohlman. That was the girl's name." She nodded, remembering that day as if it were yesterday, and in some ways wishing it were. "Yeah, that was a good day. Too bad it didn't last that long afterward. I didn't expect you to bring a picture of Mom with you." She hoped he would put it in his office at school and she wouldn't have to see it every day.

"True to form." David laughed. "It took me less than a day to touch that nerve. I know that you blame your mother for our divorce, but I've told you many times: it was as much my fault as it was hers, probably more so. I wasn't the greatest husband in the world." He still held the photo in his hand, as if he could will himself back into the picture.

Meiko avoided eye contact and continued pulling clothes and various knickknacks out of the boxes and laying them on the floor. "Yes, the nerve has been touched, and it's even more sensitive now that we're in Japan. I know what you've told me, and I know what I saw, what I heard, and what I believe. You know how I feel. She disappeared. She left us. She moved halfway around the world and essentially abandoned me when I needed her most." She was trying to hold back her anger, which was always difficult when she thought about her mother.

Her parents divorced when Meiko was nine. Because Meiko was a US citizen, her mother couldn't repatriate her to Japan without David's approval, and David didn't want to let Meiko go. So, Chieko left. She moved back to Japan and started practicing psychotherapy in Tokyo, eventually forming her own, private practice. She and David rarely talked. She tried to reach out to Meiko on several occasions, even inviting her over to Japan to stay the summer. But Meiko was always busy with one sports team or another, usually volleyball, and felt more comfortable staying in San Diego with her father than heading to Japan and living with someone she barely knew anymore. Someone she never forgave.

But here they were in Tokyo, essentially in Chieko's backyard. Meiko and Chieko talked a few times in the months before they arrived, and her mother told her how much she was looking forward to seeing her and that she would show her all around Tokyo as well as other parts of Japan. Meiko half-heartedly told her that she was looking forward to seeing her again. She lied. She dreaded it. What were they going to say after all these years? *How have you been doing since you left me? Dad says that your career has prospered. Glad to hear it. Well, I've done pretty damn well without you, and if it were up to me, we'd keep it that way.* She hated feeling so much anger toward one person, especially the person she should love as much or more than anyone in the world. She listened to what her father said and deep down knew that it wasn't all her mom's fault and that she probably was in a difficult position when she left the country. But hearing it, understanding it, and feeling it were quite different things. Her father might like to be reminded of those happier times when the three of them were together, but seeing that picture just reawakened a lot of pent-up anger and hurt that Meiko consciously, and unconsciously, had worked hard at repressing for more than a decade.

David wisely changed the subject. "We're almost finished here, and I'm tired of being cooped up in this rabbit hole all day. Why don't we go out, stretch our legs a bit, and get something to eat? Whaddya say?"

Meiko neatly folded a T-shirt and laid it on a pile of other shirts. She looked up at her father and smiled. She knew exactly what he was doing. They had these conversations occasionally, and her father worked hard at trying to convince her to not be so hard on her mother. But he also knew there was a point of diminishing returns in such discussions and readily shifted gears and got her to focus on something else, typically food or sports. It was a predictable, and yet admittedly effective, pattern.

"Sure. Let's head out. It can't be any hotter out there than it is in here."

Meiko wondered if she had made the right decision in coming to Japan. She wondered if she'd ever truly fit in here, or anywhere, for that matter. In the States, she was an Asian girl, a tall one at that. Here she was an Asian girl people knew wasn't full-blooded Japanese, and therefore, she was sort of an anomaly. Intriguing, different, and tall. The moment someone spoke to her in Japanese they knew she wasn't a native, even though she spoke quite well. She didn't seamlessly blend in anywhere.

CHAPTER 2

Dr. Chieko Tokunaga sat back in her chestnut-brown leather chair with a notepad resting on her crossed leg, pen in hand, ready to take down her observations. Behind her, the windows of her small yet tasteful office looked out onto the seemingly endless expanse of Tokyo, with the skyscrapers of Shinjuku in the distance and the immense Skytree tower looming behind them. A dense white haze enveloped the horizon, making the skyline look like a black-and-white photo.

"Miss Takeyama, in our last session, we discussed the frustration you experienced with your most recent boyfriend. If it's all right with you, let's continue where we left off."

Across from her on the dark-tan leather sofa sat Mia Takeyama. A graduate of Hitotsubashi University, she was thirty-five, single, and worked as part of the creative design team for one of Japan's most popular children's shows. The job paid well and was intellectually stimulating with plenty of room for advancement. She sat upright on the couch with her hands folded neatly in the lap of her short, black skirt. Like many Japanese women, she gave off an air of innocence wrapped in seductiveness. From all appearances, she was a successful woman who made good money, dressed well, and was, if not beautiful, then certainly attractive.

"He told me two weeks ago that he thought we should see other people." She spoke quietly, as if she was afraid of saying something wrong. "I asked him why he felt that way, and he said he needed space, that he wasn't ready to settle into a long-term relationship."

"How long have you been dating?" Chieko asked calmly.

"Almost six months."

"Was this the first time he told you that he wanted to see other people?"

"He hinted at it a few times," she said shyly, as if she were sharing a secret.

"How did you feel about his comment?"

Tears welled in her eyes, and she reached into her Chanel bag and pulled out a handkerchief and patted her eyes. Silence. "It made me so sad. I thought we had something special," she said between sobs. "He told me that he did care about me but that he just wasn't ready to settle down, that we should take things slower, see other people, and see if what we have will stand the test of time."

"How did you respond?"

"I told him that if he didn't want to commit to me, then he could see as many women as he wanted because he wasn't going to see me anymore." She openly sobbed, her torso shaking as she wept.

Chieko waited until she settled and the crying stopped.

"Miss Takeyama, we've had five sessions so far, and you have told me about all of your relationships for the past three years. Have you noticed a pattern in how those relationships begin and how they end?" probed Chieko.

"I find that I fall in love so quickly and try to do everything I can to make these relationships work, but they all end the same way. They want space, they want to see other women, they want to slow things down. It's always some excuse. I must be attracted to men who have a hard time committing to a serious relationship." She folded her hands again in her lap. "Is that what you see, Sensei?"

Chieko set her notepad and pen down on the glass coffee table next to her chair. She adjusted the sky-blue, square-frame glasses that rested on her high cheekbones and straightened the creases of her slacks and then slowly interlaced her fingers under her chin. She paused one more moment. The air needed to be clear.

"My opinion, Miss Takeyama, is that you have become trapped in a destructive behavioral pattern wherein you are trying to win back the affection of your father, who divorced your mother and left your family when you were a girl. You mentioned on more than one occasion that you blamed yourself for his leaving, even though you now admit that it probably had very little to do with you. Nonetheless, that childhood trauma has stuck with you. You have a pattern of jumping into relationships with men you don't know particularly well and have unrealistic expectations of what a real relationship can or should be. In the end, you are so consumed by a fear of being abandoned again that you suffocate the men in your relationships and they feel they can do nothing but try and escape." She consciously tried to soften her look of clinical detachment. "I know that what I have told you may be very difficult to accept. At the same time, I do stand by my conclusions. More importantly, I want you to know that there are things we can do to get you out of this vicious cycle and help you form longer-lasting, meaningful, and satisfying relationships. Does this sound right to you,

Miss Takeyama? Are you interested in working with me to do that?"

Miss Takeyama nodded emphatically. "Yes, yes, I am, Sensei. I know you're right, everything you said. Please help me. Help me because I don't want to repeat this anymore."

Chieko sat back in her chair and took her notepad and began writing.

"I ask you to trust me because what I will tell you will not always make sense and in fact will seem quite foreign to you. But if we are to get you out of these self-destructive behavioral patterns, we need to change the way you think and the way you act. If you are willing to commit to that, then I will commit to help you."

If there had been a table between them, Miss Takeyama would have slammed her head on it and knocked herself out she bowed so forcefully and deeply. "Yes, yes, I will do whatever you say, Sensei. I want to change. I know I can change if you will help me."

Chieko bowed as well, the tight bun in her jet-black hair pointing toward the ceiling. "Very well, let's plan on meeting next week at this same time and start to work on what we will call your relationship tool kit." She stood and led her patient to the door. "Until we have this relationship tool kit in place, I want you to promise me that you will resist the temptation to form any more romantic relationships without first discussing them with me. Are we agreed?"

"Yes, Sensei, absolutely. I will do whatever you say." She continued to bow as she left the room.

After Miss Takeyama left, Chieko walked over to the window and looked out at the metropolis that spread out in all directions. A light drizzle appeared to be falling. There were beads of rain on the floor-to-ceiling windows of her office. She wasn't sure what Miss Takeyama would think of her skills and tool kit if she knew that Chieko herself was divorced, that she had left her own daughter when she was a young girl. She hadn't been able to make her own marriage work, so how was she supposed to help others with theirs? It was something that every therapist dealt with. They weren't perfect. Things didn't always go according to plan, despite the best intentions. But she knew how to effectively build and sustain relationships, at least for other people. She was good at what she did. She was a successful psychotherapist and particularly respected for her work with women who struggled to balance work and family in a society that was gradually and grudgingly evolving to support such notions, not only for women but also for men.

She wondered whether her own daughter, Meiko, would fall into similar patterns of behavior because of her fear of abandonment, not by her father but by her. She knew that Meiko resented and blamed her, and she understood her emotions. They were perfectly reasonable. She would feel the same way if she were in that position. Hopefully, this year together in Japan would offer her an opportunity to get to know Meiko again, as a young woman, and just as important, allow Meiko a chance to get to know her, not only as her mother but as a person. She stared out the window a bit longer and then prepared for her next appointment. She knew that a year would go by quickly. *I've got to do my best to turn this narrative around and get Meiko back in my life, and me in hers.*

CHAPTER 3

JULY

Meiko walked down the crowded street on her way to the Nihonbashi train station, holding an umbrella in one hand and her cell phone in the other. It was still before rush hour, but Tokyo was crowded at all times of the day and night. A soft drizzle had been falling all day, and it didn't look to be stopping anytime soon. She had finished her job teaching English to businesspeople about an hour ago and had spent some quality time browsing the flagship store of the upscale Takashimaya department store. She was amazed at not only the selection but also the level of service. There were young women in crisp uniforms greeting customers and knowledgeable, well-trained staff in every department. It was a favorite stop of hers after work. There was nothing like it in the States. Even Neiman Marcus and Nordstrom in Fashion Valley mall in San Diego that she used to visit occasionally with her girlfriends seemed like half-empty cathedrals staffed with people who were more likely to be talking to each other than serving customers.

She carried a small paper bag with the distinctive Takashimaya rose pattern in the same hand she held her umbrella. Even though there was very little room in the apartment she shared with her father, it was hard to go into a store like that and not buy something. She wasn't much into expensive designer wear, nor could she afford it, but she did like to pick up a nice barrette, a unique pair of socks, or some other small accessory. She also loved stopping in the basement level where there was a dizzying array of food, from top-quality wagyu beef to fine teas, both green and black, delectable French pastries, and almost anything one could imagine.

Today's snack had primed her appetite, and despite the noise of the street, she pressed her phone to her ear to check in with her father. "Hey, Dad, wasn't sure what you were doing for dinner," she said, gradually winding her way down the crowded sidewalk. "I finished work and am on my way back."

"I'm pretty much finished here as well," David answered. "Why don't we go out? How about an *izakaya* somewhere close?"

Japanese tapas sounded perfect to Meiko. "I've got a great idea. One of the Japanese guys I teach said there's a cool *yakitoriya* place in Ginza that's only about twenty minutes from me. He said it only seats about thirty people, but their grilled chicken skewers are worth the wait. I'll get there and see if I can get us a table. They don't take reservations. It's called Takechan."

"Sounds great! I'll call you if I get lost."

"Put it in your iPhone," she said. "And bring your umbrella," she suggested. "It doesn't look like it's going to stop raining."

"Thanks, Mom," he chided. "Will do. See you soon."

"Bye, Dad." She hung up her phone and put it in her purse. His teasing had struck a nerve. Sometimes she wondered whether she had taken on a motherly role with her father. She probably had. It came naturally to her to look out for someone she cared for. She decided to hop on the Ginza line instead of walking. It would be faster, and she didn't really want to walk that far in the rain. It was still relatively early when she made it to the small restaurant, but she still needed to wait thirty minutes before she could get a seat for two. The rain wasn't bad, so she spent her time outside, checking emails, catching up on Instagram and Facebook, and strolling up and down the small side street that was lined with other small restaurants and shops.

There was a tiny Shinto shrine, about the size of a phone booth, tucked only about two feet into the white brick frame a building on the street corner near the restaurant. It was odd to see such a thing in Ginza, where land prices were some of the most expensive in the world. The outside was framed by a reddish-orange *torii*, or gate, with jagged white streamers of paper, like the tails of kites, hanging from the lower wooden crossbeam. At the back of the shrine was a black shelf lit on either side by two electric candles. Outside of the candles were two wooden figures of a fox looking toward the center. Several dolls sat on the shelf, along with three ceremonial flat-topped bowls. In the bowl on the left was sweet *mochi*. The other two bowls were empty. Meiko assumed that someone had made the offering very recently, maybe even that morning, because the rice ball was shiny and smooth. Two paper lanterns hung from the ceiling behind the candles with the Japanese characters for *Inari Jinja* written on them.

"Shrine to the rice god Inari," Meiko murmured.

The structure was just big enough for a person to step in, say a prayer, and then step back out onto the street. It was the first such mini-shrine that she had seen in her almost nine months of living in Tokyo. She found it quite cute and at the same time somewhat odd. She couldn't imagine that there were a lot of big cities in the world that would make space for such mini-shrines tucked into the sides of downtown buildings. It was one of the great paradoxes of Japan that she loved: an ancient culture seamlessly melding into an ultra-modern megalopolis.

She checked her watch. Time to try getting their seats. The restaurant didn't have any type of electronic beeper to alert you when your spot was ready. About two minutes after she was seated at the counter, her father poked his head in the doorway. It was impossible to miss a 6' 2" blond man in such a small place. She waved to him, and he plopped into the seat next to her.

"Good timing," she said as he stashed his soft leather laptop messenger bag at his feet. "I just got seated. Any problem finding the place?"

"Thanks to the wonders of Google Maps, I found it on the first try," he replied. "The hardest part was walking to and from the stations."

A waitress appeared with a large bottle of Sapporo beer and two small glasses.

"I thought you might be thirsty. I know I am," said Meiko as she poured a glass for her father and then for herself.

They touched glasses together—"*Kanpai*"—and then each took a big swallow, which pretty much finished off what was in the small glasses. She poured them another round.

"Well," David said, "I don't know what it is, but the first glass of cold beer is always one of the highlights of any day. Speaking of that, how was your day?"

She was about to respond when the server appeared to take their order.

"I haven't really looked at the menu yet," David said. "Do you know what you want?"

"Umm." She nodded. "They really only have two options, five skewers or eight. They also have a dish of assorted pickles. I'm hungry. I think we should go for eight skewers."

"Then by all means, I leave it to you. Eight sounds good to me."

Meiko proceeded to place an order with the older woman who seemed to be single-handedly serving the entire restaurant.

"Would you like another beer or something else?" Meiko asked her father.

"I was thinking of a highball. How about you?" he responded.

"Unfortunately, they only serve beer and sake," she replied. "I suggest sake after this beer." She waved down the server as she passed by and ordered a carafe.

"You know, I never really felt the urge to drink sake back in San Diego, outside of sushi restaurants, but for some reason, it goes perfectly here with so many different meals," said David, finishing off the beer in his glass and pouring the bottle's final two glasses.

"Yeah," agreed Meiko. "You don't get as full as with beer either." Sitting at a bar or restaurant with her father was a new experience for her. She had been off to college for the past four years and wasn't of legal drinking age until just before coming to Japan. It was just another thing about Japan that she had grown to love. She couldn't imagine too many things she enjoyed more than enjoying a meal with her dad.

"So, how were your classes?" asked David.

"Ah, you know, mostly businessmen who want to improve their conversational English so they can get promoted faster. There's one guy whose English is really good. He was assigned to London for a couple of years and speaks with a charming British accent." He was sort of cute too, and his accent reminded her of Benedict Cumberbatch. "He's probably going to get assigned to the States or Australia in the next year, so he's trying to build up his vocabulary. How about your day?"

"I only had to teach one class today, which left me a lot of time to do some research for my book. I spent most of the afternoon buried in books about Japanese ghost stories."

"Ooh," cooed Meiko. "Sounds scary. Actually, it sounds like a perfect day for you." She knew that her father's two favorite things were spending time doing research, preferably in a big library versus over the internet, and teaching.

"Yeah, pretty much," agreed David. "That's pretty geeky, isn't it?"

She shook her head. "You always told me that leopards can't hide their spots. You should feel comfortable with your geekiness. It's an endearing quality."

Dr. David Archer Wright was the author of three best-selling books on myth and what it teaches us, which had been translated into over twenty languages, including Japanese. He was also keenly gifted in helping translate the obscure, metaphysical, and often downright strange into something people could grab hold of and relate.

Their ceramic carafe of warm sake arrived, and Meiko poured small glasses for herself and her father. Another waitress set down a small, shallow bowl of pickled vegetables:

eggplants, daikon radishes, and cucumbers. She also set down three plates. One contained two skewered chicken meatballs, grilled to perfection with a crisp outer shell, served with a white scallion covered with a dollop of miso paste. Next to that was a plate of grilled chicken skewered with asparagus spears. The final plate held two skewers of green, translucent gingko nuts dusted with salt.

"Wow," exclaimed David. "These look great."

They started the meal the way every meal in Japan starts: palms together in a slight bow, the word *Itadakimasu*, "I will receive," murmured before they dove in.

They made their way through several plates of grilled skewers, including more of the same as well as some different ones: chicken thighs with scallions and chicken tenders lightly grilled and salted and slathered with a thin wasabi paste.

"So, why the interest in Japanese ghost stories? Is that going to be part of your book?" asked Meiko.

"I'm not sure yet," replied David. "But I've been intrigued by the things that scare us. There's a great deal of consistency across cultures regarding what we fear, although it manifests itself in different forms."

"Like what?"

"Well, for one thing, most people seem to be frightened by seeing dead people, particularly dead people who come back to life in one form or another."

She agreed that seeing dead people would be terrifying. "That would seem to be the basis for almost every ghost story, wouldn't it?"

David laughed. "It is hard to have a ghost story without ghosts. But ultimately, I think that our biggest fears have to do with loss. Loss of control, loss of loved ones, loss of our senses, our minds, our memory, and in the end, loss of our own lives. One reason that we're afraid of ghosts is that we don't have control over them. You really can't do anything to a ghost."

"Interesting," mumbled Meiko, who was finishing off a grilled chicken thigh. She had never thought that of it that way, but it made sense. "Don't forget the devil; he's always pretty frightening."

"That's true. But the devil is the most frightening in cultures that ascribe greater power to him, like in Christian societies. In Buddhist cultures, for instance, there isn't just one supremely powerful devil who is hell-bent on taking our eternal soul. There are many lesser demons that we may run into, but by and large, they aren't actively trying to get us. But there again, the reason that we are most likely so scared of the devil in Western culture is that he has the power to take something from us, specifically, our soul, which is possibly the ultimate thing to lose."

"Especially if you believe that the soul is immortal, and if you lose it to the devil, you will live out eternity in flames and agony."

"Yep," agreed David. "Not a pleasant thought." He motioned to the waitress to bring another carafe of sake. Smoke billowed from the grill behind the counter as more meat was added to it. Fortunately, there was a clear plastic screen that separated the grill from the wooden counter, and there was a powerful fan directly above it that sucked the smoke upward. Three chefs in white short-sleeve shirts, aprons, and squat, square caps efficiently worked in the cramped kitchen, prepping, grilling, and plating. Their movements were practiced and precise, with no wasted effort. There seemed to be a constant flow of orders coming in from a seemingly endless stream of customers.

David shared some of the ghost stories he had uncovered while Meiko listened intently. She loved listening to her father talk about his work. It always fascinated her. He was without a doubt the most interesting person she knew. Not only did she find the folklore itself compelling but he had a way of bringing it to life like few others could. He really had a gift. She loved her father more than anyone in the world and always relished the time they were able to spend together. She wished she could feel something similar with her mother, but she wasn't even close to having that type of relationship with her.

When they finished their meal and headed out, there was a line of about twelve people, almost all businesspeople in suits stopping by after work for something to eat and a few drinks. It was still drizzling, but it wasn't cold, and in fact, it felt quite nice. Meiko imagined that this was what it must be like in London. They hopped on the subway and made their way back to their tiny apartment in Meguro.

When they returned home, Meiko made some tea, and she and David sat at the tiny kitchen table working on their computers, David on his laptop and Meiko on her iPad. She checked emails and her Facebook page. She posted some pictures she had taken on her iPhone at Takechan that evening and made updates to her blog. When she got her job as an English instructor, she started a blog about her experiences.

She also kept a personal diary, something she had done since she was eight years old. It had helped her through the difficult times during her parent's divorce and in the years after her mother left. She found it to be a cathartic escape of sorts.

> *I'm beginning to really enjoy being in Japan, and my Japanese is definitely improving, although I spend most of my days speaking English. Fortunately, I also get to speak a lot of Japanese with students whose English isn't very good. I still miss San Diego and my friends. Every time I check Facebook, I'm reminded of them. Most everyone I used to hang out with in high school or college is now either in grad school or starting their careers. I still don't really know what I want to do at this point. Does anybody really know what they want to do, or do they just choose a path that seems reasonable and go with it? I don't know. I don't have a true passion for anything at this point. I'm pretty much over the culture shock I felt when I first came here, and I could probably stay here another year and teach English. The money is decent, and it's not hard. Besides, Tokyo is very cool, and I still want to see so many places. If I want to go to grad school next fall, I'll need to take the GRE and apply pretty soon. But I don't know what I want to major in or do once I get out! Maybe I'm using this time in Japan as an excuse. Maybe it will help me decide what I want to do. Either way, I need to decide soon.*

CHAPTER 4

OCTOBER

Meiko dipped her last crispy fried shrimp into the sweet-and-spicy dipping sauce before biting it in half and setting the uneaten part down on the wire rack next to the finely shredded cabbage that she had nearly finished. She always saved the shrimp for last. She and her mother were finishing up lunch in an upscale *tonkatsu* restaurant in the Hikarie building in Shibuya. Meiko thought it was interesting how Japan had restaurants categorized around the type of meat they served; the type of restaurant her father and she had gone to was for skewers and this one's name meant "fried pork cutlet."

Meiko had insisted that she and her mother speak in Japanese whenever possible, so she could improve her language skills. Besides, when they spoke Japanese, she didn't feel as much animosity toward her mother. At least, it was harder to vocalize.

"I don't eat a lot of fried food in the States, but I'm absolutely hooked on tonkatsu and tempura in Japan. I would never even think of eating this much for lunch if I was back home," said Meiko.

"I know exactly what you mean," replied Chieko. She passed her piece of shrimp over to Meiko, who had been covertly eying it for the past several minutes. "I can't eat all of this, and I know you like the shrimp the best."

"Are you sure?" said Meiko, with no intention of turning down the offer.

Chieko smiled. "Yes, I'm sure, it's all yours." She sipped the miso soup that came with the meal. "Hey, do you have a little time?"

Meiko finished chewing her shrimp and nodded hesitantly. She wasn't sure she wanted to spend more time with her mother. Things were going well so far, and she didn't want to push it. But she really didn't have anything going on right now and couldn't come up with a reasonable excuse on the fly. "Sure, what are you thinking?"

"I thought we could take a walk through the Imperial gardens in Shinjuku. They are beautiful this time of year, with the leaves changing."

That actually did sound pretty good to Meiko. She loved the outdoors, and besides, she could use a little exercise after lunch. "That sounds nice. I've never been there."

"Good, then this will be a real treat," replied Chieko. They both finished the rest of their soba noodles and put on their light fall jackets. Chieko paid for lunch despite Meiko's offer to treat her.

It was less than five kilometers to the Imperial gardens, and since it was a crisp fall day with clear skies, they decided to walk. They mostly made small talk, catching up on Meiko's teaching, what Meiko's seemingly ageless grandmother, Aiko, was up to, and any tidbits about interesting patients that Chieko could share.

It was early afternoon on a weekday, so the gardens weren't particularly crowded, at least by Tokyo standards. Much like Central Park in New York, there were always people milling around. At this time of day, they were mostly housewives out for lunch with their friends as well as some tourists, both from Japan and abroad.

They stopped just inside the entrance in front of a large sign that described the history and design of the gardens. Originally the residence of an eighteenth-century *daimyo*, a high-ranking feudal lord, the grounds covered nearly 145 acres and boasted more than twenty thousand trees, including nearly fifteen hundred cherry trees. The gardens blended three distinct styles, with an English landscape in the north, French formal in the east, and traditional Japanese style in the south. It was a favorite of picnickers during the summer and cherry-blossom-watchers during the spring.

They started their visit at the northern tip of the garden, winding their way along a well-maintained gravel path surrounded on both sides by maple, oak, and chestnut trees. The colors were vibrant: fiery oranges, yellows, and reds under a robin's-egg-blue sky peppered with fluffy white clouds. Although it was still early in the season, some of the leaves had already started to fall, creating a multicolored quilt along the closely manicured green grass fields.

"The leaves are unbelievable! The maple trees especially look like they're on fire," said Meiko as she looked all around her. "I've never seen colors like this in San Diego."

"It's beautiful during cherry blossom season too. But I think I prefer it during the fall. I always missed the change of seasons when I lived in San Diego. I mean, the seasons do change there, but it's pretty subtle."

"Yeah, since I've been here, I think I've seen more weather

changes than I did the past ten years in San Diego." They both laughed because it was true.

Meiko often thought about the time they spent together in San Diego when she was young, wishing that it could have continued. Despite the bitterness she felt toward her mother for abandoning her, she had to admit that she enjoyed spending time with her here in Tokyo. She was getting to see more of the real person as opposed to the uncaring, two-dimensional monster she had created in her head over the past decade.

"You haven't seen the winter or the spring yet. They're both beautiful, although it's hard to beat cherry blossom season," said Chieko as the two of them continued strolling through the gardens. They passed through the English land-scape part of the park and were just entering the Japanese portion. After stopping at a kiosk for a cup of tea, they sat down on a wooden bench underneath a vibrant elm tree whose golden leaves danced in the light breeze.

"You know, we've seen each other four or five times now, and I know there are things you want to say to me. Now is as good a time as ever to get things off your mind," said Chieko.

Meiko gently blew the steam from her paper teacup, which sat on the open palm of her right hand. *Uh-oh, here we go.* She knew that the carefree stroll through the park wouldn't last. She looked at Chieko and smiled. "It's tough having a clinician for a mother." She looked back down at the teacup, trying to determine how best to express her feelings.

"Do you know how hard it was for me when you left? You and I were so close, and then you just left me," started Meiko somewhat hesitantly.

"I know," agreed Chieko softly. "That must have been difficult for you."

"You mean, having your mother abandon you and move out of the country? Yeah, that was pretty damn difficult to deal with." It didn't take long for those deep feelings of anger and betrayal to rise up, even in a tranquil environment such as this. Unconsciously, Meiko had reverted to English. Not only could she express her anger better but it felt more natural, of course. *No use holding back at this point!*

"I wish there would have been a better option for me. I would have never left you if I felt that there was another option."

"There was an option. You could have worked it out with Dad and stayed together. Did you guys really try? It just seemed so easy for you to simply run away from your problems!" Meiko tried not to raise her voice. She didn't want to get emotional, but she knew this was what would happen when she finally confronted her mother. Twelve years of bottled up emotions were set to explode.

"We did try. Trust me," said Chieko, shaking her head. "I never wanted to leave you. It was the hardest thing I've ever had to do in my life. Knowing that I wouldn't see you grow up almost killed me."

"But it didn't hurt enough to try and stay and be my mother!" Meiko spit the words out like poison darts.

"Your father and I just had too many issues going on to maintain our marriage. It wasn't going to be a healthy environment for any of us."

What a load of crap! "I've got a lot of friends whose parents have shitty marriages. In fact, from what I've seen, most marriages sort of suck. But they stay together for their kids' sakes, right or wrong. They don't run away, and their kids at least have their mom there when they get their first period or when they have their first kiss or their first crush. Do you know how hard it was growing up without a mother?" Meiko wiped away the tears that were running down her cheek, angry at herself for losing control. *I wish I could hold it together, but I just can't!*

"I do, sweetheart. I do know that it's very difficult not having that positive female role model and influence in your life. Someone you can share your fears and secrets with."

"You only know it from your patients and your education. You don't know how it feels. Your mother was always there for you. You never had to go through it." The heartache of being abandoned by her mother, which had gnawed at Meiko as she cried herself to sleep countless nights, returned as if it had never left.

"You're right. I can only imagine what it was like because I never went through it myself," agreed Chieko. "But do you know how hard it was for me to miss your first kiss? To miss your first date or prom night?"

"Forgive me if I'm not in the most charitable mood right now." Meiko's emotions bounced between pain and anger, with the latter clearly winning the battle. "You know, sometimes I really don't even know who I am. Am I a Japanese girl living in the States or an American girl here in Japan? I'm somewhere in the middle. I don't fit in either place. I'm a misfit. Maybe my mother, the psychologist, could have helped me figure that all out. But she wasn't there for me, so I've had to deal with these feelings of inadequacy my whole damn life!" She had felt these things for so long but had never voiced them aloud. It saddened her to hear them coming from her mouth. But they were true. That's who she was, someone who didn't belong anywhere.

"I know it's difficult finding your place and knowing who you are, sweetheart. I felt the same way when I was your age. We were living in the US because of my dad's job, and while I was excited about the idea of living in the States and learning English, it was very difficult for me. I didn't read, write, or speak as well as the other students and had to work twice as hard as they did. I guess that having to try so hard helped me get through things. I didn't have a lot of time to think about who I was or where I fit. While I know that you think you might not fit in anywhere, you could also look at it another way. Unlike most people, you fit in both places. Not many people can say that."

Meiko looked down at the gray gravel beneath her shoes, not sure what to say. "It all sounds good. It just doesn't feel very good, that's all." She ran her hand through her black hair, which had fallen over her eyes. She felt confused. "I never thought about how hard it must have been for you going to school in New York. I only knew my super intelligent and educated mother who spoke fluent English and Japanese. You always seemed so in control, so confident. That's why it was so hard when you left!" She paused before finishing: "I needed your help!"

Chieko smiled softly. "Looks can be deceiving, Meiko. Part of the reason I left your father was because I lacked confidence. I felt that I was becoming a second-class citizen to the great and powerful Dr. David Wright."

"Forgive me, but 'I lacked confidence' doesn't justify you walking out on us. We all lack confidence, but we still have to take care of our responsibilities. You don't leave your family and your nine-year-old daughter because you lack confidence."

"You're right. There was more to it than that, but you are absolutely right. I ran away from my problems instead of tackling them head-on. I had to get away, and I didn't have the confidence to start a practice in the States or even to join an existing practice. I returned to Japan, which seemed safer to me at the time. I can't tell you how many times I've regretted that decision. It's something I'll have to live with the rest of my life. I'm sorry for the pain I caused you."

While Meiko's anger toward her mother had percolated for over a decade, it was only now that she realized there was probably more to it than she had ever imagined. She was so consumed by her loss and her struggles that she hadn't thought about what it must have been like for her mother. It had been easier that way. Leaving her child and moving to a completely different country couldn't have been all sunshine and roses. She had also never thought of her mother as lacking confidence or sharing her feelings of not belonging. She was still angry. But now the anger that had always been directed toward her mother was joined by self-loathing at her egocentricity and lack of empathy for a person who loved her and whom she ultimately loved as well. She wasn't sure which hurt worse.

Meiko heard laughter and turned to see two young children, a boy and a girl who were very likely brother and sister and who couldn't have been more than three and five years old, respectively. The boy was chasing the girl around a large

oak tree with flaming-red leaves. They were dressed in colorful clothing, the girl in pink stockings with black shoes and
a white dress covered with vibrant flowers. The boy wore
tan pants that seemed puffy and soft like pajama bottoms,
with a navy-blue sweater. Their young mother, who couldn't
have been more than thirty, chased after them, half-heartedly
telling them to quiet down while at the same time laughing
at their joy.

The air smelled so fresh—cold and crisp. She had never
experienced fall days like this in San Diego because, well, because they really didn't exist there, not like this, at least. Fall
air is more bracing, cleaner, and more melancholy when you
know that the cold of winter, with snow, clouds, and frigid
breezes, will soon arrive, leaving the crisp, tart-apple taste of
the fall air a distant memory.

After a long silence and a few more sips of tea, Meiko
couldn't help but laugh. The roller coaster of emotions had
run its course, and she was, frankly, spent.

"Well, thanks for the therapy session, Dr. Tokunaga," she
said to her mother. Much like her father, she used humor to
diffuse discomfort. "I guess we'll leave it here until next time."

Chieko wrapped her arm around Meiko. "I think that's
probably a good idea. I love you, Meiko. I always have, and
I always will."

Part of her wanted to pull away, while another, deeper, part
of her wanted to lean in closer and bury herself within the comfort of her mother's embrace. "I know." She wanted to say, "I
love you too," but she couldn't get the words out. She stood up
and looked around the park as if waking from a dream. "I'd still
like to visit the Japanese section of the park, if you have time."

"Of course," agreed Chieko, dusting off the seat of her pants. "I have as much time as you like."

Meiko pointed to her left. "According to the map, there is a large pond with several small islands. That might be nice." After such an emotional release, she needed to get back in control and focus on something completely mundane. She needed more time to deal with all the feelings that rushed toward her like a six-foot wave.

"Sure, let's go that way. It's very beautiful," directed Chieko.

CHAPTER 5

KYOTO
MARCH

This was the first time that Meiko had ever been in Tokyo train station, and she wasn't familiar with all the different shops. She was about to hop on the *shinkansen*, the bullet train, to Kyoto and wanted to grab something to eat along the way. Lately, she had developed a taste for fried pork cutlet sandwiches. It wasn't hard to find them in the various shops that lined the special entrance to the bullet train area. Her problem was deciding which one. She arrived at the station with plenty of time and was able to casually wander from store to store, carefully evaluating her options. She finally decided on one that looked particularly wonderful, with a thin crispy cutlet, shredded cabbage, the sweet sauce that always accompanied tonkatsu, and mayonnaise on fluffy white bread with the crusts removed. She had never seen these in the States, but over the past nine months in Japan, she had become quite the connoisseur. She bought a can of sweet, creamy iced coffee to wash down her sandwich as well as the most recent copy of *Non. no*, a Japanese weekly fashion magazine directed at women in their twenties. She wasn't much on expensive, designer clothing, nor could she afford it on her English teacher's salary, but the magazine highlighted a lot of cute, inexpensive clothes that were so different from anything she would have worn back in San Diego. San Diego was T-shirt, jeans, and flip-flop territory, and that suited her fine. But Tokyo was one of the world's most fashionable cities, and it naturally made a person evolve to dress more sharply. Besides, it was too cold and rainy for T-shirts and flip-flops in late March here in Japan.

After making her way to the platform, Meiko hopped on the long, sleek train and settled into her seat. She had splurged and purchased a green-car seat, which wasn't much more than a standard one. The seats were nicer, and there was free Wi-Fi. This was the first time she had taken a trip outside of Tokyo on her own. She and her father had taken a couple of trips outside of the city, and she also spent a day in nearby Yokohama with her mother in late November. But neither of them was available to join her this weekend, and her Japanese friends were tied up as well. She didn't want to miss cherry blossom season in Kyoto, which everyone told her was something she absolutely had to experience. She was excited to spend a few days on her own, exploring all the famous temples in Japan's old capital city.

The train pulled slowly out of the station and gradually picked up speed as it headed out of central Tokyo. Meiko decided to send some texts to her friends on LINE, a popular Japanese texting platform. She had been exchanging messages with a group of friends from San Diego for most of the year. It was just after 10:00 a.m. in Japan, but it was 6:00 p.m. the previous evening back on the West Coast.

> On the bullet train heading to Kyoto to see cherry blossoms—they only last ~ 2 wks. They are gorgeous here in Tokyo as well but to see them surrounding ancient temples and shrines is something I'm so excited about. The bullet train is so smooth!

> Just passed Mt. Fuji. Great view, snow-
> capped, looks almost purple! Beautiful!
> Everyone on that side of the train taking
> pictures—and they're from here! LOL

> Hey Meiko! Great to hear from you. Sounds
> awesome. Take a ton of pictures. Miss you!

> Meiko, of course they're taking
> pictures…they're Japanese!!! LOL Hope you
> have a great trip—lots of love. We miss you!!!

She missed her friends back in San Diego. Even though they were thousands of miles away, she felt closer to them than to anyone here. But they were moving on with their lives. Soon they would get married, start families, and move to different places. They wouldn't hang out and surf like they used to or go down to Hodad's or Rocky's to grab a burger. Or, at least, they wouldn't do it very often. Where would she end up? What was her next move?

Meiko had been in Japan for nine months already, and she still didn't know what she wanted to do. She took the GREs in October and did well on them but didn't feel like committing to graduate school, so she didn't apply anywhere. She wasn't sure whether she would stay another year in Japan or go home with her father in June. The longer she stayed in Japan, the more she enjoyed it. Her Japanese was improving rapidly because she had made some Japanese friends and tried to hang out with them as much as possible instead of falling into the trap of staying close to ex-pat Americans teaching English. But there were always those moments when she felt completely isolated, alone, and out of place. They were coming less frequently, but they still existed.

As she nibbled on her sandwich, taking her time, so she could enjoy every savory bite, she watched the rice fields and the sparsely populated train stations whip by as the bullet train careened at two hundred miles per hour on its westward trek toward Kyoto. The trip was a little over two hours, which gave her plenty of time to make it through the fashion magazine, read a couple of chapters in Haruki Murakami's *Kafka on the Shore*, finish her sandwich and iced coffee, and take a quick nap. The train slowly pulled into Kyoto station, and Meiko edged her way through the shifting tide of humanity that was part of every major train station in Japan. She took a cab to the small *ryokan* where she was staying, checked in, dropped off her bags in the small *tatami* mat room of this traditional Japanese inn, and then headed out to see some temples.

She spent the next two days exploring, taking pictures, eating local food and just taking in the magical experience that was Kyoto. Without question, this was the most beautiful places she had ever been. It was like living in a dream world. She returned to her room at the end of the second day ready to just chill out and relax a bit after so much walking. They would be bringing a traditional Japanese dinner, which was included in the price of the room, in a little less than an hour. After that, she would head down to the *onsen* on-site and slowly soak away her fatigue in the hot springs. Japanese baths had become one of her favorite things about the country. In the States, she would normally take a shower in the morning before school or after surfing. Here, the custom was to take a shower followed by a hot bath before bed. It took her a while to get used to the practice, but she eventually fell in love with it, especially in the winter. Now, while waiting for dinner, she decided to catch up on her blog. Despite being very small and over a hundred years old, the inn offered free Wi-Fi. She sat down at a small table and opened her iPad and began working on her blog.

I'm in Kyoto for cherry blossom season! This truly has to be one of the most magical places on the planet. Where else can you see a *maiko* (apprentice geisha) walking through the streets in a stunning green kimono with red and orange flowers? There were tourists, delivery people, and businessmen in their dark suits milling around, and this colorful figure from a bygone era gracefully made her way to her destination. Besides the tourists, no one even noticed.

The real stars here, though, are the cherry blossoms. It's hard to describe how beautiful the trees are. In most cases, the trunks and limbs are very dark, like the ironwood trees I remember from the deserts in Southern California. But from these dark, austere branches, white, candy-like blossoms, so small and delicate, seem to explode.

Some of the trees have thick trunks but are very low slung, with their lowest branches only two feet above the ground. The dark wooden fingers reach out, covered in what seems from a distance to be fluffy white popcorn, almost like giant baby's breath trees. Amazing!

I walked through the Imperial Park (Kyoto was the emperor's home and therefore the capital of Japan from 794 to 1868), which is filled with weeping cherry trees (*shidare zakura*). The black silhouette of these lonely trees, alone in their own space, spread out as far as their limbs can bear. The white-and-red-hued blossoms hang in strands like wisteria from a backyard canopy. The sheer number of trees, set in thick emerald-green grass wrapped with soft dirt paths, is breathtaking. You can almost imagine the emperor and his court making their way along these paths to view the exact same trees I saw today.

I sat on a bench drinking an iced coffee, so sweet and creamy, and just stared at a moss-green pond while delicate tentacles of snow white petals extended precariously over the water, nearly dipping their tips into the cold green liquid. I can just imagine a haiku master working on his poem in just such a setting, sans iced coffee, of course.

I visited so many temples over the past two days that my head is awash. In Japan, temples (*otera*) refer to Buddhist sites, while shrines (*jinja*) are Shinto. With notable exceptions, Buddhist temples tend to be more subdued, with dark, almost black, wood and green patina roofs. The Shinto shrines tend to be more colorful, in bright red, gold, silver, orange, and white. I had to go to all the big-name temples, including the Golden Pavilion (*Kinkakuji*) and the Silver Pavilion (*Ginkakuji*), as well as the Pure Water Temple (*Kiyomizu-dera*), which sits on the top of a mountain overlooking Kyoto. They were all incredible in their own way, and all of them were packed with people. I enjoyed some of the less-well-known, or at least smaller, temples better than the top five. There are fewer people, and you get a much better feel for the mood of tranquility and quiet that the temple was meant to stand for in the first place. On my way back from Kinkakuji—which was a mass of humanity—I somehow stumbled upon a secluded moss-covered temple called Honen-ji, which was built in 1680. The only noises I heard were from the water dripping in the small streams that ran through the immaculate gardens, the birds in the many trees that enveloped the temple buildings, and the crunch of my feet on the gravel paths. It was like the crowds and noise outside completely disappeared—magical! There were more maple trees than cherry trees at this temple, meaning that it would be incredible in the fall, but there were still a few solitary cherries in full bloom, carefully tucked away from the wandering hordes. I slowly strolled around the grounds, which I had almost all to myself. There was a calm, serene energy to the place that washed away the fatigue I accumulated battling through endless crowds trying to get a view of a famous temple building or a sacred tree. Next time I come, I'm going to focus on these lesser-known places.

Tomorrow is my last day in Kyoto, and I plan on seeing a couple more temples. I don't know what it is, but being here in Kyoto, which is such an ancient city, has really made me feel more Japanese, if that makes sense. Not sure if it makes that much sense to me even, but it feels that way. I hope you all enjoy the photos I've posted. More to come soon!

She published her post and planned on writing a follow-up with photos and descriptions from the temples she would see the next day. She liked to keep her blog as up-to-date as possible, when the memories were fresh. Tomorrow she would see several more temples before heading back on the bullet train late in the afternoon. She cracked open a cold Sapporo beer from the small refrigerator in the room and relaxed until dinner arrived.

CHAPTER 6

MARCH 24ᵀᴴ

After strolling around the spacious grounds of Tofuku-Ji, the head temple for the Rinzai sect of Zen Buddhism and home to the oldest Zen main gate in Japan, Meiko felt distinctly at peace, even with the crowds. Such gates symbolized the border between the land of Buddha and the secular world, and her mood was probably from that, plus the serenity and austere beauty of the medieval temple, which was considered one of the Five Great Temples in Kyoto during the fifteenth century. There were working monks, along with novices at various levels of study, making their way from their morning meditation sessions, called *zazen*. The monks moved with purpose, quietly focused on the task at hand, on being completely in the moment. Meiko had started reading more about Zen and had gone a few times to a temple close to her apartment in Tokyo to sit with the monks in silent zazen, which usually lasted one hour. While her legs usually fell asleep halfway through, she ended up feeling refreshed after such sessions. She often wondered what a monastic life would be like. What it would be like to be so disciplined, purposeful, and stoic. While there was a certain attraction to such an uncluttered lifestyle, she doubted whether she could do it for more than a month or so.

On the short train ride to the next temple, she sat and calmly absorbed everything around her, the sights, the smells, and the tourists—mostly Japanese but also many Europeans,

Americans, Koreans, and Chinese, packing the train heading to the next stop on their rigid itinerary. Visiting temples in Kyoto had become sort of a checklist event for most tourists. You had to see the "big five" temples, no matter how long the lines were and how completely removed from any type of Zen experience they provided. Everyone had seen the tranquil photos of the rock gardens at Ryoan-Ji: islands of stone floating in a perfectly manicured ocean of pea gravel. But in reality, no one ever got the chance to sit and contemplate those gardens as they were originally intended. Instead, you were lucky to be able to sit for sixty seconds on the wooden porch overlooking the garden, scrunched between two other people, before the endless throng pushed you along and out of the viewing area. After taking in those five temples, if you were able to grab a few second- and third-tier temples on the list, you really felt like you had accomplished something. This being her first trip to Kyoto, Meiko realized that she herself was among the "checklist tourists," which made her laugh, drawing odd looks from her fellow train riders. She felt both intensely immersed in the present yet also distinctly separate, like she was somehow watching everything, including herself, from a perch twenty feet above the train car. It was a feeling she was experiencing more in Kyoto than she did in Tokyo. An otherworldly, *am I really here?* sensation, that was strange but not frightening or discomforting.

She made it off the train and headed in the direction of the shrine. Even if she were illiterate, it would be impossible to miss, not only because of its massive vermillion torii gate but also because of the stream of tourists all headed in the same direction. She vowed to return to Kyoto when it was quieter. She wondered if Kyoto ever really did get quiet but imagined that it couldn't get much busier than this—at least she hoped not.

Fushimi Inari Jinja, dedicated in the eighth century to the god of rice and sake (Inari-san), stood as the head shrine for nearly forty thousand Inari shrines scattered throughout Japan, including the tiny one Meiko saw in Ginza. She climbed the granite stairs that led to the vast courtyard, at whose far end stood a bright-red-columned building guarded on both sides by two massive bronze fox statues, green with centuries of patina, each wearing a red scarf. As was the case for most of the temples and shrines she had visited, this one was thick with tourists eager to climb the four-kilometer mountain path famously lined with ten thousand bright vermillion torii, forming a long, winding fiery tunnel.

Opting to avoid the crowds, at least for a while, Meiko took off down a narrow gravel path that led into the thick forest that surrounded the grounds of the shrine. It wasn't long before the voices of the other tourists faded away, and she was deeper into the forest, following this deserted path. Suddenly, she saw movement in the distance on her right and was sure that she saw a small reddish fox run across the path less than twenty yards ahead of her. She knew that the fox was a servant to Inari and there were likely hundreds of fox statues situated around this shrine. But she never expected to see a real fox. She had never seen one outside of a zoo or in one of those nature shows. Without thinking about why she did it, she ran after it. She could hear her feet hitting the gravel as well as her breath as she ran. Everything else seemed to disappear. She saw its tail zip into the woods ahead of her, and she followed it, leaving the path, weaving her way through the dense forest, hoping that she wouldn't twist an ankle on a root or fall into some unseen recess. The leaves on the ground were moist from the morning dew, and her red Toms moccasins were already soaking wet. Up ahead, no more than thirty feet, she saw the fox stop and turn to look at her. She felt a sudden sting in her neck just as she felt her feet slide on the ground, slick as ice. Seeing herself move in slow motion, she was upended, her feet flying high in the air with the rest of her body floating horizontally, suspended momentarily. It was the last thing she remembered.

CHAPTER 7

KAWAGOE
MARCH 24TH

Aiko Tokunaga, Chieko's mother and Meiko's grandmother, carefully trimmed and shaped the tiny limbs of the cypress bonsai trees in her backyard with her pruning scissors. There were over twenty bonsai trees, of various sizes and ages, that she and her husband, Tetsuo, had cultivated over the past three decades, since returning to Japan from his assignment in the States at one of Japan's leading trading companies. The half dozen bonsai that were miniature cherry trees were already engulfed in white blossoms. The trees were originally her husband's hobby, something that he could spend his time on in retirement. Unfortunately, he passed away nine years earlier, and *his* bonsai became *her* bonsai, a constant reminder of the man with whom she had spent nearly fifty years of her life.

It was a warm spring day, and she was glad to be out in the garden after so much rain the past week. Suddenly she felt short of breath. She tried to stand up from her small garden stool but couldn't make it to her feet. Falling backward off the stool, which was fortunately only a foot off the ground, she lost consciousness. Her body collapsed onto the pea gravel path that framed two sides of the house.

She blinked as the bright sun poured into her eyes, not sure why she was staring straight up into the sky. She looked around and realized that she was lying on the ground in her garden, the wooden stool tipped over under her knees, her pruning scissors nestled in the palm of her right hand. She wore gardening gloves on both hands. The wide-brimmed cotton hat she wore to block the sun was on the ground next to her head. *Why am I lying on the ground?* She remembered trimming the bonsai and then feeling light-headed. That was the last thing she remembered. She felt her arms and legs for any pain. Fortunately, there was none. She slowly got to her knees and then gradually stood. She patted her rear end and the backs of her legs, which were damp from the moist gravel. Unsure exactly how long she had lost consciousness, she glanced at her wristwatch: 2:23 p.m. That didn't really help because she didn't know when she had started working in the garden, but she knew it was after lunch, which meant that she was likely out for less than two hours. The last time she remembered losing consciousness was almost seventy years ago, when she was a young girl. She decided not to mention this to Chieko. It would only make her worry needlessly.

She went inside to get a drink of water before continuing in the garden. Water was a "magical elixir," her doctor had told her years ago. When in doubt, drink water. She thought that was sage advice and particularly appropriate now. *Probably just got dehydrated*, she assured herself, although she didn't really believe that to be the case.

CHAPTER 8
TOKYO
MARCH 24ᵀᴴ

"Has anyone in this room ever woken up with the feeling that they couldn't move, that they were paralyzed?" Dr. David Wright asked the classroom of slightly over one hundred students gathered for his class, Making Sense of the World: The Origins of Myth and Folklore, at the international division of Waseda University in Tokyo. Approximately twenty hands went up around the lecture hall. "OK, that would seem to be between 15 and 20 percent of you." He assumed there were probably a few who were too shy to raise their hands.

"Now, of those who have experienced this phenomenon, how many have felt that there either was someone sitting on your chest or was someone or something in the room with you while you were unable to move?" Ten or so hands went up, with a murmur as students looked around the room at their classmates. "Pretty scary experience, right?" All those who were holding their hands up, as well as many others, nodded their agreement.

"Here's something that might be even more frightening. Of those who raised their hands earlier, how many of you, at the time of this phenomenon, had an out-of-body experience where you felt that you were floating above your body or that perhaps you were being touched by something out of this world, potentially an alien. You were able to watch but do nothing about it?" There was a spattering of "oohs" throughout the room as about eight hands went up.

The percentages were pretty much the same as they were in the United States, England, and France, where he had given a similar lecture.

"In our last lecture, we talked about how folklore and beliefs develop out of real-world phenomena. While the folklore, stories, and myths that emerge may appear larger-than-life and otherworldly, their foundations arise from experiences that are common, or at least familiar, to large sectors of the community or culture in which they arise. To ancient civilizations, the daily trek of the sun across the sky, a phenomenon as common as any we know, was explained in the context of their understanding of the gods who controlled the world as they knew it. For the Greeks and later the Romans, it was Apollo, the Sun King, on a golden chariot pulled by a team of four fiery steeds who set out every morning and made the long arc across the sky before returning at the end of the day. That made sense to them and fit nicely into their paradigm about the nature of the universe." The screen behind David lit up with a Greek painting of Apollo making his daily journey.

This class was a collection of lectures taken from some of his most popular classes that he taught at the University of California, San Diego. While the class was taught in English in the international studies department, students from all disciplines and departments across the university, one of Japan's most prestigious, were welcome to attend. There were some Japanese students, particularly those in the sociology and psychology departments, who were eager to attend lectures by one of the world's most well-known authors in the field of folklore and myth.

For many students, in Japan as well as in Europe and the United States, formalized religion had lost much of its appeal. Nonetheless, there was still the fundamental human need to make sense of the world around them. Understanding how myth and folklore evolved as a sense-maker throughout human existence provided comfort, a safe harbor from which to explore the world.

David pulled up a slide of a painting depicting a woman in a sheer robe stretched out on a bed with her arms hanging over the sides, upon whose stomach sat a diabolical-looking demon, along with a horse peeking out from behind curtains in the background. Nearly everyone in the classroom reacted visibly to the photo. Some of the girls covered their mouths, while some of the male students in the back smirked at the overt sensuality of the image. David knew that this photo would generate such a reaction and couldn't help but laugh.

"Quite a provocative image, right? This painting is entitled *The Nightmare* and was painted by Henry Fuseli in 1781. In fact, the word *nightmare* in English derives from the Old English word *mare*, which refers to demons and, particularly, incubi, who visit us at night." He pulled up another slide, this time a marble statue of a nude woman on a bed clearly struggling to hold off the winged demon perched menacingly on her hip. "This is entitled *Le Cauchemar*, or, in English, *The Nightmare*, by Eugène Thivier, created in 1894." The reaction to this image was even stronger than the last one. He knew that this painting always got people's attention. It was at once both demonically terrifying and erotic. The room rumbled with stray comments and uncomfortable giggles. Almost everyone leaned closer to get a better view. He knew he had them. He loved this part of teaching, the ability to captivate an audience. Getting them out of the here and now for a few minutes and entering the world of myth and legend—a world that most people unconsciously suppressed but deeply missed and, as far as David was concerned, needed.

"This phenomenon, namely, the inability to move when one awakes, coupled with the feeling that someone or something is in the room, or sitting on your chest, or even that you are floating above your own body, is referred to as sleep paralysis."

He looked out to the students. "How many of you have ever heard that term before?"

Everyone looked around as two hands went up from different corners of the room. David laughed. "Isn't it strange that about twenty of you have experienced this phenomenon but only two of you knew that it had a name?" Murmurs of soft laughter filled the room. "Of those twenty people who have experienced this phenomenon, which we will now call sleep paralysis, how many of you mentioned it to anyone else?" He surveyed the room, as did the rest of the students. Only eight hands went up, which was about what he would have guessed. "This goes to show you that even when people experience something terribly frightening and disturbing, most of us tend to keep that experience to ourselves. That's exactly where myth and legend come along to help us."

He looked quickly at his notes and continued with his lecture.

"While clearly not as common as the rising of the sun, as we have seen by our own sampling here, sleep paralysis is relatively pervasive. Depending on whom you ask, it seems to affect about 10 percent of the general population and is much higher in individuals who also suffer from sleep apnea or narcolepsy. It has been reported in almost every culture and all parts of the world. There is a sophisticated scientific explanation for the phenomenon that involves an inappropriate overlap of REM, or rapid eye movement, and the waking stages of sleep. The brain has a natural mechanism, a switch, if you will, that flips when the body enters REM cycles, the deepest stages of sleep, where dreams occur, and limits the body's ability to move. It prevents us from flailing, hitting ourselves, or doing something like twitching our legs like dogs and cats do while we dream. It also puts us in a state where we are slightly less attuned to external stimuli so that we are not woken up during these stages and can reap the benefits of the restorative REM sleep. When we phase out of REM sleep, that switch turns off, and we have normal use of our bodies. But in people who experience sleep paralysis, REM sleep is disrupted. You have a situation where your mind is in a hyper-vigilant state that interprets external stimuli as threats. At the same time, because you are still in a semi-REM sleep pattern, you are temporarily unable to move, and to top it off, your breathing tends to be more rapid and shallow. So, you perceive everything as dangerous, you can't move, you have trouble breathing, and you know it's not a dream. That's a pretty scary combination, if you ask me.

"But this explanation is one that we have come upon only very recently, within the past twenty years, with advances in neurobiology and advanced sleep research. It's not hard to imagine that people who experienced this terrifying condition five hundred or a thousand or ten thousand years ago would attribute it to a demon of some type. That would seem to be a perfectly reasonable explanation to me." David smiled. "Now, to make it more interesting, this is a condition that only affects certain people, and even among those individuals, it typically occurs rather infrequently."

He stepped from behind the lectern and came closer to the students in the front row of the lecture hall. The wireless microphone clipped to the front of his shirt allowed almost unrestricted movement. He leaned closer to those in the front of the room as if talking to them in private.

"Now, wouldn't it be natural to try and look for some cause to this affliction? Wouldn't it be very reasonable to assume that it was connected to something you did, something you ate, or maybe even from someone or something from another world trying to tell you something? Maybe even punish you for something you did?"

Smiles, giggles, and nods of agreement passed through the students. Several of the students in the first two rows had that *please don't call on me* look as they tried to stay relaxed, to avoid direct eye contact without appearing to avoid making eye contact. He was aware how intimidating it was to be singled out in front of a large classroom. But he also liked to get students involved in class rather than having them sit passively and take notes.

"So, let's think back a thousand years or so ago. It's 1000 CE in Europe. The Roman Empire has fallen; the Holy Roman Empire is taking hold in Constantinople; Vikings are marauding their way across Northern and Central Europe; Huns are pillaging and raping their way through Eastern Europe;

and the Moors have conquered much of Spain. Feudal life and castle building begins in earnest as kingdoms form and reform. It's a volatile, uncertain, and frightening time. Even in Japan, while the Heian period was characterized by relative peace and a highly refined culture, wealthy landowners employed samurai to engage in territorial battles to acquire land and wealth."

David paused. Whenever he taught to non-native-English speakers, he tried to keep his delivery slow and focused on clear pronunciations. As someone who spoke Japanese and Spanish, in addition to his native English, he knew how challenging it was to focus on complex thoughts in a foreign language. He also knew that the Japanese students in class were unlikely to raise their hands to ask a question, out of fear of embarrassment. He pressed the clicker in his hand, and an image of a young woman in medieval European peasant garb looked at the camera with a hint of what seemed to be sadness or anxiety emanating from her dark-brown eyes. Behind her lay rolling fields of pale yellow grain and a small, rural village of plaster-covered walls and thatched roofs.

"Let's go back to Europe," David continued. "At some point, someone, let's call her Maria, who experienced this sleep paralysis more than once, must have thought that she either was going mad or, more likely, was possessed by demons. She decided to mention her experience to someone else, and to her good fortune, that other person had experienced the same thing. It must have been a wonderful day when Maria realized that she wasn't alone, that there were other people, at least one, who also experienced this terrible feeling. Now, given that it only happens to about 10 percent of the population, it's likely that poor Maria mentioned it to several other people before stumbling upon a sympathetic corroborator. You can only imagine what the other 90 percent of the people she talked to back then thought about her."

He stood next to an American student in the first row. "Tamara, you didn't have your hand up earlier, so I'm assuming you've never experienced sleep paralysis—is that correct?"

She nodded sheepishly. "Yes, that's correct."

"So, imagine if one of your friends came up to you and said that she woke up last night, unable to move, with the distinct feeling that a demonic presence was not only in the room with her but actually sitting on her chest staring at her. What would be your first thought?"

Tamara thought briefly and then said, "I'd think that she had a terrible nightmare. That something was clearly bothering her, and it was showing up in her dreams."

David laughed. "Tamara, you're a psychology major, correct?"

She nodded. "Yes, Dr. Wright."

"OK." He looked out at the entire room. "I'm going to have to stop calling on psychology majors for these things." Laughter bounced around the room. "Now, for all the non-psychology majors in the room, if a friend of yours came to you and told you this, raise your hand if you would at least partially think that this person was a bit nuts." Hands shot up all over the room, perhaps as much as 50 percent of the class, along with a chorus of laughs, short asides, stray comments, and knowing glances. David winked at Tamara. She was a good student, and he knew that she wouldn't take the laughter negatively. At least, he hoped not.

"Exactly!" said David with a smile. "Remember that up until the latter part of the nineteenth century, there wasn't a concept of the unconscious mind. We didn't know about how unrealized fears or ambitions expressed themselves in our unconscious and manifested themselves in strange ways in our dreams." He paused, quieting the room. "A thousand years ago there was no such thing as the unconscious. There were demons and evil spirits, and they likely visited you because you were impure of thought or deed. So, imagining that Maria was a lunatic or perhaps just weak-minded would probably be a relatively kind-hearted reason for her affliction." He walked slowly past the front row as he continued.

"In the small communities of the time, word about Maria would spread, maybe not with the speed of Twitter, but nonetheless it would get out. It would reach a tipping point where a critical mass of people would have shared their experiences. The strange sensation wouldn't be isolated to Maria and her friend. When that happened, it would require some type of rationale to explain this collective experience. That rationale would likely come from a priest, a shaman, or some other respected person. We would now refer to that explanation as folklore or myth. It would clearly have been grounded in the prevailing religious and cultural belief systems of that society. There would need to be some explanation regarding the cause of such a malady, as well as what might be a remedy or a means of prevention. Dating back to the earliest records of humankind, we know that we as humans have an inherent need to make sense of our environment and the phenomena we experience. It's important and, I argue, an essential part of our being to make sense of the world around us. Whether that explanation turns out to be the quote-unquote truth or not is irrelevant. We lived comfortably for millennia thinking that the sun was the center of the universe and that the earth was flat. We laugh about that now, but fifteen hundred years, ago the greatest thinkers in the world had no problem accepting it. The important thing is that whatever story emerged had to explain this phenomenon, this collective experience, in a way that fit inside a paradigm of beliefs that people in that culture or society could understand."

David moved to the left of the lectern and directed attention back to the screen behind him.

"Let's see how different cultures took to explaining this universal phenomenon. Remember, we're talking about a single phenomenon, at least from a physiological or psychological perspective. The description of the symptoms of sleep paralysis is essentially identical across cultures. But as we'll see, every culture explains the exact same set of symptoms in ways that fit with their world-view, their religious beliefs, their myths, and their cultures."

Behind him a map of the world appeared, with blinking red dots scattered across the entire globe. He clicked a button on his remote, and the map zoomed in on Sweden.

"In Scandinavian folklore, sleep paralysis is caused by a woman who is cursed, called a *mare*, whose body is carried away during the night without her noticing. During this state, she sits on the chests of villagers, causing them to have what we commonly refer to as nightmares." The map zoomed in on China. "In Chinese folklore, it is believed that human breath can be stolen by a mouse, which temporarily turns that mouse into a human at night. The feeling of pressure on the chest is actually the mouse sitting near the individual's nostrils, trying to steal their breath." The map jumped to Turkey. "In many Islamic cultures, demons known as *djinn*, or *cin*, are the cause of this phenomenon. They haunt those who have not been true in thoughts and deed. To get rid of the djinn, one must pray to Allah and recite specific lines of the Qu'ran." The screen switched to the United States. "During the Salem witch trials, one of the accusations against the alleged witches was that they visited unsuspecting individuals at night, sitting on their chests to bewitch and haunt them."

The screen returned to the globe with the flashing red dots. He looked to his audience. "These are just a few examples. There are literally hundreds of others that describe both this phenomenon and its causes in surprisingly similar ways." David moved in front of the lectern, facing the classroom.

"Given what we've seen here today and what we talked about in the last class, what does this tell us about the origins of myths?" Hands popped up around the room. David pointed to a young man seated near the door. "Thomas?"

"That one way or another we are compelled to make sense of the world around us," replied the young man without hesitation.

"Excellent," agreed David. "What else?" He scanned the room and pointed to a brunette with her hair pulled back into a ponytail. "Sarah?"

"That every culture needs to fit that sense-making heuristic into their own cultural norms and paradigms," she said cautiously, with the end of the sentence coming out almost as a question.

David nodded. "I couldn't have said it better myself." He then said, "Cultures continue to build up these means of understanding the world around them, brick by brick, stone by stone, until they have created a sustainable set of values, mores, stories, myths, and beliefs to guide them. But then, as we will see in next week's lecture, there comes a time when those stable beliefs are no longer able to handle a wave of new information, and people are forced to rethink, recalibrate, and in some cases, abandon large portions of their belief systems to accommodate this new reality. As we will see, those shifts in paradigms often occur quickly, and they never come about without significant resistance."

He pulled up another slide, showing a reading assignment in their textbook along with questions for consideration. "For the next class, I'd like you to finish up chapters eight and nine and answer the questions that I've highlighted here, which are at the ends of the chapters. Those are due at the beginning of next class. Until then, enjoy the week."

He folded up his materials and unhooked his laptop as the students filed out of the classroom. He chatted with a few students who came up to him and then went to his cramped, spartan office. There was a wooden desk, an office chair, and a small bookshelf, which he had filled with books shipped from the States. Still more professional journals and books sat in precarious stacks on the floor, seemingly the result of an academic game of Jenga.

David was enjoying his time in Japan, even though the summer months had been rather stifling with heat and humidity. As someone used to San Diego's low humidity and temperate climate, he had learned to appreciate the clear changing of the seasons. Meiko was really becoming more comfortable with her Japanese roots and had made some headway in reconnecting with her mother. They were baby steps, but it was progress nonetheless. He owed it to Chieko to bring Meiko here and reunite them after almost twelve years. Chieko's mother, Aiko, had been a steadying presence and served as a faithful intermediary between Meiko and her mother. He wished that things could have worked out between himself and Chieko. But that was water under the bridge. Their relationship hadn't progressed much beyond cordial acquaintances since he'd arrived here, and that was probably where it would remain. He did enjoy reconnecting with Aiko, though. Their relationship hadn't suffered any setbacks because of the divorce.

He plopped down into the chair and stretched out his arms and looked out the lone window in the room. He watched students on their way to their various classes, walking in small groups. He relished the college atmosphere and daydreamed about his days as an undergraduate studying literature at USC. Back then, he was convinced that he would eventually write the great American novel. He smiled, thinking about his naiveté. But that innocence had also been paired with a drive and an unbridled thirst for knowledge that had pushed him to continue his education and eventually finish his PhD in anthropology from UCLA. It continued to push him to this day. He had never left the academic world, the campus environment, which every year welcomed bright new minds filled with dreams and unfettered ambitions. He was grateful that he never had to.

CHAPTER 9

KYOTO
MARCH 24TH, DAY 1

She heard his voice before she saw him.

"Hello. Are you all right? Can you hear me?"

Slowly, she opened her eyes. The sun rushing in. Her head pounding. It was like waking midway through a dream and looking around a strange room. She felt confused and disoriented.

"Miss, can you hear me?"

She opened her mouth. "Yes."

"Wonderful. Just relax. You're going to be fine. Do you feel pain anywhere?" The voice flowed through her like a warm, calming breeze.

"It feels like I was stung by a bee." She sat up and looked down at her torso, her legs, and then to her arms and hands. They appeared to be in order. She rubbed the back of her neck where the bee sting seemed to originate. "My head hurts."

"I'm not surprised," replied the ghostly voice. She still hadn't seen who was speaking. "You fell down and hit your head."

She turned and saw a white robe covering a middle-aged man with gray-streaked black hair. He was staring warmly into her eyes, a look of concern but also of caring and comfort in his dark-brown eyes.

"Where am I?" She looked around and saw that she was in the woods somewhere. Her bottom felt wet and cold.

"You are at the Fushimi shrine. Fushimi Inari Taisha, in Kyoto," replied the man. "Do you remember coming here?"

She thought for a minute, but there was nothing.

"Do you know your name?"

She looked at him. It was such an easy question, but for some reason she didn't know the answer. How could she not know her name? Her heart raced, and her chest tightened; she had difficulty taking in a full breath. She realized she was panicking and did her best to stay calm.

"That's all right. Don't worry. It will all come back to you in time." He opened a small stainless-steel thermos and poured some steaming liquid into the cup. "Here, sit up a bit, and sip this slowly. It will make you feel better."

She grasped the aluminum cup with both hands and took a sip. It tasted green, earthy, and slightly bitter.

"It's tea. There's plenty more, so drink up."

She slowly sipped the tea and felt it warm her insides and clear her head a bit. She gradually got to her knees and then stood up, unsure whether her legs would hold her. The man in the white robes held her arm to steady her.

"Be careful," he reassured her. "There's no rush. We can stay here as long as you wish."

She brushed herself off, again felt the dampness on her behind and the backs of her legs.

"I'm OK. I can walk." She looked at her clothes and those of the man next to her, wondering which of them was out of place. Probably her, she thought. *I bet he at least knows his name.*

"Good. Let's go to the administration building and get some information about you and see if we can help you find your way."

He led her slowly to a narrow dirt path. Her head was clearing some. This looked oddly familiar, yet completely new and foreign at the same time. What country was she in? What language were they speaking?

"What language are we speaking?" She hoped that didn't sound too odd. After all, how could you communicate in a language and not even know what language you were speaking?

The man stopped and looked at her with concern and compassion in his eyes. "We're speaking Japanese. Aren't you Japanese?"

Again, it seemed like a simple question, but she didn't know the answer. She had another burst of panic but did her best to hold it together. *Just keep walking*, she told herself.

"I guess so. I'm not sure."

They moved along the path. Everything was a blur. Her legs felt shaky, and she did her best to keep her balance, focusing on every step.

"Well, you look Japanese, and you speak Japanese, so I'm going to assume that you are Japanese."

That seemed like sound enough logic to her.

The path opened into a massive granite courtyard littered with bright-red buildings. There were dozens, maybe hundreds, of people walking around. None of them seemed to pay attention to them, intent as they were on taking pictures of the spacious grounds, the buildings, and the bright torii-lined path leading up the mountain. The man guided her to a large, two-story building.

"This is the administrative building," he said, moving them forward. "We'll have a seat, fill out some paperwork, and see if we can find out a bit more about you."

Several men dressed similarly to the man she was with

worked at desks and bowed ever so slightly as the pair headed to a back room. He poured another cup of tea into a ceramic cup and handed it to her.

"I'm not sure if it tastes any better drinking from a real cup, but it's certainly more refined."

He sat behind a simple metal desk that might be found in any schoolroom or office building and took out sheet of paper from the top drawer and began taking notes.

"I'm going to ask you some questions. It's all right if you don't know the answers. I have to make a record of what has happened. This won't take long, and we will have you on your way shortly."

She nodded, sipping the tea.

"What is your name?"

She thought as hard as she could, but nothing came to mind. She shook her head. "I don't know."

"That's all right. For our purposes, would you mind if I called you Hana?"

She thought for a moment. Considering that she had no idea what her name really was, Hana was as good as any. "Yes, that's fine." *Hana's a nice name*, she thought. It meant "flower" and was as good as any she could think of. At least it would give her something to latch on to. It was important to have a name, after all.

"Good. OK, Hana, do you have a wallet, a purse, a cell phone, or anything else that might help us identify you?"

She patted her pockets. There was nothing. "No, I don't have anything." She figured that was probably odd; most people would have at least some of these things. But she had no idea what was normal or not at this point.

"Do you have any money or a credit card with you?" He looked concerned.

"No."

He made notes on his sheet. "Do you remember coming to this shrine?"

She thought hard again. "Not really."

"What is the last thing you remember?"

Again, she searched her memory for anything. It was blank, as if she had been born that morning, which of course she knew wasn't possible. Full-grown adults didn't appear out of nowhere. She felt nauseous and tried to control it by sipping on the warm tea. Another panic attack engulfed her. If she weren't already sitting, she would have collapsed. Nothing made sense, and his questions seemed only to punctuate the desperate nature of her predicament.

"I don't remember anything." She burst into tears the moment she heard the words leave her mouth.

"Do you know where you live? Do you have any family members?"

After a pause, tears still filling her eyes. "I don't know." She held her head in her hands and wept. What was she going to do? *Why can't I remember anything?*

He handed her a red handkerchief. "Here. Don't worry. I'll help you."

He pulled a business card from inside his desk and wrote on it and then handed it to her. "My name is Takagi, Shusaku Takagi. I am the deputy priest of this shrine. I wrote my personal cell phone number on this card. Please feel free to call me anytime you need anything."

She took the *gonguji*'s card and looked at it. "Thank you. You're very kind." The white robes now made sense. Given that she didn't have a robe on, it was clear that she wasn't a priest. But what was she, let alone who was she? Nothing came to mind.

The priest continued. "Until we find out who you are and where you live and your other family members, then you are my responsibility because you passed out at our shrine."

The priest reached into the drawer and pulled out several other items.

"This is a prepaid cell phone. We keep them on hand for emergencies and for some of our priests who don't own cell phones of their own. I'm going to enter my contact information in here, so you will always be able to call me. I'm not exactly sure how long this will last, but I think it should be good for at least a month or so, depending on how much you use it."

He pulled out a stack of crisp yen notes.

"Here is ¥50,000. This should help you pay for food and find a reasonable place to stay for a while until your memory returns. Unfortunately, we can't let you stay here. I can recommend some inexpensive inns nearby that are clean and nice. Hopefully, you won't need to stay very long."

She took the phone and the money and stared at them.

"I don't know what to say. This is very generous. I don't how I will repay you." She had no idea if this was a lot of money or not, but he seemed to think it was enough to buy food and a place to stay for at least a little while. What would happen when that money ran out, though? She wouldn't feel right asking him for more.

"There's no need to repay us. Think of it as a bit of good-will for someone who needs help." He fished around his drawer and pulled out several more items. "I have a few more things for you, and then I will let you go."

He held a small rectangular packet made of white silk with Chinese characters written in black letters. There was a thin silk cord attached to it, forming a necklace.

"This is an *omamori*. Are you familiar with omamori?"

She nodded. "They're good luck charms, right?" She wasn't sure why she knew that, but for some reason she did.

"Exactly. Many people probably see them as foolish super-stitions, but we see them as an extra means of protection, to help guide and protect us through our lives. I blessed this one just this morning. It would be my honor if you would wear it at all times, at least until your memory returns and you are safe back at your home." He gently handed the charm to her.

She received it in both hands and then slid the cord over her head and let the charm rest on her chest, under-neath her blouse. It was very fragrant, with hints of bergamot and rosemary and some other spices that were unfamiliar. It had a calming influence on her. She felt less anxious than she had just moments earlier.

"It smells nice."

"Yes," the priest agreed. "It contains some local herbs and flowers that the priests pick and dry. I blended this one my-self. I guess you could call it my signature fragrance." He laughed. "People tell us that smelling it is very calming to their nerves."

He wrote a name on a small sheet of paper and handed it to her. "This is the name of a local hospital. I think it makes sense for you to go and get checked out. In fact, you should go there immediately. I can arrange to have a taxi take you right after we finish here. If they ask you to pay or to provide your health insurance information, please just refer them to me, and I'll handle it."

She nodded.

"Finally, I have a small purse for you to hold your belongings in. It's not fancy, but it should do until you find something else. I've put some tea packets in there for you as well. This is the same tea that you've been drinking. It is very calming, and that is important for you right now. I know that it must be very frightening not remembering who you are. The tea will help you relax, and that will allow your memory to return quicker. Please put one tea bag in hot water and allow it to steep for two or three minutes. You should drink at least one cup in the morning, another around midday, and another with dinner. But feel free to drink more if you like." He handed her a light-brown, woven silk pouch embroidered with little white foxes.

She took the purse and looked inside. There were about a dozen small mesh packets of what looked to be tea and herbs. It smelled much like the tea she had been sipping since she woke up. She placed the money and her cell phone in the purse.

"I don't know what to say. I, I feel so stupid. I fell down, and now I can't remember anything, and you're being so kind to me." Tears welled in her eyes again. She dabbed them with the handkerchief.

The priest stepped from behind the desk, knelt next to her, and gently took her hands in his. "Hana, you are going to be fine. I promise you. I will help you along the way. I'm going to say a prayer now and then let you go. Please close your eyes and listen closely." He recited a prayer in a way that seemed to be halfway between talking and singing. His deep voice was calm and soothing. She felt herself drifting away as the prayer continued. She lost track of time as his voice resonated through her head. She felt like she was floating in the clouds. It was peaceful. She didn't want it to end.

When he finished, she opened her eyes. The priest was still kneeling next to her.

"How do you feel?" he asked, clearly concerned.

"I'm hungry," she replied meekly.

The priest laughed. "I'm sure you are. I'll tell you what—there's a small soba shop near the entrance to the shrine, close to the train station. The noodles are very good. They will give you strength. The owner is a nice man who will help you. His name is Masaharu Fujiwara. After you get something to eat, then you can call the taxi and go to the hospital with you. Is that OK?"

She nodded. He stood and helped her to her feet.

"Are you all right to go, or would you like to rest here a bit longer?"

"No, I'm fine, just really hungry. Thank you for everything." She was definitely not all right, but she didn't want to impose on the priest anymore. Besides, she needed to get started on her adventure if she was ever going to remember who she really was.

"Please call me when you're finished eating, and I'll meet you at the soba shop. Until you get back to normal, don't hesitate to call me, day or night."

"Thank you."

He led her out of the administration building and pointed her toward the exit to the shrine. She looked back once and saw him standing there with his hands in prayer, bowing to her slightly. She returned his bow and headed down the stairs. She was on her own now. The journey had begun.

CHAPTER 10

Hana exited the shrine grounds, crossed the street, and walked in the direction of the train station. Just as the priest had indicated, there was a small soba restaurant next to a row of souvenir shops. It was halfway between lunch and dinner, and the shop wasn't particularly busy. She slid the latticed wood-and-glass door open and entered. There was a dark wooden counter with a row of chairs, much like a sushi bar. Several gray-haired men sat in the chairs hunched over bowls of soba, making loud slurping sounds. There were also traditional tables set on tatami mats with dugout places for one's feet to rest underneath the table. It looked to her that the place could probably serve thirty people at a time. It smelled like green tea and straw.

A hostess welcomed her and asked her if she wanted to sit at the counter or at a table. She said that she'd prefer to sit at the counter, but in the corner, if possible. She didn't say that she didn't want to sit next to the old men. She didn't need to—they weren't who she was here to see. The hostess gave her a knowing smile and led her to a seat at the end of the counter and handed her a small menu.

A man wearing a white apron, who looked to be in his early forties, stood behind the counter directly in front of her. He set down a glass of water and asked her for her order.

She looked up at him and asked, "This is my first time here. What would you recommend?"

The man thought for a moment and then said that most people liked the cold noodle tempura set.

Without taking her eyes off the man, she nodded. "That sounds delicious. I'll have one of those."

The man grunted, took her menu, and made his way back into the kitchen. She looked around the small restaurant. It was clean and orderly and looked like it had been in business for a great many years. The wood on the counter was smooth and polished from the oils of the hands and forearms of the patrons who had enjoyed their noodles over the decades. At this time of day, there didn't seem to be very many employees. The hostess was busy wiping down the tables and setting them up for the next round of customers. Hana sipped her water. It was cold and tasted clean and pure. The hostess came by and filled it up for her.

After ten minutes or so, the man emerged from the kitchen with a red lacquered rectangular tray, which he set in front of her. There was a wooden square plate with a rolled bamboo mat heaped with long light-gray, brown-flecked square-cut noodles topped with thin strips of green seaweed, *nori*. On a separate plate, sitting on a square white piece of paper, were several pieces of tempura: batter-fried shrimp, pumpkin, eggplant, and lotus root. Next to the tempura sat a small mound of sea salt and a second mound of green tea powder. A large lacquered dipping bowl with a fragrant soy-based soup sat in the corner of the tray.

The man looked at her. "I hope you enjoy. Let me know if you need anything."

She looked up from the tray and nodded. "Thank you. I certainly will. This looks wonderful."

Over the next twenty minutes, she proceeded to dip the noodles in the soup and slurp them up with gusto, in the style that the Japanese find most pleasing to the senses. The tempura was crisp and flavorful. The shrimp was sweet, even the crunchy tail—especially the crunchy tail. The lotus root was crisp and sounded like a carrot when she chewed. She dipped some in the salt and green tea powder and some just in the soup. Both approaches worked well. Occasionally, the man would walk by behind the counter or peek out from behind the kitchen curtains to see how she was progressing. When she was finished, she laid her chopsticks on the tray and dabbed her lips with the paper napkin. She was full and felt wonderful.

The man immediately emerged from the kitchen and took her tray away, as if he'd been waiting for her to finish. "How did you enjoy it?" he asked.

She hesitated, as if thinking hard for the right answer. "I don't think I've ever had better soba noodles in my life." Her eyelashes fluttered, purposefully giving off a look that was shy and coy and yet uniquely seductive.

The man tried to maintain his cool appearance, although he was obviously pleased to hear such high praise and couldn't help but be stirred by her appearance. "Thank you. Are you from Kyoto, or did you come from somewhere else to see the cherry blossoms?"

"I don't really know actually," she said, sounding as scared and vulnerable as she could. "I fell while I was at the Inari shrine, and I seem to be lost. I'm not sure what to do at this point."

"Do you have a place to go?"

"Not really. I don't have any money," she lied. "I used most of my money to eat lunch because I was so hungry." Tears welled in her eyes.

The man handed her a napkin. She wiped away her tears.

"Don't worry about me. I'm sure I'll find my way somehow."

"I can't just let you leave without any money or any place to go. Let me help you. First off, consider this my treat, an unofficial welcome to Kyoto."

"I hate to impose, mister." She hesitated. "I don't even know your name. You must think I'm just some silly girl who's lost her way. I feel so stupid."

"Nonsense. My name is Masaharu Fujiwara. I own this place," he said with pride. "I'd be happy to help out, at least until you get back on your feet. This is our slow time. Give me a minute, and I'll get you set up."

He went behind the curtain and emerged shortly thereafter, sans apron, and it looked to her as if he'd run a comb through his hair. He said something to the hostess, who nodded, gave a suspicious glance toward Hana, and then proceeded tidying up the restaurant. Mr. Fujiwara motioned to Hana to follow him outside. They stepped outside the door and walked toward the train station. "I'm sorry, I didn't get your name."

"Hana. My name is Hana. I don't know my last name." She looked as lost, helpless, and afraid as she could. She knew it was an irresistible combination.

He looked at her protectively. "That's OK, Hana, I'll take care of you. I'm sure you'll remember your last name soon enough. But first, let's find a place for you to stay."

† † †

Light shone onto her closed eyes, warming them. Hana opened her eyes and saw it was morning light streaming in through a window. She looked around the small room. She didn't recognize it. She turned her head on the pillow and saw Mr. Fujiwara fast asleep beside her, his bare chest rising and falling with his breath. She gently lifted the futon cover a few inches. They were both naked. *That's odd*, thought Hana, although she didn't panic, which would have been Meiko's reaction to finding herself naked in a bed with a man she had just met. But Hana didn't feel any concern. She felt a strange sense of something, but she wasn't sure what. Satisfaction was probably the closest emotion. She decided to go back to sleep. She'd try and figure things out when she woke up again.

CHAPTER 11

TOKYO
MARCH 26TH, DAY 3

Chieko's cell phone rang. The caller ID indicated that it was her ex-husband, David. *I wonder what he wants.* She debated whether to take the call or just let it go into voice mail. Her next patient wouldn't arrive for another hour, but she wasn't particularly interested in talking to David. After three rings, she took the call.

"Hello, David, how are you?" She tried to sound friendly.

"Sorry to bother you. Are you with a patient? Can you talk?"

So much for the pleasantries. "No, I have some time. What is it?"

"Have you heard from Meiko?" He sounded concerned.

"No, she hasn't called me. How was her trip to Kyoto?"

"That's just it." There was a hint of panic in his voice that she rarely ever heard. "I haven't heard from her in two days. She was supposed to be back yesterday, and she hasn't called, emailed, or texted, which isn't like her. I called her cell phone, and it went directly to her voice mail. I left a couple of messages and texted her several times. I thought she might have contacted you."

Sure, as if she'd call me before you. "No, the last I heard from her was on her blog, three days ago." Something wasn't right. Meiko might not be her mother's biggest fan, but she always stayed in touch with her father. They were very close, something that Chieko admittedly envied.

"Yeah, me too. That's the last time I heard from her. I'm worried." Again, that note of concern, even panic, screamed through the phone. It made the hairs on her neck stand up. "Meiko is usually really good about keeping in touch. If she was going to be late, she would have definitely called."

"OK, let's stay calm. There's probably a very reasonable explanation for this." Her training as a clinician and her natural tendencies as both a woman and a mother took over. She needed to calm David down and alleviate his fears. "I'll check with my mother to see if she's heard anything. She and Meiko seem to have formed a good relationship." *Better than the one she has with me, at least.* "Let's give it one more day, and if any of us hear anything, we'll let the others know. I bet she comes back tonight with some crazy story to share."

When she hung up the phone, Chieko had a strange feeling that something wasn't right. Her training as a therapist helped her prevent others from engaging in irrational thinking. It didn't mean that those concerns, such as David's, weren't real and justified. She remembered one of her abnormal psychology professors used to say, "Just because you're paranoid doesn't mean the bastards aren't really after you." She could hear the fear in David's voice. She didn't blame him. Meiko had always been a very organized and responsible girl, even from an early age. The few times they had met while in Japan, she was always punctual. This was definitely out of character. She tried not let her imagination run wild. There was probably a reasonable explanation for all of this. Meiko probably lost her cell phone, and maybe her wallet had been stolen, so it was hard to get in touch with anyone. Those, at least, would be simple problems to fix.

CHAPTER 12

KAWAGOE
MARCH 26TH, DAY 3

Aiko was in her kitchen cutting pickled daikon for her lunch when the phone rang. The caller ID showed that it was Chieko's cell phone. It was strange for Chieko to call this early in the afternoon. She had probably forgotten something, or she was going to miss dinner. She pressed the speaker button on her phone. Kotetsu, her cat, was asleep on a cushion next to the dining table, rhythmically extending and contracting his paws in some unconscious dance.

After Chieko filled her in on her conversation with David, Aiko hung up the phone, and a chill ran up her spine. There was something wrong, of that she had no doubt. Something had happened to Meiko, something bad, perhaps very bad. She had learned long ago to trust her instincts, and right now sirens were going off in her head. She thought about what Chieko had said. The last time anyone heard from Meiko was Friday evening. Aiko wondered if her sudden loss of consciousness on Saturday afternoon had any connection to Meiko's disappearance. It wouldn't be the first time that something like that had happened to her. She put the sliced daikon away in a ceramic container with a plastic lid, her appetite having slipped away.

She sat down on a cushion next to Kotetsu and softly stroked him. Slowly waking from his afternoon nap, he purred and rolled his head to meet her hand and voiced a few soft meows. Kotetsu had shown up on her doorstop on the morning of July 7, a year after the death of her husband, Tetsuo. July 7 was the date of Tanabata, the Star Festival. Legend had it that Princess Orihime, a seamstress, wove beautiful clothes by a heavenly river, represented by the Milky Way. Her father, a god of the heavens, arranged for her to meet Hikoboshi, the cow herder who lived on the other side of the Milky Way. They fell in love instantly and were married. Their love was so deep that Orihime stopped weaving and Hikoboshi ignored his cows, who in turn wandered the heavens aimlessly. Orihime's father became angry and forbade the lovers from being together. Orihime pleaded with him, and because he loved his daughter, he agreed that the two lovers could meet once a year, on the seventh day of the seventh month. On the first day that they were supposed to meet, they found crossing the Milky Way river too difficult. But a flock of magpies made a bridge for Orihime to cross. It is said that if it rains on Tanabata, the magpies will not come and the two lovers must wait another year to meet. For that reason, Japanese always wish for good weather on Tanabata.

Tanabata was significant for Aiko, much as it was for Orihime and Hikoboshi. She and Tetsuo met each other at a Tanabata celebration in Kawagoe. It was their unofficial first date. Every year, Tetsuo did everything in his power to be together with Aiko on Tanabata, even if that meant taking the shinkansen from Kyoto or wherever his business had taken him.

When Kotetsu first arrived on her doorstep, the cat sat and cried until she came to the door. She looked down upon the small gray cat with three white paws and a white spot on his forehead. There was something about this tiny cat that brought a warmth to her heart. He was different from the other strays that roamed the neighborhood. He wove his way between her legs, rubbing against her ankles and purring loudly, as if he belonged with her. She knew that it was probably a crazy idea, but in that instant, and ever since, she felt that Kotetsu was the reincarnation of her lost husband. She wasn't one to get lost in silly superstitions or crazy belief systems, yet she also wasn't one to ignore what stared her in the face. She gave him the name Kotetsu, which meant Little Tetsuo.

She often sat and talked with him when she wanted to work things through in her head or when she felt lonely. He was good company. Somehow, she felt that his presence helped her think more clearly. In any case, he comforted her. She needed that right now.

CHAPTER 13

TOKYO
MARCH 27TH, DAY 4

Chieko finished up her last appointment of the morning and was tidying up the office in anticipation of David's arrival. She buzzed him up from the front entrance of the building to her tenth-floor office in the Toranomon district of Tokyo. She hadn't seen David in several months and hadn't planned on seeing him any time soon. Their mutual concern about Meiko's recent disappearance necessitated their get-together. Chieko wanted it to be on her turf and recommended that he swing by so that they could make the call to the police together.

She waited for him to ring the bell and then opened the door to her office, his first visit. He seemed nervous; so did she.

"Come in, David. It's good to see you," she lied. "I wish it were under different circumstances."

"Yeah, me too. Good to see you as well. Beautiful office." He walked over to the large windows overlooking the Tokyo skyline. "You have a great view. Business must be good."

"I get by." *I busted my ass to build this practice from scratch, so yeah, after more than a decade, you could say that business is good. You wouldn't have said that if you would have seen the crappy offices I started in.* She led him to a chair next to a coffee table with a phone sitting on it. "I thought we'd just do this through speakerphone, so we can both hear what they have to say. How's your Japanese?"

"It's OK, not great. I should be able to follow most of what is said."

The ever-confident Dr. David Wright, she thought. Knowing him, his Japanese was probably very good. He was one of the smartest people she had ever met. Things seemed to come so easily to him, which bugged the hell out of her.

"If you have any questions or want me to ask them anything for you, just let me know." She had always been impressed by his flair for language. Unlike her, he wasn't afraid of making mistakes, which greatly accelerated his communication skills. It also led to some awkward encounters as well.

"Will do."

She dialed the number for the Kyoto police department and explained to the operator that they wanted to speak to someone about their daughter, who had gone missing. They were transferred to two more individuals who each asked them again to explain who they were and what they were calling about, how long the girl had been missing, what her name was, and other basic information. Finally, after about ten minutes, they were transferred to a fourth person, who they were told would be able to help them. At this point, Chieko seriously doubted that.

"This is Detective Nomura. I've been told that your daughter is missing." He sounded bored. "Who am I speaking with?"

"This is Dr. Tokunaga, and I have on the phone with me Dr. Wright from Waseda University."

"Very good," he replied, seemingly unimpressed with their credentials. "And I am to assume that you are the girl's parents?"

"Yes, that's correct."

"Is she a Japanese citizen?"

"No, she's half Japanese, but she is a US citizen." Chieko felt like she was apologizing for her daughter mixed-blood status.

"When did she come to Kyoto, and when was the last time you heard from her?"

Chieko thought Nomura sounded like a recorded message, dry and detached.

"She arrived last Thursday to see the cherry blossoms. The last time we heard anything from her was Friday evening."

"And how did she communicate with you at that time?"

"She posted some notes on her blog and sent us a text message with some pictures."

"She also gave me a call and told me about her day," piped in David. This was news to Chieko, who glared at him for withholding this information. He looked down at the coffee table. She simmered with anger but focused on the task at hand.

"I see. When was she supposed to arrive back in Tokyo?"

"Yesterday afternoon."

"When you talked with her on Friday evening, did you notice anything unusual?"

"No, she said she was tired from all the travel and sightseeing but that everything was beautiful. She was excited about seeing more temples the next day," replied David, his Japanese rough but understandable. "She called right before bed. We didn't talk very long, maybe three minutes." David ignored Chieko's glare.

"Can you provide me with a physical description of her, including any discernible features?"

"Yes, she's tall, 170 centimeters"—while Chieko spoke, David checked her math in his head to make sure she had said their daughter was the equivalent of 5' 7"—"attractive with an athletic build, twenty-one years old. She looks more Japanese than Western, but she also has some Western features. I can email you some photos, if that would help."

"Yes, that would be useful. Include anything else you can in the email, such as what she was wearing, where she was likely to visit. Anything that might help."

"We will. Thank you. Will you get in touch with us if you find out anything?" asked Chieko.

"Yes, we will. Of course, technically, she's only been missing for one day, since she was supposed to return yesterday. So, by official standards, at least, she's not missing. We don't consider an adult to be missing for at least three days."

Here we go, thought Chieko. This was the typical BS that epitomized bureaucracies. "We're here to help" really meant "We're not going to do much of anything about this unless you know someone who can make us do something."

"Let me ask you one more question," said Nomura, "and I apologize in advance if it seems rude. Is Meiko the type of girl who might have met a young man and might be staying in Kyoto for a few days with him?"

"Not at all," responded Chieko, jumping to Meiko's defense. "She's not that type of girl. She's friendly, but she's also very responsible. She wouldn't let some guy she just met convince her to stay in Kyoto and not contact her parents. Besides, she was supposed to be at work today. It's definitely not like her to miss work."

"Fine. Good to know. Please contact me with anything else that might be useful."

Great, thought Chieko. He probably thinks she's some slut who shacked up with some guy for the weekend, and we're her naïve parents wondering why we keep finding condoms in the wastebasket.

"Thank you for your time, Detective. I'll email you some photos in the next hour," replied Chieko.

She pressed the button to end the phone call.

"Jesus Christ, David, why the hell didn't you tell me that you actually talked with her on Friday?"

He shrugged. "In all honesty, it slipped my mind. I was so worried about not hearing from her, I sort of forgot about it. It was a very short call, and she was tired. It's no big deal."

"You made me look like an idiot."

"Well, we can't have that, can we, Chieko. I know how important your image is to you."

"You're such an ass, David! This isn't a game, you know. Our daughter is missing, and you're so damn absentminded, you can't even remember talking to her." She was so angry at him that she wanted to scream or, better yet, punch him in the face. He never appreciated how important it was to save face in Japan. He never would, either, because he just didn't care.

"In any case, what do you think we should do at this point? I brought a few photos of her, like you asked." He laid a stack of photos down on the coffee table. "Can you scan them and send them to the detective?"

"That's exactly what I plan on doing. I don't place a lot of faith in Detective Nomura, though. He sounded like we just woke him up from a nap. I'm sure he's laughing at us right now."

"Well, it's all we've got at this point. I'm sure she'll show up soon. It's just so unlike her not to contact me. Or you," he added.

"Let me scan these and send them off. I've got another appointment in an hour, and I need to review some notes beforehand."

"Keep the photos for now. I can always pick them up later. In fact, you're welcome to keep them." He stood up to leave. Chieko stayed seated, sorting through the photos. Somehow, seeing Meiko's face, even in photos, made her feel better, like she really wasn't that far away. "Also, I'm sorry I didn't tell you about the call with Meiko. It really did slip my mind."

"Thank you. I'll get them back to you later." She said after a pause, "Thanks for stopping by the office."

"Call me if you hear anything," David said, seeing himself out of the office.

"I will. You too."

After he left, she scanned the pictures. She looked at Meiko's smiling face in the photos. She remembered talking with her two weeks earlier. *What in the world could have happened to her to make her disappear?* She hated how David could push all her buttons. But Christ, he could be so nonchalant and forgetful. It's like he didn't take anything seriously. Of course he would say that she took everything too seriously. When they first started dating, their different personalities added humor and fun to their relationship. Over time, it had turned to frustration and animosity.

What she hated most was that he made no attempt to change his behavior, in any way, to accommodate her. She knew that she was a perfectionist and constantly worried about doing things correctly or somehow not meeting other people's expectations. David, conversely, seemed to float through life on his own carefree magic carpet, following whatever interested him at the time. It angered her even more because she envied that quality in him and hated her own inability to master it, or even experience it. She also hated the fact that the world rewarded him for his nonchalant attitude.

CHAPTER 14

KYOTO
MARCH 29TH, DAY 6

Hana emerged from the bathroom of the small hotel room wearing seductive, black-laced lingerie. Her lips were bright red; her mascara, eyeliner, and false eyelashes gave her eyes a seductive feline look, like Cleopatra. She leaned temptingly against the bureau, pushing out her perfectly shaped butt. "Do you like it?"

Fujiwara sat on the edge of the bed in his white underwear, his excitement apparent. "Wow, you look beautiful."

"Thanks, baby. You did a good job of picking out my size." She bent over, exposing the black thong running up her backside. "Do you think it fits all right?"

"Yeah, it fits fine. Now I want to tear it off you." He stood up and grabbed her by the waist. He gently kissed her neck.

"Mmm, that feels good." She rubbed her body against him. She slowly turned around and kissed him deeply, playfully nibbling on his tongue. Gradually, she made her descent, kissing his neck, his chest, slowly licking his nipples and his belly. She moved to her knees and began to remove his underpants. Fujiwara closed his eyes and moaned.

† † †

They lay on the bed, sweaty and exhausted. Fujiwara smoked a Lucky Star cigarette. Hana eventually got up and wrapped herself in a plush bathrobe.

"Did you enjoy that, love?" she purred.

"Are you kidding me? It's the greatest sex I've ever had. I thought I was going to pass out at one point."

"Well, we can't have that. You're going to have to give up smoking if you want to keep up."

"Yeah, maybe."

It was time to ratchet this up a bit and get this guy to shell out some more cash. "Babe, I don't like this hotel anymore. It's too small, and the walls are too thin. I feel self-conscious when we're having sex. It makes me inhibited." She pouted.

"Christ, if that's inhibited, I'd hate to see what you're like when you feel freer."

"Really? You wouldn't want to see how I could take care of you if I wasn't constantly thinking about who's next door?"

"Just of a figure of speech, babe. Of course I'd like to see that. Then I might really have to give up smoking to survive."

"Can you get me into a nicer hotel room soon? Maybe even tonight? I need some new clothes too. I've been wearing the same things for so many days." In reality, she hadn't been wearing much at all most of the time. But this place was small, and he could do better—besides that, she deserved better.

He fidgeted, snuffing out his cigarette. "We went shopping the other day, sweetheart. What else do you need?"

"I was hoping to get another outfit or two, something sexy for when you take me out to a nice dinner. I also want a Louis Vuitton bag. Everyone seems to have one. They look so nice."

"Yeah, they are nice. They're also crazy expensive. Babe, I'm not sure if I can afford all of these things right now."

This was going to be a bit more challenging than she initially thought. But not much more. She pouted, tears welling up in her eyes. "I thought you cared about me and wanted to take care of me and treat me right. I guess those were only words. Maybe we should just stop seeing each other, if that's how you really feel."

"No, no, that's not how I feel. You know that. It's just hard for me to take out so much money without my wife eventually knowing about it." He pulled out another cigarette from the pack and lit it shakily. "Don't worry. I'll figure out something. I've got money in savings that I can pull out. I'll get you into a nice hotel tonight, and then we'll go out shopping and to dinner downtown."

Good boy, that's more like it. She ran over to him, her robe coming open in front, and wrapped her arms around his neck.

"Yay! Thank you, babe!" She jumped up and down like a five-year-old with their first bike. "You know how much I love you. I know you'll take care of me. I don't have anyone else, only you. I can't wait to see you again. I'll show you something extra special next time." She had no idea what else she could possibly show him, but he didn't need to know that. The plan didn't involve telling the truth, now, did it? She smiled, knowing that the hook was fully set. It was just a matter of how fast she wanted to bring the fish into the boat. Sooner would be better. After all, she had bigger fish to fry. She smiled, thinking that the fishing analogy worked well.

He snuffed out his cigarette as they fell back onto the bed.

CHAPTER 15

Meiko rubbed her eyes as she awoke. She was lying on a large bed with a fluffy down comforter, her head resting on thick, soft pillows. It looked to her like she was in a hotel room, a nice one. She rolled out of bed wearing a silky nightshirt that hung to just above her knees, and nothing else. Rubbing the sleep out of her eyes, she tried to figure out where she was.

She walked to the bathroom, passing several department store bags filled with boxes and a distinctive orange-and-brown bag with *LV* printed all over the outside. Inside the box she found a brand-new Louis Vuitton bag, deep brown with a long strap. *What in the world is all of this? Whose stuff is this?* It felt like waking up in someone else's body, like her soul had jumped to a completely different person.

She entered the bathroom and looked in the mirror. The face was familiar. She had seen it before, but it didn't bring back any memories or sense of self. *Who am I? What am I doing here?* She had so many questions and so few answers. She felt a little wobbly, like she might faint. She turned on the faucet and let the water run into the sink and then splashed cold water onto her face, hoping that it would help her wake up out of this nightmare. It didn't work. She patted her face dry and looked again in the mirror. Nothing. She vaguely remembered having this feeling of complete blankness before but couldn't remember when.

Lying on the desk next to the bed was a small tan silk purse with little white embroidered foxes on the outside. Inside there was a cell phone and a stack of bills. There was over ¥200,000 in cash. She wondered whose money this was and how it got here. Could it be hers? There weren't signs that anyone else lived here. How could all of this be hers without her remembering any of it? There were also five small mesh packets that looked like tea bags. *I do remember those.* That, at least, was a positive.

She flipped open the cell phone, hoping that it would have some information about who she was. She pressed the contacts icon. There was only one number. Without any idea who would answer, she called the number.

"Hello, Hana?" answered a man's voice.

"Um, hello. Who is this?"

"It's Takagi, the priest from Fushimi Inari Jinja. Hana, are you all right?" He sounded concerned.

"Um, I'm not sure. Is that my name? Hana?" She wondered why he knew more about her identity than she did. But if he knew who she was, then he could help her get her memory back. It was more than she had a minute ago.

"Well, we're not sure right now, but that's the name I've given you temporarily, until you remember your real name."

"My real name? Why don't I remember my real name? Where did we meet?"

"We met at the Inari shrine. You passed out. I think you must have hit your head, because you couldn't remember anything. Is everything all right? Where are you right now?"

"I feel all right, a little groggy, I guess. I think I'm in a hotel room somewhere." She opened the desk drawer. "The stationery says the Grand Prince Hotel. Does that make sense?"

"Of course. It's a beautiful hotel. I'll tell you what—I can be there in less than an hour. I'll explain to you what happened, and we can try and figure out what to do, so you can get your memory back. Do you remember meeting me?"

"I think so. It's one of the only things I do remember. Did you give me the fox purse and some money?"

"Yes, very good. I also gave you that cell phone. You can trust me, Hana. I'll help you get better. Why don't we meet in the lobby of the hotel in an hour? We can have tea and talk."

"OK, that sounds good." A sense of relief rushed over her. He was going to help her figure this out. She wasn't alone.

She hung up the phone and stared at it for several seconds. She set it down and decided to take a shower.

She dressed and made her way down to the front desk, where a sharply dressed woman, her hair in a tight bun, greeted her. "Good morning, ma'am; how can I help you?"

"Good morning, I'm in room 719. Out of curiosity, what name do you have on the reservation for that room?"

"Of course, let me look it up. It's under the name of Tanaka, a Miss Hana Tanaka. You checked in last night. Is everything to your liking with the room?"

"Yes, yes, the room's very nice." At least she knew her name, although it didn't really mean anything to her. But the priest had also called her Hana, so that was good. The key would be to start fitting together pieces that connected, like a jigsaw puzzle. It would eventually lead her to a place where everything came together and made sense. At least she hoped so.

"Wonderful. Is there anything else I can help you with?"

"Yes, is there a bookstore near here?"

"There's one about a five-minute walk from here." She pulled out a map and explained the best route.

Meiko headed out the front door, which was opened for her by a uniformed doorman. The street was busy with cars passing by as well as fellow pedestrians on the sidewalk.

"Would you like me to call you a taxi, ma'am?" asked a hotel valet.

"No, thank you. I'm fine." The air felt fresh on her face, and having a clear destination in mind gave her a sense of purpose. The panic she felt earlier was subsiding. She would get through this.

She found the bookstore, which was brightly lit and laid out with aisle upon aisle of multicolored books and magazines. She felt a sense of comfort here, although she wasn't sure why. After browsing the magazines, many of which seemed familiar to her, she purchased a blank journal, a copy of a magazine titled *Weekly Woman* with a smiling young woman on the front, and a pen. There was a Starbucks next to the bookstore. She ordered a cup of coffee, tasted it, and decided that it needed milk and some sugar. She found a small table in the corner, took out her notepad, and began writing.

This was day one of her journal. She wrote down the date, which she copied from the receipt, the time, the location, and everything she remembered about that morning, every person she saw or talked to, the bookstore's name, her hotel's name and room number, as well as the name Hana Tanaka, which she assumed must be her. She also noted the priest's name and that she was going to meet him in the lobby of the hotel. He had mentioned that she fell at an Inari shrine and hit her head and that was probably why she couldn't remember anything. It felt good to write all of this down. It made her feel much more at ease, in control of something, at least.

† † †

Meiko sat on a comfortable, deep-cushioned sofa in the spacious, modern lobby of the Prince Hotel. She saw a man in a dark-blue suit and dark wool cap walk through the revolving door of the hotel. She didn't pay attention to him except that he smiled as soon as he saw her and made a beeline to where she sat. *Must be him. His face looks familiar.* He looked friendly. She was feeling better already. Things were starting to come together.

"Hello, Hana, how are you?" he asked. His eyes looked warm and friendly to her.

"I guess I'm fine. I just can't remember anything." It seemed odd for her to say that she felt fine, given the circumstances, but other than having no memory, she did feel fine.

"Do you remember me?" He looked at her with warm, caring eyes.

She looked at him intently. "Yes, now I remember you. I don't remember too much, but I remember sitting and talking with you in an office. We drank tea."

"Yes, that's correct. That was almost a week ago. Do you remember anything since then?" He looked concerned.

She shook her head. "No, nothing until I woke up this morning. I don't even know how I ended up in this hotel."

He looked around the lobby. "Well, it's certainly a nice hotel. You're lucky to be staying here. Would you care for some tea?"

"Um, sure, I guess so." Even though she had just finished her coffee, she didn't mind some tea. It might settle her nerves a bit.

He opened his leather satchel and pulled out a thin, stainless-steel thermos. He poured her a small cup. "Here, you seemed to like this when we met. It's very calming."

She took the cup in both hands. It was warm and smelled familiar, which was a plus. "Aren't you going to have any?"

He shook his head and laughed. "I've had too much already today. My doctor tells me I drink too much tea. It's funny because tea is actually very good for you. But like many things, too much of a good thing is a bad thing. I limit myself to a few cups in the morning and a few in the evening. Other than that, I just drink water. But you're young, and this is a very good tea. It's good for your soul."

She sipped the tea. She remembered the taste. It comforted her. She needed more things that comforted her. Being with him brought back more memories than she had had all day. She felt confident he could help her work out this puzzle, which also put her at ease.

"Do you have a hot plate or a warming thermos in your room?" he asked.

"I'm not sure. I think I saw a thermos plugged in with some tea cups and a teapot next to it."

"Perfect." He reached into the satchel and pulled out a handful of homemade tea bags. "I knew you liked this tea, so I brought some bags with me, so you can make it on your own. This tea is very medicinal. Please drink one or two cups in the morning, a couple at midday, and several more in the evening, around dinnertime. It will relax you. Hopefully, that will help you get your memory back."

That made sense. She felt better already. She took the tea bags in her hand and put them into her small, silk pouch.

"I see you have the pouch I gave you. Obviously, you also have the cell phone because you called me. Is it charged? I think I gave you a charger, right?"

"I'm not sure. I think I saw a small charger in the room. I'll plug it in when I get back." Even though she didn't really know this man very well, he did seem to care a great deal about her well-being. He was also the only person she remembered.

"Good. Just in case it's not the right charger, I brought another one for you." He pulled out a charger from his leather satchel and handed it to her.

"You said that you found me at the Inari shrine. What was I doing there?"

"Yes, you were on one of the many trails. I imagine that you were there like most people, to visit the shrine grounds, to climb to the top of the mountains through the ten thousand torii gates, and to see the cherry blossoms. I found you lying on the ground. That was Friday afternoon. Today's Thursday, so it was almost exactly one week ago."

She nodded. Meeting him at the shrine seemed like more of a hazy dream than a memory. Maybe if she went back there, more of her memory would come back. She'd try and do that tomorrow. It was not like she had any other plans.

"Do you have enough money? I have some if you need it." He tapped his satchel.

"No, I seem to have a lot of money. I don't know where I got it, but it's there, along with a lot of new clothes I've never seen before but that fit me perfectly, along with a brand-new Louis Vuitton bag still in the box." *I must sound like an absolute idiot. He probably thinks I'm crazy.*

"That's odd. You must have met someone. You didn't have any money when I found you. I only gave you enough money to get you through a week or so in a modest hotel. It certainly wouldn't have paid for expensive new clothes, a designer bag, or even one night in this hotel. Do you remember meeting someone?"

"No. But you must be right. Somehow or another someone bought me these clothes and got me my room." Why would someone do that for her?

They sat in silence while she sipped the tea. She remembered the taste of the tea. It was familiar to her, which was good because so few things seemed familiar. It also put her at ease, calmed her. It was like being with an old friend. She was glad this man had brought it with him. It made a lot of the angst about losing her memory wash away. He poured her another cup from the thermos. Around them, businessmen greeted each other, exchanged courtesy bows, and then led each other off to the lobby bar, one of the hotel's restaurants, or out into the street. There was a young couple along with two sets of older people, most likely their parents. They were probably here planning their wedding. While Meiko had waited for the man, she had seen a bride and groom getting their picture taken in the lobby next to a vase of cherry blossoms.

"Do you remember anything else?"

She shook her head. She started to feel a little dreamy and forgot about her loss of memory and just went with the warm sensation that flowed through her.

"Close your eyes." His voice was soothing, rich, and warm. "Stay very calm. Try to ignore the noises around you and let your mind go blank. Maybe you will remember something in a quiet moment."

Two minutes passed in silence. Meiko sat still with her eyes closed. The priest sat next to her, waiting patiently. She opened her eyes slowly.

"Anything come back to you?"

"I'm afraid not. I remember seeing you at the shrine. I remember how nice you were to me. I remember drinking tea and seeing cherry blossoms and an enormous orange building. Other than that, there's not much of anything."

"Well, at least it's something. That building you remember is the main building at Fushimi Inari. It's the administration building where I have my office. Don't worry; it will come back eventually. In the meantime, enjoy this delightful hotel. If you need anything at all, please call me. I will come at once."

"Thank you. You're the only person I know. You've been so kind to me." She felt safe in his presence. She could trust him.

"Well, Inari is a god of protection. He protects rice fields and ensures an abundant harvest. But we extend that philosophy beyond just agriculture, to people."

He reached into his satchel. "Do you still have the omamori I gave you?"

"I don't think so." She didn't remember having one.

He handed her another charm on a silk necklace. "Here, wear this. It was blessed this morning. It should bring you luck and help protect you."

She put it around her neck.

"Remember to drink the tea. It will help as well."

"I will, thank you."

"Now, close your eyes again, and I'll say a prayer to protect you and to get your memory back soon."

She closed her eyes, and he began a slow, rhythmic incantation in a deep baritone. She could feel the sound waves traveling through her head, not knowing what the words meant but luxuriating in their warm resonance. She floated on a warm river of silver, perfectly relaxed and content, as time stopped. The sound stopped, and she opened her eyes. The priest was standing in front of her, his satchel over his shoulder.

"Goodbye, Hana. You will be fine. Let me know if you need anything." He bowed to her with his hands in prayer position in front of his chest. She bowed to him in return.

"OK. Thank you again." She was glad he came. At least she had someone to lean on.

With that, he turned and left, walking past the doorman and through the revolving doors.

CHAPTER 16

MARCH 31ST, DAY 8

Hana stepped out of the cab dressed in a black, tight-fitting dress that stopped high on her long, shapely thighs. She wore tall black Prada pumps and a rose-gold Cartier watch. This was a bustling area in the center of Kyoto's entertainment district. Neon lights made the darkness of evening seem like a black velour backdrop. She confidently walked up to a plain door in a row of cabarets, hostess bars, and nightclubs and pressed the intercom button. A voice came over the box: "Yes?"

"Tanabata is in July," she replied without hesitation. She heard deadbolts unlatching, and the door slowly opened, just enough for her to slip through. She proceeded down a flight of stairs and then emerged into a small casino complete with blackjack, poker, craps, baccarat, and roulette tables. Servers in low-cut French maid costumes carried drinks and cigarettes to the gamblers, most of them male. The women present were mistresses, hostess bar girls, and escorts, spending an evening with their catches. At least, that's what they looked like to Hana. She looked forward to making all of them feel inferior. She scanned the room and estimated that there were over two hundred gamblers involved in various games of chance, along with dealers, pit bosses, and waitresses. Gambling of this type was illegal in Japan, and therefore these types of underground clubs ran much like speakeasies in Prohibition-era America. The fact that it was an illegal club interested her. It made everything just a bit more risqué. There were two rows of slot and video poker machines against the right wall, but most of the room was set up for table games. The sound of cheers at the craps tables and roulette wheels rolled in waves over the smoky room.

Slowly she strolled between the tables, ignoring the turned heads and gawking looks she received as she passed. Like a leopard on the prowl, she focused on her elusive prey. Then she stopped, having spotted her target.

He stood at the shooter's end of the craps table in a dark-gray pinstripe suit with a white shirt and a loosened navy necktie, lording over several stacks of chips. She watched him from two tables over. He roared loudly when his numbers hit and the chips were pushed his way, exclaiming to anyone within earshot that he "knew" that number was going to hit. He waved over a waitress, leered down her top, and ordered another of whatever he was having. It appeared to be whiskey and water. *There's my boy.* She readied herself to go in for the kill.

She gradually made her approach and eventually ended up standing slightly behind and to his right. "Wow," she purred, "you must be very good at this game. You've won so much money."

He turned to her and almost spit out his drink. Trying to remain cool, he nodded, "Yeah, babe, I'm damn good at this. I'm good at a lot of things," he added with a sly smile.

She was going to enjoy taking this pompous clown down. "I'm sure you are. I can tell just by looking at you." She nudged closer so that her hip gently pressed against his leg. She pulled a cigarette out of her bag and put it to her mouth; she made no attempt to light it. In a move of bar-room chivalry, he whipped a thin, chrome-plated lighter out of his pants pocket and lit it for her. She took a pull from it, her red lipstick staining the white filter, and blew out a thin stream of smoke. "Thank you, sweetheart." She leaned closer, whispering in his ear, "Would you show me how to play? I've never really seen such a successful craps player."

He nodded confidently. "Of course. Stick by me, and I'll show you how it's done."

She couldn't help but smile. He had it wrong; she was the one who was going to show him how it was done. His problem was that he didn't know what game they were playing. She cooed and snuggled next to him when he won, squeezing his arm and clinking glasses with him, sipping champagne in a tall flute while he sucked down one tumbler of whiskey and water after another. Over the rest of the evening, he raised his bet by more than 50 percent what it had been when she had arrived at the table, trying to impress her with his largesse, which was exactly what she'd hoped. This was only the start of raising the stakes. Despite a couple big misses, he ended the evening on a positive note, tipped the dealer, and left the table with Hana on his arm, nodding knowingly to anyone who looked at them as if to say, "Yeah, that's right, she's with me." They popped into a taxi and headed to her hotel. It was just after eleven in the evening.

† † †

They lay in bed, sweaty and exhausted while they both pulled on their cigarettes.

"My God, Hana, that was the greatest sex I've had in my life. You're amazing!"

"Thank you, honey. You're an incredible lover too. I wish you could make love to me every day." Men were such idiots, she thought. Tell them they were great in bed, and they thought they were Superman.

"Me too, but unfortunately, I have to get back to my wife. She thinks I'm out with guys from work. I can't come home too late."

She pouted, sticking out her lower lip. "I'm so tired of this hotel room. I wish I had an apartment of my own where you could come by after work every day, and we could have some fun. I just don't have enough money to get a nice apartment."

"Babe, I wish I could help you out. I have to save money for my son's education and other stuff."

"I understand. I thought maybe we could have something special, but I know you'd prefer to be with your family than me." She lay with her head on his chest and swirled the thin, black hair just above his navel with her fingers. He was nibbling around the bait, playing hard to get, but he couldn't hold out much longer. She wondered if she were being too subtle for this oaf.

"That's not what I'm saying at all. I'd much prefer to be with you. My wife's a nagging bitch, and my son is a lazy kid who takes everything I give him for granted."

"I don't think it would take too much money. I'd like someplace nice, maybe close to your office, so it would be convenient for you. We could meet for lunch and play around a bit, go out to dinner. I could even cook for you."

"We could do all that stuff while you stay here. This is a beautiful hotel. What's wrong with this place?"

"It's just a room, and I'm tired of it." She pulled away from him and sat on the bed facing the other way. "I want someplace I can call my own, with a kitchen, a living room where I could relax, and a nice bedroom. Maybe I was under the wrong impression about you. You seemed so confident and successful at the casino. That's what most attracted me to you. I like strong, confident men who are willing to take care of the women they love. I can't stand weak men who hide behind their families."

He grabbed her by the shoulders and turned her around to face him. "I am strong! I'll prove it to you. I think I know how I can get some money to set you up nicely."

"Really? You're not going to rob a bank or anything like that, are you?" She didn't care how he got the money, just that he got it, and lots of it.

"No, nothing like that. I have a lot of control over the money that comes into our company. I can shift some money around, and nobody would even know. For a company our size, it's a trivial amount of money, but it would set us up nicely. Let me look into it."

She snuggled closer to him. "You could really do that? You must be very high up in your company." He didn't know it, but he had swallowed the bait in one huge gulp.

"High enough. I can make it work. Leave it to me. I'll find a really nice apartment for you close to my office."

"Sweetheart, that would be wonderful! I want to spend as much time with you as I can. I can show you some things that will blow your mind. I promise."

He stood up and kissed her on her forehead. "Looking forward to it. Now, I really must get going. I'll call you in a day or two and let you know what I've found." He pulled on his pants and buttoned his shirt. He reached into his pocket and pulled out a business card case and extracted a crisp white card. "This has my email and office phone number, as well as my cell phone number. Please don't call me at work unless it's urgent. If you do, say that you're a policy holder and you were referred to me by your agent."

She took the card and looked it over. He was vice president of business development, life and property division, at an insurance company she had never heard of. "I won't call you, dear. I'll wait to hear from you. Please don't wait too long to call. I miss you already."

After some passionate kissing and hugging, she closed the door as he left. It was just after 1:00 a.m.

CHAPTER 17

Chieko and David took an early Saturday morning bullet train from Tokyo to Kyoto to retrace Meiko's steps. Meiko had provided David with her expected itinerary before she left, although they both agreed that it was likely to change based on the weather, how crowded different temples were, recommendations from taxi drivers and other tourists, as well as her energy level. But nonetheless, it was a start.

The plan was to visit each of the temples and shrines that Meiko had on her list and ask the priests or anyone else there if they had seen a young woman who fit Meiko's description. It had been five days since they contacted the police in Kyoto, and they hadn't heard anything. They were done waiting for the bureaucracy of the police department and decided that they needed to take matters into their own hands. Chieko hoped they weren't too late.

A little over three hours after arriving in Kyoto, they had visited six temples, and in all cases, they found no one who remembered seeing Meiko. This wasn't particularly surprising, given the millions of tourists who flocked to Kyoto during cherry blossom season, as well as the fact that there were over two thousand temples and shrines in Kyoto. But at least they had distributed copies of Meiko's photo as well as their contact information at each place they stopped. The priests and administrators at each of the temples they visited had mostly met them with kindness and genuine compassion and empathy for their situation. Each promised to circulate Meiko's photo among their employees and let them know if anything turned up. Still, Chieko hadn't found even one person who remembered seeing her, which frustrated her to no end. They decided to stop for lunch and then continue their search on a full stomach. Chieko suggested they stop for soba noodles.

The taxi dropped them off in front of a small, nondescript soba shop with a line of people waiting outside. One of the tourist books that Chieko had bought for the trip recommended it. It wasn't in David's English-language version, which Chieko insisted was a good thing, helping confirm its authenticity, and hopefully reducing the wait time a little. After standing in line almost twenty minutes, they were led inside to a small, square table. Chieko sat cross-legged on the tatami mat while David tried to unfurl his long legs under the low-slung table, without much success.

"I'm not sure I'll ever get used to these types of seats," said David as he stretched his legs straight ahead of him and settled his butt onto the small cushion.

"Unfortunately, they really weren't made for people with long legs," admitted Chieko.

He followed her lead and ordered the cold noodles with the soy-based dipping sauce along with a side of tempura. She stuck with the water that the waitress brought to the table while David ordered a beer.

The sound of enthusiastically slurped noodles filled the air. Loudly slurping noodles in Japan was a sign that the noodles were good, and in no way was it considered bad manners. It had taken David a while to get used to it when he first came to Japan with Chieko over twenty years ago, but Chieko had made it simple for him. Slurp Japanese noodles; don't slurp spaghetti.

"God, I wish Meiko were here. She loves soba," said David, attempting to break one of the many uncomfortable silences.

"If you would have joined her on her trip, you could be enjoying soba with her right now," said Chieko bitingly.

"Are you trying to blame me for letting Meiko come here on her own? You think it's my fault she's missing?"

"I don't know, David. I'm frustrated, and I'm extremely concerned. On the one hand, yes, I partially blame you for not going with her. On the other, I realize that she's a grown-up and should be able to travel on her own."

"Actually, I wanted to come with her. I just couldn't come last weekend because I'm behind schedule on my book and needed to catch up."

She glared at him. "There it is, your career taking precedence over everything else. I see that not much has changed, has it?"

"That's a shitty thing to say, and you know it. If she had come home on time, then you wouldn't have thought twice about her going on her own. But now that something's gone awry, then suddenly, I'm a self-focused jerk. Why didn't *you* go with her?"

"Because she didn't ask me, that's why. If she had, I would have dropped everything to spend time with her. If you don't believe that, then you don't know how much I long to spend time with my daughter. I know I can never make up for the past decade, but I'm trying." Chieko tried to control her anger, but it was hard. David would never know what it was like to walk away from her daughter's life because he would never have to.

"I know," said David, looking down at his beer. "I know it's been hard on you, and I know that Meiko still blames you for leaving."

"I left because we got divorced! That's what people do when they separate, David—they leave. If I could have taken her with me, I would have, and you know it." Some of the customers at nearby tables looked over at the couple having the animated conversation in English. Chieko flushed with a combination of anger and shame at having made a scene.

"I know, but at the time, I didn't want her leaving the country. I felt that she should stay where she was from. I thought it would be too confusing for her to move to a foreign country at that age."

"I wasn't that much older than she was when my family moved to the States."

"True, but you had no choice, and you also had a mother who stayed home and took care of you. Who was going to take care of Meiko while you built up your practice?"

"Let's not come up with alternative histories, David. My mother could have looked after her, and you know it. You didn't want to let go of her, and you used the legal system to keep her with you. I understand that, and if I were in your position, I would have done the same thing. But don't ask me to like it."

A waitress came to the table to clear their plates. She returned with two cups of hot tea made with the water used to cook the soba noodles as well as a wooden pitcher filled with more tea.

"Chieko, I've tried to raise Meiko to think for herself, to make good decisions, to be independent. She went away to college for four years on her own and never ran into problems. If I didn't think that she would have been safe coming here on her own, I would have never let her come. You understand that, don't you?"

"I don't know what I understand," Chieko admitted in frustration. "You've done a wonderful job raising her, and you've formed a relationship with her that I am admittedly envious of. Maybe I'm just a bit more protective than you, I don't know."

"I've done everything I can to protect Meiko. I think that teaching her to think for herself and make good decisions is the best defense I can give her. There's a fine line between being protective and suffocating, and I'm sure you are aware of that, given your profession."

"No, you're right. I guess that deep down I'm terrified of making a mistake and something going wrong." For some reason, Chieko decided to share a story with David that she had never shared with anyone, not even her mother. "Did I ever tell you the story of Taro the dog?"

"Taro? No, I don't think so. Is it a Japanese children's tale?"

"In a way, I guess it is. It's a story about my childhood. I was somewhere between four and five, closer to four. It's hard to imagine that anyone would remember much from that age, but I remember it like it was yesterday. We used to live on a side street that was right off one of the main streets in Kawagoe. I never really thought of it as busy, but in retrospect, I guess it was. It was the sixties, and there were a lot fewer cars than there are now. But there were also a lot fewer highways too. Our street connected one main street to another, and depending on traffic, you could save some time by going down our street. Of course, I didn't know that at the time. I used to play with the kids next door, two girls who were both older than me, and a couple of other kids, younger and older, who lived down the street.

"Way down at the far end of the street, closest to the main street, lived a young couple. I don't remember them moving in, but I remember them not being there, and then suddenly, they showed up. Things happen like that when you're four. My parents always warned me about getting close to the main street and told me never to go there without an adult, or at least a teenager, with me. The man, and I don't remember his name, was in his late twenties or early thirties. He seemed really cool to me at the time. He wasn't like a lot of the other grown-ups who don't have much time to spend with other people's kids, or even care to if they did have the time. He was always friendly to me and was glad to see me when I ventured down the street, either alone or with a friend. Back then, little kids roamed all over, and no one gave it a second thought. It wasn't unusual for us to walk or get on bikes and just go out and play somewhere. We always came home in time for dinner, and I never heard of any kids getting hurt bad or running into any serious trouble. Sure, you'd fall and bang up your knee or something like that, but that was just part of being a kid."

Chieko took a sip of her tea. The background noise of the busy soba shop drifted away as the memories flooded back to her.

"The greatest part about visiting this guy was that he had a big dog named Taro. I'm not sure what type of dog Taro was—I think some type of Akita mix. It was the biggest dog I'd ever seen. He was bigger than me at the time. He was brown and gray with a big thick curly tail and tall black ears. I'm pretty sure he was just a puppy, less than a year old, and he was very friendly and loved to play. We'd stand in the small backyard and throw a ball to Taro, and he'd bring it back to us. The man threw it more than I did because I couldn't throw a ball very well back then. I'm not sure I can throw one very well now, either." Chieko smiled, thinking of the times that she and David had played catch with a baseball. His throws always seemed so effortless, and they came in straight and fast. Hers always had an arc to them no matter how hard she tried to throw them in a straight line.

"I remember how cool it was that Taro would sit facing him, waiting in anticipation. His eyes focused on the ball, like nothing else existed in the entire world. Then he would sprint away after it and bring it back, drop it in front of the man, all covered with slobber, and then they'd repeat the process."

David filled up their cups with the hot, sweet tea, without breaking the flow of her story.

"For me, if I wasn't watching him throw the ball to Taro, I would just spend my time running around his backyard, rolling on the ground with Taro or just sitting and petting him. The man also let me just hang out and watch him do things like water his flowers or dig a hole or whatever he happened to be doing. I was pretty good at watching people do stuff.

"One day during the summer I went down to see them. I walked to the side of his house where there was a fence and called the man's name. He called back and said to come to the backyard. I don't really remember passing through a gate, and I don't remember opening or closing any gate, but there must have been one there. He was in the backyard working on a motorcycle. It was the first time that I'd ever seen a motorcycle up close. He was doing something to it; to this day I couldn't tell you what. I sat and watched him, and we talked for a while. I'm not sure how long it was, maybe five, ten minutes, tops." Chieko stared at her hands, sadness creasing the skin around her eyes.

"Then, suddenly, we heard this loud screech of tires in the road. Someone had slammed on their brakes. I remember the man immediately looked up with panic on his face. He yelled, 'Taro! Taro!' He asked me, 'Did you shut the gate?' Like I said, I didn't remember there being a gate, and I don't remember what I said. He got up and ran to the front of the house, and I followed him. He was bigger and a lot faster than me, and by the time I got to the front, he was sitting in the road, holding Taro in his lap.

"He was petting his head, and he was crying. It was the first time that I had seen a grown-up cry. Taro must have run out into the street and gotten hit by the car. I ran up, and by this time, I was crying too. I asked if Taro was all right. I can still see his face. He just shook his head, with tears streaming down his face, and he said, "No." He was holding onto Taro's limp body and rocking back and forth in the middle of the street while cars passed around him.

"I didn't know what to do. I was overwhelmed with sorrow and, worse, guilt. It was my fault. I left the gate open and let that beautiful, happy young dog run into the street. Now Taro, the first dog I ever loved, and a dog that this wonderful man loved dearly, was dead. I ran home crying. I remember going into my room and crying until I couldn't cry any more. I never went down to that end of the street again. We moved to another house later that year when my father got transferred. I never saw the man again, and I never had a chance to apologize to him for killing Taro." Tears welled in her eyes. She blotted them with one of the small paper napkins on the table. There were tears in David's eyes as well.

"I never want to leave the gate open again, David. I'm scared to death of being responsible for something terrible happening to someone I love. That's probably why I'm so protective, and that's why I'm so scared about Meiko."

"We'll find her, Chieko. No one left the gate open this time. She's out there. We'll bring her back."

† † †

After finishing lunch, Chieko and David visited three more temples before walking up the long set of stairs to the Fushimi Inari Jinja. They found the administration building just off to the left of the main building in the center of a large, granite courtyard. Chieko told the young priest working behind the desk about Meiko and asked if anyone had seen her. Unsure of how to handle the situation, he asked them to wait while he got his boss. He scurried past several other priests who were busy at desks working on various tasks. Chieko thought that it could have passed for most small business offices in Japan. Moments later, the young priest emerged from a back room followed by an older priest, whom she assumed was his boss. Both wore their everyday white robes with bright vermillion *hakamas*; worn also by practitioners in some martial arts, such as aikido, they always reminded David of a pleated skirt or kilt. The senior priest had a darker complexion than the younger one, with a round, black mole on his left cheek. They stopped in front of Chieko and David. The senior priest looked first at Chieko and then at David and then back to her. Appearing none too happy to be interrupted from whatever he was doing, the senior priest broke the silence.

"How can we help you?"

"Yes, thank you for seeing us," Chieko began, apologetically. "We believe that our daughter, Meiko, visited this shrine last week. She has disappeared, and we wanted to see if anyone here might remember seeing her or hearing anything about her." She held a picture of Meiko out to the priest, who grudgingly pulled his hand from his sleeve to accept the photo. He looked at it briefly.

"I don't remember seeing this girl." He turned to the younger priest and handed him the photo. "Have you seen her?"

The young priest looked at the photo, glanced briefly at the senior priest and then to Chieko. "I'm sorry. I don't remember seeing anyone who looks like this either."

"Please remember," added the senior priest, "we get thousands of visitors here every day. If we can keep this photo, we will pass it around and post it."

"Thank you," Chieko replied, trying not to stare at his mole. "Here's my business card. Please call or email me at any time if you hear anything about her. Her name is Meiko."

The senior priest received the business card with both hands, as was tradition, scanned it, and then handed it to the junior priest.

"We will be in touch if we hear anything." He stared at Chieko coldly, penetrating straight through her.

"All right, thank you again." She hesitated. "Would it be possible to get a card so that we can contact you in the future?"

The priest hesitated and then nodded to the junior priest, who pulled a business card from his desk and handed it to her.

Chieko accepted the card, and she and David both bowed to the priests and then turned to leave the office.

"Well, he wasn't the friendliest guy in the world, was he?" said David as they made their way down the steps and out of the temple grounds.

"No, not at all," agreed Chieko. "Compared to the other priests we've met, he was downright rude. There's something very dark about that man, like he's hiding something."

"I felt sorry for the younger priest. I can't imagine that guys a lot of fun to work for. Maybe he was pissed off because you were staring at his mole." David laughed.

"I was not staring at his mole! What a terrible thing to say."

"I know." David smiled. "Just kidding."

"You're terrible," replied Chieko, unable to hold back a smile. They continued toward the train station, on their way back to Tokyo.

† † †

For the first twenty minutes of the train ride back to Tokyo, David and Chieko sat mostly in silence.

"David," Chieko said finally, "is there anything that you can think of that would make Meiko not return without contacting one of us? Anything?"

"No," replied David, shaking his head. "I've been thinking about it for a while, and this is completely unlike her. She's the most responsible young woman I know."

"That's what I thought. It doesn't make me feel any better, though."

"I know. As much as I hate to admit it, I believe that something serious has happened to Meiko. We have to stay positive, though. She's a very resourceful and intelligent girl," David said, trying to sound confident both for himself as well as Chieko.

"Tell me more about what she was like after I left. I feel like there's a twelve-year void where I don't really know anything about her. When I left, she's was a precocious nine-year-old, and then suddenly here she is as a young adult."

"She's a wonderful daughter. Straight-A student; very good at sports, especially volleyball and tennis. She was captain of both of her high school teams. She's an avid surfer and has a lot of close friends." A thin smile appeared on David's face. "But it's more than that. She's just such a good person. She used to volunteer at the San Diego Humane Society. They have some very nice rooms where they keep cats that are up for adoption. They're sort of like small, glass-enclosed bedrooms, with chairs, places for the cats to sit, almost like a person's house. Many of the cats, especially the older ones, will never find homes. Meiko used to go there a couple of times a week to sit with the cats, pet them, read to them, and just keep them company. She also volunteered to walk the dogs, most of which were pit bulls. A lot of the female volunteers shied away from them and would walk the Chihuahuas and smaller breeds. Meiko was fearless. She would walk them for two hours once or twice a week whenever she had time. She absolutely loved the animals there, and everyone loved her. I talked with some of the people who worked there, and they had nothing but great things to say about her."

"It sounds like you did a very good job of raising her," said Chieko.

"I'm not sure I had that much to do with it," admitted David. "She's just such a special kid—kind and caring. She made me a much better person, not the other way around."

They sat in silence, looking at the scenery passing by.

"David, I'm scared. I just got my little girl back. She's hated me for so long. We were just turning a corner." She dabbed the tears that had started to flow from her eyes. "I don't want to lose her again."

David's eyes were moist as well. For the first time in over twelve years, he reached out and took Chieko's hands in his. She didn't pull back. "Chieko. People tend to hate the people they love the most because it's safe for them to rebel. Because they will always be accepted back. No matter how shitty they treat them, no matter the animosity they display, they will be cared for by those loved ones, who will ultimately accept them back. No matter what." He smiled, looking at the ceiling of the train, trying to be strong. "We'll find her. I will never give up on her." He lowered his gaze back to his ex-wife's, tightened his lips, and confidently nodded. "We'll find her."

CHAPTER 18
APRIL 2ND, DAY 10

Hana poured tea from a small pot into a blue ceramic cup with no handle. She put the cup to her mouth and sipped gently. A silk robe draped around her otherwise naked body.

In the other corner of the room, Masaharu Fujiwara, the soba shop owner, sat on a chair in his underwear, sipping from a can of Kirin beer. His eyes were red and swollen as if he'd been crying, which in fact, he had.

"Hana, you have to understand that I am literally running out of money, and my wife knows that I'm seeing someone. It's terrible going home now because all she does is accuse me of seeing my 'girlfriend,' whether I've been spending time with you or not. I've already blown through most of my son's college savings."

She raised her head and glimpsed him lazily as she sipped her tea. "I thought you wanted to buy me nice things," she said, inspecting the polish on her nails. *I should get them redone today.* "No one forced you, darling."

"I know, I know. I'm not blaming you. I wanted to buy you stuff and take you out and make sure that you stayed in a nice place. I'm just saying that it's all coming apart now." He took a long draw from his beer and then looked down at the carpet. "I just don't know what to do. Once my wife finds out about all the money I've spent, she'll want a divorce. I'll lose my shop and my family. It's a complete mess." He began getting dressed.

Hana poured herself another cup of tea. "I'm sorry that it's worked out this way, sweetheart. You know I'd love to spend more time with you, but it doesn't sound like that's possible anymore. I think it's probably best that we stop seeing each other."

He stood up and held her in his arms. "I don't want to stop seeing you. I need to be with you, Hana! I just need some time to work things out."

She gently pulled away from him.

"We'll see, darling. I need a man who can support me, who wants to spend time with me. We had a lot of fun, but it doesn't sound like you're that man anymore. I'm sorry, dear, but I have a manicure scheduled, and I have to get ready. Call me when you've worked things out."

"Worked things out! I don't know how I'm going to work things out. My life is essentially ruined."

"Don't worry, darling. I'm sure you'll find a way. You're very clever. Now, I really need to take a shower and get going. Take care, sweetheart." She kissed him on the cheek and ushered him gently toward the door.

"When can I see you again?"

"That's up to you, darling. Hope to see you soon." She shut the door before he could respond.

She poured herself another cup of tea. It was lukewarm now. She finished it in two sips. Letting the robe slip to the floor, she headed to the shower.

CHAPTER 19

KYOTO
APRIL 3RD, DAY 11

Detectives Nomura and Saito pulled up to the crime scene in their black Nissan Skyline GT-R. The scene was already roped off with yellow crime scene tape. Four uniformed policemen were on hand, keeping a crowd of onlookers at bay. The crime scene investigators hadn't yet shown up. *Here we go. This isn't going to be pretty,* thought Nomura.

They stepped out of the car, slipped on their white gloves, and ducked under the tape, flashing their badges to the nearest officer, who gave a respectful bow. Splayed out on the pavement in front of them lay a face-down male wearing jeans and a white shirt, with a dark pool of congealed blood beside his head.

The senior uniformed officer, Miyama, informed them that they had not touched the body and had no information about the victim. Dispatch had received a call from a passerby who saw a man fall from an apartment building. Two squad cars arrived on the scene shortly thereafter and secured the area, waiting for backup and the CSI team to arrive. Nomura grunted unintelligibly, and Saito nodded approval as Officer Miyama went back to focus on securing the area. Unfortunately, Japanese police departments were getting very adept at handling things like this with the increase in suicides following the 2009 recession. Most people jumped in front of trains, but sometimes they jumped from buildings.

Nomura bent next to the victim, careful not to break the chalk outline, and with Saito's help, gently turned the man onto his back. Both men grimaced. The man's face was a pulpy mess, and his limbs flopped in directions that nature never intended, clearly broken in several places. It looked like he had instinctively extended his arms to try and break his fall. Nomura wished it got easier seeing smashed bodies, but it really didn't. He was glad he had had a light breakfast and wondered how Saito was holding up. In the victim's shirt pocket was a surprisingly neatly folded piece of lined paper. Nomura carefully removed it, unfolded the paper, and found a photo of a young woman. He read the handwritten note.

It's time for me to leave. I can't go on. My life is ruined. If I had never met you, Hana, would my life be better? Am I better off having met and fallen in love with you? I don't know, but I can never go back. Now that I can't be with you, what's the point in living?

Yukiko, I'm sorry. I tried to be a good husband, but I have failed in so many ways. I hope that you can move forward without me weighing you down. You deserved better.

Ichiro, my son, I hope you will remember me as a father who loved you and tried to do his best for you. Even though I tried, I failed. I hope you can forgive me. I never meant to hurt either one of you. Goodbye.

Well, at least we have a motive, Nomura thought. *You just gotta wonder how some people screw up their lives so bad.* He handed the note to Saito while he studied the picture of the girl. She looked to be Japanese, although it seemed to him that she probably had some Western blood as well. She was standing in the street in a tight-fitting dress and high heels, holding a small black purse with a miniature padlock on the leather handle. Her hair was dark and hung past her shoulders. She had an alluring smile that Nomura had to admit was quite seductive.

After Saito finished the letter, he handed the photo to him. "I'm guessing this must be Hana," grunted Nomura.

"She's very attractive, isn't she?"

"Yeah, pretty young too. I bet she's under twenty-five." *Definitely not worth ruining your life over.* He took the photo back from Saito and put it along with the piece of paper into a plastic evidence bag.

"That looks like an Hermes purse she's holding. Those aren't cheap. I bet that cost over $7,000."

"I'm impressed. I didn't know you had such expensive taste. Wanna take bets as to who bought it for her?"

Saito grinned. They stood up and stepped away from the body.

"Let's see if anyone here knows him. Once CSI gets here, they can take fingerprints and get a positive ID." Nomura looked up to the apartment building next to them. "In the meantime, our best bet is that he jumped from this building right here."

Saito nodded. "Let's get statements from anyone who saw him fall or who might know him."

After slightly more than thirty minutes of wading through the gathering flock of onlookers, asking if anyone recognized the man or saw him fall, they came up with a few leads. The woman who called the police said that she was on her way to the market when she heard a noise and looked up to see a body falling from the sky. He landed not more than ten feet from her, with a terrible thump and crack. She was still sobbing uncontrollably, and the paramedics were treating her for shock. She didn't know the man, but she did confirm that he probably fell out of the apartment building Nomura had targeted. She had heard him scream on the way down. Nomura could only imagine what this woman felt. It was bad enough for professionals like himself and Saito, but it had to be truly terrible for civilians to see something like this. He wondered how his wife would react. He imagined that she would have nightmares for weeks. Most people would. You just didn't forget things like this.

Several others had heard the sickening "thwack" when he hit the pavement and came to see what caused the noise. They didn't see him fall or know who he was. No one, it seemed, knew who he was.

They were finally able to contact the manager of the apartment building and showed him several pictures of the victim that Saito had taken on his iPhone. After he had failed to prevent himself from throwing up his breakfast at the sight of the mangled face in the photos, the poor manager was able to identify the man as one of his tenants. *That was pleasant.* Nomura couldn't help smiling. *Surprised that more people don't blow chow after seeing something like this.* After making a short trip to the restroom to clean up, the manager led the detectives into his cramped office on the first floor of the building. He spent the next several minutes rummaging through a file cabinet with multicolored folders. He leafed through a couple of them before pulling out a folder and setting it on his desk. In the folder was the apartment application, a photo of a man and a woman, the rental agreement, and some other papers. It was hard to make a positive identification based on this single photo, but he did seem to roughly match the victim. Masaharu Fujiwara, forty-five years of age, owner of a local soba shop. His wife's name was Yukiko, forty-two years old, also employed at the soba shop. They had a son named Ichiro, who was ten. They had lived in apartment 814 for the past eight years.

The apartment manager called the number listed for the apartment and let it ring until it went to voice mail. He left a message for them to call his cell phone. He then led Nomura and Saito to the Fujiwaras' apartment. After the manager unlocked the door, Nomura told him to wait in the hallway. The manager complied, grateful not to have to step into the apartment, still embarrassed at puking in front of the policemen.

Nomura and Saito wore protective booties over their shoes and put on their white gloves again. It was a simple apartment, much the same as where most middle-class people in Kyoto or other large cities lived. This one was neat, although a bit cramped, but that was normal.

"Here we go, Saito. Let's see if we can find anything that will lead us to the lovely Ms. Hana," grunted Nomura as they stepped into the room. "Probably some escort he fell in love with who eventually bleed him dry."

Saito nodded. "Wouldn't be the first, and won't be the last, for that matter."

Sometimes Nomura wondered if half of Japan lived in apartments just like this one. You could probably come home drunk, walk in and go to sleep, and not realize it wasn't your place until the next morning. Even then it might take you a while. The small kitchen next to the living area with a table, a couch, and a TV didn't offer many clues. There were two bedrooms and a bathroom with a shower and Japanese bath, or *ofuro*. One bedroom looked like it belonged to a young boy. It had posters of baseball and soccer teams on the walls, a baseball glove and bat leaning against the wall. They walked into the other, larger bedroom, which they assumed belonged to the parents. There was a dresser filled with clothes, men's on the left and women's on the right, neatly folded. A small desk sat in the corner of the room and looked like it had recently been used. Nomura carefully looked through the drawers while Saito stepped out onto the balcony. There were mostly ledgers and receipts for the soba shop as well as some home finances in the drawers, nothing uncommon for a small-business owner.

There were envelopes with old receipts, lists of vendors, and tax documents. An envelope was stuffed inside one notebook. He opened the envelope and found numerous photos of the same young woman as the one in the picture they found in his shirt pocket, some alone, and some with him in the picture, smiling, toasting glasses of champagne, her kissing his cheek. There were also numerous receipts. He often wondered why married men kept photos of their lovers and receipts of items they bought with cash. Why even print them out at all? What was the purpose? He thought that it was like a serial killer who kept a memento of each victim, a locket, a ring, something to remember the victim and allow them to reexperience that moment of ecstasy again and again. There was also the widely held belief that deep down, people like this ultimately wanted to get caught.

Nomura thumbed through the photos and receipts. It looked as if Saito had been right about the Hermes purse. It was called a Kelly handbag and cost $8,500. *Didn't know Saito knew so much about women's fashion. I'll have to give him some shit about it later.* There were also several dinner receipts at high-end restaurants, each more than $3,000, various department store receipts in the $3,000 to $6,000 range each, and payment for a suite at the Grand Prince Hotel. That was the best lead so far. *Mr. Fujiwara certainly went out of his way to show his young girlfriend a good time. Probably went bankrupt paying for all this stuff.* Nomura had seen it happen before. Middle-aged man, bored with his life, somehow gets hooked up with a young, attractive girl who sees him as a sugar daddy. He's happy to play the role and probably feels more alive than he has in decades. In the end, it all falls to pieces. Sometimes, even in suicide.

Saito walked into the room as Nomura riffled through the contents of the envelope.

"Looks like we got the right place. He landed directly below the balcony here. You'd have to be in pretty dire straits to jump from eight stories. Can't imagine what goes through your head on the way down." Saito shook his head at the thought.

"I guess, on the positive side, it's a relatively quick death," replied Nomura, not looking up from the receipts. Twenty years as a detective, and these things still turned his stomach. But he'd learned not to show weakness, even around his partner. Maybe especially then. "Our friend here seems to have rung up some serious debts with this girlfriend of his. She's the next person we need to talk to. We've got several photos to go by, and I've got a receipt for a hotel room at the Grand Prince. We can start there."

"Yep," responded Saito. "We'll see what this young lady can tell us about her beau."

"My guess is that this is some married guy who fell in love with the wrong woman, spent himself into debt, and then at some point realized that he was so far in the hole it was easier to just end it. Hopefully we can put a bow on this and wrap it up quickly." Investigating suicides took up a lot of their time, but they were usually able to wrap up the investigation of each one in a day or two. This one didn't seem particularly challenging.

"Um," Saito said, "we'll need to contact the spouse. Not sure what she knew about his affair. Another one of those lovely conversations we find ourselves in."

"I know," grunted Nomura. That was part of the job he didn't enjoy. "Sometimes I feel like those soldiers who were responsible for telling the families that their son died in battle. But in this case, there's nothing positive to say. It's not like you can say your son died bravely defending his country." Poor lady probably didn't suspect that her husband was cheating on her. Or maybe she did and either didn't care or was afraid of confronting him. A lot of women were afraid of repercussions, like divorce or physical abuse, and just sucked it up and stayed silent. *I bet she didn't know about all the money he spent, though. What an asshole this guy was.* The more Nomura thought about it, the more pissed off he felt.

"No," snickered Saito. "More like, 'Hi, ma'am, wanted to let you know that your husband has been banging this young girl and running up huge bills that have probably put your family into financial ruin and then decided it was in his best interest to kill himself. Sorry for your loss. Oh yeah, and since this was a suicide, the insurance isn't going to pay anything either.' Yeah, that'll be a nice conversation."

Nomura couldn't help but chuckle. "You've got a nice bedside manner, Saito. I think you should be the one who delivers the message to the widow."

"Thanks for the encouragement."

Nomura put the envelope and its contents into a plastic evidence bag.

"Let's get the hell out of here and let CSI wrap things up. We'll need to start the paperwork on this thing." Over the years, he'd come to accept the drudgery of filling out endless reports, answering an exhausting list of questions from his superiors. He used to love solving the puzzles that challenging cases presented. But years of trudging through the politics-infested bureaucracy of a large-city police department had worn down his curiosity and enthusiasm and replaced it with acquiescence.

CHAPTER 20

Thin plumes of incense wafted in the soft breeze, the aroma dense, sweet, and pungent. Dusk's lasts breaths held the night at bay. The priest knelt deep in prayer before the fox statue, his voice a barely audible groan emanating from deep within his soul. His crisply pleated orange hakama puddled on the white cloth he had laid on the granite base of the small shrine. Lights from two small candles flickered and illuminated his frame, his face mostly obscured by the darkness, except for the black mole on his left cheek.

The main shrine was closed, and most of the other priests were wrapping up for the day or had already retired to their dormitory. The mountain stream ran strong in the valley below, providing a permanent white noise that enveloped the mountains. The negative ions from the flowing stream along with the dense forest canopy added to the sense of serenity.

The mother fox and her baby looked down from their stony perch at the silhouette below them, silently listening to the man's prayers, steeling themselves for the cold evening to come.

CHAPTER 21

APRIL 4ᵀᴴ, DAY 12

Detectives Nomura and Saito entered the spacious, modern lobby of the Grand Prince Hotel, the first stop of their day. The hotel looked like an oval-shaped football stadium encircling a castle, complete with two towers at either end, which could be mistaken for turrets, encircling a tree-lined park. It was quite spectacular, a place that neither Nomura nor Saito could afford. They showed their badges to an employee at the reception desk, as well as a photo of Masaharu Fujiwara and the woman known as Hana from a happier moment than Fujiwara's last. The woman at the desk looked at the photo carefully and said that she recognized both people in the photo.

"Would you mind if I get my manager?" she asked timidly.

"Not at all," replied Nomura. He looked around the lobby while they waited and wondered how much you would need to make to afford to stay in a place like this. More than he made, that was for sure.

The desk manager walked in with the woman and efficiently and discreetly ushered the detectives to a conference room, out of sight of paying customers. Police asking questions about hotel guests was never good for business, especially in a luxury hotel.

The manager introduced himself as Mr. Yoshio Katayama, and the woman who greeted them introduced herself as Ms.

Yumi Ando. They exchanged business cards with the two detectives.

Nomura looked at Ando. "You said that you recognized both people in this photo. What can you tell us about them?" Another employee entered the office and set ceramic cups of steaming green tea in front of the detectives and then silently exited.

After first looking at her manager for approval, the woman from reception responded.

"The woman was a guest of the hotel. She checked out yesterday. The man in the photo paid for her entire stay in advance. In cash," she added.

"Do you know the name of the woman?"

The manager pulled a record book and verified the information.

"Her name was listed as a Miss Tanaka, Miss Hana Tanaka. We did not have a registered name for the man in the photo."

"How long was she a guest?"

"She was with us for five nights," replied the manager. "As Ms. Ando stated, she checked out yesterday."

"Was she alone when she checked out, or was there someone with her?"

"I was working yesterday and checked her out," replied Ando. "She called down from her room to confirm that everything was current on her bill and that she would be checking out. There was a substantial amount paid up-front, and she had a credit of approximately $2,100. She stopped down and picked up a copy of the receipt and her credit and then left. She was alone."

"Did she seem upset in any way? Was there anything unusual in her demeanor?" Saito asked while Nomura sipped his tea. Nomura liked to take turns with his partner questioning witnesses. It kept the witnesses on their feet. Besides, it gave him time to think.

"No, nothing special. She didn't say much, but she was polite. She was very nicely dressed and had several pieces of luggage with her. I recall that she was carrying a black Chanel bag. She was wearing a very stylish dark-blue dress—I'm not sure of the designer—and she was also wearing large Prada sunglasses and high heels. She was tall for a Japanese."

"Do you remember how much luggage she had with her? Was it taken by a porter somewhere?" continued Saito.

"Yes, when she called down to check out, she asked to have a bellhop take three pieces of luggage down for her."

"Do you know where they took them?"

"I can check for you." Katayama placed a call to the porters' desk. When he hung up, he reported to the detectives, "I should know shortly."

"Would it be possible to review her bill?"

"Of course. Ms. Ando, please bring us a copy of the bill."

"Yes, sir." She excused herself and left the room.

"Is it unusual for people to pay for a full week's stay upfront, and in cash?" asked Nomura, leaning back in his chair.

"It is somewhat uncommon, but it does happen on occasion."

"So you didn't see it as strange?"

"You can imagine, from the hotel's standpoint, that if a customer is willing to pay for their entire stay, as well as a significant deposit against incidentals, up-front in cash, that's not a negative thing." Katayama gave them an uncomfortable smile as if to say, "As long as they pay, we don't ask questions."

Nomura wondered how many secret affairs were going on this minute, not only in this hotel but in luxury hotels all over Kyoto. Much easier to pay with cash from some hush fund. No trail, nothing to explain. Except, that is, when the money runs out, like it did for Mr. Fujiwara.

Ando returned to the room and handed copies of the receipt to the two detectives as well as her boss.

"Phew," exclaimed Saito. "That's a heck of a bill. If I'm reading this correctly, it looks like the charge for the room was $1,500 per night, plus taxes. That must be a pretty nice room."

"Yes, Miss Tanaka was staying in one of our city-view suites. It's one of our nicer rooms," explained Ms. Ando.

"I also see two charges for Beaux Sejours. I'm assuming that's a restaurant?" asked Saito.

"Yes, Beaux Sejours is one of our fine-dining restaurants. It specializes in French-and-Japanese fusion cuisine," said Ando, as if quoting from a well-practiced script.

"The total for those two meals is over $2,000."

"The price of the dining experience at restaurants such as Beaux Sejours is largely impacted by the wines that are selected. We have a very extensive wine cellar, with many wines, especially the older French ones, running well over $1,500 each," replied Katayama proudly.

Nomura couldn't imagine paying $1,500 for a bottle of wine. He was a beer and *shochu* man. You could drink for half a year for $1,500, maybe longer. "There look to be other charges for room service. Some of these are pretty expensive as well," stated Nomura.

"If you'd like, I can get an itemized copy of the receipts from Beaux Sejours as well as room service," Katayama said. "That will detail what was ordered."

"You keep a copy of all of that?"

"Yes, just in case there are any disputes regarding the bill. Also, it helps with our inventory management."

"Yes, that would be helpful," agreed Saito.

Katayama nodded to Ando, who excused herself again.

"Do you know the name of the man she was with?" asked Nomura.

"I'm sorry, I don't recall getting a name from the gentleman. I'll ask Ms. Ando when she returns. Detectives, may I ask why you are asking questions about Miss Tanaka and this man?"

"We're investigating a possible suicide. We're not at liberty to disclose the man's name at this point, but he was found dead late yesterday afternoon outside of his apartment. We're trying to find out if Miss Tanaka could provide us any information that might help us understand what happened."

Color drained from the manager's face, and Nomura thought that he might pass out. "My God, that's terrible. What a tragedy. If there is any way that we can be of further assistance, please let us know." Which really means, thought Nomura, "Please don't mention our hotel to the press."

Ando returned with neatly stapled copies for the detectives and her boss.

"Thank you," said Nomura. "You've been very helpful. Ms. Ando, do either of you remember seeing any other men with Miss Tanaka during her stay?"

"I do recall seeing one or two other gentlemen with her while she was here. Not at the same time, but on separate occasions, I saw them in the lobby together," replied Ando.

"Would you recognize them if you saw them again?"

"I'm not sure. I didn't really pay that much attention. Like I said, Miss Tanaka was always very stylishly dressed, and she caught my attention whenever I saw her. If you had a picture of the gentlemen, then I might be able to provide you more information."

The phone rang, and Katayama picked it up. After a brief back-and-forth, he hung up.

"That was the bell desk. He said that Miss Tanaka met another man outside the lobby, and they left together in a taxi. He mentioned that he had seen the man coming into the hotel once or twice over the past week but didn't think anything of it. He looked like a normal businessman."

"Did he hear them tell the taxi where they were going?" asked Saito.

"No, he didn't. He loaded her luggage, and she thanked him."

"I'd like to talk with him and get a physical description of the man," said Nomura, finishing his tea. "I also want to see if we can talk with some of the cab drivers who normally service the hotel."

"Absolutely. I'll set that up for you," replied Katayama.

"Thank you, that would be helpful," responded Nomura. He and Saito stood up and got ready to leave. "If you happen to see Miss Tanaka or recognize any of the gentlemen who were with her, please call me immediately."

Before leaving the room, Saito hesitated and then turned to the manager. "I should have asked this before, but do you have surveillance cameras monitoring activity in the lobby or the entrances?"

Katayama nodded. "Yes, we do. I completely forgot about them. Would that be helpful for you? I'm sure I could have a copy of the video for the time of Miss Tanaka's stay released to you, but I believe that I would need some sort of subpoena or a formal request from the police department."

"We can arrange that," said Nomura, feeling a bit embarrassed for not asking for the video in the first place. "In the meantime, would it be possible for us to view the video of Miss Tanaka leaving the hotel with the gentleman?"

The manager thought for a moment and then said, "Yes, if you give me about fifteen minutes, I believe I can arrange for a tech person to bring in a laptop that has access to the video feed. Does that work for you?"

"Absolutely, that would be very much appreciated," agreed Nomura.

Nomura and Saito sipped more tea and checked emails on their cell phones. Right on schedule, fifteen minutes after the manager left the room, he returned with a young man carrying a laptop. After brief introductions, the tech, a Mr. Hagiwara, pulled up the surveillance footage and started scanning through the previous day. Ando returned to the room and sat next to the tech. She was the only one who had seen Miss Tanaka, so both detectives felt that she would be best prepared to review the footage. Hagiwara set the video to the approximate time that Ando remembered checking her out. They watched for about five minutes before Ando told the tech to hit the pause button. He rewound it briefly and played it back in slow motion.

The detectives huddled around the screen. They saw a sharply dressed young woman along with a middle-aged man walk to the front entrance of the hotel, where the outside camera picked them up. They didn't wait long because there was a black taxicab already waiting for them. The back doors to the cab opened, and Miss Tanaka slid into the backseat. The man she was with walked behind the car and entered the other side.

They ran the video back several times at even slower speeds. Nomura prompted the tech when to pause the video. He asked if he could get screen captures made. The tech said that he could. He also offered to print out those captures on a color printer in the technology room. After he said that, he looked toward Katayama to make sure that it was all right. The manager nodded his approval. In total, they grabbed six photos. None of them was particularly informative. All of them turned out to be better photos of the woman than the man, who seemed very nondescript, nothing to distinguish him from most businessmen. He wore a dark-blue suit with what appeared to be a dark-blue or black tie, as well as a dark wool cap. His face was blocked by Hana's shoulder, as she was several inches taller than him. Nomura wondered if he knew they were under surveillance. He hoped that the CSI folks could apply some facial recognition software as well as increase the resolution. It wasn't much, but it was the best lead they had so far.

Nomura turned to Katayama. "Can you get us a copy of the video covering the two days before Miss Tanaka's stay through the end of today? We'll take care of getting the authorization necessary."

"Absolutely. We're happy to help in any way that we can," said the manager. Nomura thought that Katayama would be happy to have them out of his hotel and get this wrapped up as soon, and as discreetly, as possible.

Saito and Nomura got up to leave. Ando, the tech, and the manager gave them both a well-practiced formal bow, in unison, as they left.

The conversation with the bellman didn't provide much additional information. All he could remember was that the man who left with Hana was of average build, probably in his early fifties, and wore a dark-blue suit. He carried a well-worn, brown leather messenger bag with a matching leather strap over his shoulder. It was exactly the man they had seen in the video footage.

Nomura asked the bellman to put together a list of the taxi companies that serviced the hotel. The bellman said that he would email over a list shortly.

Hagiwara met them outside the front of the hotel with a manila envelope with the photos he had printed off. They thanked him and headed to their car.

"Jeez, she ran up a bill of over $15,000 in a week, and Mr. Fujiwara paid for all of that in cash," Saito commented as they hopped in the car.

"I'm willing to bet that most of her designer clothes were also paid for in cash by the unfortunate Mr. Fujiwara. I counted receipts in excess of $20,000 from his room yesterday, not counting the hotel bill."

"What did you think about the report from forensics that found a tattoo of a fox on his ankle?" asked Saito.

"Yeah, I saw that this morning. I was planning on asking

Mrs. Fujiwara about that tattoo when we talked with her again today." He wasn't sure what to think about the fox tattoo. It was odd for middle-aged men to have tattoos. It was odd for anyone in Japan to have one. Tattoos were still considered part of the underground culture and mostly associated with Yakuza members. Most Japanese, even those in their teens and twenties, avoided tattoos because of this connection to the mafia. Many hot spring resorts and public baths had strict policies forbidding guests with tattoos, no matter how innocuous, from entering.

"She was pretty broken up yesterday," Saito said of the widow. "Poor lady."

"Can't blame her. It's going to be rough for her to run the soba shop and take care of her son at the same time. At least she has a business to work in. A lot of widows aren't that fortunate," lamented Nomura.

"What do you think makes a guy throw his entire life away for a woman?"

"Saito, that's a question that men have been asking since the beginning of time. I'm not sure there's a good answer."

† † †

Nomura returned to his desk with two cups of coffee in his hand. He had run a couple of errands for his wife and swung by a coffee shop close to the office before returning to work. He set one in front of Saito.

"Thanks," said Saito, looking up. "By the way, I heard back from the cab company that picked up Miss Tanaka and her male companion at the Prince."

"That was quick," replied Nomura. "What did they have to say?"

"The driver remembered picking them up. He dropped them off at the Kyoto train station."

That wasn't surprising, thought Nomura, as he settled into his seat across from Saito. "Did he see them go into the station?"

Saito smiled. "You know, I actually asked him that same question. He said it was busy, and as soon as they paid and left the cab, he had to move on."

"Hmm," grunted Nomura. "Why did you ask him that?"

"One, because I try to be as thorough as I can, and two, because I knew that you'd ask me," replied Saito with a grin. "Why wouldn't they go into the train station? Why go all the way there on not get on a train?"

Nomura sat back in his chair and ran his fingers through his hair. "Most likely they did get on a train. But it's also one of the easiest places to disappear in the crowd and grab another taxi."

Saito looked confused.

"I doubt that's what happened, but if I wanted to cover my tracks and throw off nosy detectives like us, then that's exactly what I'd do. It's essentially untraceable."

"Hmm." Saito nodded. He pulled the lid off his coffee, blew on it, and then took a sip. "Never thought of that. But that would be clever. It would also mean that they expected to be followed."

"Exactly," agreed Nomura. "Let's keep digging." He had expected this to be a routine case of suicide, but it was turning out to be something more than that. He hadn't worked on a case that made him really think in a quite some time. Most of his work was quite mundane. A part of him had to admit that he was grateful to be presented with something more than another open-and-shut case.

CHAPTER 22

KAWAGOE
APRIL 5TH, DAY 13

Chieko sat on a cushion at the square table set about a foot off the tatami mat floor, with her feet resting comfortably in the recessed area below the table, reading the paper while Aiko finished preparing breakfast. In the winter, Aiko put a small space heater into the recessed area and laid a quilted blanket over the table, which covered their legs and kept them warm and snug in the century-old house that lacked central heating.

Miso soup with sliced daikon radishes was simmering on the stove while two salmon filets broiled in the small oven. Aiko moved around the small kitchen with an efficiency honed over a lifetime. She made her miso soup from scratch, no instant abomination for her. Although both Aiko and Chieko had spent over a decade in the United States, they still preferred a traditional Japanese breakfast, rich in fish protein, pickled vegetables, and white rice, to Western breakfasts.

Aiko put the finishing touches on the meal, served up the steaming hot rice, and settled herself down at the table. Chieko set down the paper, and both started the meal the way every Japanese person starts a meal, with a tiny bow and the word *Itadakimasu*, which roughly translates to "I will receive." They ate without speaking. The sounds of the wooden chopsticks clicking against the ceramic bowls, the sipping of the miso soup, and the crunching of the crisp homemade pickled daikon radishes and eggplants filled the room, along with Kotetsu's occasional light snoring. Aiko knew that Chieko was preoccupied with her concern about Meiko. Upon her return from Kyoto, nearly four days earlier, Chieko had shared her frustration about David and her lack of success in turning up anything that might help them. They still hadn't heard anything from the detectives or anyone at the temples.

"Did you get any feelings when you were at any of the temples? Did anything strike you as odd or raise your alertness?" Aiko finally asked without introduction, crunching loudly on a pickled eggplant.

"You mean, did I get a sixth sense or anything like that while I was there?"

"Exactly. You said that no one seemed to remember seeing Meiko, but did you *feel* anything anywhere that might be a clue?"

Chieko smiled. "I'm not as mystical as you, Mother. I'm more a cognitive behaviorist than a shaman."

"Don't discount your senses. Even with all of your education, you have to admit that there is a lot that modern science can't explain about how the human brain works and how we perceive danger."

"Well, outside of a priest at Fushimi Inari Shrine who clearly didn't want to have anything to do with David or me, there was nothing that made the hairs on my neck stand up, if that's what you're implying."

"Did you get the feeling that he knew more than he was willing to share?"

"Not really. I got the feeling that he didn't approve of

interracial marriage, or maybe he's just a fundamentally negative person who takes his insecurities out on anyone he can."

"Hmm," grunted Aiko, finishing off the last of the grilled salmon. "That shrine's probably worth another visit at some time. Maybe you can talk with someone else."

"It just seems like we're making no progress at all. We didn't find out anything while we were there. No one remembers seeing her. I bet that the moment we left, they went back to business as usual and completely forgot about Meiko."

"You planted the seeds. Sometimes that's all you can do. A lot of people have Meiko's picture, and they know that not only is she missing but people care about her and are looking for her. That's a start. Now we have to wait a while and see what becomes of it."

"I can't stand just sitting here and waiting!" Chieko replied, her voice rising in exasperation. "I feel so completely helpless. I hope that Meiko is all right, but with every day that passes, I become less optimistic."

Aiko knew her daughter better than anyone. Chieko had many gifts: ambition, intelligence, and a strong work ethic. Patience, however, was not something that came naturally to her. "I know," she said, trying to calm Chieko. "But remember, Meiko is strong, and she's smart. We can't lose hope. We have to let things come to us and be open and ready to see any sign or clue when it does arise."

"You're probably right, Mom. It's just that I'm so worried about her." Chieko set down her chopsticks, put her palms together, gave a slight bow, and said, "*Gochisosama*," to close her meal—"I have partaken." She pushed herself out from the table and stood up. "I have to get to the office. I have a full day of appointments. At least they allow me to focus on something other than my missing daughter."

After Chieko left, Aiko returned to the table to finish her tea and the newspaper. It was part of her morning routine. On the third page of the paper, there was a short article that caught her attention. It was about a forty-five-year-old man named Masaharu Fujiwara, the owner and operator of a soba shop in Kyoto who plunged to his death from an eight-story apartment window. Police believed that it was a suicide. He left behind a wife and young son. Mr. Fujiwara was originally from Izumo in Shimane prefecture in western Japan and had moved to Kyoto twenty years earlier. While suicides were not uncommon in Japan, they still showed up in newspapers across the nation. It wasn't unusual for her to read about two or three of them every day. What struck her about this story was that the man was from Izumo, where she had been born.

She finished the rest of the paper, spending considerable time solving the daily *shogi* problem, and then cleaned the dishes. She gave Kotetsu the broiled salmon skin that she had saved for him. It was one of his favorite treats.

CHAPTER 23

TOKYO
APRIL 5TH, DAY 13

Chieko hung up her phone and then immediately called David's cell phone.

"Hi, Chieko. Have you heard anything about Meiko?"

"David, do you have a few minutes to talk?" Chieko could hear the panic in her voice, and she hated to appear so vulnerable, especially in front of David, but she didn't have any choice.

"Of course. Is everything OK?"

"I'm not sure. I just got off the phone with Detective Nomura from the Kyoto police, the man we talked to last week."

"Yeah, I remember. Did he share anything about Meiko?"

"He didn't have any news regarding Meiko's whereabouts, but he asked me some very strange questions and told me some things that are very disturbing."

"That doesn't sound good. What did he say?"

"First off, there was a middle-aged married man who committed suicide two days ago. He jumped from his apartment building and died instantly."

"People commit suicide here all the time," replied David, sounding confused. "What's that got to do with Meiko?"

"Hold on," replied Chieko. "Here's the strange part. He had several pictures of himself with a girl that the detective said matched the photo of Meiko that we left with him. The guy wrote a suicide note saying that he was in love with a girl named Hana, but the detective said all the photos looked just like Meiko. He also said that the man had a tattoo of a fox on his ankle." Chieko paused before continuing. "Do you know if Meiko has any tattoos?"

"Hmm, not that I know of. I mean I haven't seen Meiko naked since she was about eight, so I can't say for sure, but I've never noticed any tattoos on her arms or legs. I think she would have told me if she got a tattoo."

Chieko wondered if it might have been something she got in college and was embarrassed to share with her father.

"I asked if he could text or email me the photos, but he said they are police evidence and part of an active investigation, and he can't share over the Internet or even mail them to us at this point. Police protocol or something ridiculous like that. He did say that if we came down to the precinct office, we could see the photos, the scrapbook this guy kept, and any notes he made, including the suicide note."

David paused, skimming his calendar. "I can't take off for another two days, but I could go down on Thursday. Does that work for you?"

Chieko looked through her schedule as well. "Yes, I can shift some appointments. I think it's best that we go down together. David, do you know anything about Meiko having any relationships with married men, either here or back in San Diego?" It was a question she would never have thought to ask about Meiko if it hadn't been for the call from the police.

"Again, not that I'm aware of. If she has, then she's certainly done a good job of keeping them a secret from me. I just don't think it's likely. If she was planning on going down to visit a married man in Kyoto and staying for two weeks, then she would have come up with a better excuse than she did. For one thing, she would have called her employer and asked for some time off. She didn't do that. It's very unlike her to be late for anything or to miss one of her commitments. Another is that she would have packed more. She only took a very small suitcase with her."

That's what she was afraid of. Having an affair with an older man would have explained a lot. And in the larger realm of possibilities, it wasn't the worst thing that could happen to a young woman. "Do you think it's possible that she got lured into some sort of relationship from a chat room or something like that? There are a lot of sexual predators out there looking for victims. I've treated several patients who were victims of that sort of thing."

"No offense to your patients," replied David, "but I think Meiko is too sharp to be caught up in something like that. Until we see the photos, we have to assume that it's a girl who looks a lot like Meiko, instead of actually being Meiko. Anyway, if he was a sexual predator, wouldn't it be odd for him to commit suicide?"

Despite his assertion that Meiko was somehow too sharp to be caught by such a predator, his second observation was quite astute, thought Chieko. Her clinician mind clicked in automatically. "First of all, a lot of very intelligent people get caught by sexual predators. These individuals target victims who are trusting, naïve, and most often in the wrong place at the wrong time, but not necessarily unintelligent. To your question, the answer is typically yes, it is odd. But there's a great deal of repressed shame and guilt in some of these individuals. They know what they're doing is wrong, but they just can't control their impulses. Some of them commit suicide as a form of penance. Often, its part of a murder-suicide."

"It's worth checking out. It's all we've got at this point."

"I agree. Let's take the 8:15 a.m. shinkansen on Thursday."

"I'll be there," David said. "And Chieko, don't worry too much about this until then. There's nothing we can do until we get there. We might even hear from Meiko in the meantime."

"I know. Thanks."

She had to grudgingly admit that she was happy that David was here, and they could search for Meiko together. Despite all they had been through, she still enjoyed his company and his sharp mind and gentle sense of humor. It took the edge off her tough exterior. Having to do all of this by herself would have made a terrible situation almost unbearable. She also knew that David was likely just as panicked as she was but he was adept at covering up his more sensitive emotions.

CHAPTER 24

TOKYO
APRIL 7TH, DAY 15

David met Chieko outside of the small izakaya tucked between several other eating and drinking establishments on a narrow side street in Ikebukuro, one of Tokyo's wards. Metropolitan Tokyo was the most populous area in the world. It consisted of twenty-three wards, or districts. Tokyo was not only a metropolis but a prefecture, or state, the only one of its type in Japan. Hidden gems such as this tapas restaurant were common in a place at once so sprawling and so dense. There was a large red Japanese lantern on the outside of the small sliding door with the name Benke on it. That was the only marking to differentiate it from the dozens of other nondescript places on that street.

David slid open the wood-and-glass lattice door and ducked under the dark-blue curtains that framed the entrance. It was just after seven in the evening, and the place was packed, mostly with businesspeople in dark suits sharing beers, shochu, and a wide range of tapas. All eyes turned to him as he entered. While foreigners in Tokyo were not a particularly rare commodity anymore, it was still unusual for a blond 6' 2" *gaijin* to enter a small neighborhood restaurant, even if that "neighborhood" ran into the hundreds of thousands and even millions of people.

Chieko entered closely behind David and waved to a man behind the counter. He smiled and spoke to one of the servers, who showed the pair to a small table tucked in the corner.

All the tables in that section shared a bench, so the two edged their way past a group of businesspeople sitting at one end and settled into their places. Chieko ordered two draft beers. This restaurant served Kirin. Since many Japanese restaurants have contracts with one of the major breweries, it wasn't necessary to specify the type of beer you wanted, just whether you wanted it in bottle or on draft, and in some cases large or small.

"How were you able to get us a reservation? It's pretty packed." David munched on some of the edamame that had been set on the table when they arrived.

"I come here a lot after work, just to unwind, sit at the counter and have a beer or two and get something light to eat. They don't officially take reservations, but they're willing to hold a spot for a little while for people they know."

The beers arrived, and Chieko ordered some tapas for them. Grilled meat was always one of David's favorite foods, so she ordered an assortment, from the more traditional chicken thighs with scallions and beef tenderloins to some more exotic offerings like chicken gizzard, liver, and her personal favorite, chicken cartilage. She also ordered some grilled *shishito* peppers, marinated eggplant with grated ginger, and fried sardines.

They clinked their beers together, which was customary before the first sip. It felt weird to be with Chieko in Japan, especially just the two of them at dinner at a restaurant. He saw her in her native environment, strong, confident. As successful as she was in the States, it seemed to him that she fit in much better here. She had moved on without him, which was ultimately what he wanted, but it still seemed odd, and bittersweet.

"So, we're all set for tomorrow," said Chieko. "The train leaves at 8:12 from Tokyo station. I already bought two green-car tickets. I'll be arriving at 7:35 from Kawagoe and will meet you just outside the entrance to the shinkansen." She handed him a train ticket. "If something comes up, just text me. We can always catch the next train."

David took the ticket and put it in the zippered pocket of the small leather bag that he had bought in his first month in Tokyo. It wasn't something he would likely wear in Southern California, but in Tokyo, everyone had one, and he had to admit that it was surprisingly useful.

He couldn't help but smile at how organized Chieko was. She never left any detail to chance. Left on his own, he would probably, no, most certainly, have just arrived at the station in the morning, unaware of the train schedule, and attempted to buy a ticket for one of the trains that left every hour. He didn't love structure and hated to be tied down to specific schedules. But in Japan, where everything ran on precision, there was a benefit to planning ahead and a definitive penalty for not doing so. It reminded him how Meiko used to kid him that he was smart, but she was smart and organized. It seemed like such a long time ago that he last saw her. He missed her terribly.

The first order of skewered meats came, along with a dish of a fiery-red miso-based sauce that paired well with the beef. David made his way through several skewers, finished his beer, and signaled to the waitress for another. He opened his bag and pulled out a small notepad.

"After we talked the other day, I reached out to some colleagues who do research on Japanese folklore. I also did some research on the internet and went over to ICU. That fox tattoo got me thinking. Turns out there's a lot of folklore associated with the fox in Asia and especially here in Japan. Are you familiar with any of it?"

Chieko munched on a crispy sardine, which she had dipped in mayonnaise sprinkled with hot pepper flakes. She knew that International Christian University had an excellent English-language library and that that was why her ex had gone there. "I'm familiar with a few superstitions, nothing much. Enlighten me, Professor."

David continued, ignoring her casual tone. "The *kitsune* has been part of Japanese folklore since the fifth century BCE. There seems to be two common classifications of the *kitsune*: one is benevolent and associated with the god Inari, while the other is mischievous and even malicious. The foxes you see at the Inari temples, like Fushimi Inari, where we met that charming priest, are benevolent servants of Inari, the god of rice, sake, and fertility."

Chieko listened, crunching on a piece of grilled chicken cartilage, which sounded like she was eating carrots. It always amazed David how she could eat and drink as much as he did and keep her figure. It was something that had always attracted him to her, even now.

David took a sip of his beer and glanced at the two men working at the grill, carefully turning the skewers and watching to make sure that everything was cooked to perfection, while smoke billowed up from the long, boxy stainless-steel *yakitori* grills that were black from years of constant use. The waitress moved through the restaurant, taking orders on a tiny notepad from men with gradually reddening faces as the level of alcohol increased and serving small plates of grilled meats, fish, and vegetables as well as beers, shochu, and highballs.

"Maybe that priest didn't get the message about which type of fox he's supposed to worship," Chieko said.

David wasn't sure if she was being playful or cynical— probably a bit of both. "Yeah, whatever god he's worshipping, it certainly isn't one god of warmth and kindness," David agreed. He chewed on a piece of the cartilage. It was crunchy and chewy at the same time, much as you would expect from cartilage. Not much meat, but there was something about it that grew on you. He doubted that it would ever become his favorite, but he wouldn't turn it down either.

"You'll love this," he continued with a grin. "It was a common belief in medieval Japan that any woman encountered alone, especially at dusk or in the evening, could be a fox." He took a sip of beer and looked in her eyes. "Didn't we first meet at night?"

"Ha-ha," she said, shaking her head at his joke. "No, we met during the day, and I was with some friends at the time, so I think you were safe."

"Just checking." He took another swig and continued. "Fox possession was noted as a disease as early as the eleventh century and continued to be classified as such through the early twentieth century."

"I've heard of *kitsunetsuki*. You don't hear about it in the West, but I have read accounts of it here, although they are rare and almost exclusive to rural areas. It's a form of demonic possession, which we would now most likely classify as a form of psychosis or schizophrenia."

"From what I'm told, entire families were ostracized by their communities after a member of the family was thought to be possessed. Girls who come from a fox-possessed family find it hard to get married. As in many other patriarchal societies, Japanese women are often seen in the benefactor/bane duality. They are either to be venerated and protected or seen as dangerous, manipulative, femme fatales."

"Are you speaking from personal experience or sharing what you've learned?" asked Chieko, eating a grilled shishito pepper.

"As a folklorist, I need to take in information from all sources," replied David.

"Some of the goals of the trickster kitsune include seduction, theft of food, humiliation of the prideful, or vengeance for a perceived slight. It's said that those who kill a fox risk being bewitched by the fox's kindred or even the ghost of the fox."

"I'll have to check with my mother to see if she's killed any foxes in the past year or so," said Chieko with a laugh. "David, these are all interesting stories. You know that I respect your work and think there is a lot of value in understanding the origins of our beliefs, but what practical use does this have for us?"

He sat back, folding his arms. "I know you take a more clinical and pragmatic approach to behavior than me. I think it's important to understand everything we can about the belief systems of those around us. Hidden within these myths and legends are deep-seated fears and possibly hints of truth. I'm not sure what is going on with Meiko, but a man that the police think is associated with her just committed suicide.

He also had a tattoo of a fox on his ankle. While we still don't know if this has anything to do with Meiko, I don't see those as just coincidences."

"Surely you're not suggesting that Meiko is possessed by a kitsune or anything ridiculous like that."

"You of all people should know that people's beliefs, whether rational or not, guide their behavior. I don't necessarily believe in fox possession, but I'm sure that some people do believe in it, and those people act upon those beliefs. It doesn't have to be true to be real."

Chieko nodded. "So, what you're saying is that this man may have believed that Meiko was possessed by a fox?"

David shrugged. "I'm not sure at this point. I honestly don't know what to believe. I just have a feeling that there's something here, and we should keep our minds open."

"Leave it to you to turn this into something to do with spirit possession and voodoo."

David had heard derision in her voice many times before. It used to annoy him to no end, but he had learned to ignore it.

"More likely than not, the man's tattoo has nothing to do with Meiko any more than the fact that he owned a soba shop. We don't even know if the pictures he had are of Meiko."

"All true." David finished his beer. He waved to the waitress and ordered a highball. "But you have to admit that this fox folklore is interesting. At the very least, it provides me a nice chapter for my book."

"I'm glad to see that you haven't let Meiko's disappearance affect your professional goals," she said.

"Hey, you still see patients, right? That's your job. Mine is to teach classes and write books. I can't just curl up in a corner and wait for some detective to solve the crime."

"I know. I'm just scared. You're right."

"Don't worry. We'll find her." He knew that most of her snarkiness was caused by Meiko's disappearance—most, not all.

"You really think so? I've started to have my doubts lately, and I hate thinking that way." She sounded much less confident and much more vulnerable than usual.

"I'm confident we'll find her. I don't have anything to base that on other than the fact that Meiko is very smart and resourceful. Wherever she is, she will get in touch with us." He tried to sound confident even though deep down he was scared to death as well. But he had always been good at putting on a positive veneer.

"I hope you're right, David."

"Me too." He ate another skewer of beef with the spicy miso sauce and looked around. People were leaving and then were immediately replaced by new customers. He often wondered if working in a restaurant gave you a sense of déjà vu. He remembered something he forget to mention earlier. "Hey, just when you thought that I couldn't get any crazier, one of my colleagues gave me the name of a shaman in Kyoto who specializes in fox possession. I contacted her and set up a meeting for us tomorrow while we're there."

"Jesus, David! A shaman!" Chieko couldn't help laughing. "You really don't leave any stones unturned, do you? The next thing you know, you'll be telling me that you've set up an appointment with a fortune teller, a witch doctor, and a palm reader to help us."

"I'm not ready to go there yet, but if I thought it would help us find Meiko, I certainly would." The bubbles of the highball felt fresh and clean as David drank. There's just something about that fox tattoo and all the related mythology that has piqued my interest. It can't hurt, and we may learn something."

"And it will give you something to write about as well."

"That's not nice. My motives are pure. But yes, I imagine that it will add a little spice to the chapter. Don't blame me for being resourceful."

"I won't. I'm happy to blame you for many worse things than that." Chieko sipped her beer. "Do we need to fast before we see the shaman or eat some mushrooms or anything?"

He had to smile. He missed Chieko's sharp wit. They had a wonderful relationship for over twelve years and a crappy one for three. A lot of that, he knew, was his fault. But he had never stopped loving her. Spending so much time with her over the past two weeks reminded him of that. "I have no idea, but I don't think that hallucinogens are part of the Japanese shaman's repertoire. I'm personally looking forward to having a pork cutlet sandwich on the train for breakfast. I've grown quite fond of those since I've been here. In fact, Meiko introduced me to them."

† † †

After finishing their dinner, David and Chieko headed their separate ways. David's train ride was less than five minutes while Chieko's was forty-five. When she returned to Aiko's house, she found her mother sitting at the kitchen table working on a Sudoku puzzle.

"Welcome back," Aiko greeted Chieko and poured a cup of green tea for her.

Kotetsu greeted her by rubbing himself against her arm and meowing loudly. She tickled the top of his head, which he always seemed to enjoy.

"Thanks, Mom," she said, settling herself at the table.

"How was your date with David?"

Chieko scowled. "It wasn't a date, and you know it." She knew her mother secretly, or maybe not so secretly, wished that she and David would get back together. "Anyhow, true to form, David has gone down the supernatural path and is convinced that Meiko's disappearance has something to do with fox possession."

"Really?" Aiko replied without looking up from her puzzle.

"He even got us a meeting with a shaman in Kyoto tomorrow who specializes in fox possession. I think it's a ridiculous waste of time, but I've got no better ideas, so I just have to go along with his craziness."

Aiko laid her puzzle on the table and removed her reading glasses.

"Chieko, you are a very bright, well-educated woman. Don't let that education get in the way of learning new things or seeing things from other perspectives. You may find some value in the most unlikely places."

"Oh no, you sound just like David! He didn't call you while I was on the train, did he?"

"No, he did not. But I do know that there are ancient sources of wisdom and knowledge in this world that go well beyond our current scientific paradigms. I think that seeing a shaman will be very enlightening."

"Well, I will try and keep an open mind. I'm headed to bed. I have to leave early tomorrow."

"I'll have breakfast for you before you leave."

"Thanks, Mom. Are you going to be up long?"

"Not much longer. You know I can't leave a Sudoku unfinished once I start it. Besides, I only sleep about five hours anymore, so it's still a bit early to go to bed."

"Well, good luck with the puzzle and good night."

"Good night, Chieko," replied Aiko without looking up from her puzzle. Kotetsu curled up next to her, purred loudly for about a minute, and then fell asleep.

CHAPTER 25

The train ride to Kyoto was uneventful. Chieko caught up on some professional articles related to sensorimotor psychotherapy. As planned, David ate a fried pork cutlet sandwich and washed it down with a black coffee from Starbucks, both of which he bought at the train station. To Chieko's dismay, he also spent part of the time reading some articles that he had printed out on fox possession. At least he didn't feel compelled to share any of the information with her, which she had feared he would.

For the last forty-five minutes of the ride, Chieko noticed David reading a Japanese novel, *Spring Snow*, by Yukio Mishima, a book she had read when she was in college. It was part of a trilogy and dealt with two of Mishima's favorite topics, suicide and reincarnation. Of the three books, *Spring Snow* was Chieko's favorite. When David put the book down, she couldn't help but ask how he was enjoying it.

David looked down at the well-worn paperback in his hands and then at Chieko.

"It's the second time I've read it, and it's just as hauntingly beautiful as I remembered it to be."

She agreed that was a great way of putting it: a hauntingly beautiful novel.

David continued, "I've come to the conclusion that great Japanese fiction, whether it's in novels or in movies, is like the English countryside."

"That's an interesting comparison," said Chieko. David always had a novel take on things, whether she agreed or not. "How so?"

"They sort of flow onward with no clear beginning or end. There are hills and valleys, but they're subtle. No tall mountains like the Alps or the Rockies. It's never extremely cold like the frigid plains of Minnesota or burning hot like the deserts of Arizona. There's an ethereal, timeless quality to them. They pull you along slowly. You want to reach out and touch their beauty, but it's just out of your grasp. There's a sad longing to the muted tones that is best viewed from a distance. You feel calm, almost hypnotized, as they roll onward, sucked into a misty green haze that smells fresh and ancient at the same time. You're not captivated or enthralled; rather, you gradually melt into them, blurring the lines of reality and fiction. When it's done, you're not sure what happened or why, but you're sad that it's over—and in most cases, you're moved somehow."

Chieko listened to David without interrupting. Despite their differences, she found herself entranced by his observations. She herself would have never made that comparison, but now that it was laid out in front of her, it was a perfect analogy.

"I never thought of it like that," she said. "But I think you're right. Japanese gravitate toward subtlety, both in our language and our behavior. We also hold a special place in our hearts for the comingling of beauty and sadness. We find it hard not to think of one without the other. Like cherry blossoms: so beautiful and yet so fleeting."

David nodded. They remained silent as they pulled into the station.

From the train station, they grabbed a taxi to the police station in central Kyoto. Chieko explained to the man at the main desk that they were there to see Detective Nomura. After they had waited for a few minutes, a detective who seemed to be in his mid-thirties emerged from behind a set of closed doors.

"Good morning." He bowed to them. "I'm Detective Saito, Chief Detective Nomura's partner. We've been working on this case together. Thank you for coming. I hope you understand that we couldn't send the pictures and other information over the internet. I'm sorry for the inconvenience. I know you both must be busy."

"No, it's nothing at all," replied Chieko, returning his bow. "We appreciate you letting us know about the pictures." She and David both introduced themselves to the detective, exchanging business cards. They had decided to let Chieko do most of the talking because her Japanese was so much better. But David was "allowed" to jump in whenever he liked, and she would help explain any questions that he might have. She warned him about bringing up his fox possession nonsense so as not to embarrass them, especially her.

"I've got everything laid out for you in one of our conference rooms. Chief Detective Nomura is waiting for us. Shall we?" Saito led them through a large room with aisles of desks set close together. There were several uniformed officers, but mostly the room was occupied by what must have been close to thirty detectives in dark business suits and ties. At the far end of the large room was a conference room where Nomura awaited them. He stood in front of a rectangular table upon which lay several photographs and several pieces of paper.

Detective Nomura nodded slightly to them as they entered the room.

"Thank you for coming. I hope that we didn't call you here on a false alarm."

"Any lead is important for us to look into. We're happy to come," replied Chieko.

"This is what we found in the apartment of the victim, a Mr. Masaharu Fujiwara. He was the owner of a small soba shop here in Kyoto. We'd like you to look at the pictures and see if they match your daughter." Nomura motioned to the photos, receipts, and what Chieko assumed to be a suicide note.

There were eleven photos in all. David and Chieko both gasped as they looked at the photos. Without question, they were all photos of Meiko. Five of them included a man, whom they assumed was the victim. There was a photo of Meiko and the man dressed up at what seemed to be a nightclub. They were sitting at a small table, toasting with champagne glasses, a bottle of Dom Perignon Rose on the table. There was one of her kissing his cheek as he smiled. There were two of them standing underneath cherry trees that were exploding with tiny white blossoms. There was another of them sitting next to each other at a fancy restaurant.

The photos of Meiko by herself were the most disturbing to David and Chieko. In three of the photos, she wore skimpy, expensive-looking lingerie. In another, she stood outside of Mitsukoshi department store holding a yellow Hermes bag, a huge smile on her face. One photo showed her posing in a short, sexy dress with high heels outside a restaurant. It appeared to be the same outfit she wore in the photo with the victim inside the restaurant. There was also a photo of her in tight jeans and a white sweater under a cherry tree.

In each of the photos, she wore more makeup—provocative, seductive makeup—than either David or Chieko had ever seen her wear. There was an alluring look in her eyes in every photo. It was as if they were looking at Meiko's twin sister—her evil twin sister.

After laying down the final photo, Chieko spoke.

"These are definitely our daughter, Meiko. I, I just don't know what to say. We've never seen her dress like this." Chieko stumbled over her words, trying to make sense of what they had just seen. "We had no idea that she was having a relationship with this man, or any man, for that matter." Chieko felt intense pressure in her chest, which she knew was a sign of a panic attack. She focused on taking deep breaths and staying in the moment. She needed to stay clearheaded and figure out what had happened to her daughter.

David spoke for the first time, in passable Japanese. "Like Dr. Tokunaga said, these are clearly photos of Meiko, but these are not her clothes. If I didn't know better—and I hate to say this—but I would have to say that these are the clothes of an escort, a prostitute. Definitely not anything that Meiko would wear."

"May we see the suicide note?" asked Chieko, trying to piece all of this together.

"Of course," replied Detective Saito, handing her the wrinkled paper. "We found this in the victim's shirt pocket."

"Thank you," said Chieko, taking the note in her hand. She read the note aloud, given that David's spoken Japanese was far superior to his reading comprehension, especially when something was handwritten.

"He refers to Meiko as Hana," said Chieko to no one in particular. She turned to David. "Has she ever used Hana as a nickname?"

He shook his head. "Not that I know of. I've never heard her referred to as that."

"Odd," continued Chieko. "Obviously, she has taken on some alias and seems to have assumed almost a separate personality from the Meiko that we know." She paused, lost in thought. "I just can't imagine why she would do that or what might lead her to take on such an alias." The term *multiple personality* ran through her head, and she tried to push it aside. That was not something she wanted to consider at this point.

"Just to confirm," interrupted Detective Nomura in a businesslike tone, "you both agree that these photos are of your daughter, Meiko. Is that correct?"

David and Chieko both nodded. "Yes, that's correct," added Chieko.

"It's also true that you have never known her to dress in these types of clothes, associate with middle-aged men, or use the name Hana. Is that also correct?" he continued.

"Yes, those are all true statements," agreed Chieko, although she started to feel that Meiko was now being seen more as a suspect than a victim. Her feelings of confusion and panic morphed into anger. Her protective instincts as a mother were taking over.

"Do you have any leads with regards to where Meiko might be—a hotel room, anything?" asked Chieko, trying to redirect the conversation back to finding Meiko.

"At this point, all we know is that she was staying at the Grand Prince Hotel under the name of Hana Tanaka. Her entire stay, which seems to be five nights, along with two dinners at an expensive hotel restaurant, was paid for in cash by Mr. Fujiwara. Your daughter checked out of the hotel five days ago with three pieces of luggage as well as a black Chanel bag and got into a taxi with another man. We have yet to identify that man nor do we know where they went." Detective Saito debriefed Chieko and David on what they knew so far. "The hotel bill was slightly over $15,000. In addition, we found receipts totaling an additional $21,000 in Mr. Fujiwara's apartment. Those included the black Chanel bag as well as the Hermes bag, which by itself cost $8,500."

Chieko listened in disbelief. This couldn't be her daughter. Meiko had never showed any interest in designer bags or clothes. She was more of a flip-flops–and–jeans girl, more tomboy than seductress. It was a whirlwind of information swirling around them. Chieko felt nauseous.

Nomura nodded toward Saito, who asked them to focus on a white screen on the wall. He then pulled up the footage from the hotel. Saito explained what they were about to see and played the tape for them in slow motion.

Chieko watched in shocked amazement as her daughter, dressed in beautiful designer clothes that she had never seen her in before, exit the luxury hotel.

After they watched the footage through, Nomura asked them, "Can you confirm that the woman in that video is your daughter?"

Both Chieko and David confirmed that it was indeed her. Chieko held back tears.

"Have you ever seen the man that she was with?" continued Nomura.

Chieko shook her head. "No, I've never seen him before." She turned to David, who also said that he had never seen the man before.

Saito handed David and Chieko blown-up, high-resolution screen captures of both Meiko and the man she left with. Chieko and David confirmed that it was Meiko in every photo. They couldn't place the man. His face was never clear in any of the photos. They mostly saw his face in shadows or from the side, never a clear shot.

"You're welcome to keep those photos," said Saito.

Chieko nodded. "Yes, please. I'd like to keep them." An awkward silence fell on the room.

"Detective," said David, breaking the temporary silence. "You mentioned that there was a tattoo of a fox on the victim's ankle. Would it be possible to see a picture of that?"

"Oh, good lord, David!" said Chieko in English. "We talked about this. You promised!"

"Humor me for a moment," David replied in English as well.

"Yes, we have several photos," said Saito, handing three close-up photographs to David.

"Hmm," he grunted. "Would it be possible to get a copy of one of these? It doesn't show the victim's face, just the tattoo, so that should be all right, correct?" Without waiting for a response, he added, "Also, if we could get copies of any of these photos of Meiko, not the ones with the victim but just by herself, that would be helpful for us."

Saito turned to Nomura, who nodded his approval.

"Yes, I'll get some copies for you," replied Saito, heading out of the room.

"Chief Detective Nomura," continued David, "I know this may be an odd question, but are you familiar with a phenomenon referred to as fox possession?"

"David, please!" implored Chieko, flushing with a combination of embarrassment and anger.

Nomura rubbed his chin for a moment before responding. "Yes, I've heard of it. In fact, I've heard of cases where people who have committed crimes said they were possessed by fox spirits, which caused them to commit the crimes. It's not very common. When you've been a detective for twenty years, you hear all kind of things, Dr. Wright," he said, with a slight laugh. "But people claiming to be possessed by foxes are no more common than people claiming to be attacked by vampires or zombies. In fact, given the recent popularity of some movies, we've started to see an increase in that sort of behavior." He held up his hand to clarify. "Not actually anyone being attacked, mind you, but just people saying they were. Most are just delusional individuals, many of whom are trying to come up with an excuse for their bad behavior."

Saito returned and handed David an envelope containing a copy of one of the photos of the fox tattoo as well as five photos of Meiko.

"I have to tell you both that at this point we have to assume that your daughter is a person of interest in the suicide of Mr. Fujiwara. She may not be directly linked to his death, but we would like to find her and bring her in for questioning."

"But she's not a suspect; she's a victim. She's a missing person!" blurted Chieko.

"I understand your position," replied Nomura, remaining calm and unemotional. "You are in a very difficult position. However, we both want to find your daughter. We will continue to search all our leads. We will share what we find with you in the hopes that it will help us find her. We would appreciate it if you would contact us with anything you find as well."

David put his hand on Chieko's shoulder, attempting to calm her down.

"Thank you, detectives," said David with a bow, trying to diffuse the tension.

"Yes, thank you," added Chieko. "We refuse to believe that Meiko had anything to do with Mr. Fujiwara's death, but we understand your position. Please keep us informed. We can be here in less than half a day."

"Thank you. We appreciate your help and your time." Nomura bowed. Saito escorted Chieko and David, both of whom were dazed and agitated, to the exit. They bowed once more and then the two of them headed into the street.

The moment they were outside of the police office, Chieko couldn't hold back her anger.

"Can you believe they think that Meiko is a suspect in this guy's suicide? First off, people commit suicide for any number of reasons. We have no idea how mentally unstable he was. Second, unless Meiko pushed him out of the window, she's no more to blame for his death than anyone else. It was a suicide, not a homicide."

David nodded. "I know, and I agree with you. It's frustrating to have the focus turn from victim to suspect so quickly. Still, I guess it's positive that they seem to have renewed interest in locating her. If they see her as a suspect, perhaps they'll put more manpower on it to try and find her."

"And you!" fumed Chieko. "I can't believe you asked about fox possession! They must think that we're raving lunatics! We talked about that before we went in. You just couldn't help yourself, could you?"

"I'm telling you Chieko, there's something more here than meets the eye. It's piqued my curiosity. Let me just run with it a bit. It will probably lead nowhere, but I have to learn more." They continued walking down the street aimlessly. "Speaking of which, we should probably hop in a cab and make our way to the shaman. I'd like to see what she has to say about this tattoo."

"Lead the way, Professor. It can't go any worse than it did with the police." Chieko's head was swirling with too many unpleasant thoughts to argue with David.

David flagged down a taxi, and they both hopped in.

As they traveled, Chieko couldn't stop thinking about the way Meiko looked in those pictures. It was like looking at a completely different person but one who looked just like her daughter. The woman in those pictures looked seductive, manipulative, materialistic, and overtly sexual. She would never use any of those adjectives to describe Meiko. Perhaps there was a side of Meiko that neither she nor David was aware of, a hidden side that had somehow been released. The term *multiple personality* surfaced again. It wasn't something she wanted to consider because she knew how terrifying that truly was. But she couldn't overlook the possibility either. She prayed they would find Meiko before this other side of her took over her identity for good.

CHAPTER 26

APRIL 8TH, DAY 16

Neither David nor Chieko knew what to expect when the cab pulled up to the driveway of the shaman's house in a residential neighborhood on the outskirts of Kyoto. It was an older house than many in the neighborhood, prewar, but it didn't seem out of place, nor was it the oldest house in the area. There was a small stone statue of a fox in the front courtyard, which wasn't odd. To the casual observer there was nothing to identify it as the house of a shaman.

In his travels, David had met with numerous shamans, fortune-tellers, spiritualists, and storytellers, and it always struck him how comfortably they fit into their cultures, regardless of whether they lived in a rural place or in the middle of a city. It always impressed him that even in modern societies such as Japan, there was a place for such custodians of myth, legend, and occult belief systems. They had their place in society, albeit an obscure and largely unknown one. There seemed to be a timeless, ethereal quality to them, as though they would have been equally comfortable living a thousand years earlier or a thousand years in the future. As if they had always been there and also were just passing by. There was also a calmness that seemed to shroud their very being, a confidence based on some hidden wisdom. People who sought their advice inevitably found them without consulting a directory, although there were plenty of spiritualists and fortune-tellers who did actively advertise. In

David's experience, those were largely charlatans who played on the fears of insecure people. It always impressed him that even in modern societies such as Japan, there was a place for such custodians of myth, legend and occult belief systems.

David and Chieko walked on a stone path, past the fox statue, and came to the front door. David turned to Chieko before pressing the doorbell. She looked detached and disgusted, like she wanted to be anywhere but there. David had seen that expression more than once toward the end of their marriage.

"I know that you think this is a waste of time, but please try and be respectful. This is your culture after all," he admonished.

"Of course I will be respectful. Just because I think you're delusional doesn't mean that I'm going to be rude." She responded like a petulant teenager.

"Perfect. Also, try not to roll your eyes when I ask questions that bother you. It makes me feel bad." David and Chieko had agreed in the car that he would take the lead in asking questions but that he might need Chieko's help if he didn't understand something that the shaman said. Chieko said she would be more than happy to let David take the lead.

"Aww, poor baby," Chieko responded to his snip. "I'll be on my best behavior, I promise."

"Good. Besides, it's rude to do that."

"You're pushing your luck. Ring the bell."

David nodded. She was right, he thought. But it was rude. He pressed the bell, and gentle, recorded chimes rang within the house. After a few moments, the door opened, and they were greeted by a woman, whom David estimated to be in her mid-sixties, dressed in an indigo *samue*, a cotton two-piece outfit commonly worn by Buddhist monks when performing physical labor. Over that she wore a maroon *hanten*, a padded three-quarter-sleeve quilted house jacket made of cotton. She wore maroon slippers, and her graying hair was pulled into a bun.

David and Chieko introduced themselves and apologized for bothering her, a traditional greeting when entering someone's house in Japan. The woman said that she was expecting them and led them into the house. David's size-thirteen feet hung over the edges of the slippers that were set out for them next to the door, as they did every time he wore house slippers in Japan. They followed the woman into a back room, where she motioned for them to sit down on cushions set on top of the tatami mats around a small, lacquered table. The smell of incense permeated the entire house—a combination of sandalwood and something David couldn't identify but that was sort of sweet. From a stainless-steel thermos on the table, the woman poured hot water into a cast-iron teapot with a goldfish pattern on the side. She casually waited a full minute without saying anything while the tea steeped in the pot and then carefully poured tea for each of them in small celadon-colored ceramic cups. Although the silence was both calming and uncomfortable, David felt that it was best to let her start the conversation. Shamans didn't mind long periods of silence. In fact, they seemed to enjoy them.

"I was told that you wanted to talk with me about your daughter, who is missing. Is that correct?" When the woman finally spoke, her voice was calm, emotionless, and yet somehow soothing.

"Yes, that's correct," responded David.

"What can you share with me? Do you have a photo of your daughter?"

"Yes," David replied, handing her a photo of Meiko before she disappeared.

The shaman received it gently with both hands and looked at it carefully and then closed her eyes, holding the photo close to her face. David thought she might be smelling it, like an old book, trying to gain some additional insights. She set the photo down on the table and then reached into a small wooden box and pulled out a single stick of incense. Without comment, she stuck the stick into a square stone with a circular opening in the center and then pulled a wooden match from a separate drawer in the incense box and slowly lit the stick of incense. She shook out the match, extinguishing the flame, and set it down on the table. White-gray smoke from the incense snaked gently upward.

"Do you have any additional photos?" Her eyes were gentle and warm and yet piercing, like she was looking deep inside of David. She made you feel like you were the only person in the world, like nothing else mattered. It was a talent that few people had.

David nodded and handed her the five photos that the police provided them of Meiko, or the girl who went by the name of Hana, but whom he knew was Meiko. The shaman deliberately and slowly repeated the same process with each of the photos, looking at each one closely and then closing her eyes and seeming to absorb its essence. She set each of them down in a row, placed her hands on the table, and then slowly sipped her tea.

"You have something else for me, don't you?"

"Yes." David nodded. "This is a copy of a tattoo that was found on a man who committed suicide. He had these pictures of our daughter with him."

The shaman's eyes noticeably enlarged when she saw the photo of the fox tattoo before she repeated her viewing process. She set the photo down on the table but kept it separate from the other photos. She closed her eyes, breathing quietly while her body slowly oscillated left and right. A deep, soft hum emanated from her. This continued for at least three minutes. David couldn't make out what she was saying and doubted if Chieko could either. He intentionally avoided making eye contact with Chieko, afraid that she would roll her eyes in disgust. Slowly, the shaman opened her eyes and looked first at David and then at Chieko.

"I'm sorry to say, but your daughter has been possessed by the fox spirit. She is currently suffering from kitsunetsuki." She looked sad and concerned. "How long has she been missing?"

David looked at Chieko and then responded. "The last time we heard from her was slightly more than two weeks ago. Sixteen days, to be exact."

"This tattoo is a very powerful fox symbol. It is rarely seen anymore. I haven't seen this symbol in almost twenty years. It is very evil." She paused, looking down at the photos on the table. "I am sure that the woman in these photos has a similar tattoo on her body."

"How can you be sure of that?" asked Chieko, unable to remain quiet.

"Nogitsune is a very powerful fox spirit. It only possesses women, and then those women seduce and destroy men. No man would willingly get this tattoo put on his body unless he was under the influence of a woman controlled by Nogitsune." The shaman looked directly at Chieko. "The woman in these pictures you have shown me is very different from the innocent girl in the first photo. This woman is a seductress, a temptress set out to destroy her victims. She is ruthless, uncaring, and unrelenting. She will use her sensuality to lure her targets to her and then systematically ruin them. This man may be her first victim, but he certainly will not be the last."

"Why would this fox spirit, Nogitsune, possess our daughter?" asked David. Obviously, what she said concerned him, yet at the same time, he felt vindicated. His "crazy" ideas about fox possession weren't so far off base after all.

"Inari Mountain here in Kyoto has been a site of worship of the god Inari for centuries before the founding of the Fushimi Inari shrine in the eighth century," the shaman began. She went on to review the differences in foxes who hung out around Inari, as David had with Chieko, saying good ones served the god and evil ones were drawn to his power. "The current Fushimi shrine is the parent shrine to all Inari sites in Japan and has immense power associated with it. It is the most powerful Inari shrine in the world. It attracts many helpful kitsune, but it also attracts evil kitsune, even Nogitsune. For some reason, Nogitsune found your daughter in a moment of weakness and was able to possess her."

"So, what are we supposed to do? How do we break her possession?" asked David. He looked at Chieko, who was staring at the table. *Probably trying not to laugh…at him!*

"You must find her, and you must find her soon. If she remains possessed for thirty straight days, she may never come back. She may never return to her previous state. If you find her, I will help you." The shaman said this in a serious tone, as if what she was saying sounded completely rational, even obvious.

"What do you mean, she may never come back?" asked Chieko, her skepticism apparent.

"There are women roaming this world who are permanently possessed, and they will never come back. After thirty days, your daughter will stop knowing who she is. She will always be controlled by Nogitsune. I pray that you can reach your daughter before that happens. If you can break the spell by then, you can get her back."

David tried to redirect the conversation while Chieko glared incredulously at the shaman. He was glad to have been vindicated, but he hadn't been expecting to get such a negative prognosis. This whole fox possession thing was a hell of a lot more serious than he had ever imagined.

"Can you give us any clues as to how we might find her? Where would Nogitsune try and take her?"

"She will be near the mountain, near the shrine. That is where Nogitsune's power is strongest. There will be other men who fall victim to her seduction. Look for them, and you will find her."

Well, that's sort of what we have been doing, thought David. He had hoped that the shaman could give them a bit more direction.

The incense stick burned out. The woman pulled a small cloth pouch from the pocket of her jacket. She turned the stone receptacle over, poured the ashes from the burnt incense into the pouch, and then pulled the two braided white strings tight and tied them into a knot, sealing the pouch. She handed the pouch to David.

"This should serve as a good luck charm for you as you search for your daughter. I know you were hoping for more from me. This is all I can give you at this point. Keep it with you at all times." She sounded apologetic that she couldn't do more.

"Thank you. We appreciate your time." David took the pouch and placed it inside the pocket of his coat.

The shaman turned to face Chieko, her eyes warm and gentle.

"I know that you don't believe what I have told you about Nogitsune. You probably see me as a superstitious old woman. You may choose to believe what you wish. That is your choice. But I can tell you that the tattoo you have shown me, as well as the photographs of your daughter, are unmistakable signs of Nogitsune's possession. No matter what you believe, you must find your daughter—and find her soon. Before it's too late."

Chieko bowed slightly to the woman. "Thank you for your time."

David pulled an envelope with $300 in yen from his coat and set it down on the table. That was the amount that he had been told by his colleague was appropriate for a consultation with the shaman. "You've been very helpful. Thank you."

The woman bowed to them.

They left the woman's house and headed back into the street. Chieko called for a cab.

"What do you make of what she said?" asked David.

"I think it's all superstitious nonsense," Chieko replied, looking down at her feet. "But I have to give it to her—she's very convincing."

"So, you don't think there's any possibility that what she is saying is true?"

"David, I'm a psychologist, a scientist. Demonic possession is a prescientific way of understanding mental illness. You know that as well as I do." She paused. "But I do agree with her that we need to find Meiko soon. The girl in those photos appears to be an alternate personality of Meiko. The longer that she is in that persona, the more likely that the dissociation will strengthen. That will make it harder to get the real Meiko back."

He didn't like hearing the prognosis any better from Chieko than he did from the shaman. They needed to do everything they could to save their daughter.

CHAPTER 27

APRIL 16TH, DAY 16

The late-afternoon sun silhouetted Hana's lithe figure, covered only in a thin silk robe, as she stood in front of the large window. She turned to Yoshimitsu Watanabe, who was lying on the bed smoking a Lucky Star cigarette.

"Darling, I love this view! It's wonderful!" she said in a voice dripping with sensuality.

The man blew out a plume of white-gray smoke. "I'm glad you like it, babe. It sure didn't come cheap."

I'm sure that's the case, she thought. She was also sure that it was just the start of the money he was going to be spending.

She strolled to the bureau beside the wall and pulled out a cut-crystal glass, dropped three ice cubes in it with stainless-steel tongs, and then poured two fingers of an amber liquid from a crystal decanter. It smelled sour and sweet at the same time. She swirled the ice cubes with her finger and then slowly sauntered over to the man and handed him the drink.

"I know, sweetheart. This must have cost a fortune. It's such a beautiful place. I don't think I've ever been in such a nice apartment. We're so high up too. The view is amazing! I can't wait to see it at night."

She knelt by the man as he sipped the smooth, sweet-tasting bourbon that surely burned slightly as it went down, and started drawing a soft circle on his chest.

"How long do we have this place, darling?" she mewed.

"I paid for three months in cash," he replied.

Perfect. She doubted she'd need it that long, but it was nice to have a roof over her head. He would be long gone before three months passed. Of that, she was certain. "I really appreciate it, love. How did you come up with the money?" she asked innocently.

He chuckled confidently. "Well, I told you that I'm pretty much in charge of one of our largest departments. Even today, most people choose to pay their insurance premiums in cash. We have collectors who go out every day and bring back envelopes full of cash that gets counted and then recorded. I worked something out with one of the guys who reports to me. Basically, we set aside a certain portion—not much in the grand scheme of things, really—and just don't record it for a while. Of course, we'll eventually need to record it, but we can push things for a month or so here and there. We bring in hundreds of thousands in payments every day, so by setting aside 3 percent every day for two weeks, I can put aside a nice little slush fund. That will give me time to win back the money at the craps table or at blackjack and pay off that debt. The money will get recorded, and no one will be the wiser. I'm also drinking buddies with one of our internal auditors, so I can keep him looking elsewhere for a couple of months."

"Wow, you have so much power. You must be a very important person at your company to be able to do something like that. It's such a turn-on! Isn't it dangerous, though? What if you don't win enough at gambling?"

"Well, that's part of the fun, isn't it, babe?" He took another sip from the glass and pulled out two cigarettes from the pack and offered one to Hana. She took the lighter from the nightstand and lit both of their cigarettes.

"If there was no risk, then life would be boring. If you always won at gambling, then they wouldn't call it gambling, would they?"

"I guess not," she said, blowing out a long white stream of smoke. He hadn't exactly been tearing up the tables since she met him. He had dug a nice, deep hole for himself. It would be interesting to watch him try and get himself out. Of course, she was there to help—help dig a deeper hole, that is. It made her smile, thinking of it. "I think that's why I'm so attracted to you. You like to live life on the edge. Take chances. Live large."

"Some guys are content with simple, boring lives. That's not me. I want to taste everything the world has to offer, even if there is some risk involved. Especially if there is risk involved. But there's a difference between taking calculated risks and being reckless," he continued. "I'm a smart gambler who plays the odds and knows when to bet big and when to sit tight. It's a risk, but it's one that I'm willing to take."

"That's incredible, babe. You're so smart. I find that very sexy in a man," she purred as she rested her head on his chest.

He ran his fingers through her long, dark, silky hair.

After a few minutes, she lifted her head and said, "Darling, I feel like going out to someplace nice for dinner tonight. I've heard that Nagaragawa is a nice restaurant."

He smiled. "Yeah, it's a great restaurant, top-end *kaiseki*. Very expensive too."

"If it's too much money for you, babe, we don't have to go there. I just wanted to go somewhere really nice with you." Earlier in the day, she did a web search of the most expensive restaurants in Kotyo, and that one popped to the top. *Let's see how high Mr. Big Shot wants to fly.*

"Sure, we can go," he said. "Why don't I take you shopping before that, and then we can go to dinner?"

She knew that he was just trying to sound nonchalant while his internal calculator was working overtime registering his rapidly expanding debt. She could smell his fear. It gave her a warm feeling of accomplishment. The wheels were slowly coming off.

"Ooh, that sounds fantastic, darling! Maybe we can go to that club afterward, and you can show me how to play blackjack. I've always wanted to learn."

"Sure, babe, I'd love to."

"Then we need to work up an appetite before we go out, don't you think?" she said with a conspiratorial smile that was a combination of girlish innocence and unadulterated sexuality. He could show her how to play blackjack, and she'd show him what she was good at. Besides, having sex was preferable to talking to him.

"Sounds like a good plan to me, babe."

CHAPTER 28

APRIL 8TH, DAY 16

Chieko and David walked from the train station up the long staircase and through the large orange gates of Fushimi Inari Jinja.

"The administration offices are over there." Chieko pointed to a two-story building with a green roof to the left of another large gate and a brightly colored orange-white-and-red shrine in the middle of the sprawling granite courtyard. The crowds were already filing in, which was common during cherry blossom season.

"I wonder if that charming priest will be there to lay out the red carpet for us like last time," David commented, trying to keep pace with Chieko, who, despite being almost a foot shorter than him, was able to move at a surprisingly fast clip.

"Let's hope not. I don't want you to get the idea that all Japanese priests are jerks. Most are quite friendly, although somewhat reserved," she continued, not breaking stride.

"I've learned over the years not to generalize," replied David. "Still, it would be nice to deal with someone else this time around."

She agreed as she pulled open the door of the administration building. Several priests were working at their stations, performing various administrative tasks. A young priest with sleepy eyes greeted them and asked if he could help.

"Yes, I'm Dr. Tokunaga," Chieko responded with confidence. She handed him one of her business cards. "If possible, we would like to talk to the priest in charge, about a rather delicate matter."

"Yes, Sensei. Let me see if he is available." The young priest scuttled past his coworkers into a back room.

"Dr. Tokunaga, huh?" chided David. "Didn't take you long to pull rank on the poor fellow."

"In hierarchical systems, it's good to establish the pecking order early on," she replied.

"Well done, Sensei," David said, giving her a slight bow. The term *sensei*, while most commonly translated as "teacher," is widely used in Japan to denote anyone in a position of specialized expertise and responsibility.

The young priest returned, followed by an older priest in a crisp white robe and orange hakama. He was thin, was slightly taller than Chieko, and appeared to be in his late forties or early fifties, with dark hair streaked with gray.

"This is Takagi San, the priest in charge," said the young priest. He bowed to both Chieko and Takagi before excusing himself.

"It's a pleasure to meet you, Dr. Tokunaga, and uh…" he said, trailing off, bowing to both David and Chieko. He held Chieko's business card in his hand.

"Wright, Dr. David Wright," replied David, handing the priest his business card.

"Dr. Wright and I used to be married," added Chieko.

"I see," replied the priest, effortlessly handing each of them one of his business cards, which he pulled from the expansive sleeve of his robe. "It's a pleasure to meet you both."

His business card indicated that he was the gonguji, who reported directly to the *guji*, or head priest. At such a large shrine as this, this was a very senior-level position. He could be the head priest at almost any other Inari shrine in Japan, should he wish to be.

"The young priest indicated that you had something sensitive that you wished to talk with me about. Perhaps we could talk more openly while we walk a bit. I've been cooped up inside all day and could use some fresh air and a little exercise. It's a very beautiful time of year. I hope you are able to enjoy the cherry blossoms." He motioned gently toward the door without overtly directing them.

"Yes, that would be nice," agreed Chieko. He had a calm demeanor that put people at ease, she thought. He was a much better representative of a Shinto priest than his colleague they met two weeks prior.

The spring sun was bright, especially as they emerged from the darkness of the building. The priest directed them toward a less crowded path away from the main shrine area.

"So, how can I be of assistance to you both?"

Chieko pulled out a photograph of Meiko and handed it to the priest.

"We came here two weeks ago looking for our daughter, Meiko, who has gone missing. We believe that she might have come here to view the cherry blossoms. We were hoping that you might have some information about her whereabouts and be able to answer a few questions that concern us."

The priest looked at the photo of the young, smiling Meiko before handing the picture back to Chieko.

"I remember that one of our priests mentioned that a girl had gone missing and that her parents had stopped by. I remember seeing a similar photo before. Unfortunately, I don't know anything more about her disappearance. I'm very sorry about your daughter. This must be very difficult for you."

"Yes, we're very concerned," agreed Chieko. "In fact, we think that the situation may have gotten worse. We were called down to meet with some detectives, and they think that Meiko may now be involved in the suicide of a soba shop owner."

"That sounds very strange," remarked the priest, raising an inquisitive eyebrow.

They continued strolling slowly down a winding stone path, occasionally passing several small stone shrines framed in bright orange and white wooden structures and guarded on all sides by stone fox statues.

"That's what we thought. But they have some additional photos of Meiko that would suggest that she has turned into a very different person." Chieko handed the priest the five photos of Meiko that the detectives had provided them. She didn't provide him the one with the fox tattoo, nor did she provide him the screen captures of Meiko and the man leaving the hotel. The priest stopped and examined each photo carefully before handing them back to Chieko.

"They look to be the same girl as in the first photo, but she has definitely changed. Not only her outward appearance but her eyes seem to draw you in—and I apologize for saying this if it offends you—in a lurid and seductive way. If I had seen all of the photos without any background information, I would think that they were two completely different people."

"Exactly." Chieko nodded. "It's as if she has an alter ego or a separate personality that somehow has taken over."

David cleared his throat. "Please show Mr. Takagi the photo of the tattoo."

Chieko nodded reluctantly, concerned with how far David would take the entire fox possession angle. She handed the photo of the victim's fox tattoo to the priest. "This tattoo was found on the suicide victim's ankle. Does it mean anything to you?"

The priest studied the photo impassively and then handed it back to Chieko. "I've never seen such a tattoo before. I understand that tattoos are becoming more common among younger people these days. Unfortunately, I don't have any expertise in the area."

"Are you familiar with the concept of kitsunetsuki?" blurted David, ignoring Chieko's stern glance.

The priest smiled. "Yes, it is not something that we hear very often, but I am familiar with the concept of fox possession." They continued their walk slowly down the path as he spoke. "As you can imagine, given the nature of this shrine, we have received people who believe that they are possessed by the spirit of the fox. We used to see it more commonly when I was a younger priest, twenty years ago. I used to hear stories from some of the older priests that they used to get at least one person a month who was supposedly possessed and wanted us to dispel the evil spirit." He led them to a stone bench in the shade of an ancient cherry tree whose branches were exploding with delicate white blossoms, and gently invited them to sit.

"Have you ever performed such an exorcism?" queried David.

The priest looked off into the distance before turning to Chieko and David. Some of the blossoms floated slowly and gracefully to the ground. It was like the first snow in December, delicate and elegant.

"There are several ceremonies or rituals that we perform to try and drive away such spirits. In most cases, it is enough for us to say a simple prayer, burn some incense, and provide the 'possessed' individual and their family with some type of omamori. There is a much more formalized ritual, however, that I have seen performed several times and I have myself performed twice. It is a longer ceremony, typically involving three priests. It lasts almost an hour. It's not a particularly pleasant experience for anyone, including the priests."

"May I ask what you mean by that?" probed David.

The priest nodded. He was facing them but seemed to be looking beyond them at some undefined target in the distance. Tiny white cherry petals softly landed on them like confetti at a New York City ticker-tape parade.

"As you can imagine, the individuals who need such an intervention are very ill and disturbed. They truly believe they are possessed by an evil spirit. They scream, swing their arms frantically, froth at the mouth, spit, and shout invectives. We not only need three priests to perform the ritual—we need at least one or two other people, younger priests, preferably, or family members, to restrain the individual during the ceremony. It is a very emotionally draining process for everyone involved." He pursed his lips.

Chieko thought that he looked like he was trying to contain some hidden emotion, perhaps pushing down a painful memory. His eyes suddenly looked sad to her.

"Do you believe that these individuals were actually possessed by the spirit of the fox?" asked Chieko.

"I saw that your business cards say that you both have doctorates. Might I ask what fields they're in?"

"I'm a psychologist, and David is an anthropologist," replied Chieko.

The priest nodded his understanding before continuing.

"I'm sure that it might seem to the outside observer that priests like myself are insulated from the modern world and focused only on centuries-old rituals and beliefs. But many of us, and certainly the younger priests, receive some education in things such as psychology and anthropology, although not to the extent of either of you. If you were to ask that same question to any of the priests here forty or fifty years ago, I'm sure that all of them would have said that, of course, they believed in fox possession. I think you would get a much more mixed response now, if the individuals were willing to express their honest opinions."

He reached into his sleeve and pulled out a small square wrapped in white silk with a braided silk string. There were small orange foxes printed on the outside. He held it on his open palm.

"This is an omamori that we sell here. It's quite simple, really. We make them ourselves, although we have the silk woven for us at a factory in Nagoya. The head priest and I bless hundreds of these every day. I believe that they can be very powerful, and I keep at least one with me at all times. They are much like a cross to a Christian or prayer beads to a Buddhist. They carry power because people believe they are powerful and blessed. I'm not sure that it would be particularly powerful or useful to someone who doesn't believe, just as a cross would likely be seen as just a piece of wood by a Buddhist.

"People have a need to believe in something beyond themselves. I would say that it is fundamental to our very being. I believe this small omamori is more than an attractive piece of silk and wood. I believe that it helps protect me and guide me along a purer path. Can I prove that? Is there scientific evidence to confirm it? No, of course not. But does that make it any less powerful to me? Again, the answer is no." He folded his hand over the omamori and put it back into his sleeve before turning back to them.

"I do believe that there are powers beyond our physical world. We still pray to the god Inari. In earlier times, he was the most powerful god in all of Shinto. His messenger and servant is the fox. In ancient times, the fox was considered a beneficial animal in the rice fields because it helped control the rodents. Unfortunately, the fox has also been linked to mischievous behavior.

"Do I believe that fox possession is real? Yes, I believe it is real because people believe it to be real, and that belief influences their behavior. If a young woman believes that her behavior and thoughts are in some way being controlled by the spirit of the fox, then in many ways, she is indeed possessed by the fox. I believe that there are gods who influence our world and our life. If I didn't, I wouldn't be a Shinto priest. But I also think that people are often too quick to attribute inappropriate behaviors or their own misfortune to the intervention of the gods."

Chieko nodded as the priest presented his worldview. After all, it was almost identical to hers. It was also satisfyingly in complete contrast the superstitious nonsense that the shaman had just presented to them. She wondered what David thought of the priest's perspective.

David remained quiet during the priest's discourse. At

the end, he posed a question. "We talked with a shaman earlier today who saw the photos of Meiko and said that she was possessed by a particular fox spirit known as Nogitsune. Have you heard of that?"

The priest nodded, looked to the ground with a smile, and then turned to David and Chieko.

"Nogitsune is supposedly a very powerful and evil fox spirit who attempts to completely possess and ultimately destroy her victims. Given the photos that you showed me of your daughter, it isn't surprising that a shaman would think that she is possessed by such a spirit."

"Do you believe that is possible?" continued David.

"What I can tell you is that I performed an exorcism on a girl about a decade ago who was supposedly possessed by Nogitsune. She had turned from a very pleasant, innocent girl into a seductress seemingly bent on seducing and destroying as many men as she could. She put herself in many dangerous and compromising situations that concerned her family and friends greatly. It was a very shocking transformation. She seemed to be a completely different person."

The priest pulled the omamori from his sleeve and casually turned it over in his palm. Chieko noticed this and thought that it must be a behavioral tick that he had developed to help cope with stressful experiences and memories. She saw this a lot among her patients.

"Upon my urging, the family took her to see a medical doctor as well as a psychologist and, I believe, a psychiatrist. Nothing seemed to change her behavior, and in fact, every intervention seemed to push her further away from her previous self. In the end, after they had exhausted all other options, including visiting a shaman, I agreed to perform the exorcism. The shaman was convinced that the girl was possessed by Nogitsune and unsuccessfully tried to dispel the spirit herself. The shaman attended my ceremony, upon my request."

"What happened to the girl?" inquired Chieko.

"We performed the ceremony. The girl screamed, she spit at me, she pulled chunks of her hair out to the point that her scalp was bleeding, and she fought with the priests who were trying to restrain her, one of whom received a pretty nice black eye. She collapsed to the ground several times, and she vomited. In the end, she was exhausted, as was everyone there, including myself. But, from what I heard from the family, she returned to her previous self." The priest continued to turn the omamori in his palm and look to the cherry trees in the distance.

"Doesn't that make you believe that she actually was possessed by a fox spirit and possibly even Nogitsune?" asked David.

"Something definitely happened that affected that young girl immensely. I know that many of the people who were there, including many of the priests and certainly all of her family members, were convinced that I exorcised the evil spirit from her." The priest paused, shaking his head slightly. "I'm not sure if there really was a spirit there or not. She believed that she was possessed, and she also believed that I had the power to expel that spirit. In the end, that's all that mattered."

"You sound more like a psychologist than a priest, Takagi San," said Chieko, trying to lighten up the conversation a bit. "Perhaps you have missed your calling."

"Hmm, maybe so," he said with a smile. "Perhaps we serve the same function in society from different perspectives.

People come to both psychologists and priests to find comfort and fix something that is wrong in their lives. We approach the problem differently but in the end hope to have the same outcome."

The priest stood, and Chieko and David followed.

"Dr. Tokunaga and Dr. Wright, I truly hope that you find your daughter. Obviously, something is troubling her greatly. That is clear from the photos. I don't personally believe that Nogitsune is the cause of her transformation. But I think it is important for you to find her, and I will do whatever I can to help. If it turns out that you need my help from a spiritual perspective, then I am at your service. However, I believe that the real problem is much more mundane than fox possession." He continued walking with them along the path back to the main gate. They walked mostly in silence, oblivious to the intoxicating beauty of the cherry trees around them and the petal storm that enveloped them.

"You have my card, and I have yours," said the priest when they arrived back at the administration offices. "Feel free to contact me with any questions you have. I will keep an eye out and instruct my priests to do the same. If we hear anything, we will contact you immediately. If it's all right, I ask that you keep me abreast of what you find. Perhaps it will help us find your daughter. I sincerely hope so."

They bowed to each other. Chieko and David expressed their appreciation for his time.

"Well that was refreshing," commented Chieko as she and David walked toward the train station, sounding as upbeat as she had in weeks. "I've never heard a priest sound so reasonable, rational, and scientific."

"I agree," said David. "But it seems odd to me that he was so, I guess the word would be secular, in his perspective."

"It seemed perfectly reasonable to me."

"That's the point, really. Don't you find it strange that a Shinto priest, let alone the second-highest-ranking priest at one of the country's largest shrines, would view his own religion more like an anthropologist or a psychologist? Why become a priest if you don't believe that there are divine spirits who influence our lives, a higher power, beyond reason? I mean, he explained possession more like a psychologist than a priest. It just strikes me as odd."

Chieko was frustrated that David couldn't accept the priest's progressive ideology. "Maybe it's because he's an intelligent, modern man with a realistic perspective on where religion and science meet. I certainly felt more comfortable hearing his perspective on this fox possession nonsense than I did that of that witch doctor we talked to earlier."

"I guess that's what bugs me. It's almost like he said everything we wanted to hear. Like he tailored his conversation to exactly what would appear most attractive to us. I just wonder if that's what he really feels or if he is somehow playing us in some way."

"To what end?" Chieko wondered what David was getting at. "He didn't sound like he was making things up on the fly. His observations seemed well-thought-out and well-reasoned to me. What would he gain from trying to convince us that fox possession isn't real?"

"I'm not sure. Maybe to direct our attention away from his shrine. After all, the shaman said that this mountain and this shrine were centers of power for Nogitsune. That can't be good PR for the shrine, especially if it's somehow related to the spirit possession of young women."

Chieko shook her head. "David, you just want to believe that this folklore is true. You're ignoring what contradicts your viewpoint and only accepting those pieces that are in alignment with it. You're using conditional reasoning." She stopped in front of the ticket machine and purchased two tickets back to Kyoto.

"And you're not?" asked David. "I'm just saying that he has a vested interest to direct negative attention away from his shrine and his religion. That's all. You have to admit that it's a possibility."

They passed through the turnstile as they continued their conversation in English. David's Japanese was quite good, but whenever they covered complex topics like this, it was easier to do it in English. It also had the advantage that most of the people in the station couldn't listen in on their conversation.

"It is. But wouldn't he also have a vested interest in convincing us to believe that Meiko is possessed so that he and his priests could somehow save her? You know those types of things don't come cheap. At the end of the day, they are running a business."

"Hmm. That's a logical argument as well. It's just something we should keep an eye on. There's something about him that seems too good to be true. He also hasn't really helped us find Meiko either."

"At this point I'll take 'too good to be true' over 'too weird to be true.' But you're right. We need to keep our eyes open. There is something that I do agree with that shaman on. We need to find Meiko soon. If she is experiencing some type of deterioration in her personality structure and is taking on an alternate personality, then that can be very damaging to her psyche and hard to reconcile. The longer it goes on, the harder it will be to get the old Meiko back intact. It's hard to imagine that there won't be some residual effects on her personality."

"I agree. We need to figure out a way to get in touch with her and try and bring her back. I just don't know how."

They waited for the train largely in silence. Chieko tried to process everything that she had seen and heard that day. The possibility that Meiko was suffering from multiple personality disorder was something she didn't want to think about because of the terrible implications it would have for her future mental stability. It wasn't something you got over easily, if at all. But she couldn't ignore the possibility. In some ways, she wished it were fox possession. In her mind, that would be a lot easier to resolve. They had to find Meiko, and they had to find her soon. That was her only hope.

CHAPTER 29

KYOTO
APRIL 9TH, DAY 17

Meiko woke up, rubbing what felt like a month's worth of sleep from her eyes, and tried to focus on where she was. She did her best to remain calm, or at least as calm as a person could be when they had no idea who or where they were. What she did know was that she was lying in a very comfortable bed with soft, fluffy pillows. The comforter was light but warm. It was probably filled with down of some sort, she thought. She lifted the covers and saw that she was wearing a sheer, silky, black negligee. She had no recollection of putting it on, let alone ever owning something like this. Her eyes moved around the room, desperately looking for something that looked familiar. No luck.

She gradually slid out from under the covers. Her bare feet sunk into the dark-tan carpet. A fluffy pink robe sat on top of the wooden bureau in the bedroom. She pulled that over her bare arms. The material felt soft and warm. Each drawer in the bureau was filled with clothes she'd never seen before, including underwear, bras, socks, and more lingerie. She closed the drawers and walked into the bathroom attached to the bedroom. She looked at her face in the mirror. It seemed familiar and yet she failed to recognize the person staring back at her. The drawers below the sink were filled with an assortment of makeup: lipstick, fingernail polish, fake eyelashes—all of them looked expensive. There were cotton balls, a hair dryer, dental floss, toothpaste, and several hairbrushes. On the counter below the mirror was a toothbrush leaning in a glass. She assumed it must be hers and squeezed some toothpaste onto the brush and started brushing. The routine task felt comforting. She'd done this many times before. It felt normal. After she finished, she spit out the toothpaste and rinsed her mouth with water. She opened the glass shower door and saw several bottles of shampoo and conditioner, facial masks, scrub pads, and liquid soap. There was a small tub next to the shower with an automatic reheating unit attached. She closed the shower door, left the bathroom, and returned to the bedroom.

The door to the bedroom was open, and she walked into a large living/dining room. The blinds were open, and light bathed the entire room in a bright, warm glow. She looked around at the dining table with four chairs and a leather couch, coffee table, and flat-screen TV on the wall. None of it rang a bell. There were boxes piled up next to the dining room table with labels she'd seen before in magazines and store windows but had never owned: Hermes, Louis Vuitton, Chanel, Christian Louboutin, and Versace. Some were empty while others contained shoes—gorgeous, exotic, expensive-looking shoes—or purses or dresses, the latter of which were very short and very seductive. All were things she would never buy for herself. Her head was spinning. *Whose apartment am I staying in?* She went to the kitchen and opened the refrigerator. Outside of two bottles of champagne and what looked to be a large jar of caviar, it was empty. She opened a cupboard and found a clean glass and filled it with water from the tap. She took a long drink and then filled the glass again.

Sitting on the dining table was a notebook with a pen on top. She sat down at the table, still sipping her water, and opened the notepad. There were a few lines on the first page in a handwriting that looked oddly familiar to her.

Today is Thursday, March 30. It's 11 in the morning. I'm in the lobby of the Grand Prince Hotel in Kyoto. I'm not sure who I am or what I'm doing here. I called a number on a cell phone and am waiting for the man, a priest, who answered to meet me. Hopefully, whoever he is can help me figure out who I am and why I'm here.

She decided that she needed to keep moving. It was no good sitting in this apartment. She headed to the bathroom, got undressed, and hopped in the shower. The warm water pounding down on her made her feel calm and less afraid. She took her time, carefully soaping up and rinsing off, shampooing her hair and just letting the water try and bring her back to normalcy.

As she soaped and washed her legs and feet, she noticed a tattoo of a fox on her ankle. She didn't remember ever getting a tattoo. But she found it neither surprising nor disturbing. It was just another of the many odd things that seemed new and strange to her. Maybe she'd always had it. In any case, she didn't mind it. It must mean something because people didn't get tattoos for no reason. It was something else she'd need to figure out.

She toweled off, dried her hair, and headed to the bedroom to find some clothes. Most of the drawers and closets were filled with clothes she would be embarrassed to wear in public, at least in the daytime. She found a pair of jeans, a pair of Toms slip-ons, and a black sweater. Not sure what the weather was like outside, she grabbed a thin black jacket with a tag that said Chanel. She took the black Chanel purse that contained cell phone, a wallet with a surprising amount of cash in it, as well as packets of tea. She found keys conveniently hanging next to the front door.

She rode the elevators to the ground floor. The doors opened on a lobby where people milled about, either heading out of or into the building. She stepped outside, and the sounds of the city hit her squarely. Cars and people passed by. The sun was bright, and she reached into her purse and found a pair of Chanel sunglasses to put on. Not knowing where she was going, she chose to go left and get lost in the stream of pedestrians. She passed a wide range of small shops, boutiques, and several restaurants. On the next corner was a convenience store, and she had an idea. She walked up to the woman working at the counter and asked if there was an internet café anywhere nearby. The woman indicated that there was one about four blocks from where they were, on the next street over. After paying for a pork cutlet sandwich and a can of iced coffee, Meiko thanked her and set out on a mission that gave her a sense of purpose for the first time that she could remember.

She arrived at the internet café, which was larger than she expected. At rough count, there must have been at least twenty cubicles, each with an office chair, a small desk, and a desktop computer with a flat-screen monitor. The staccato sounds of keyboards and mice filled the air. The man working at the reception desk next to the vending machines assigned her cubicle number eighteen, at twenty-five dollars per hour.

She settled in, putting her notepad on the tiny desk next to the keyboard and monitor. There was a hook on the cubicle wall to hang her purse and jacket. She logged in using the username *wakaran* (I don't know) and the password *tasukete* (help me). She browsed around the internet trying to find anything that might remind her of who she was and what she was doing here. There were several icons for Japanese and international news sites, Yahoo Japan, MSNBC, and Google, among others, that seemed mildly familiar. She clicked through these and read the headlines. Nothing. Nothing brought back any memories at all. Then she had an idea.

For some reason, the word *blog* came to mind, so she typed that into the browser, and several pages of options appeared. After skimming a couple, she chose to start her own blog. Blogbuilder.com seemed to be a good choice. After creating an account with the same username and password she had used to log in (although she had to add numbers at the ends of both because they were either already in use or they required numbers) she started writing her first entry: "Help Me Find My Identity." She found it natural to type in Japanese, especially given the keyboard.

> I'm in Japan, Kyoto, to be specific. I'm female and in my twenties. I seem to be taller than most of the girls I see. I can speak, write, and understand both English and Japanese. I'm not sure why. I don't know which is my native language and which is my second. The main problem is I don't know who I am or why I'm here. I seem

to be caught up in some type of dream. I completely lose consciousness for days at a time and then only reappear intermittently. I'm sending this out in one of those periods where it seems that I have some ability to reason and figure things out. If you can help me in any way, please respond to this blog. For now, I'm going to use the name Hana Tanaka because I found something in my purse with that name. I have no idea if that's my real name or not, but it's as good as any.

Thank you,
Hana

She made careful notes about the website, her log-in information, and the time and location of the internet café in her notebook. She spent another forty-five minutes skimming all the news sites she could find. Still nothing. She ate her sandwich and finished off the iced coffee. They were both delicious. She logged off, paid for her user fee in cash, and then headed back to the apartment.

When she got back to her room, she put her notebook in one of the drawers in the bathroom. She was tired, exhausted, really, although she wasn't sure why. She filled the bathtub and took a long, hot bath. She wanted to hop in the bed, but a small handwritten note beside the teapot in her bedroom caught her attention.

Mix one bag of tea in a pot of hot water.

Let it steep for at least five minutes

Drink at least *two cups in the morning, two at midday, and* at least *two cups before bed.*

It will help you relax.

There were about six of what looked to be homemade tea bags, like the ones she had found in her purse, next to the teapot. Not sure what it all meant but looking forward to some calming relief, she tossed one of the tea bags in the teapot and filled it with hot water from the electric water heater that seemed to have plenty of hot water in it. She waited for the tea to steep and then poured herself a cup and sipped it in bed, hoping that it would indeed calm her down and provide some clarity. She skimmed through the channels on the TV and stopped on a show called *Science for Everyone*. They were talking about the best way to slice raw fish. It was a welcome diversion. She finished her third cup of tea before falling asleep with the TV on.

CHAPTER 30

APRIL 9ᵀᴴ, DAY 17

Detective Nomura sat in the passenger seat while Detective Saito parked the black Nissan in a metered parking spot a few doors down from a small tattoo parlor in downtown Kyoto. Since tattoos weren't that popular among everyday Japanese citizens, there weren't that many establishments to search. Of course, the scarcity also meant the parlors were not easy to find. Much like a favorite hole-in-the-wall restaurant, most didn't advertise. Their clientele knew where to find them. Because of the parlors' association with organized crime, most metropolitan police departments kept tabs on these establishments. This was the fifth tattoo parlor that Nomura and Saito had visited this morning. There were only three more on their list.

The door to the tattoo parlor was locked, but there was a buzzer, which Saito pressed. A voice blurted through the speaker above the buzzer, "Yeah?"

"This is Detectives Nomura and Saito from the Kyoto Police Department. We'd like to ask you some questions," replied Saito.

Nomura heard a grunt from the other side of the speaker and then a click that signaled that the lock had been opened. Saito opened the door, and the two detectives walked into a dimly lit cave-like environment that smelled of cigarette smoke and cleaning fluid.

"I wonder why these places are so damn dark," said Saito as they took off their shoes and put on the guest slippers by the entrance.

"Probably for the privacy of their clientele," replied Nomura. "Let's hope they have more light focused on the areas of interest that they're working on." Nomura knew tattoos were not only for Yakuza members, but that didn't mean he liked them. He thought they made a person look dirty.

The detectives moved into the parlor. A scruffy man who looked to be in his late thirties sat reading the morning paper on a low-backed chair next to a small, round glass table. He had a ponytail and an attempt at a goatee, but it was more of a thin black mustache and a tuft of hair on his chin, each struggling in vain to connect with each other. When he saw the detectives, he set the paper down on the table and pulled out a cigarette from a pack lying next to an ashtray.

"Gentlemen, here for some ink?" He smirked as he lit his cigarette with a Zippo lighter that he snapped shut with a practiced motion.

"No, not today, not enough time," responded Nomura. He and Saito both showed the man their badges and then returned them to their jacket pockets. "We'd like to ask you about an unusual tattoo we've found. Wanted to know if you might have drawn it."

"Well," replied the man, blowing a stream of smoke through his nostrils, "you'll have to be a bit more specific than that. You got a picture of this 'unusual' tattoo?"

Saito grinned and set a photograph of the fox tattoo on the table. "Have you seen this before?"

The man looked at the photo without picking it up. He didn't need to look long. "Yep, I've seen it before." He pushed the photo to the edge of the table, and Saito picked it up. "Where'd you find that one?"

"We found this on the ankle of a man who recently committed suicide. Are you saying that you were the one who did the tattoo?"

"I can't tell you for sure that I did that particular tattoo, but I can tell you that I've done several of them recently." The man rubbed the hair on his chin and took another draw on his cigarette and then blew out a thin white stream. "And I have to agree with the word you used originally, Detective: *unusual*."

"How so?" asked Nomura.

"Well, up until a few weeks ago, I'd never done that tattoo before. In fact, I'd never seen anything like it before. Then, a little over two weeks ago, a pretty young girl comes in here, hands me a picture of that tattoo you just showed me, and says that she'd like it on her ankle. She was a looker, I tell you that: tall, gorgeous legs. Probably an escort or, at the very least, a hostess at some high-priced bar. No doubt out of my price range."

"So, the first time you saw this tattoo was when this girl showed you a photo?" continued Nomura.

"That's right."

"And was she the first person you ever put that tattoo on?"

"Yep."

"You said that you've done others since then. Can you explain? "

"That's what makes this sort of unusual." He laughed. "I've been doing this for about fifteen years, eight of them here in my own place. Up until two weeks ago, I'd never seen that tattoo anywhere, not even in magazines or on the internet. And then, since that first time, I've already done two more."

"So, you're saying that you did the ink on the man in this photo," said Nomura.

"Like I said, I can't be 100 percent sure because you didn't show me his face, but I think so. I did two more since her. He coulda been one."

Saito handed him a photo of the man's face, one that his wife had provided. The one from the crime scene wasn't a good example of what the man had looked like. "Here's a photo of the victim. Was this the man you inked?"

The man studied the photo more carefully than he had the previous photo. He handed it back to Saito.

"I would say yes, that's the guy. I did his tattoo on a Monday morning. I think it was the twenty-fifth. It was exactly a day after I did the same tattoo for the girl. He came in with the same photo as the girl and said he wanted to get it on his right ankle. Hell, I learned long ago not to ask questions. If you want a tattoo, I'll do it for you, wherever you like it. Ankle's not the most unusual place that I've done 'em."

Nomura could only imagine the strange requests a guy like this had received in fifteen years. "You said that there were two individuals since the girl came in. The man in this photo is one. Who was the other?" probed Nomura.

"Again, my clients aren't really big on names, and I'm not one to go asking. I'd say a little over a week and a half ago, a big guy comes in here. Real cocky, arrogant type. He hands me the same photo, and I look at him, and I remember laughing. He didn't like that and asked why I was laughing at him. I told him he looked a lot like one of my cousins, and I apologized. He was a lot bigger than me, and besides, he was a paying customer. As you gentlemen know, many of my clients don't take kindly to being laughed at. I couldn't help it, though. It was just too strange. First, this hot, young girl; then a day later, in walks some guy; and then not more than three days after that, this big guy shows up with the exact same photo. It was all I could do to keep a straight face when I asked him where he wanted it."

"Let me guess—the right ankle?" said Nomura.

"Well, forgive me for saying this, because I'm sure you're good at your job and everything, but you don't need to be a detective to guess that one." He laughed and lit up another cigarette. "When he said he wanted it on his right ankle, that's when I just about lost it. I pretended to cough and told him that I needed to go to the back to wash up. I laughed my ass off. I'm thinking, *I wonder what that gorgeous girl is up to.* Maybe it's some strange form of S & M that she and her gentlemen friends are into. In any case, I pulled myself together and inked the tattoo for that gentleman."

"Have there been any others who have come in asking for that tattoo?"

"Nope, just those two. Well, I guess, three, including the girl."

Saito handed him one of the pictures of Meiko, the one in the sexy lingerie. "Is this the girl who came in?"

The man stared at the photo before handing it back. "Damn, she is beautiful. That's her. I'd never forget that face, or that body."

Nomura handed the man his business card, as did Saito.

"I'd like you to call us the next time someone comes in here and asks for that specific tattoo. If possible, get their name."

"Now, like I said, not all of my clients are particularly jovial men. If word got out that I called the cops to report on a customer, my business would dry up pretty quickly. And I might find myself with some knee damage, know what I mean?"

"Yes, I do indeed." Nomura nodded with an understanding smile. "We're not interested in your Yakuza clientele, at least not at the moment. We have reason to believe that the men who got these tattoos are involved in some other type of ugly business and that their lives and the life of that girl are in danger. So, you can either call us the next time someone comes in, and I mean call us quickly, or I'll make sure that there's a uniformed police officer who swings by your shop a couple times a day, and a few times at night as well, just to ask you in person. That probably wouldn't be very good for your business either. It's up to you."

The smile left the man's face, and he nodded. "All right, next time someone comes in here to get that tattoo, I'll contact you guys. Can't promise that I'll be able to get his real name, though. Please don't make this a habit. I run a respectable business, pay my taxes, and keep my nose clean. I can't be responsible for what some of my clients do any more than the person who serves them ramen noodles or pours them a beer."

"We appreciate your cooperation. We will do our best to keep everything discreet," replied Nomura calmly. "Thank you for your time."

As the door to the tattoo parlor closed and locked shut

behind them, Saito turned to Nomura. "That was a pretty good Dirty Harry impersonation there."

"Yeah, I used to love that character. The key is to keep your voice low and never appear that you're upset. It's much more intimidating that way," replied Nomura. The two detectives hopped into the car and headed back to police headquarters. At this point, there didn't seem to be any reason to call on the other three parlors.

"From what our friend there said, we've got another victim pretty much lined up. It seems like this girl, Meiko, or Hana, is branding her victims in some ritualistic manner. She's either doing it on her own or someone is directing her actions. Either way, the outcome hasn't been very positive. What we need to look for now is some sort of pattern, something that links these men together." He dialed his cell phone as Saito drove through the streets of Kyoto.

"I'm going to call Dr. Tokunaga and let her know about the tattoo."

Saito nodded and continued driving.

CHAPTER 31

Aiko picked up the phone after the second ring. She'd been anxious to hear from Chieko. She sat down at the kitchen table and took out a notepad and started scratching out details from what Chieko shared with her. She let her daughter speak without interrupting.

When Chieko got to the part about the fox tattoo, Aiko tensed. "Do you have a copy of the fox tattoo with you? Can you take a photo of it and text it to me, now?" She caught herself holding her breath even after she finished talking, and she tried to relax.

A moment later, a text appeared on her phone. She opened it, albeit hesitantly, knowing what it would look like before she ever saw it. Aiko reviewed her notes, no longer surprised by any of the details. She listened while Chieko shared her concern that Meiko was being considered a suspect and not the victim. Aiko could hear the pain and anger in Chieko's voice. She made more notes.

"Don't worry, dear. We know that Meiko is innocent," Aiko said. "The truth will be her ally. In some ways, this could be to her advantage, because police are much more motivated to find potential killers than they are to protect victims." She paused, not sure if she wanted to ask the next question. She asked anyway.

"What did you find on your trip to the shaman?"

Aiko could almost see Chieko rolling her eyes as she

talked about Nogitsune and a thirty-day deadline. "Chieko, I want you and David to come here tonight for dinner. We need to talk about some things that might be relevant." Aiko tried to speak with a steady voice. It was a challenge.

"Mom, I've got a ton of things to pull together. I was just planning on heading to my apartment, grabbing something quick to eat, and doing some work tonight," Chieko protested.

Aiko remained calm but firm. "Chieko, listen to me. We need to talk, and we need to talk tonight. David needs to be here as well. I know you're busy. Trust your mother on this. Do this for Meiko, if not for me."

Chieko grudgingly acquiesced, after checking with David, who seemingly had no plans for the evening and always enjoyed Aiko's cooking. "We'll be there. I think we can get there a little after six."

"Good. I'll have dinner ready at six thirty."

Aiko hung up the phone and held her face in her hands. She looked down at her notes and then made a few additional comments. This was exactly what she had feared. She would have to take a much more active role in finding Meiko and getting to the bottom of this whole thing. That was very clear to her.

CHAPTER 32

APRIL 9TH, DAY 17

David and Chieko arrived at Aiko's house just after six thirty. Aiko was putting the final touches on dinner. It was early spring and cold at night, so she thought it was still a good time to make *nabe*. Japanese hot pot was one of Chieko's favorites, and Aiko wanted to make something that would relax and comfort them after what they had learned about Meiko, as well as what she was going to share that evening. It was a communal form of eating that helped bring people closer together. She made small chicken meatballs out of ground chicken, scallions, ginger, as well as some soy sauce and *mirin*, a seasoned vinegar. She knew that David preferred that to the more traditional cod. She did as well. She also had shiitake, eringi and maitake mushrooms, baby bok choy, rice noodles, and tofu chopped and ready to go. As an appetizer, she had a simple plate of sashimi: tuna and yellow tail, with freshly grated wasabi and plenty of pickled ginge. She preferred beer with nabe and had a few bottles of locally made Koedo beer chilling in the refrigerator. Koedo, or Little Tokyo, was the nickname name given to Kawagoe over two centuries earlier. There also was Japanese sake and shochu in case David preferred something other than beer.

Chieko slid open the door and entered the house, followed closely by David. They took off their shoes and put on the slippers that were waiting for them. Chieko had her own indoor slippers, and Aiko had kept the ones she got for

David years ago, before the divorce. She felt that would be nicer than having him use guest slippers. Besides, they were larger than normal slippers.

"You both must be exhausted," said Aiko, washing the cutting board in the kitchen sink. "Chieko, there's beer in the refrigerator. I thought you might want to try something from the new microbrewery. It's actually quite good."

"Um," responded Chieko half-heartedly. "David," she asked as David made himself comfortable at the small dining table on the floor, "would you like a beer or maybe some sake or shochu?"

Chieko knew that her mother had always liked David and wished that they had stayed together. Whenever he came to her house, she still treated him as Chieko's husband. Aiko expected Chieko to serve him as if she was still his wife. Chieko accepted that role; it was expected of her, and it was her culture. Aiko knew that while Chieko accepted that role, she didn't necessary enjoy it. But sometimes you had to do things because they were the proper things to do, not because you liked them. She had learned that lesson many times over. Besides, she secretly hoped that Chieko and David might find a way of getting back together.

"Whatever you are drinking is fine with me." David responded to Chieko's offer with a smile, stretching his long legs into the recess in the floor under the *kotatsu* and settling the comforter Aiko kept there to ward off the chill over his legs. He always enjoyed coming to Aiko's house because not only did he like his mother-in-law a lot but she treated him like a king. He suggested, "I'd love to try some of the local beer."

Chieko brought several bottles to the table and poured small glasses for the three of them.

Aiko sat down with them and served herself some sashimi before talking for a while about the cherry blossoms here in Kawagoe, as well as in Tokyo and Kyoto. Aiko purposely avoided getting into anything too serious until they finished dinner. She put the hot pot on a small gas heater on the table along with the vegetables and chicken balls. She added an assortment of vegetables, mushrooms, and a dozen chicken balls to the boiling liquid and let it simmer for a while. Chieko brought dipping bowls for the three of them and poured dark vinegar into each one. They spent the next thirty minutes enjoying the warmth and flavor of the nabe and sipping their beers. After they had finished the vegetables and chicken dumplings, Aiko added some thick udon noodles to the remaining stock, and they finished off the meal slurping noodles.

Aiko was adept at small talk and asked David about his research and teaching and Chieko about her practice. Having spent years as the wife of a "*shosha* man," someone who made his living by facilitating business and negotiations between others, she was a master at getting people to talk and, more importantly, to relax.

Aiko and Chieko cleaned up the dishes from dinner. Aiko pulled out a large bottle of shochu made from sweet potatoes and set that, along with three glasses and a tub of ice with tongs, on the table. Chieko fixed drinks for each of them. It was time to talk about their experiences in Kyoto.

Aiko sipped her shochu as she listened to David and Chieko share their adventures in Kyoto with the police, the shaman, and the priest. They showed Aiko the photos that the police provided of Meiko. Through it all, Aiko listened quietly, occasionally asking questions to clarify or to prod them on, but otherwise she didn't interrupt. It took them the better part of an hour to share everything. By that time, Chieko and Aiko had switched to green tea while David continued to sip shochu and water.

Aiko cleared her throat. The floor was now hers.

"What you have learned about Meiko is very troubling. I know that you are both concerned about her. I don't know if what I am about to tell you will make you feel better or worse, but it's something that I feel I need to share."

David and Chieko both straightened up when they heard this. Aiko was never one to exaggerate.

"I was pretty sure that I would take what I am going to say to you now to my grave. I thought that would be best. But it's clear that is impossible now." She looked at Chieko. "I always told you that I was born here in Kawagoe and that your grandmother's name was Kumiko." Chieko nodded. "That isn't entirely true," continued Aiko. "I was born in Izumo, in Shimane prefecture. My mother's first name was Hana. We were forced to leave our small village when I was a young girl."

"What do you mean, forced?" inquired Chieko.

"I'm sure it's hard for you to imagine since you've always lived in big, modern cities and are both accomplished scientists. But back when I was a young girl living in a very rural village in western Japan, things were quite different. People were much more superstitious. Certainly, the world was becoming more modern and there was a place for science, but old beliefs linger much longer in the countryside. My mother was a very beautiful woman, at least from what I remember. Many of the other women in the village were jealous of her beauty. So jealous, in fact, that they accused her of being possessed by the spirit of the fox."

Chieko interrupted. "Why would they think she was possessed just because she was attractive?"

"It's because women possessed by the fox are supposed to be seductresses, overtly attractive to men," replied Aiko.

"That makes sense," responded Chieko. "Sorry to interrupt."

"At first it was just some rumblings," continued Aiko. "Just women whispering things as we walked by. As time went on, though, we faced several seasons of drought when the fields failed to produce enough food, and we all lived in dire hunger. People became angry and started pointing fingers. The accusations got to be more serious and their words more venomous. People threw rocks through our windows at night and either avoided us or actively tried to make us leave. Children stopped playing with me, and I was often chased or even beaten by both boys and girls who accused me of being a fox. I remember nights in our home, sitting with my mother as she cried, asking her why people were so mean to us. She said that there was a long history of supposed fox possession in her family. As many as five generations of the women in my family had been accused of being possessed by the fox spirit. They had been forced to move from village to village to avoid persecution. Eventually, someone would hear about our family, and the troubles would begin again. I was a young girl and knew nothing of it at the time. I saw the pain that my mother lived through. She wanted the nightmare to end and apologized for bringing this curse onto our family.

"They eventually burned down our house and chased us out of the village. You have to understand that this was 1945, Hiroshima had just been bombed, and Japan had lost the war. There was a lot of tension, poverty, and fear. I'm sure people were ready to blame anyone who was an easy scapegoat. Unfortunately, that scapegoat turned out to be my mother and me. We had no choice but to pack up what little we had and leave the village.

"We spent the better part of the rest of that year making our way from village to village looking for work and food. My father was a hard worker and was willing to do any job to try and make enough money to keep his family sheltered and alive. Living in the country, we had the advantage of grabbing vegetables from the fields, often at night when no one could see us. We slept in the fields or the woods with little or no shelter other than some simple straw mats and cotton sheets that we carried with us. But then word would spread about a woman and her child possessed by the fox, and we would be forced to leave again.

"After almost a year of bouncing around from one village to another, a woman came to visit us. I don't know how she found us; my mother must have gotten a message to her somehow. The woman's name was Kumiko, and she was at least twenty years older than my mother. She was my mother's aunt, her mother's younger sister. I remember that night after she first arrived, my mother sat me down and told me that I was to go live with Kumiko in a city called Kawagoe, far from Izumo and close to Tokyo. We both cried together.

It was the only time in my life that I saw my father cry. I remember my parents waving to me with tears in their eyes as Kumiko and I drove off in a car driven by a man I never saw again. We rode on trains for more than two days and finally arrived here in Kawagoe, which was by far the biggest city I had ever seen. I never saw my parents again."

Both David and Chieko remained silent for the entire story. David was the first to speak.

"Aiko-san, I can't imagine what that was like for you. It must have been hard for you to keep this a secret for all these years."

"Yes, it was difficult. Kumiko was a wonderful person. She and her husband didn't have any children of their own, and they treated me like I was their daughter. I truly owe them my life."

"Why didn't you ever share this with me?" asked Chieko. Aiko could sense both sadness and anger in her voice. She didn't blame her.

"I guess I was ashamed," replied Aiko, looking down at her tea.

"Ashamed of what? You did nothing wrong!" Chieko protested.

"You of all people should know that you don't have to do anything wrong to feel shame or guilt." She looked at Chieko directly. "You can't imagine what it was like to spend most of your childhood being ostracized by other children, being scorned by their parents, and watching your family terrorized. Don't children who were abused feel guilty? Don't they internalize the pain and wonder if it was something they did to deserve it?"

Chieko nodded. She had been so focused on her own emotions that she forgot what it must have been like for her mother.

"Yes, many do. I'm sorry, Mother, I was being insensitive. I can't imagine the trauma that you went through."

"I was six when we were forced to leave our village, and it was just before I turned seven when Kumiko came and picked me up. I was formally adopted into her family."

Aiko slid her right leg from under the comforter and rolled up the pant leg. She was wearing dark-blue socks with pink sheep on them. She rolled down the sock and exposed her ankle to David and Chieko. What they saw made them both gasp.

On her ankle was a tattoo of a fox that was identical to the one that they had seen on the victim's ankle.

"Mother, what?" Chieko couldn't even put together a full statement. Aiko could only image what was racing through her mind.

"Shortly before we left our village in Izumo, some of the villagers kidnapped my mother and me while my father drank at a bar with some of his few remaining friends. They took us to a house where a man put this same tattoo on both of us. I remember that we were both screaming and crying. It hurt so much! They tied gags around our mouths and held us while he made the tattoos. I watched as he tattooed my mother, and they forced her to watch as he tattooed me. They said that this would serve as a sign so that everyone would know who we really were."

"But I, uh, I've never seen this tattoo before," said Chieko in shock.

"I know. I did everything I could so that you would never see it. Did you ever wonder why we rarely went to an onsen or even to a *sento* together?"

"I do remember going to an onsen in Nikko with you and Dad, but I never saw that tattoo."

"I wrapped it up and told you that I had twisted my ankle. You didn't question it."

"Did Father know?"

"Yes. I explained everything to him before we married. He was a smart, modern man and didn't believe in such superstitious nonsense. I think he may have taken pity on me. In any case, we agreed that it was better that you should never know."

"Mother, I don't know what to say."

"I don't either. But what I do know is the fact that Meiko has this exact same tattoo is no mere coincidence. We must find her. She is in a lot of danger."

CHAPTER 33

KYOTO
APRIL 10TH, DAY 18

The taxi pulled up outside of a ten-story building in the Nishi-Kiyamachi district of Kyoto. It was just after nine at night, and the neon lights of the numerous bars, restaurants, and pachinko parlors made the night come alive. Hana paid the driver and stepped out of the taxi and into the lobby of the building. She confirmed the name on her cell phone with the one on the directory next to the elevator, Kokuchou, or Black Swan, three stories below. At B3, the doors to the elevator opened, and she stepped out into a darkly lit room. She sauntered toward one of the empty seats at the small bar, her skin-tight black Versace dress extending only to her upper thigh, and her long legs ending in black Christian Louboutin pointed-toe pumps with red soles and four-inch heels. She held a small black-and-red Cartier clutch; her neck was wrapped in an elegant, silver fox stole. Her hair was pulled up in a tight bun with a long, golden chopstick-like pin holding it in place.

She gracefully sat down on the cushioned leather barstool. Behind the vanilla onyx bar, underlit with tiny halogen lights that made the entire bar look like it was filled with bubbles, was a built-in cabinet with glass shelves stocked with dozens of scotches, bourbons, ryes, shochus, grappas, cognacs, and vodkas. A bartender, dressed in a crisp, white, open-collared tuxedo shirt with silver cufflinks, a gray vest, and skinny black jeans glided toward his newest guest.

"Welcome to Kokuchou. How can I help you?"

Hana smiled at him, her false eyelashes fluttering. "I'll have a glass of Yamazaki single malt, on the rocks," she replied not breaking eye contact.

"Very good choice. The twelve- or eighteen-year-old?"

"Eighteen," she said without hesitation.

"Excellent, I'll have that right up," he replied, clearly impressed by her choice of one of the world's finest whiskeys, especially one that retailed for over $700 in Japan. It was $70 a glass here in the bar. It wasn't that unusual among his clientele, but it was rare for a young woman to order something like that, especially a woman on her own.

While the bartender set to work expertly hand-chiseling a large ball of ice from a four-inch cube, Hana slowly scanned the interior of the establishment. It was small, with eight small black leather booths, all with circular polished wood tables, elegantly lit with tiny halogen lights that hung from thin cords from the ceiling. Most of the patrons were men in suits: wealthy-looking businessmen enjoying a fine cigar and a glass of good whiskey or cognac after work. She didn't give them a second thought. They weren't why she was here, and if she was anything, it was focused. There was only one other woman in the bar, seated with three other men, probably coworkers. Soft jazz played through ceiling speakers. She didn't recognize the music, but she liked what she heard. It fit the place: sophisticated, hip, and elegant. She opened her purse and pulled out a thin, golden cigarette case with a matching lighter. As she put a cigarette to her lips, the bartender arrived, placing before her a crystal tumbler with an amber-colored liquid gently engulfing a perfectly round orb. His timing was perfect, or, more precisely, hers was.

"Here, allow me." The flame from his silver lighter was ready to light her cigarette.

She took the first pull on her cigarette and gracefully blew out a long, thin cloud of bluish smoke, like Lauren Bacall after getting a light from Bogie.

"Is this your first time here?"

"Yes, it's very nice," she replied.

"Well, welcome. I'm the owner. My name is Kanie, Sanjuro Kanie." He looked to be in his late thirties or early forties, with thick black hair combed straight back, a small black soul patch under his chin accompanying a thin mustache.

"Pleased to meet you. My name is Hana."

"Your name matches your beauty. Certainly, even the most beautiful of cherry blossoms are no match."

"You're quite the charmer, Mr. Kanie. I'm flattered." She took a slow sip of her whiskey.

"You have good taste in whiskey, Hana. Not many women know to order that whiskey, and even fewer have it on the rocks."

"Are you saying that women don't appreciate good whiskey, Mr. Kanie?" she said, looking slightly defensive.

He laughed. "Touché. No, that's not what I'm saying at all, but it probably sounded like that." He scratched the back of his ear. "What I meant to say is that not many women order that particular whiskey."

"I'm not like most women." He would find that out soon enough. She took another draw on her cigarette and casually blew it out while she slowly swirled the large glass ball around her glass with her index finger. "When women do order this whiskey, don't most of them have it on the rocks?"

"Yes, in fact, they do." He nodded. "And I can see that you aren't like most women. Anyone could see that, Miss Hana." He handed her a bar menu. "If there is something you'd like, please let me know. I have to make a few drinks."

"Of course. I can see that you're busy. Thank you." She set the menu down without looking at it. She wasn't particularly hungry, and besides, she wanted to focus on the task at hand. Kanie spent the next ten minutes chiseling ice balls, pouring drinks, and occasionally mixing up cosmopolitans and martinis. He pretended not to look at her, but she could see that he would peek out of the corner of his eye occasionally, probably to make sure that she didn't go anywhere. *Don't worry, Kanie,* she thought. *I don't plan on going anywhere—at least not alone.*

After finishing his other orders, Kanie returned to Hana with a small plate of smoked and dried squid jerky. "These go very well with whiskey, especially Japanese whiskey."

She looked at the plate in front of her and then to the bartender. Delicately, she took one of the strips and nibbled on it lightly, biting off a third of it and then setting the rest down on the plate. She chewed the delicacy, and slowly she sipped her drink, enjoying the moment as well as the tense pause that it created.

"It's very good, thank you, Mr. Kanie." He knew his stuff. This did go very well with the smoky whiskey.

"Please, my friends call me Sanjuro."

"Am I to assume that we are friends then, Sanjuro?" she said playfully, glancing up from her drink.

"I certainly hope so. It would be an honor to count you as a friend."

"Thank you, Sanjuro. I feel the same." She played with the frozen orb in her glass for a moment and then looked at him. "But there are many types of friends, don't you think? I wonder what type of friends we will be." She let the words linger and reached for another cigarette, which he again lit for her.

"Um," he stuttered, trying to sound confident. "I would hope that we could be the closest of friends."

"That sounds nice."

"Would you care for another glass, or would you like something else?"

"I'm afraid that I will become too tipsy if I have another glass of whiskey, and I wouldn't want that to happen." She gave him a look that oozed with mischief. "Perhaps a glass of champagne would be better for me."

"Of course. I have one that I think you would enjoy. Allow me to offer it to you as a gift of our new friendship."

"That sounds lovely," she cooed. Things were going exactly as she had planned.

CHAPTER 34

After waking up that morning with her new friend, Sanjuro Kanie, Hana spent the afternoon with a distraught Yoshimitsu Watanabe, the insurance executive. She sipped her tea distractedly and listened while Watanabe frantically paced back and forth in the apartment he had leased for her, drinking Jack Daniel's highballs like water.

"I can't believe this happened! Someone called our head of accounting and told them that I was skimming money! The shit hit the fan this morning. I walked into my boss's office, and there were two guys from accounting standing there with him. They looked at me like I had killed someone." He threw back his drink and went over to the makeshift bar in the living room, tossed some ice cubes in his glass, filled it halfway with Jack, and topped it off with some Pellegrino. His sipped that and continued pacing, sweat beads forming on his forehead. The armpits of his blue-and-white-striped cotton shirt were soaked. He'd unbuttoned the top button, and his silver tie hung loosely around his neck.

Hana was studying the small chips in her fingernail polish during his rant. *I'll need to get these done after he leaves*, she thought. *I think I'm going to try a new color this time.*

"I spent the next hour answering questions as we scoured daily statements, customer payments, deposits, and every transaction known to man. They had me down to the last yen, for God's sake! How could they have known?"

Hana looked up at him. "I don't know, sweetheart." She sounded genuinely concerned. "Maybe someone at work is jealous of how successful you are. You know how coworkers can be. Everyone is envious of a man with money and power."

"I don't know." He ran his fingers through his hair, trying to make sense of it all. He took another swig from his glass. "The thing is, I never told anyone about this." He paused. "The only person I've told is you."

She looked hurt. "Baby, you don't think I said anything!" She started sobbing. "Why would I say anything to anyone? You've been so good to me." She stood up, grabbed a tissue, wiped the tears from her eyes, and blew her nose. "Anyway," she continued between sobs, "I don't even know anyone at your company."

He put his arms around her as her shoulders shook.

"Of course not, babe. I never thought that it could be you."

"I feel so bad," she sobbed. "I don't know what I can do to help. Did they say who called?"

"No, they said it was an anonymous caller. A man. That's all they said."

"Do you think everything will be all right?" She was pretty sure it wouldn't be.

"I don't know, babe. I think it's more likely that I'm going to lose my job, probably my pension as well. They may even file criminal charges. I have no idea. Do you know how hard it will be for someone my age to find a decent job? Especially if they do a reference check on my current company, and they tell them why I was let go. No one would ever touch me. I'll be lucky to get a job at a convenience store, for God's sake!"

Hana took his empty glass and made him another drink. Then she made one for herself. She needed a little buzz to watch him fall apart.

"Babe, you are so smart and successful. I know you'll find a way out of this. Maybe you can negotiate with your boss, tell them it was a one-time thing, that you were trying to pay off some gambling debts, that you need professional help, and that you'll pay it all back." She stood by his side and gently rubbed his shoulders and sipped her highball, looking out the window. It was getting dark, and she was hungry. She wondered when he was going to leave—hopefully soon.

"Well, that's just it. I have no idea how I'm going to pay back the money. I'm out like $50,000! Do you know how long it takes me to save up $50,000 after taxes? I tried to win some of it back, but I've been on a cold streak and pissed away another $10K. It'll take me three years to pay back $60K, assuming I have a decent job!" He grabbed a cigarette from a pack on the dresser and lit it with shaky hands, took in a long draw, and blew out a huge cloud of smoke, laced with his future, his dreams, his life.

"Babe, I know it's not the right time to ask, and I know it sounds selfish, but how long did you pay for this apartment?" She tried to sound scared as opposed to overly self-serving.

"Uh, shit, I think I paid for the whole month. You should be fine, babe. I'm not sure what we'll do after that. I should lay low for a while. My wife will probably throw me out when she finds out. I may have to stay here with you for a while. Either that or I might end up jumping from your balcony. That's probably the easiest way out of this damn mess."

She thought that another balcony would be better. She wrapped her arms around him. "Don't say that, sweetheart. I'm sure you'll come up with something. You're so smart. You're the smartest person I've ever met. Of course you're more than welcome to stay here. You paid for it, after all."

"Yeah." He threw back his drink. "Thanks." He grabbed his gray suit jacket from the couch and put it on over his sweat-soaked shirt. "I need to take off, babe. I'll call you soon. I've got a lot of things to think about, and I need some time to myself."

"I understand," she purred empathetically. "Just be careful, my darling."

"I will, babe," he muttered, as he slipped on his shoes and headed out the door.

Ticktock, ticktock, she thought as he left.

CHAPTER 35

Meiko awoke with a pounding headache. She stumbled her way into the bathroom, searched the medicine cabinets for pain relievers, and washed down two Advil with water from a ceramic cup used for mouthwash. She looked in the mirror and again felt that disorienting feeling of not knowing who she was looking at. When she opened the second drawer in the bathroom, she found a notebook and leafed through it quickly. It had a date and some notes. She took the notebook with her to the kitchen for a cup of coffee.

Based on what her watch told her, the last entry in the notebook was made three days earlier. She wondered why she would wait three days to write in her journal, as well as what she had been doing for the past three days. She had no recollection. She looked around the apartment: crystal tumblers sitting in the kitchen sink, half a dozen bottles of bourbons, Jack Daniel's, shochu, and expensive-looking champagne on the living room credenza. She didn't like hard liquor, so she wondered who had been drinking them.

There wasn't much of anything to eat in the refrigerator, so after washing her face, throwing on a pair of jeans and the least provocative-looking blouse-and-jacket combination she could find, she headed downstairs and into the street, her notebook at her side. She stopped at a corner convenience market and bought a rice ball with tuna inside, wrapped in nori, and a bottle of green tea. She made a direct path to the internet café, whose address was written in the notebook. She paid for her cubicle, logged in to the blog website using the information in the notebook, and started scrolling. The first thing she found was a blog post that she had written three days earlier. To her surprise, there were five people following her blog, and some of them had commented on it already.

Comment: Don't worry, Hana—everything will work out for you. I'm praying for you. T. Yamaura

Comment: Hana, you sound very beautiful. I can help. Call me 488-27-8159 —Yoshi.

Comment: Stay positive and keep writing your blog. It will help. Yumi

She unwrapped the plastic covering the rice ball and took a bite and sipped the green tea. She began writing a new blog post.

It's been three days since my last post. I have no idea where I've been or what I've been doing over that time period. I found my notebook, which led me to this website. I am thankful for those of you who have started following my blog. It means a lot to me. Please keep thinking of me.

I feel very lost and confused right now. I'm not sure when I will be able to come back to this blog or feel like I do now. It's like I disappear for days at a time and then suddenly I reappear again. It's like I'm living some terrible nightmare that I can't wake up from. If you know anything, anything

at all, please contact me through this website or the email
account I will be creating shortly. I'll post the email here
on my blog. If you don't know anything, please keep me
in your thoughts and prayers. It helps.

Hana

She hit *Post* and opened another window and went to
Google, which was a name she remembered. She followed the
instructions and soon had a new email account. She went back
to the blog and created a new post, sharing her email address.
She also went to the settings menu and figured out how to
take and attach a photo to her blog. She wasn't sure if it was
the right move or not, but she was willing to risk any negatives
if someone would recognize her. It wasn't a great photo. She
had woken up less than an hour ago. But it was something.

She wrote everything down in her notebook: when she
posted, her email address, the date and time, that she attached
a photo, what she ate and drank. *Now what?* She decided to
clear her head a bit by walking around. Hopefully she would
remember something. At least the fresh air and the cherry
blossoms would help her feel better.

This entire time she hadn't thought to look at her phone.
When she did, there was a message on her cell phone from
the priest. She would call him later that day. He'd been so supportive to her. Maybe he had some information that might
help her. She was also running low on the tea he gave her.
She found herself craving that tea more than she liked to
admit. There was something about it that kept calling to her.
It comforted her.

CHAPTER 36

KAWAGOE
APRIL 13TH, DAY 21

Kotetsu stretched out on his side in a patch of sun on the table, as comfortable as any living thing had the right to be. Only occasionally would he let out a meow in his sleep. Aiko sat beside him, focused intently on the MacBook Pro in front of her. Chieko had bought it for her two years ago as a birthday present, a replacement for the aging Toshiba laptop that Aiko had used for the better part of a decade. She wasn't one to replace something if it worked just because it was old, and slow, even though she had to reboot it once a day because it locked up so much. It had taken her a little while to get used to using a Mac instead of a Windows-based computer, but fortunately they had copied so much from each other over the past thirty years that it was hard to distinguish one from the other. Besides, it wasn't like she used it for anything too sophisticated. Browsing the internet, checking emails, reading the latest shogi strategies was pretty much the extent of her usage.

Since her dinner with David and Chieko, she had spent the better part of each morning and late into the evening scouring the internet for any clues regarding Meiko's status. She and Meiko had emailed each other regularly in Japanese ever since Meiko was a junior in high school. Aiko also followed Meiko's social media accounts and the blog she had written since moving to Japan. In other words, when it came to internet savviness, she wasn't what most people would expect of a seventy-six-year-old Japanese grandmother.

Again, Aiko ran through her list of sites to check, and again, Meiko had made no new posts.

Aiko stood up from the table and stretched her back. Kotetsu let out a small, monosyllabic, meow-like grunt that sounded more like "ma" without opening his eyes. Aiko couldn't help but smile. In the kitchen she opened a small cherrywood cylinder, scooped dried green tea leaves into a ceramic teapot, and filled it with hot water from an electric thermos that kept the water at exactly 94 degrees Celsius all day long. The hot water bubbled through the flaky leaves, releasing an aroma like fresh-cut grass. She carried the small pot to the table and set it beside her handle-less celadon-green ceramic teacup. She watched Kotetsu sleep as she waited for the tea to steep. Kotetsu made soft movements with his paws, stretching them out and then closing them rhythmically. Aiko had read somewhere that kittens make that movement against their mother when they want to feed. Doing so without the mom present must release some deeply ingrained feeling of security and comfort. She envied Kotetsu, wishing that there were some simple movements she could do that would release the stress she felt about Meiko.

After a little over a minute, Aiko poured a cup of tea. She held the cup in both hands with her elbows on the table. She stared at the computer screen and slowly sipped the tea: fresh, clean, and slightly acidic. She felt frustrated. It seemed like there was nothing she could do to help Meiko, whom she knew needed her help.

She poked around in vain for another hour, trying to find anything—news stories, user groups—that might help. She exhausted all the possible search criteria she could think of and started getting mildly delusional with fatigue mixed with frustration. Perhaps it was too much tea. By this time, Kotetsu had awoken and was walking back and forth, bumping the side of his head against the corner of the laptop. She knew it was one way that cats marked their territory, but it was still annoying. And then she saw something.

There was a blog site, however, one that she hadn't visited before, nor even thought to visit. She wasn't even sure how she stumbled upon it, but there it was: a blog from Hana Tanaka, the name Chieko said the detectives had shared. If Aiko hadn't been convinced it was her granddaughter writing the blog, the photo she found attached to the second post confirmed it. After reading her blog, Aiko could only imagine how scared and confused Meiko must be. She copied the website address and included it in an email to Chieko. Then she sent Meiko an email.

> Meiko, this is Aiko, your grandmother. I know you are feeling lost. Your mother, father, and I can help you. Let us know where you are. Please call any of the following numbers or email me. We love you and can help. Everything will be all right. Please be careful whom you trust. I believe there are people out there trying to hurt you.

Aiko included Chieko's and David's cell phone numbers and email addresses as well as her own. She then called Chieko. She felt a rush of adrenaline as the phone rang. Meiko was alive, and they would soon find her. She was sure of that. Kotetsu looked up at her, with what she would have sworn was a smile, and let out an extended meow. "Kotetsu!

We found her! We're going to get her back. I won't rest until we do, I promise!"

Growing up a Buddhist, Aiko had been taught that the transmigration of souls, reincarnation, was something real. She had always questioned it. But seeing Kotetsu here made her reconsider her beliefs. Was her dead husband somehow reincarnated as this cat? Was he helping her find Meiko? Although it sounded crazy, somehow it felt plausible.

Chieko answered, and Aiko told her everything in a rush. She told her that she and David should also reach out to Meiko both in Japanese and in English. She wasn't sure which language might be better at helping her remember who she was. Aiko had written her message in Japanese, but that didn't mean that reading something in English wouldn't help snap Meiko out of whatever spell she was under. They decided at this point not to mention anything to the police in Kyoto, at least until they talked with David and got his perspective. After three weeks, this was the first real sign of hope, and they both felt it. They both hoped that this nightmare would soon be over.

CHAPTER 37

KYOTO
APRIL 14TH, DAY 22

Hana placed her polished silver knife on the edge of the white plate as she finished the last bite of the filet of wild turbot, dressed in an exquisitely delicate yuzu foam emulsion. It was the fourth of eight courses on the menu at the elegant restaurant Chez Morlet, the top French restaurant in Kyoto. She patted the corner of her mouth with her napkin. Her hair was done in an elaborate twisting braid, which had taken the better part of two hours by an expensive team of expert stylists earlier that day at one of the finest salons. She wore a thin platinum chain with a large light-purple tanzanite that dipped slightly into her cleavage, accentuating her swan-like neck. The purple Tanzanite necklace, along with its matching bracelet, contrasted beautifully with her dark-blue, tight-fitting Dolce & Gabbana dress, all gifts of one of her numerous, and now tragically in-debt, admirers.

Sanjuro Kanie sat across from her, finishing his turbot and looking longingly at the gorgeous woman across from him. The past four days had been a whirlwind of passionate, mind-blowing sex and elaborate shopping sprees. She had returned to his bar several times, but this was the first time they had been to dinner. It took some arm twisting and calling in favors from people he knew in the industry to get a table at this restaurant on such short notice.

"Are you enjoying the meal, sweetheart?" he asked.

"Mmm," she purred, "I am. It's absolutely wonderful. I can't believe you were able to get us a table on such short notice. You must have a lot of pull in this city." Her brown eyes drew him ever deeper into a state of euphoric hypnosis. She relished having that effect on men.

"Ha, not much." He laughed. "But enough. Cheers." He raised his glass of Grand Cru Burgundy, which was part of the wine pairing accompanying the chef's tasting menu. They touched glasses and finished off what remained in their glasses.

Kanie extended his right hand across the table with his palm turned up, and she gracefully set her hand inside his gentle grip.

"Hana, I want you to move in with me. I want to be with you all the time."

"I know, baby, me too. You know I'd love to do that." Hana paused, letting the silence carry the depth of her sadness. "But I'm trying to get away from my old boyfriend, and he won't let me go. In fact, he's so jealous that I'm seeing you, he started to hit me again." Tears filled her eyes, and she pulled her hand away from his and dabbed her eyes with her napkin. The server came and removed their plates without paying attention to her tears.

"I've been trying to break up with him, but he just won't let me go. It's getting worse and worse. He's stalking me. I'm afraid that he's going to kill me." Her eyes filled with tears.

"Have you gone to the police?"

"Yes," she said, "of course. "But they say that until he does something terrible, they can't really do anything. They are hesitant to get involved in domestic violence cases." She sniffled and patted her nose with her napkin, drying her eyes as well. "I feel so helpless. I don't know who to turn to." She looked at him pleadingly.

"OK, let me take care of it," Kanie said.

"But I don't want you to get hurt, sweetheart! He's very strong, and he's a third dan in judo. You need to be very careful. He's a dangerous man."

"Don't worry. I'll be careful. Sometimes in my line of work you have to deal with people who are less than savory. It comes with the territory. I know some people who might help."

"Oh, darling," Hana gushed and grabbed both of this hands in hers. "If you can do this, then of course I will move in with you. But promise me you'll be careful."

"I will. Don't give it another thought," he said. "After dinner, give me a photo of him, where he works, where he likes to hang out, the dojo he works out at, his address, phone number, anything you've got that will help me find him. Then just leave it to me."

Hana smiled at his feigned confidence. She knew that deep down he was probably scared to death. Hopefully, that fear would make his attack that much more ruthless, sealing his own fate in the process. *Two birds, one stone.* It was an elegant solution.

The server came with two fresh Burgundy glasses, and a second server poured them glasses of Clos Vougeot Grand Cru Burgundy.

"I don't want the thought of him to ruin your meal in any way." Kanie smiled longingly and raised his glass. "Here's to our future."

"To our future, cheers," Hana said, the tears gone and her eyes shining.

The server set down their next course: crispy veal sweet-breads with a Burgundy reduction sauce.

Before Hana took a bite, Kanie gave her a devious smile. "I have a surprise to show you later."

"Ooh, I like surprises," she said. "Can you give me a hint?"

"Well, let's just say I paid a visit to your friend at the tattoo parlor today."

"Wonderful. I can't wait to see it."

"I can't wait to show it to you." They both laughed and sliced into the crispy, succulent sweetbreads.

CHAPTER 38

KAWAGOE
APRIL 15TH, DAY 23

Aiko headed out for her morning walk and a visit to the graveyard where her husband, Tetsuo, was buried. She enjoyed walking to the local Buddhist temple early in the morning when the weather was nice. It was about two kilometers from her house, and the route took her past a few old friends. Occasionally they would be outside their houses, and she would stop and chat for a while. On this day, she didn't run into anyone she knew, just people heading to the train station on foot or by bicycle, on their way to work. She liked the temple too, especially on weekday mornings. It was almost empty except for some of the priests going about their daily activities. It wasn't a large temple, but the grounds were well kept, and it was tranquil. In the back, there was a small graveyard filled with dark-gray granite stones. There were probably several thousand people buried there, but unlike Western graveyards she had seen, the space was much more compact. Everyone in Japan was cremated, and therefore entire families, three to four generations, could fit into a three-foot-square space. Tetsuo was buried here, as was his father, mother, and grandparents. Aiko would eventually join him here. She found it comforting—she would be by her husband's side, where she had been for almost fifty years of her life.

She set a small bouquet that she bought on the walk on a stone wall, filled a small plastic bucket with water from the nearby tap, and grabbed a long-handled wooden ladle. There were almost a dozen such buckets and cups lined up against the wall. They were the property of the temple for use by visitors who came to pay their respects. She carried the bucket to the grave, removed the old flowers from the stainless-steel vase, which fit neatly into a recess in the granite gravesite, and set them on the ground. After dumping the dirty water from the vase and rinsing it out with fresh water from the bucket, she poured two cups into the vase and set it back into the stone recess. She then ladled clean water over the granite surface of the gravestones, making sure to wash away any dirt that had accumulated since the last time she was there.

Once the grave was sufficiently clean, she returned the bucket and cup to their place by the spigot and threw the old flowers in the trash. She took the fresh flowers to the grave and put them in the vase. It was spring, and she liked daffodils. They were bright yellow and seemed to welcome the warm weather that was to come, a sign of renewal. Tetsuo never cared one way or another about flowers, but she knew that her mother-in-law had always liked daffodils as well. Closing her eyes and putting her palms together, Aiko asked the spirits of her deceased loved ones for their help in finding Meiko and ensuring that she would return home safely and unharmed. She thanked them for everything they had done for her in their lifetime and vowed to serve them better in the future.

Returning home, Aiko found Kotetsu curled up on her cushion by the dining table. She decided not to disturb him and instead sat down on the other side of the table and opened the newspaper that she had picked up on her walk back. She was studying the latest shogi problem in the paper when her phone rang. It was Chieko.

"I just got off the phone with Detective Nomura in Kyoto." Chieko's voice was higher pitched than usual, and she was speaking rapidly—she sounded scared. "He said that they were called to investigate a second suicide last night. A man hanged himself in his bedroom. His name was Yoshimitsu Watanabe, and he worked for a large insurance company in Kyoto. He left a note apologizing to his wife and to his company. In the note, he described his obsession with a girl named Hana and how he did everything, including embezzling money from his company, to win her love." Chieko started crying. "It was just like the other man who jumped from the building. He realized that he made a mistake but that his life was ruined and he would never be able to repay the money he owed the company or make amends with his wife and son. He thought it was better for everyone that he was no longer alive." Chieko paused, sniffling. She was obviously trying to hold it together. "They also found the exact same fox tattoo on his ankle that the previous victim had."

Aiko forced herself to remain calm. It was one of her strengths. She was able to stay clear-headed in the face of tragedy. She often thought that going through what she did as a young girl helped steel her against becoming rattled. "Hmm," grunted Aiko, taking notes. "Was there anything else?"

"Yes, Detective Nomura said that he received a call from the man who runs the tattoo parlor just this morning telling him that another man came in to get the same fox tattoo."

"What else did he say? Have they learned anymore about Meiko's whereabouts?"

"No, but he said that they want to bring her in for questioning. She's now the lead suspect in the deaths of both men." Chieko broke down and started crying uncontrollably. Aiko waited. "Oh, Mom, I don't know what to do. I feel completely helpless. There's no way that Meiko would cause these men to do all of these things and ruin their lives. She must be under the influence of someone…or something!" Chieko halted, and sobbed into the phone.

"Chieko, be strong." Aiko knew that for all her education and training, Chieko still looked to her for strength in times of stress. "We will find Meiko. We need to find out who is controlling her. Her blog is our best bet." Aiko was calm, calculating their next move. Despite what she said to Chieko, she didn't like just waiting around until they heard from Meiko again. "Please tell David what you told me. Let me know if he has any thoughts." Then, with a comforting tone, she said, "Chieko, why don't you come home tonight and have dinner with me? I don't want you to be alone."

"OK, I'll let David know. I'll be home tonight, Mom. Thank you." She sounded more like the sensitive young girl Aiko raised rather than the cool, confident clinician she had become.

"Chieko, we will find her. I promise you," she said with a calm yet determined confidence.

After she hung up the phone, Aiko folded up the paper and looked at the cat.

"Kotetsu, I need your help. We need to figure out what is going on down there in Kyoto." The cat looked at her when he heard his name called and let out a short chirp before returning to his curled-up ball.

CHAPTER 39

KAWAGOE
APRIL 16TH, DAY 24

The previous night, Aiko took Chieko to a local yakitori restaurant that was an easy fifteen-minute walk from her house. She felt that going somewhere familiar and spending some time together was what Chieko needed right now to help calm her. It was a hole-in-the-wall place that only sat about fifteen people, most of them at an L-shaped wooden bar where they could watch the lone chef/owner grill the various skewers of chicken, meat, and vegetables. Taka was the owner's name, and he greeted Aiko and Chieko from behind the counter when they came in. Aiko had called ahead and reserved two seats at the counter. They only took reservations for regulars and, even then, not for everyone. Aiko and Tetsuo visited this restaurant two or three times a month for over fifteen years. Aiko remembered Taka as a young man who worked at the restaurant with his father and mother before they passed. Aiko now came alone or with some of her shogi friends. Taka hadn't seen Chieko in well over six months, and the three of them chatted casually while Taka manned the grill, turning skewers, salting new ones before they went on the grill, and then plating while his wife, Asa, served. They drank beer and shochu and feasted on a wide range of delicacies that were Chieko's favorites. Aiko knew that Chieko would enjoy visiting this place. Hopefully, it would bring back memories of a simpler, happier time. Six months seemed like an eternity given the events of the past month.

After dinner, they walked back to the house and the two of them stayed up late talking, drinking green tea, and playing shogi. Despite giving Chieko a three-piece handicap, Aiko won handily each time, but Chieko was making good progress, and by the third game, she had Aiko on the ropes a few times. It was a good diversion.

Aiko woke early to make them a traditional breakfast of rice, *natto* (fermented beans), broiled salmon, pickled daikon and eggplant, and miso soup with cubes of tofu. After breakfast, Chieko headed off to catch the train to Tokyo.

Aiko cleaned up the dishes from breakfast and sat down at the kitchen table with her laptop, a notepad, and a cup of green tea along with a small teapot. Kotetsu was in his usual spot, curled up on the cushion that Chieko sat on for breakfast. Aiko had given him some of the leftover salmon, which he loved, and he was now settling into his morning nap. She booted up the laptop and then started searching the internet for any news about the second suicide victim, Yoshimitsu Watanabe. There was an article in the Kyoto news about him. It didn't say much, although it mentioned some family information and where he was born. It was that piece of news, his place of birth, that hit Aiko like a punch to the gut.

She took out her notepad and scanned her notes about the first victim, Masaharu Fujiwara. Yes, both victims were born in Izumo, in Shimane prefecture. It was the same place that she had been forced to flee as a young girl. She started making a chart of the similarities in the victims' backgrounds. Both had been born in Izumo, a rural area where belief in fox possession was still likely to be if not prevalent, then at least ingrained in the belief system of the locals. They had lived and worked in Kyoto. Both had fallen in love and had extramarital affairs with a girl named Hana, who was undoubtedly some alter ego of Meiko. In both cases, those affairs had led to their financial or professional ruin, which in turn had led them to take their own lives. If that weren't enough, both had identical fox tattoos on their ankles. The very same tattoo that was inked on Aiko's ankle, against her will, before she and her family were forced out of Izumo. There was no way that these could just be coincidences. But it was hard to tell what connected everything. Aiko's mind was working rapidly.

She remembered that she had an old corkboard in storage, and using it to help organize her thoughts may be helpful. After pushing various dust-covered boxes out of the way, she found the corkboard, some index cards, and some pushpins, just what she needed. She brought everything back to the kitchen table and started assembling a makeshift war room. By the end of an hour, she had assembled a workable storyboard that she could continue to review and update. It comforted her to start putting the pieces of the puzzle together even if she didn't know what the final product looked like. To her, it was a logic puzzle, and she had always enjoyed working on those. She came up with a list of questions as well as some ideas on how to get them answered.

She organized everything and stored loose notes and other items in a neat pile on the corner of the table and decided to leave the corkboard where it was. She knew that Chieko would think that she was nuts for pursuing such a strange path, but Chieko's thought processes were always very linear. Her daughter didn't like thinking about things that didn't fit her neat understanding of the world. Aiko never had had that luxury.

CHAPTER 40

KYOTO

APRIL 16TH, DAY 24

Tamotsu Sasaki stumbled out of the tiny bar along with the gaggle of friends with whom he had spent the better part of the past four hours drinking Suntory whiskey highballs and chewing on dried squid and roasted soybeans. It was Friday night, and there was no work the next day, which didn't necessarily make that much of a difference because he found himself in this local watering hole two to three nights a week, work or no work. Divorced and living alone, he did not have a lot to draw him back to his house at the end of the day. Then again, the reason for his divorce, among many other things, was that he rarely came home at a decent hour, or sober, even though his wife had spent hours preparing one of his favorite dishes. The pack said their goodbyes and headed on their homeward treks. Two of his friends lived close by, another needed to decide whether to walk five minutes to the train station, hail a cab, or make a thirty-minute walk. His choice became much easier because there was a taxi idling at the corner waiting for the light to change. He got the driver's attention and hopped into the backseat, waving to Tamotsu as the door automatically closed and the taxi pulled away.

Left alone in the misty cool of the night, after the smoky warmth and noise of the bar, Tamotsu lit a cigarette and pulled his suit jacket closed. It wasn't supposed to rain, and he hadn't brought an umbrella with him. Fortunately, it was only drizzling, which felt nice on his face. He made his solitary, slightly buzzed walk toward his apartment, face turned down toward the sidewalk directly in front of him to help keep his cigarette from getting wet and his left hand cinching the lapels of his jacket together to help keep warm. It was an easy fifteen-minute walk home, and as long as the rain didn't get any heavier, it shouldn't be a problem. In fact, he kind of liked walking by himself on nights like this. It gave him time to clear his head and decompress after a hectic workweek. It was a little after midnight, and the narrow back streets were pretty much empty, either too late for most people to be walking around or too early for more serious partiers, who would be in the bars and clubs for a few more hours.

Tamotsu was lost in thought when he heard a quick rush of feet on the wet pavement behind him on the left. *Some poor bastard trying to catch a train.* He turned to look over his left shoulder when he felt something or someone smash into him from the side, which reminded him of being tackled in rugby when he was in high school. Then, unlike during rugby, there was a sharp pain in his lower ribs, and then another, and another. He had no idea what had happened. He wasn't sure if he had been shot, stabbed, or what, but he knew he was falling to the ground. He crumpled under the weight of the attack and felt that sharp pain in his stomach two more times. Still unaware of what was happening, trying to shake off the whiskey buzz, he realized that there was a man in a dark hooded sweatshirt on top of him sticking a short, bloody knife into him. *What the hell is going on?* His instinct took over, and he attempted to curl up and protect himself. He felt the man get off him and then felt several strong kicks land on his curled-up back and legs—definitely uncomfortable but an improvement over the searing pain of the knife wounds. He was losing consciousness quickly and wasn't sure if he was ever going to make it home. At this point, he didn't care. He just wanted the pain to stop and whoever had attacked him to leave him alone, so he could die quietly.

Just before he passed out, he heard a man's voice by his left ear.

"This is for Hana, asshole! If you come near her again, I will kill you. Understand? Leave Hana alone!"

He felt the man stuff something under the lapel of his suit coat, heard sneakers running away from him on the wet sidewalk, and then there was just silence. He could barely make out the sound of the rain. He curled himself up as tight as he could and started to shiver. The last thought he had was *Who the hell is Hana?* Then everything went black.

CHAPTER 41

*S*he sat with her legs wrapped around her short board, bobbing gently in the cool Pacific water as the ocean tides moved past, and waited. On her left was a girl she had grown up with—the name Laura came into her head. They both wore thin, neoprene wet suits, although several other surfers nearby wore only rash guards. That morning's "June gloom," the marine layer that covered most of the coastline, had burned off, leaving clear blue skies and a consistent, if not spectacular, surf.

Joining her and the girl potentially named Laura were two other friends, both male—Alex and Todd were names that seemed to fit. They chatted on and off while they waited for the right wave to come in. A key difference between experienced surfers and novices, besides the ability to carve a wave, was that novices weren't adept at choosing their waves. Experts didn't waste their energy going after waves that didn't catch their eye. Catching five good waves in an hour wasn't a bad session at all. So, you waited. She didn't mind waiting. It was peaceful. You were at one with the ocean, just like the seagulls and pelicans that skimmed the surface or dove violently head first into the surf to grab a fish they spotted. There was the occasional seal or dolphin that swam past, ignoring the surfers sitting on their boards. The air smelled briny, and the sun on her face felt warm.

The four of them faced outward, away from the coastline, keeping an eye out for a swell that would appear in the distance *and might turn into the perfect wave. They all had similar surfing styles and liked the same type of waves. Todd nodded in the distance and gave a quick shout: "I think we got one."*

The others saw the same thing and gradually turned their boards around toward the beach. They kept looking over their shoulders as they slowly started to paddle. The swell grew larger as it got closer and gradually started to change shape from a smooth mound into something whose front face grew quickly while the backside remained low, pushing the face forward. She could see the telltale sign of the foam starting to form on the top edge as the wave continued to develop. Paddling faster, she felt her practiced strokes propel her ahead without disrupting her balance. She felt that unmistakable push as she matched the speed of the wave. And then she was up on her board, cutting across the front face of the wave, her friends riding the same wave off to her left. She cut quickly to her right and then again to the left as the wave continued to push forward. She crouched low on the board, and her trailing hand dragged along the face of the wave while her other arm remained outward, helping her balance. There was no thought at this point. She just reacted. She was part of the wave. Her cuts just came to her, nothing premeditated. She made several more turns and then felt the power of the wave subside. She fell softly to her left as what remained of the wave washed over her. The roar of the surf filled her ears, and the brisk salt water awakened her from her temporary flow state, where time had seemed to stand still.

Meiko held her breath and opened her eyes slowly, not sure whether she was still underwater. She blinked and looked around what appeared to be a dark room with slits of light coming in through the blinds. She was in bed, a strange bed, but one that she remembered sleeping in before. She realized that she was still holding her breath and let it out. Where had she been? The feeling of being on the ocean with people she knew, riding a wave, cutting through the water, all seemed so real. In fact, this bed, this room, every part of where she was right now seemed much more like a dream than where she had just been. She got out of bed and looked around and felt déjà vu. Clothes, all of them expensive, most of them provocative, hung in closets or were neatly folded in dresser drawers. Boxes with designer names, lined with richly colored paper, surrounded expensive handbags, shoes, and purses. She counted over ten pairs of shoes in her closet, but she didn't remember buying or ever wearing any of them. There was lingerie in dressers and closets that made her blush. She couldn't imagine wearing any of them. There were bottles of champagne in the trashcan, unopened ones on a table in the living room along with several bottles of bourbon and other whiskeys that she never remembered drinking, and frankly, didn't even like. Packs of cigarettes lying around, along with butts in ashtrays throughout the apartment. White-filtered cigarette butts with deep-red lipstick marks lay haphazardly alongside tan-filtered butts. She had never been a smoker and didn't remember ever smoking these either. But she had seen these same things before and felt exactly the same way now as she had then. The only comfort was knowing that she had experienced this state of absolute confusion before.

She felt so alone, so completely alone. Who was living her life? What did she do with all of these clothes? Who did she see? Who saw her? And why did she wake up now and start asking questions again? She spent the next half hour cleaning ashtrays, throwing away empty bottles, and washing glassware. There was very little to eat in the apartment except for some light snacks: sesame crackers, nuts, and chocolate-dipped pretzel sticks in red-and-white boxes that said Pocky on the outside. There was a Keurig coffeemaker with some K-cups next to it.

After she finished cleaning up, Meiko went to the bathroom, washed her face, and as she was drying it with a towel, remembered something. She opened one of the drawers in the bathroom and found a familiar-looking toiletry kit. Below it was a notepad. She had seen it before even though she didn't recall putting it there. It made her feel good to make sense of something in this nightmare that she found herself in. She took the notepad back to the kitchen table and made a cup of coffee.

There, right in front of her, was confirmation that she wasn't crazy. It was like the pages were talking directly to her. She vaguely remembered writing the words on the page. They made sense to her. As far as she could tell from the date on the last entry, it had been five days since she had written in this notepad. All the same emotions she felt that morning—the bewilderment and confusion about her strange surroundings and clothes—were written down in that little notepad. She could have written them this morning. She had felt these exact same things before. She had felt them here in this apartment and had probably written her notes at this same kitchen table. She skimmed through the notes. It appeared like her true self, or her current self, reappeared every five to seven days and made notes in this journal and then disappeared. She wondered, then, if she appeared the other days as a completely different person, someone who lived in this apartment, wore these clothes, smoked these cigarettes, and apparently drank a lot of high-priced alcohol. She shuddered to think what else she did when she was in that role. But why was she popping in and out of different personas, and what did that dream about surfing have to do with any of them? It had seemed so real. An actual memory with faces that she remembered, even names.

She wrote everything down, everything she felt, her dream, how she cleaned the apartment, whatever came to her head. After she finished writing down as much as she could, she decided to head out to the internet café that was listed in the pages of the journal and update her blog. She also wanted to see if she could figure out anything about either of her identities, hoping that there were only two. After finishing the last gulp of her now tepid coffee, she threw on some jeans and the most modest-looking blouse she could find. She chose a deep-blue Hermes bag, pulled out the pack of cigarettes and laid them on the kitchen table, and then started outfitting the bag with her essentials: an orange Hermes wallet that contained ¥100,000, all in large bills, a cute white silk pouch with a fox pattern that held tea bags, the key to her apartment and her cell phone, as well as her notepad and pen. She headed out the door and down the elevator.

She made it to the internet café listed in her notebook with a cup of Starbucks coffee and a blueberry scone in a paper bag, greeted the woman working at the counter, and laid down a 10,000-yen note to secure a cube. She didn't have a credit card, which she thought was a bit odd, but at least she had cash—plenty of it. She imagined that she must strike an odd figure, pulling out 10,000-yen notes from an Hermès handbag at an internet café. Oh well, she had more important things to think about at this point than the impression she made on complete strangers.

After settling into her cube and before going to her blog site, she logged into her email account. She pulled the scone from its bag and took a small bite from the corner and then set it down on the desk, using the wax paper as a plate. She took a sip of coffee but almost spit it out when she saw all of the new emails in her inbox. There had to be at least fifty of them, maybe more. She set the coffee down next to the scone, afraid that she might spill it, and began reading through the comments.

Three threads that pointed in the same direction came from a man named David, a woman named Chieko, and another woman named Aiko. They claimed to be her parents and grandmother, respectively. They attached photos of themselves with a girl that certainly looked a lot like her, and they all referenced each other. David's emails were in English, and Chieko's and Aiko's were in Japanese. Although she didn't even think twice about it, Meiko realized that she could read both languages easily, and English was easier. David's messages mentioned that they lived in San Diego and were here in Japan for a year while he taught cultural anthropology classes at Waseda University in Tokyo. He also sent her links to books that he had written.

Meiko thought about her dream. It had taken place somewhere on a coast, and even though she hadn't thought of it before now, the dream had been in English. Could that have been a memory from San Diego? Chieko's and Aiko's messages brought on very different emotions. Somehow, she felt a warmth and comfort in Aiko's messages. She wasn't sure why, but Aiko felt familiar, and safe. Chieko's message made her feel sad and angry, for no apparent reason. There was something in her past with Chieko that just wasn't right. She didn't get that feeling from David's or Aiko's messages. But Chieko's messages touched her somewhere deep, an unprotected and vulnerable place in her psyche. Feelings of loss, resentment, longing, and love mixed together in a peculiar chowder of emotion. She wasn't sure whether to run from Chieko or move closer to her.

There were other messages, from a man named Hiroshi, that also included photos of a girl who looked a lot like her. He said that she was his girlfriend and that she had gone missing a couple of weeks ago. He said that they had been dating for more than two years and provided a lot of specific information about places they had visited together and things that they had done. She wasn't sure which were legit—maybe all of them, maybe none. Could someone actively be trying to take advantage of her? If so, what would they get out of it?

After reviewing the links to David's books, which seemed quite interesting, she decided to take a chance. What did she have to lose, really? She sent David an email and suggested that they meet at a local Starbucks, two days from now. She hoped that she would still be here in this current state in two days, but she wasn't sure. Anyway, that would give him time to check his email, work out his schedule, and hopefully make time to come and see her. She told him to try and bring some things with him that would clearly identify him as her father. She also sent an email to Aiko, thanking her for the information she had sent and encouraging her to continue emailing her. She considered inviting her to come visit as well, but if Aiko, David and Chieko were all related anyway, it didn't seem necessary. She decided not to respond to Chieko or Hiroshi just yet.

After reporting on her blog that she was optimistic to finally meet someone who might be able to help her, she logged off the computer and finished the scone that she had completely forgotten about in all the excitement and then headed outside. She decided to take a walk to help clear her head. It was a beautiful spring day, the air was fresh, and the birds chirping in the trees made her feel alive and whole. It was the first time in as long as she could remember that she started to feel "normal."

CHAPTER 42

Detectives Nomura and Saito sat patiently beside the hospital bed of Tamotsu Sasaki, who was in critical but stable condition. Tubes and wires were connected to him at various key locations while an electronic monitor flashed his vital signs. He had been brought in by ambulance in the early hours of the morning and had undergone four hours of surgery to patch up five knife wounds that had lacerated one lung, sliced through his stomach wall, and filleted enough muscle fiber to make breathing, sitting, and standing excruciatingly painful for the next month or so. At the moment, though, he was connected to a powerful morphine drip and was experiencing no pain whatsoever.

Fortunately, or at least as fortunate as anyone who had been attacked in the dark by a knife wielding assailant could be, none of his wounds were fatal. The knife had missed his heart by less than a centimeter. He would have bled to death in the street if it weren't for a pair of businessmen making their way home after a night of heavy drinking. One of the men heroically puked about two liters of shochu and grapefruit juice on the pavement upon seeing the victim curled up in a fetal position in a pool his own blood. At least he had missed Sasaki with his expulsion. His partner had the wherewithal, and the stomach, to refrain from puking and call an ambulance from his cell phone.

It was almost evening again, and the doctors felt that Sasaki would be stable enough to answer five minutes worth of questions, but no more. Nomura and Saito had waited thirty minutes for the patient to regain consciousness long enough to see if they could get something from him. They had been called to the hospital because of the photo of the fox tattoo that paramedics found stuffed in the folds of the victim's jacket.

"Mr. Sasaki, my name is Detective Nomura, and this is my partner, Detective Saito. We're from the Kyoto police department and would like to ask you a few questions." Nomura spoke softly, close to Sasaki's ear. He knew from experience that the victim wouldn't be able to talk loudly, and it was important to listen closely.

"It appears that you were attacked late last night or early this morning. Do you remember anything about that?"

Sasaki looked at him with fish-like glassy eyes floating under the influence of the morphine. Nomura wondered if he even knew where he was.

"Umm," he mumbled.

At least that was a start, thought Nomura. "Yes, do you remember anything?" He prodded.

"I, uhh, walking home from bar," Sasaki rasped in a forced staccato, his voice little more than a whisper. "Something hit me. Don't know what." His eyes closed. "It hurt. Hurt bad. Three, four times, in my side. Happened so quick." He took several long breaths, pulling in the oxygen from the tubes in his nostrils.

"Do you have any idea who it might have been?" asked Nomura.

He shook his head, his eyes still closed.

"Do you remember anything about the person who attacked you? What did he look like?" Nomura assumed that the attacker was a man. Most were. Considering that Sasaki was a pretty big guy, it would have taken a very strong woman to overpower him, even with a knife. Although you could never rule out a jealous lover, Nomura was willing to bet that the person who attacked Sasaki was a man.

Sasaki shook his head. Then he moved his lips, trying to form words. "He said, 'Leave Hana alone, or I'll kill you.'" His eyes popped open suddenly, which startled Nomura, who was leaning in closely to hear every word. "Don't know any Hana." Sasaki looked confused, tired.

Nomura looked at his partner, who was taking notes. "You said that he told you to leave Hana alone, or he would kill you. Is that right?"

Sasaki nodded, his eyes still closed. "Yeah, Hana. He said Hana a couple of times."

"Do you know anyone named Hana?"

He shook his head. "No."

"Do you have any idea who might have attacked you?"

He shook his head as he drifted back into a morphine-induced sleep.

Nomura turned to his partner, and they nodded to each other. That was all they were going to get today.

"You got all that, right?"

"Yep, got it all," replied Saito, closing his notepad.

"Lovely, now our mysterious Hana isn't only causing men to take their own lives, she's making them try and kill other people," responded Nomura, standing up from his chair.

"We need to call her family, don't we?" asked Saito.

"Yeah, we need to find this girl, and find her soon. She's starting to get under my skin." Nomura was genuinely agitated. At the same time, he had to admit that this was as engaged as he had been in his work for as long as he could remember.

The detectives bowed as they exited Sasaki's room and headed out into the corridor. When they made it outside the hospital, Nomura dialed Chieko's cell phone number to share the latest news with her.

CHAPTER 43

Aiko sat at the end of the kitchen table pointing to the corkboard, which was filled with photos, names, and handwritten notes, all attached with various-colored pins. She had invited Chieko to come by after work, so Aiko could go over everything that she had put together over the past several days. She had received information about the latest victim from Chieko the previous evening and had already gathered some information about him. This was the first time that she had shared this information with Chieko. She wanted to have it as complete as possible. She knew her daughter wouldn't be able to help herself from trying to poke holes in her logic. It was an annoying trait but one that she grudgingly admired. Chieko sat on the other side of the table, sipping green tea, listening intently.

"These three people at the top are the three victims, two suicides and one stabbed multiple times, although still alive. I've listed the dates that the first two committed suicide as well as the time of the attack on the third victim. Below each one I've done a brief historical biography that shows where they were born, when they moved to Kyoto, what they did, the names, addresses, and in some cases phone numbers of their closest relatives."

"How in the world did you get all of that information?" Chieko asked incredulously. "The police have been very hesitant to share any of that with us, especially since they consider Meiko to be their primary suspect."

"Some of it I was able to get over the internet. It's amazing all of the personal information you can get access to. For the pieces I couldn't get, I remembered that the son of one of your father's subordinates works in the records department at the city hall in Kyoto. I guess you can say that I called in a favor. Your father was very well liked and respected. It didn't take much to work through the father to get to the son. He was more than happy to help out."

"But disclosing those types of records is illegal, isn't it?"

"There's some gray area." Aiko shrugged. "Remember, these two cases are considered suicides, not homicides. That opens things up quite a bit. Also, the third victim is still alive. I was just asking for information that should be publicly available, at some point at least, nothing too sensitive," Aiko replied, confident that her methods wouldn't land her in too much hot water.

"Anyway, I called as many of the relatives of these victims as I could, posing as a journalist who was writing a story about the growing number of suicides following the financial crisis in 2008. No one raised an eyebrow. They were happy to share whatever information they could with me."

Chieko grunted and poured more tea into her cup.

"It turns out that all three of these victims were originally from Izumo, in Shimane prefecture. They moved to Kyoto, but all of them still have relatives who live in Izumo. Now, you have to remember that Izumo isn't that big of a place, and it's quite rural. There's a lot of collective history, shared gossip and the like, that seems to linger for decades. When

I mentioned to each of the relatives that the suicide victim had a tattoo of a fox on his ankle at the time of death, there was a quiet but very real fear that I sensed on their part. If I told you that someone had a tattoo of a fox on their ankle, the normal reaction would be to think that was strange, right?"

Chieko nodded. "Yes, that's how I would react. In fact, that's how I did react when you showed me yours."

"Exactly," agreed Aiko, ignoring any accusation that Chieko was trying to make. "Well, in almost all of the cases, that's not how they reacted. It was as if it didn't surprise them at all. When I pushed a little and asked them if they thought that was odd, most of them didn't want to say anything. But a few of them, especially some of the older women, said that they suspected something like that might have happened."

"Something like what?"

"That the victim was under the influence of a woman possessed by the fox spirit. Three of the women even used the word *Nogitsune* when they referred to the spirit," Aiko replied and took a sip of tea, knowing full well that would get a response out of her daughter.

"Oh my God! You can't be serious! You sound like that crazy shaman David introduced us to," responded Chieko. "Mother, even though you and your mother have the same tattoo, you don't really believe that either of you were ever possessed by some demonic fox spirit, Nogitsune or not?"

Aiko had expected Chieko to respond exactly this way and remained calm. She continued, "I didn't say that I thought that the men were possessed by a fox spirit. What I'm saying is that the women I talked to thought that it was very reasonable that these men were under the influence of a woman possessed by a powerful fox spirit and that she had led to their demise. In fact, they seemed somewhat relieved, in a strange sort of way. It was as if it took responsibility away from the victims. They were no longer men who had affairs with some woman, squandered their life savings, ruined their families, and then took their own lives. They were helpless in the face of this powerful evil spirit. It was the inevitable conclusion. That all made sense to them."

"Hmm." Chieko nodded, not sure what to think but still quite skeptical of the whole fox possession angle.

"I know you think all of this fox possession stuff is nonsense. But just because you don't believe it doesn't mean that it might not have something to do with Meiko's current situation," admonished Aiko. Aiko was always amazed how closed-minded Chieko could be. David was much more willing to accept things that defied conventional thinking.

"So, I started probing a bit more about what they knew about fox possession, if there was any history of it in their family, things like that." Aiko paused. "Guess what I found."

"Don't tell me—someone in their family had been possessed by the fox spirit, and it had driven them mad," replied Chieko, sarcasm dripping from every word.

"No, interestingly enough," Aiko said, ignoring Chieko's tone, mostly because she had anticipated it, "none of them had any history of fox possession in their family. However, several people mentioned hearing stories when they were young girls about how people in their family, usually their grandparents or a great-aunt or great-uncle, talked about how their village had been possessed by the fox spirit and how they had chased it out of their village. They had essentially exorcised the evil spirit by kicking out families they thought were possessed."

"Did they share the names of any of the people they expelled?" asked Chieko, suddenly more interested in where this was heading.

"No, but in each case, they talked about how their ancestors had branded the offending woman and in some cases her female child with a tattoo of the fox, in order to warn other people that they were possessed. These were stories that their grandparents had shared with them when they were very young girls. Sort of like ghost stories."

"Do you think these people were involved in ostracizing our family from Izumo when you were a little girl?" asked Chieko.

"I'm not sure. But based on the ages of the women involved, and the ages of their grandparents, it wouldn't be out of the question. In fact, I would say that there's a strong possibility that's exactly what happened."

"But how does any of this make sense? Are you suggesting that these men have somehow been cursed by the fox spirit because of what their ancestors did seventy years ago?"

"You have to admit that there are a lot of connections here just to be a coincidence. Like I said, Izumo is a not a large place. The fact that all three of these individuals came from Izumo, went to Kyoto, and then were somehow fatally linked to a woman, who we believe to be Meiko, who is my granddaughter, and two of them have a fox tattoo, identical to the tattoo I have on my ankle, seems a bit strange, doesn't it? If you include me coming from Izumo, then everyone who has been involved in these incidents—Meiko, the two suicide victims, and the man who was attacked—had direct relatives who came from Izumo. It wouldn't surprise me if the person who attacked the last victim also came from Izumo, or at least had ties there." Aiko added, "And I definitely wouldn't be surprised if he had a fox tattoo on his ankle."

"Mother, this just all seems like some crazy conspiracy theory coming to fruition. I don't disagree that it's very strange that all of these victims have ties to Izumo, but isn't it just as likely that they also somehow knew each other, maybe because they were originally from there, got to know each other, and got involved in some strange, and perhaps even illegal, activities that led to their downfalls?"

"Maybe so," agreed Aiko, thinking through every possible angle. "How do you explain the fox tattoos?"

"It could be some sort of gang initiation or some strange religious cult. Whatever it is, it's not some evil fox spirit taking over these men."

"Chieko, it might not be. But until I know the answer, I want to keep all lines of inquiry open. Until something rules out fox possession completely, then it's worth at least considering."

"I've never known you to be someone who believes in the occult."

"Exactly. That's why you should know that I'm not some hysterical extremist who points to voodoo dolls and palm readers whenever something strange happens. This is just a logical line of inquiry. I think it's premature to rule anything out at this point."

"Hmm," Chieko acknowledged.

CHAPTER 44

Chieko and David found themselves once again sitting together on the bullet train on their way to Kyoto. This time was different, though. They weren't going to meet with any priests, police, or shaman. If all worked out as planned, they would finally meet up with Meiko and bring her back to Tokyo safely.

Over the past twenty-four hours, David had shared emails with Meiko and they had agreed to meet with him and Chieko at a Starbucks near the train station in Kyoto. It was a location that Meiko had recommended. He sent her a few pictures of them together, here in Japan as well as in San Diego. He also provided her with a history of who she was and where she came from. After several emails, a cautious, yet hopeful, Meiko was willing to trust him and meet, albeit in a very public place. She hadn't shared her cell phone number with him, though. In addition to the emails and blog posts from David, Chieko, and Aiko, she had also received half a dozen emails, complete with photos that looked like her, from various men who claimed to be her boyfriend, fiancé, and in one case, her husband. She wasn't sure who to believe, but David had helped gain her trust with detailed stories and explanations about her life, as well as about Chieko and Aiko, who were also emailing her, corroborating his story.

Although it was always difficult to admit, Chieko knew that the bond between David and Meiko was much stronger than the one that existed between herself and her daughter, so she let him take the lead in setting up the meeting. She would have plenty of time to continue working on her fractured relationship with her daughter once they were all back, safe and sound, in Tokyo.

They didn't say much on the train ride down, not wanting to jinx their meeting with Meiko. There was some good, positive energy working, and no one wanted to be the one to break the spell. David had provided a description of himself, as well as several photos of himself, to make it easy for Meiko to recognize him. Chieko had done the same. If Meiko was in some amnesic state, they figured it would be better to let her feel like she was reaching out to them as opposed to two people, whom she might not recognize, coming up to her and potentially scaring her off. They obviously didn't need any photos to recognize Meiko, so assuming all went as planned, they would sit down, have a cup of coffee, and Meiko would come and join them. If not, plan B was for them to forcibly try and bring her back to Tokyo, hopefully without causing too much of a scene or upsetting her any more than was absolutely necessary.

The train pulled into the station, and the passengers started preparing to get off.

"Well, this is it," remarked David. "Hopefully, in an hour or so, we'll be heading back to Tokyo, and Meiko will be with us."

"I'd give anything for that," replied Chieko. "I hope she's not too scared and disoriented. I can't imagine what she is going through."

"Isn't that what psychologists are supposed to do?" joked David.

"Funny." Chieko smiled as she made her way down the aisle and out the door.

It was midmorning, and the train station was bustling with commuters and sightseers. Meiko had chosen a Starbucks that was only a three-minute walk from the south exit of the train station. Chieko and David merged into the pack of passengers who were heading up the staircase and outside. The air was fresh, with a slight chill. It was going to be a beautiful day, which helped reinforce their optimism.

As David reached the top of the stairs, he felt a sharp pain on the back of his neck, like a bee sting. Reflexively, he reached his right hand back to the dot of pain on his neck while he let out an "Ouch" that went unheard within the din of the crowd and the street. Chieko, who was walking behind him, didn't notice anything, focusing on the granite stairs in front of her.

At the top of the stairs, David stumbled. Then David crumpled, hard, to the ground; he started convulsing. There was a gasp as the commuters watched. Disoriented and in shock, Chieko was momentarily frozen, trying to make sense of what had just happened. Then she realized that David was in a critical state. She knelt beside him and tried to talk with him. He was shaking and completely unconscious. She laid his head on her purse to cushion it and made sure that his airway was clear. Turning to a businessman who had stopped to help, she implored him to call an ambulance while she saw to David. There didn't appear to be any serious injuries to his body. Perhaps he had a sudden heart attack or even a stroke. She felt helpless kneeling by David's side as a crowd circled them. She put her ear close to David's nose to listen for breathing. Fortunately, he was still breathing, although it was faint and irregular. She reached around to adjust his head and felt something sticking out of the back of his neck. She pulled on the tiny object; it looked like a dart, no more than two centimeters in length and slightly thicker than a hypodermic needle, with a red tuft of what seemed to Chieko to be tightly trimmed feathers at the end. This didn't make any sense to her. She reached into her purse and pulled out a pack of tissues and quickly wrapped the strange dart and put it into her purse.

Time seemed to stand still while Chieko knelt beside David. *How could this have happened right now?* Then her mind started working. There was no way that this was just a coincidence. Was her mother right? Was there a madman roaming Kyoto, engaging in some crazy killing spree? Was he using Meiko? None of it made sense. She looked around the crowd, trying to identify anyone who looked suspicious. It was hopeless. It wasn't like some madman with a blowgun would be standing there smiling at them or anything. Her chest felt tight, and she forced herself to take deep breaths to avoid hyperventilating. Everything they had planned was crashing around her.

The ambulance pulled up next to the sidewalk with sirens blaring and lights flashing. Two paramedics quickly and efficiently put David on a stretcher after first checking his vital signs. They transported him into the ambulance and motioned for Chieko to join them. The back door closed, and the ambulance weaved through traffic toward the hospital. Meiko would have to wait.

CHAPTER 45

Meiko sat in the corner of the Starbucks with a black French roast coffee. It was dark and slightly bitter and helped steady her nerves. She was both nervous and excited about meeting the man who claimed to be her father, as well as her supposed mother. Before suggesting to meet, she had done a Google search for both David and Chieko, and what she could find online seemed to match what they had shared. They seemed to be normal, and David certainly had a lot of information about her. He was able to describe her to a tee, at least how she looked. Beyond that, she wasn't sure if any of what he said was true because she wasn't in touch with who she was or how she felt. He said that she had grown up in San Diego, loved to surf, and was an excellent tennis and volleyball player. He said that she was warm and funny and loved animals. She remembered the dream about surfing. Maybe she really had experienced that. It was all such a blur, difficult to tell what was real and what was an illusion.

Meiko checked her watch. They were late. She would give them another fifteen minutes, and if she didn't hear anything from them, then she would leave. But she hoped that they would show up. She was lonely—lonely, confused, and scared. What if she never found out who she really was? What if she remained in this state of intermittent conscious-ness forever? Showing up every few days in a new place, sleeping in a strange bed, wearing strange clothes, with no recollection of the time between her last awakening? She wasn't sure how long she could live this way. Perhaps she was slowly losing her mind. But she didn't even have a point of reference to know what normal was like. Were these the feelings that schizophrenics lived with every day? She had no idea. She held out hope that David and Chieko could help her understand who she was and where she belonged. The one thing she was sure of was that she didn't belong here.

Another few minutes passed when she saw a familiar face appear in the front door to the café. It wasn't who she was expecting, though. It was the priest from the Inari shrine, the one who had been such a big help to her. He smiled when they made eye contact, and he walked directly to her. Since he was dressed in a black suit, she would have thought him a businessman if she hadn't known better.

"Hello, Hana, we need to get out of here rather quickly," he told her quietly and with an air of urgency.

"But I'm waiting for someone." The words escaped her lips before she thought about them. It seemed important to push back. His anxiety put her further on edge.

"I know, but the people you think are your parents are imposters. They are very dangerous people who run an illegal sex ring." His tone was oddly calm.

It was like a sharp punch to the gut. "But he had pictures of us together and told me a lot about my past. It seemed to make sense," Meiko said.

"Yes, but all of that is just a bunch of lies to lure you in. If I hadn't come in time, they would have kidnapped you and made you into a sex slave either here in Japan or, more likely, in China. I've been watching organizations like this.

They obviously saw your blog, your photos, and realized not only how vulnerable you are but how attractive you are and how much money they could make off you. They will stop at nothing to get you under their control." He looked around as though watching for them.

Meiko was having a hard time catching her breath and felt like throwing up. Her heart was racing. She choked out two words before he cut her off. "But I—"

"I'll explain everything in detail later. But right now, we have to get out of here. It's not safe. I'm not sure if I could stop them if they found you. Come on—let's go." The priest directed her toward the door with a gentle but firm hand to the center of her back.

She had no idea what was happening. It all seemed so surreal. They had seemed so legitimate. This whole nightmare was continuing. She just wanted it to stop. Was what he said even possible? It seemed farfetched. But ever since she had awoken on the trail at the Fushimi shrine, the only person who was always there for her was the priest. He took care of her, gave her advice, even money when she had none. She had no one else to trust.

The smell of coffee, which just a few minutes earlier had seemed so warm and welcoming, now seemed acidic and turned her stomach even more. She glanced longingly at the people sitting in the café, oblivious to her situation, talking or working on their laptops. She envied their normal lives.

They walked briskly away from the Starbucks, and the priest hailed a taxi. They got in the back, and the priest told the driver the name of a hotel that Meiko had never heard of.

"Where are we going?" she asked, her head spinning in a whirlwind of emotion.

"We've got to get you into a different place. These people are very clever. They may have already figured out where you are staying. I think it's safer for you to stay somewhere new, at least for the time being."

"But all my things are at the apartment," she protested.

"I know. That won't be a problem. I'll swing by after we get you checked in and bring everything you need to the hotel." He tried to sound reassuring. He seemed to be almost as anxious as she was.

"How did you know that I was going to be at Starbucks this morning?"

"Don't you remember that you called me last night? You were very excited about possibly meeting with your parents."

She didn't remember that at all. But that was the problem, wasn't it? She didn't remember a lot of things.

"We talked for a while. You told me about your blog and how you found these people. You were very excited. After we hung up, I did some research. I've worked with the police a lot over the past several years on cases such as this. They call me in to counsel the girls and help them get their lives together. You're lucky I found you in time. I didn't want to call and alert you because you wouldn't have believed me. I thought it was best that I came in person. I'm so sorry that it turned out the way it did, but it is better than the alternative, Hana."

"I just can't believe it. I mean, how could they have known so much about my past? How could they have had so many photos of me?" Was it possible that someone would go to those lengths to kidnap her and sell her as a sex slave? Did that sort of thing really happen in Japan?

"With Photoshop and other technology, it's easy to make things appear real. They clearly took some of the pictures you posted online and then went to work making up a story that would lead you to them. Don't worry—you're safe now. We'll get you set up in a nice little hotel—very private—and you'll be safe. If your real parents are out there, they will find you. We just need to be careful. There are people who will use your situation against you."

Meiko listened. At first it had sounded strange, but the more he talked, the more plausible it seemed. It certainly wasn't any crazier than her losing her identity or blacking out for several days or even weeks. They pulled into the stone driveway of a small, older hotel. The priest paid the taxi driver and helped Meiko check in.

"If you don't have any money on you, I can pay for everything right now. You can pay me back later."

"No, I've got money with me. I can pay cash right now. How long should I stay?" She pulled out her Chanel wallet filled with 10,000-yen notes. Her confusion had subsided slightly, and she was now in survival mode. She would get through this latest setback and keep pushing forward. Next time, she would be more careful. She would check with the priest before she made any rash decisions. At least she could count on him to look out for her.

"I think you should plan on staying for three nights. After that, we can think about whether you can go back to your apartment or look for something else permanent. After you get settled in, I'll go back and get some of your things. You should rest."

After she paid for a room, the priest led her to her room. He reached into the leather satchel that he had with him and pulled out a dozen small bags of tea as well as a new omamori. "I brought these just in case. I'm sure that you are confused and frightened right now. I'll make some tea for you. It will help settle your nerves."

He handed her the charm, which she put on over her neck. He seemed so caring and gentle.

"I asked the head priest to bless it especially for you this morning," he said calmly while he poured hot water from the electric thermos. "I was very worried about you. I'm sure that you think that these omamori are silly, but I believe that they have power, and it makes me feel better knowing that you are wearing one."

He brought the tea over to Meiko, who was sitting on one of the floor seats next to the table.

"I'll be back within the hour with some of your things. Is there anything special that you need from your room?"

"Yes, there is more money in one of my purses that is in the safe. The combination is 719." She sipped the tea. It was one of the few things in her life that seemed normal and comforting.

"Is that a special number for you?" he asked.

"Not really. It was the number of the first hotel room I woke up in. It was easy to remember."

"Hmm, I guess that's right," he agreed. "Oh, by the way, here's a new phone for you," he said, pulling a cell phone from his leather satchel. "I have to take the other phone back to the shrine. I went ahead and put my number into the contacts list."

"Takagi-san, thank you for everything," Meiko said, her eyes tearing up as the emotion of the past hour flooded over her. "I don't know what would have happened to me without you this morning. You've been so helpful to me ever since this happened. I don't know how I can ever repay you."

"Hana, I'm a priest. I've given my life over to serving others. I feel obligated to help you. Somehow, destiny has brought us together. I will continue to protect you until you remember your identity. Until then, just rest."

CHAPTER 46

Shusaku Takagi returned to the small inn that he had brought Meiko to earlier in the day. With him he carried a large Luis Vuitton suitcase, a Gucci duffel bag, and three designer purses. He had stuffed as much of Meiko's clothes, shoes, and lingerie in the luggage he found in her apartment. Meiko let him in when he knocked on her door. She had changed into jeans and a light-pink pullover, so he wondered if she had napped and maybe even showered.

"How are you feeling, Hana?" he asked, sounding genuinely concerned.

"Better, I guess. At least better than I felt this morning." She walked back into the small sitting room and took a seat on the floor next to the table. The TV was turned on to some cooking show. Takagi set down her luggage on the floor in the room.

"I brought everything I could. I think there are a few odds and ends back at the apartment, but I got almost everything. I'd be happy to help you unpack it, if you'd like."

"No, that's fine. Thank you so much for bringing everything here. I didn't mean to trouble you this morning. I'm still so confused about everything that happened." Meiko had spent the past few hours trying to piece together everything that happened. It was such a whirlwind of emotion. She spent part of the time just crying at the hopeless nature of her situation.

"It's my pleasure. I'm just glad that you're safe." He looked at the teapot sitting on the table next to a teacup. "Have you been drinking the tea I brought?"

"Yes, I've had several cups already. It's made me feel better, although I'm starting to feel a bit sleepy."

"That's natural, Hana. You went through a very traumatic and emotionally draining experience this morning. It's best that you drink some more tea and then just take it easy for the rest of the day. You can make a fresh start of things tomorrow morning."

"Do you really think those people meant to kidnap me and sell me as a sex slave?"

He nodded. "Unfortunately, yes. I wish it weren't the case, but this world is filled with so much evil. There are people looking to take advantage of innocent victims whenever they can." He sat across from her on the floor.

"Let's try and forget what happened this morning." His voice was calm and reassuring. He poured more tea for her and watched as she drank the rest of the pot. He filled it up again with hot water, dropped in a new tea bag, and brought it back to her.

"Aren't you going to have any?" she asked, offering to get another teacup.

"No, not now, Hana. I mentioned to you that I tend to drink too much tea during the day, and I've been trying to limit how much I have. You're still young and don't have to worry about these things. But when you get to be my age, it seems like you have to be more careful about what you eat and drink. I'll wait until I get back to the shrine later this afternoon, and then I'll probably drink too much." They both laughed.

For the next hour and a half, they sat and talked and watched a cooking show as well as one about some small town in Italy. By that time, Meiko felt only semiconscious, like an opium user on a blissful high. Takagi turned off the TV and sat close to her.

"Hana, close your eyes and listen to me closely." His voice was warm and soothing.

"Take hold of your omamori and breathe in its wonderful fragrance."

She did as he asked.

"That is the smell of peace and harmony that will protect you. Together, we will bring justice and peace to the world. We will eliminate evil wherever it lurks." His voice was rhythmic, hypnotic. Her entire upper body swayed gently side to side and back and forth as he spoke. "We have immense powers. We are strong, stronger than our enemies. Together, we cannot be defeated. It is our mission and our obligation to remove the evil we see. We are strong. We are right. We are blessed." He repeated these words over and over again, slowly, with a resonant baritone voice that was round, warm, and calming.

When the priest stopped speaking, Meiko's eyes slowly fluttered open. She was vaguely aware that Takagi pulled out a small pad of paper and a pen from his bag. There was a photograph of a man tucked into the pad. He wrote a man's name, address, and phone number on the pad, along with some instructions, and set that along with the photo in front of Meiko.

"Hana, this man, Akinori Kitasako, is evil, and we need to destroy him. He has done many terrible things, and we are now called by Inari to ensure that his evil does not continue. When you wake, you must seek him out and destroy him. He is a kimono maker and is very well off. You must ruin him, completely."

Hana listened, her eyes closed again, a smile now on her lips.

Takagi made sure that she had enough packets of tea, and then he let himself out.

† † †

Back at the Inari shrine, Takagi, in his full priestly robes, knelt in front of the small stone shrine, hands together, and prayed silently. The two stone foxes at the top of the shrine stared down at him as a gentle mist turned the granite black.

CHAPTER 47

Chieko sat by David's hospital bed, waiting for him to wake up. He had been taken out of the ICU the previous day but was still considered to be in serious condition, and he was still intubated and monitored. His vital signs when he reached the hospital were of a man in a coma and very close to death. Now he was in a medically induced semi-cryogenic state, his temperature at the lowest that his body could tolerate, which would hopefully slow the absorption of the toxin they had found and allow the treatment to gradually take effect.

After running a spectrometer analysis, the technicians found that the tip of the dart that had lodged in David was coated with a very powerful and lethal toxin. Dr. Morioka, the ER doctor on call, said that it was a type of bufotoxin, similar to what was found in the glands of blowfish. Symptoms of being dosed with the chemical included cardiac arrhythmia as well as ventricular fibrillation, and in some cases death. There was no antidote, but Dr. Morioka said that digoxin-specific fab fragment had proven effective at treating bufotoxins. He said that they still got one or two people a year, usually drunken businessmen, who came in with blowfish poisoning. Nothing, though, was close to the level of toxicity that David received. Based on what Dr. Morioka told her, they were very lucky that they identified the toxin in time. Another hour without treatment, or potentially just

15 percent more of the toxin entering his system, and he would have been dead.

While David was in the ICU the previous day, Chieko had gone to the Starbucks near the train station. By that time, however, several hours since their meeting time had passed, and Meiko was nowhere to be found. Chieko could only imagine how hard it would be to regain her trust. She wished they had a cell phone number for her, but Meiko hadn't been willing to share it. Chieko showed one of the people working behind the counter a photo of Meiko. The girl said that it had been busy, as always, but she did remember seeing a tall girl who looked a lot like the girl in the picture sitting in the corner. She didn't recall anything more about her, when she left, or whether she was with anyone. Chieko received similar results when she questioned the store manager who had also been working at that time. He recalled Meiko leaving with a man but couldn't say much about him except that he looked like a normal middle-aged businessman. They didn't have surveillance cameras in the store. Chieko had doubted that she would find anything on this errand, and that turned out to be the case.

Now, David slowly blinked his eyes. It was the first real sign of life she had seen from him since before the dart hit him. He blinked more rapidly and moved his head, oxygen tubes running below his nose and a plastic tube down his throat, and turned to face her. He managed the hint of a smile.

"David," she said, holding his cold hand. "Can you hear me?"

He nodded, closing his eyes.

"Are you in pain?" she asked, although she was sure that he was under such strong sedation that he tired from the mere effort of responding.

He shook his head slightly. His lips moved, but no sound came out. Chieko put her ear down to his lips.

"Where am I?" he whispered, the words distorted because of the intubation tube, sounding more like three staccato grunts as opposed to words. But Chieko knew what he was trying to say.

"You're in the hospital. You've been here since yesterday. You were shot with a poison dart." She realized how absurd that must sound. "Do you remember anything?" She knew that David would prefer her to be straightforward and not try and sugar coat things.

Again he shook his head, closing his eyes.

"The doctors said that you will be fine in a day or two but that you need to stay here for observation until you are fully recovered."

He mouthed, "Cold."

"I know. You should be warming up over the next several hours. It's best that you rest now." She could only imagine how confused he must be. One moment he was walking toward a meeting with his daughter, and the next he was waking up ice cold in a strange bed with a tube down his throat.

"Meiko?"

"I don't know where she is. Whoever did this definitely didn't want us to meet up with her. They could have killed you. We're obviously dealing with a very sick individual or group here. They aren't playing around. Somehow they must have known that we were coming to meet Meiko, and they wanted to stop us."

The previous day, Chieko also met with Detectives Nomura and Saito, whom she had called once David's condition stabilized. She explained what had happened, and they received a full toxicology report from the hospital. They also took the dart with them as evidence. While respectful of David's condition, Detective Nomura expressed his displeasure to Chieko, in no uncertain terms, about the two of them setting up a clandestine meeting with Meiko without notifying him. He insisted that she share every piece of information she had regarding Meiko, including her blog, and all the emails that had been exchanged between Meiko and anyone in her family. Chieko obliged, apologizing for failing to notify him. She and David wanted to find Meiko before the police did. They wanted to save Meiko and take her back to Tokyo, while the police wanted to arrest her. She couldn't have imagined that things would turn out the way they did.

Now, Chieko left David and notified the attending nurse that David was awake. The nurse came to check on him and recorded the information on his chart. She told Chieko that the doctor would be around soon to check on David but that his condition seemed to be improving.

Chieko felt more alone than ever. David wouldn't be there to help her, and it was perfectly clear that whoever was controlling Meiko was ruthless and not afraid to kill to keep them from her. But why would anyone want Meiko so badly? What was her value to them? Chieko needed to talk things through with her mother.

CHAPTER 48

Based on an anonymous call they received earlier in the day, Detectives Nomura and Saito approached the entrance to Kokuchou, the small whiskey and cigar bar. It was late in the afternoon, and the bar had just opened. There were three young women sitting in a corner booth and two older men in business suits sitting at the counter, but other than that, the place was empty. The detectives made their way to the bar, behind which a thin middle-aged man with black jeans, a blue dress shirt with the sleeves rolled up, and a tan, silk vest worked.

"We'd like to speak to a Mr. Kanie, please," Detective Saito said to the man, who was preparing brightly colored mixed drinks. The man turned to them with a smile that quickly disappeared when he saw the two detectives standing in front of him.

"Welcome to Kokuchou. I'm Kanie—how can I help you?"

"I'm Detective Saito, and this is Chief Detective Nomura from the Kyoto police. We'd like to have a word with you"—he looked around the bar—"in private, if possible."

"What is this in regard to?"

"We'd prefer to discuss that in private, if that's all right. It's a sensitive subject. Do you have someone who can watch the bar for you?"

"Hang on," Kani replied, setting the unfinished drinks on the work surface. He went back into what appeared to be a small kitchen or storage area and returned with a tall young man with a short ponytail, black pinstriped slacks, and a button-down shirt. He motioned to the man, who nodded and then took over with the half-finished cocktails.

Kanie led the detectives to a table in the far corner of the bar, as far away from his customers as possible. "We can talk over here. Hopefully this won't take long. We will start to get our first wave in the next hour or so."

"That depends on how our discussion progresses, Mr. Kanie," replied Saito warmly. The three of them squeezed into the booth, Kanie on one side, Nomura and Saito on the other.

Kanie lit a cigarette and reclined against the soft leather of the booth, trying to look nonchalant.

"Mr. Kanie, are you familiar with a man named Tamotsu Sasaki?" asked Saito, matter-of-factly.

"No, that name doesn't ring a bell. Should it?" Kanie took a deep pull from his cigarette.

"Other than the fact that you tried to murder him two nights ago," Nomura interjected. "Listen, Kanie," Nomura continued, before Kanie could start his denial, "we have every reason to believe that not only did you attempt to murder Mr. Sasaki but you did it on behalf of a girl who goes by the name of Hana. We can make this easier on you if you cooperate, or we can make it much harder. The choice is yours." He gave a slight nod to Saito, who pulled a crumpled photo of the fox tattoo. He set the photo on the table in front of Kanie, who took in a quick breath and then pulled on his cigarette to steady himself. "We found this on the victim," continued Nomura in a slow, calm tone. "Now, I'm willing to bet my badge that you have a tattoo just like this on your ankle. And I bet that I can get the man who gave you that tattoo to testify that not only did he give you that tattoo but he also gave it to the woman named Hana and two men who mysteriously committed what appear to be suicides. We're not convinced they were suicides. We think they might be homicides. It's possible that you may have even been involved—who knows." Nomura folded his hands in front of him on the table. "So, Mr. Kanie. We'd like to hear everything you can tell us about this matter, and it better be the truth; otherwise, I'm sure we can find ways to connect you not only to the most recent attempted homicide but also to these other two. What will it be?" Smooth jazz floated in the background. Nomura thought it was Miles Davis, but he wasn't sure. It gave him something to listen to while he waited for Kanie to break. He didn't think it would take long.

Kanie took another long drag on his cigarette and stubbed out the end in the glass ashtray on the table while he blew out a stream of white smoke. His hand was shaking.

"I had nothing to do with those other men. I have no idea who they are." His head fell into his hands as he stared down at the table. "I know the man you're talking about. Well, I don't really know him, but yes, I, I did try and hurt him. I didn't plan on killing him, just send a message. He was going to hurt Hana. I had to protect her."

"Tell us more about Hana. How did you meet her?"

For the next forty minutes, Kanie answered every question posed to him as honestly as he could. He admitted that it all sounded crazy, how he had fallen in love with this beautiful girl named Hana, so much so that he was willing to do anything to be with her, to win her love. He just couldn't let her go—she was like a drug to him. He was completely obsessed. He discreetly showed the detectives his tattoo and calmly explained his plan for attacking Sasaki. He told them everything he knew about Hana, about the apartment they would go to and have sex, about taking her out to expensive dinners and buying her designer clothes, anything she wanted. By the end, his eyes were red and his cheeks wet with tears. He knew that somehow, he had allowed himself to ruin his own life, to throw away everything he had worked for, and for what? The love of a young girl? He had beautiful girls coming into the bar every night. He had never been at a loss for a date or a good time. But somehow Hana was different. He repeated how she was like a drug. He gave them the address to her apartment, showed them the photos he'd taken of them together on his phone. He also gave them her cell phone number.

They agreed not to make a scene but insisted that Kanie come with them to police headquarters. He had admitted to the assault, which was potentially attempted murder, of Tamotsu Sasaki and would need a lawyer. He would also be placed in jail until the time of his trial, or until he posted bail, if that were an option. The detectives assured him that his cooperation would be taken into account and that he would hopefully be able to receive a much lighter sentence, given the extenuating circumstances. Fortunately for him, it looked like Sasaki would live.

With Kanie in the backseat and Saito driving to headquarters, Nomura called forensics to find out where Hana's phone was located. He expected that the team would have a precise location by the time they arrived. They'd also be able to pull her phone logs. It was only a matter of time before they'd come face-to-face with the elusive Hana.

After dropping Kanie off at headquarters, Saito filled out the appropriate paperwork while Nomura visited with the forensics team. A little over an hour passed, and a dejected-looking Nomura plopped down in his chair across from Saito.

"You don't look very cheery," said Saito, putting the finishing touches on his paperwork.

"Well," replied Nomura, running his hand through his hair, "that particular phone doesn't seem to exist anymore."

"Doesn't exist?" asked a confused Saito.

"Nope. From what forensics can determine, that phone has been destroyed. Even if it were turned off, it would still be connected to GPS, and we could trace it. But this Hana is smarter than we think, or the guy taking care of her is. They were able to pull call and text logs from that number. She made calls or texts to four unique numbers." He looked at Saito. "Want to take a guess?"

"Hmm," Saito said, leaning back in his chair. "I think I can guess three of the four. I'd say, Kanie, Fujiwara, and Watanabe. But I have no idea of the fourth. Was it the guy in the hospital, Sasaki?"

"Good guess, but no," grunted Nomura. "You did get the first three, though. The fourth is registered to Fushimi Inari Jinja. But just like Hana's phone, the shrine's doesn't exist anymore. They've both been destroyed."

"At least we can call the shrine and see who might have used that phone," suggested Saito.

"That's exactly what I did. Turns out that it's one of the loaners they let some of their priests borrow. There are about four of these phones with prepaid plans. They don't use a formal system for checking them out, so they sort of come and go on an as-needed basis. We'll need to swing by there and interview all of the priests and see who has used the phones in the past few weeks." Nomura summarized his past hour of seemingly useless effort. He had thought they were so close.

"Makes sense. At least it's something," replied Saito.

Nomura had to smile at his partner. He admired his ability to put a positive spin on even the bleakest news.

They decided to call it a day and head to the apartment complex that Kanie told them about first thing in the morning. Neither one felt like going out for a drink before heading home.

CHAPTER 49

Despite her better judgment, Chieko found herself on her way to the shaman's residence, this time alone. David had convinced her from his hospital bed that she needed to ask for her advice after all that had happened since their last visit. While Chieko was no more a believer in shamanistic prophesies than before, she admitted that she didn't have many options available. A call to her mom had sealed the deal. Though David would be in the hospital another day or two, the doctors removed David's intubation tube late that morning, which made it all the easier for him to smile when Chieko hung up the phone, knowing that Aiko was also in favor of seeking the shaman's help.

The taxi dropped Chieko off at the shaman's house, where she was expected. The door opened almost as soon as Chieko pressed the doorbell, and a familiar smell of incense emanated from the house.

"Welcome," said a voice from behind the door.

"I hope I'm not bothering you," Chieko said as she mechanically took off her shoes and put on the slippers that were waiting for her.

"Of course not, dear," said the woman as she led Chieko into the sitting room where she and David had first met her. "Please have a seat." The shaman knelt on a cushion next to the table and quietly poured hot water into a black metal teapot, allowed it to steep for slightly less than a minute, and then poured steaming green tea into ceramic cups. Only then did she look at Chieko with calm, sad eyes. "I'm sorry to hear about what happened to your husband. Will he be all right?"

"Thank you. Actually, he's my ex-husband. But yes, it appears that he will make a full recovery and be out of the hospital in the next day or so."

"That's good to hear. Please tell me everything that has happened since we last met."

Chieko spent the next fifteen minutes explaining everything she knew, from the second suicide victim, to the police finding the man at the tattoo parlor, to Meiko's blog, to the emails and the attempted meeting, and finally to what happened to David. The shaman sipped her tea calmly while listening intently without interrupting. After Chieko finished recapping the past two weeks, the shaman folded her hands and looked at Chieko with warm, caring eyes and a hint of a smile.

"Tokunaga Sensei, I know that you question the veracity of what I believe to be true. You're a scientist, after all. Talk of evil spirits and possession must seem like something from a distant age when superstition ruled over logic and science."

"I, uh," Chieko started to reply, but the shaman held up her hand gently.

"No, I'm not criticizing you in any way. In fact, I think your perspective is quite reasonable. I myself often struggle with the clear facts of modern science and a belief in a spirit world that runs counter to most scientific beliefs. Despite the apparent inconsistencies, I know what I have seen and experienced. It's hard not to believe in things, however strange, when you have seen them firsthand. I truly believe that your daughter is somehow under the influence of Nogitsune, either directly or indirectly. Everything that you have told me just now makes that seem even more likely."

"What do you mean, directly or indirectly? How could this fox spirit control her indirectly?" Chieko wondered if the shaman was trying to be intentionally vague, a common trick among fortune-tellers and the like.

"As I explained earlier, Nogitsune is a very evil and powerful spirit force. She works through any means that she can. My experience has shown me that there is almost always an assistant, an enabler, so to speak, who helps her control her victims. In many ways, the enabler is just as dangerous as Nogitsune herself. I'm sure that enabler is the one who shot your, uh, ex-husband with the poison dart."

"But why would anyone do such a thing?"

The shaman poured more tea for the two of them. "Surely, Dr. Tokunaga, you have seen in your clinical practice cases of people who become involved in less than savory activities. It happens for many reasons. Nogitsune is a master at playing on people's greatest fears, on their anger and resentment, anything that will help her gain control. Why do terrorists strap bombs to themselves and blow up cafés filled with innocent people? As a psychologist, you of all people would know the power a charismatic and powerful force has in guiding human behavior."

"So, what you're saying is that there is someone out there trying to help this Nogitsune achieve her goals through Meiko." Chieko ignored the shaman's tone. The idea that some fanatic was behind all of this seemed very reasonable. It didn't make it any less disturbing, but it was at least logical and didn't require jumping off into the realm of demons and evil spirits. "If that's the case, then we not only have to find Meiko, we have to find this enabler."

"Indeed. And while I don't know exactly who this person is, I can assure you that you have already met him or her. Be especially suspicious of anyone who has tried to win your trust during this entire experience. And, I must reiterate, be very careful. As you have seen, this person was willing to murder Dr. Wright. He or she will not hesitate to kill you if you get too close."

"You said he or she. I thought that Nogitsune only possessed women."

"That is true in the sense of possession. However, the enabler could be a man or a woman. They would be under the influence of Nogitsune but not truly possessed. Nogitsune is the gun, but this person pulls the trigger. It's a subtle difference, I know, but nonetheless, that is what I have seen."

"Is there anything else you can do to help us find Meiko?"

"At this point, you will need to think carefully about who has tried to help you and then work backward from there to determine what you really know about them and what motive they may have for helping Nogitsune. Remember, this person is just that: a person of flesh and blood, like you and me. They have no special powers other than they're following a very clear directive, however despicable and unreasonable it may seem to us, to help Nogitsune in any way possible. They have the advantage of knowing who you are and that you are trying to save Meiko. However, you now know that they exist. It will not likely be more than one person. Nogitsune always uses just one enabler when she possesses someone. You need to find this person and help them lead you to Meiko. When you find Meiko, then I can help you."

Chieko's head was swimming. Not only did she need to find Meiko, but now, according to the shaman, she needed to be on the lookout for some homicidal sociopath who was willing to do anything to prevent her from saving Meiko. She wished David were there. She wished her mother were there. Aiko would have some suggestions.

Her time with the shaman was over. Not knowing exactly what her next step was, it was clear that she needed to work on identifying this enabler. She left her donation on the table. Chieko called a taxi to pick her up. As she got ready to leave, the shaman gave her some final words to take with her.

"Remember that Nogitsune is a coward. She preys on the weak and vulnerable and uses deceit and lies to lure her victims and her enablers. Like most cowards, she runs from confrontation. No matter how confused and frightened you might be, you must remain strong in your beliefs and your desire to save your daughter. It will not be easy, but you have people to help you, and you are obviously a strong-willed woman. That will serve you well in your fight."

"Thank you. I admit that I question the whole concept of spirit possession. It runs counter to all my training. But everything you have told me so far appears quite reasonable. I know for sure that someone is in control of Meiko, and that they don't want David or me to save her. I need to find out who that is in order to find her and free her of this terrible 'spell' that she appears to be under." Chieko smiled. "I just used the word *spell* because that's all I can really call it at this point."

"You don't need to believe in Nogitsune to believe in her enabler. In any case, you must find her soon, my dear. There is not much time left, I'm afraid," said the shaman solemnly.

"I know. Thank you for your help."

Chieko climbed into the taxi and told the driver to take her to the hospital. She wanted to get David's help in solving this. Along the drive, she called her mother and summarized her meeting with the shaman.

† † †

David was well enough to sit with Chieko at a small table in his hospital room. He was making steady progress. The treatment was obviously working. Chieko had arrived twenty minutes earlier and explained her encounter with the shaman. The two of them were now trying to come up with Nogitsune's enabler.

"There just aren't that many people we have encountered regarding this whole situation," reasoned David. "Off the top of my head, there are the two detectives, Nomura and Saito. Then there's the Shinto priest we met at the Fushimi shrine. I forget his name. There are a couple of other priests we met when we first came down here. Other than them, you, me, and your mother, there isn't anyone else."

"What about the shaman herself?" questioned Chieko.

"Sure," agreed David. "If we're going to throw the two of us and your mother into the list of possibilities, we have to include her."

"I think for the sake of narrowing things down, we can exclude the two of us and my mother," suggested Chieko.

"Agreed," said David, "although after we got divorced, I bet your mom wouldn't have minded shooting a poison dart in my neck."

"Are you kidding me? She always blamed me for our divorce! If she was going to shoot anyone, it would be me."

"Well, your mother is a wise woman. I have always valued her instincts," said David with a sheepish grin.

"You're just lucky I didn't throw you under the bus and tell her about all of your indiscretions."

"I've always loved that about the Japanese. The ability to take responsibility for mistakes, whether it's truly their fault or not. A very noble trait, and a rarity in modern society, I might add."

"Thank you. I'll take that as a compliment. Now, let's get back to what we're here for." One of David's gifts was his ability to add levity to any situation, however stressful. Chieko knew that it was a well-developed defense mechanism for avoiding uncomfortable emotions, but nonetheless, it worked. It was one of the things that first attracted her to him. She continued, "The shaman said that the enabler would be someone who has been nice to us and has tried to win our trust. To me, that leaves us with four people. The shaman herself, Nomura and Saito, and the priest, Shusaku Takagi. The shaman suggested we start hypothesizing potential motives for each person."

"Whether there is a fox spirit of any type involved in this or not," David added, "it would seem that Meiko is being used as a vehicle to get at these victims."

"Exactly," exclaimed Chieko. "Meiko is the tool for some ulterior motive. Whoever is behind this wanted these men to be killed, or at least to ruin their lives. They are using Meiko to accomplish that goal, but the burning question remains: why would someone want to destroy another person's life?"

"At the risk of stating the obvious, revenge would be a primary motive, wouldn't it?"

Chieko nodded. "Yes, when I studied forensic psychology in graduate school, most crimes, especially premeditated ones like this, usually come down to a few primary motives, and revenge is certainly one of them. But revenge for what? It also doesn't explain why this individual would use Meiko as the tip of the spear, so to speak."

"Clearly, this person is smart. They want to remain in the background. They likely have a respectable job to hide behind and don't want to be discovered. That's why they've worked through a third party. In this case, Meiko."

"Being a priest or a cop is an excellent subterfuge for a sociopath. They are in positions of authority, given a lot of leeway in society, and often have access to confidential information as well as individuals who are in vulnerable situations. A shaman would also fit the bill nicely in that regard," added Chieko. "David, I promised my mother I would keep her updated. She's following up on a couple of leads she's come up with."

"By all means," agreed David. "We can use all the help we can get. I'm supposed to do a bit of walking anyway. I'll be back shortly." He stood up gingerly from the chair and slowly walked toward the door. "I hope I don't startle too many of the patients. I doubt many of them expect to run into a tall blond guy."

"Probably not. But I'm sure the nurses won't mind seeing you in your robe," Chieko said with a smirk.

"Be nice," admonished David.

"Couldn't help myself." Chieko grinned as she waited for her mother to pick up the phone.

CHAPTER 50

Detectives Nomura and Saito pulled into the underground parking lot at the luxury apartment building in downtown Kyoto. Based on information provided by the bar owner, Sanjuro Kanie, Nomura contacted the apartment's manager and set up an appointment to talk with him and hopefully gain access to Hana's room. The parking lot was spotless, and the elevator quietly took them to the main floor, where the manager, a Mr. Kenjiro Yamada, was going to meet them.

As the elevator door opened on the main floor, the detectives saw a thin man wearing wire-framed glasses and an impeccably tailored gray suit with a blue tie and matching pocket square. He was leaning against a marble wall nervously smoking a cigarette. As soon as he saw the two men, he extinguished the cigarette and threw it into the tall stainless-steel ashtray by his side.

"Would you be Mr. Nomura, by chance?"

"Yes, I'm Chief Detective Nomura, and this is Detective Saito," responded Nomura as they both showed their identification to the man. "I'm assuming you would be Mr. Yamada."

"Yes, that's me. We, uh, don't get a lot of police in this building, and as you can imagine, we'd prefer to keep everything quiet so that we don't upset our residents."

Nomura could see that Yamada was a perfectionist and didn't appreciate people toying with the fine workings of his apartment complex.

"I totally understand, Mr. Yamada. If you would be able to take us to the apartment in question and allow us to have a look around, we will be very discreet, I assure you," said Nomura.

"Thank you. It's much appreciated." Yamada pulled out a crisply folded sheet of paper from the pocket of his suit jacket. "From our conversation, you said that you wanted to get into apartment 1607, is that correct?"

"Yes," replied Nomura, confirming the apartment number that the bar owner gave them. "We were given that apartment number and believe that the person who leased it may be involved in one or more serious crimes. Can you tell us anything about who leased it, when, and for how long?"

"Yes," responded Yamada. "After you called, I pulled up some information. That apartment was rented on Sunday, the seventh, and one month's rent was paid up-front, in cash, as well as a security deposit that was also paid in cash. The apartment was rented under the name of a Miss Tanaka, Hana Tanaka."

"Did you actually meet with this Miss Tanaka when she signed up for the apartment?"

The manager shrugged. "She came in with a man who did all of the talking and actually paid for the apartment. She was with him, though. I've seen her several times since then but only in passing."

Nomura nodded to Saito, who handed Yamada a photo of Hana. "Does this look like Miss Tanaka?"

The manager took the photo in his hands and glanced at it for a moment before handing it back to Saito. "Yes, that is Miss Tanaka."

"Good," grunted Nomura, who again nodded to Saito, who in turn pulled out three other photos and handed them to Yamada. "Do you recognize any of these men?"

Yamada looked at these photographs and nodded in recognition.

"Yes, this is the man who paid for the apartment." He handed back the photo of Yoshimitsu Watanabe.

"I've also seen this man in the building once or twice, but I've never met him." The manager handed back the photo of the bar owner, Sanjuro Kanie. "I've never seen this other one before," he said, returning the photo of the first suicide victim, Masaharu Fujiwara.

"Thank you, Mr. Yamada, that is very helpful," Nomura continued. "Now, if it would be all right, we'd like to visit the apartment."

"Certainly," agreed Yamada as he pressed the button to the elevator.

As they rode up to the sixteenth floor, Saito asked, "Is it common for people to rent apartments here for one month at a time, and with cash?"

"Well, it's not uncommon, I guess," replied Yamada. "Most of our residents live here for more extended stays, but there are occasionally individuals who opt for a month-by-month engagement."

"Is it common for an older man, like the one in the photo, to pay for an apartment up-front and put it into the name of a younger woman, like Miss Tanaka?" Saito quizzed Yamada.

"This is a very prestigious property," responded Yamada. Nomura could tell that Yamada was becoming more uncomfortable with the line of questioning. "The privacy of our residents is very important to us. They demand a certain level of discretion, and we provide that. It's not my place to judge why someone might be renting an apartment. But no," he admitted, "it's not uncommon for an older man to rent out a nice apartment for a girlfriend or a mistress." Yamada stared at the floor of the elevator. "Again, it's not my place to judge what others do, as long as they carry on their private affairs in a manner that doesn't affect our other residents."

Nomura nodded. "I understand. Makes total sense."

They arrived at the sixteenth floor, and Yamada led the way out of the cramped elevator.

"It's right down here. It's one of the nicer apartments. It has a beautiful view of the city, as do most of our apartments."

"I'm sure it's lovely," replied Nomura. It was certainly more than he could afford.

"Here we are," said Yamada as they stood outside of the door to room 1607. He pressed the buzzer on the intercom panel on the outside of the door, and the three of them waited for a response from inside, which never came. He pressed the buzzer again and held down the talk button on the panel, "Miss Tanaka, it's the apartment manager, Mr. Yamada. Are you there?"

When no response came, Yamada pulled out a plastic key from his pants pocket and inserted it into the lock. A green light flashed on the panel, and he slowly turned the doorknob and poked his head inside. "Miss Tanaka, are you home?" He waited a few seconds before opening the door fully and stepping inside, followed closely by the two detectives.

It was a very nice, modern apartment with a state-of-the-art kitchen and a large, at least by Japanese standards, living area with a flat-screen TV on the wall and a tan leather couch, a glass coffee table, and a bar with an assortment of alcohol bottles, glasses, and a stainless-steel ice bucket on top. All three men instinctively removed their shoes, and the two detectives pulled on white gloves that they had been carrying.

"I ask that you not touch anything," said Nomura to Yamada as he and Saito spread out and began scouring the apartment for clues as to the identity and whereabouts of the inhabitant. Outside of the main living area they had seen from the doorway, there was a kitchen, with a small, attached dining area, and a spacious bedroom with an attached bathroom, complete with a Japanese bathtub and shower. There was also a small bathroom off the living room. As they carefully opened the closets and dresser drawers in the bedroom, they found very few articles of clothing. There were several empty boxes, from designers such as Hermes, Louis Vuitton, and Chanel, strewn on the floor. There was an unopened bottle of Taittinger champagne in the refrigerator but little else to suggest that anyone lived there.

Nomura looked through the bathroom cabinets and found several towels, along with a few boxes of tissue, some unopened toothbrushes, and some dental floss; there was toothpaste and mouthwash on the ceramic counter. There were half-used plastic bottles of shampoo, conditioner, and soap in the shower, along with a nylon scrub towel. The bath had been drained, but there were still drops of moisture, suggesting that it had been used not too long ago. Frustrated at how little they had found, Nomura opened the bathroom cabinets one more time. He was about to leave the bathroom but picked up one of the packets of tissue, the type handed out in small plastic packets on the street as a means of advertising. As he picked it up, a business card fell to the ground.

The front of the card provided information about a priest.

SHUSAKU TAKAGI
DEPUTY PRIEST
FUSHIMI INARI JINJA
752-31-4416

When he turned the card over, there were some handwritten notes.

Tamotsu Sasaki—your boyfriend; need to get him taken care of. Works at Yamazaki Electric, 16–35 Takasago

Important! Tea 3x per day

Call me with Qs (489-25-5412)

Bingo! thought Nomura. *Talk about a smoking gun!* He made his way back to the main room where Saito was inspecting the cocktail glasses and whiskey bottles to see if he might be able to pull some fingerprints.

"Saito, check out this card," said Nomura, carefully handing the business card to his partner.

Saito read the front and back of the card. Nomura watched as Saito's mouth dropped open. Saito handed it back to Nomura, who placed it in a plastic bag to take back to the forensics lab.

"I didn't tell you, but I received a call from a woman who claimed to be Chieko Tokunaga's mother—I believe her name was Aiko Tokunaga. She said that she was convinced that a priest with the same name as the man on this card was the mastermind behind everything. She was quite persistent."

"I see," replied Saito. He wasn't going to call out his senior partner, but Nomura could tell that he was caught off guard by this disclosure. "Why didn't you say anything earlier?" asked Saito.

"I was going to, but you know how many calls we've been getting lately with people volunteering all sorts of information, crazy theories and what not. I was planning on following up but got sidetracked a little," explained Nomura, a bit sheepishly. Even though he was the senior partner and didn't need to offer any sort of apology, he knew that he should have shared the information with his partner. If Saito had failed to mention this, he would have come down hard on him, just like his superiors had come down hard on him during his younger days.

"I know," acknowledged Saito. "I must have gotten ten calls yesterday. Two of them confessed to murdering the men. When I asked them the simplest questions about how they died and when, their stories completely fell apart. They couldn't even get the times and locations correct."

Nomura grunted. It wasn't unusual in Japan for criminals to turn themselves into the police after committing crimes. Guilt, shame, and honor were deeply ingrained in Japanese society. Even those who didn't commit actual crimes often turned themselves in, as some form of perverse penance for completely unrelated, and typically noncriminal, offenses that they had committed.

"It would seem that Ms. Tokunaga may have been onto something. We need to find this priest," said Nomura, focusing on the task at hand. "I'll call Ms. Tokunaga on the way and get more information about what she knows. In the meantime, I think we have enough evidence here to get a warrant for a crime scene crew to get down here to start lifting fingerprints and whatever else they can find. I'll call that in as well. Why don't you drive us to the shrine?"

Saito nodded agreement, and the two detectives headed toward the doorway. The manager was standing in the hallway, smoking a cigarette nervously.

"Mr. Yamada, we're going to have to seal this room off," explained Nomura. He knew this wouldn't please Yamada, but he really didn't care. "This is officially considered a crime scene. No one, other than the crime scene team who will be coming later, is allowed into this room. If anyone comes by trying to get in, I want you to contact me immediately."

The manager extinguished his cigarette in a portable metal container that he carried around for storing butts until he could throw them out. "I understand," stammered Yamada. "If possible, it would be appreciated if they were as discreet as possible. I'm assuming there won't be uniformed officers coming."

"The CSI team will be wearing Tyvek suits with hoods, masks, gloves, and booties. They will look more like a pest control team than police officers, if that's any comfort," replied Nomura. He could only imagine how this would look to the wealthy residents in this upscale complex. "Do you have any tape that you can put on the doorway to block it off until the CSI team gets here?" asked Nomura as they walked toward the elevator.

"I'm sure I can find something," agreed Yamada.

The ride down in the elevator was quiet and tense. Nomura thought about their next steps. He had a feeling they were getting close. But somehow, they were always one step behind. That would have to change.

CHAPTER 51

After leaving the vacant apartment, Nomura hopped into the passenger side of their sedan, so he could make phone calls while Saito drove. The first was to the district attorney assigned to this series of cases to get an immediate search warrant for the priest's residence. Once he described everything found in the apartment and texted over a copy of the business card, the DA assured him that there would be no problem getting a warrant quickly.

The second call was to Aiko Tokunaga. Nomura let her know that they had found some incriminating evidence against the priest and wanted to hear more about her theory. Aiko shared everything she found in her research, much of which seemed somewhat outrageous to Nomura, but he was also amazed by what she had been able to collect. They'd had a team of analysts working on this for almost a month, and this old lady from Kawagoe had pulled together more evidence than their entire department. He smiled, shaking his head in admiration mixed with exasperation. If her theory was correct, then they needed to find the priest, and there was no time to spare. He assured her that he would follow up with her after they visited the priest's residence.

Before they went anywhere, they needed to swing by headquarters to pick up the warrant, which gave them time to grab a quick lunch of ramen at a small place next to the police station, which was a favorite of Nomura's. The noodles were thick and fresh, and the pork belly was slowly braised and succulent, an irresistible combination. The two detectives ate mostly in silence, sipping ice-cold water and eating hot noodles. They both had a lot of things swirling in their minds that needed proper fermentation. Besides, crowded ramen shops weren't the ideal place to share sensitive police information. After they finished lunch and caught up on some preliminary paperwork, they had the signed search warrant in hand and were back on the road.

Saito parked the car in the lot next to the train station in front of Fushimi Inari Jinja, and they walked up the long flight of granite steps. It was Saturday, and the grounds were crowded with visitors, tourists, and cherry blossom enthusiasts. They made a beeline to the administration building where they asked one of the young priests if they could speak to the head priest, or the highest-ranking person currently on site. Their request was aided greatly when they flashed their badges. The young priest went into a back room and returned following an older man who looked to be in his early sixties.

"Good afternoon, gentlemen. My name is Takamotsu, and I am the head priest at Fushimi. How may I be of service to you?" He was both gentle and commanding at the same time. Exactly what Nomura would expect from a head priest.

"Good afternoon, Mr. Takamotsu. I'm Chief Detective Nomura, and this is Detective Saito, from the Kyoto police department. We would like to talk with one of your priests, a Mr. Shusaku Takagi."

The head priest nodded calmly. "I'm afraid Mr. Takagi is not here right now. Is there something that I could assist you with?"

Nomura pulled the folded paper from the inside of his suit jacket and handed it to the priest. "Unfortunately, our interest is with Mr. Takagi. We have a search warrant for his living quarters."

The older priest read the document and then carefully handed it back to Detective Nomura. He remained surprisingly calm for a man served with a search warrant for one of his employees. "Of course—I'd be happy to show you the way. If you will excuse me for a minute, I have to get the duplicate key to his apartment that we keep in the back office."

"Certainly. We'll wait here," replied Nomura.

They waited almost five minutes before the priest returned, making small talk as they waited. The priests working in the office mostly kept their heads down, focused on their work, occasionally sneaking a glance at the pair of detectives in their midst.

"You been to this shrine before?" asked Nomura.

Saito nodded. "I came here with my parents when I was younger, and I've brought my family here a couple of times since then. My kids like to climb to the top of the mountain and go through all those painted gates. What about you?"

"Yeah, we've come here a couple of times, mostly in the spring or the fall. My wife likes seeing the leaves change, so we cart the family around in November to the various temples and shrines. I've always found the orange color of the gates a little tacky, but that's just me," added Nomura, which made both of them smile.

Takamotsu returned with a stoic expression on his face, as if taking police detectives to search another priest's apartment was something that happened every day. *This guy would be a hell of a poker player*, thought Nomura.

"It took me a while to find it," said Takamotsu with a smile. "Don't remember the last time I actually had to open Mr. Takagi's apartment. It must have been almost ten years ago. I hope there isn't any trouble with him."

"Well, we're just following up on some leads at this point," explained Nomura as they followed the priest around the outside of the main building. Courts didn't issue search warrants unless there was something going on, so the priest must have known that Takagi was in trouble. Nomura thought he was just fishing for more details. Takamotsu led them down a path that wrapped around the administration building and then down several flights of stairs toward another building that was largely invisible from the rest of the shrine area. "What can you tell us about Mr. Takagi?" asked Nomura.

"Mr. Takagi is my second in charge here at Fushimi. When I retire, he is in line to be the head priest. I've known him for a little over thirty years. He's a good man, devout in his faith, respects and enforces the rules. The young priests look up to him, and he is good at keeping things running smoothly. He's very organized. A good administrator."

"Have you ever had any problems with Mr. Takagi?"

"None whatsoever. He's been an exemplary priest and member of Fushimi ever since he arrived."

"What do you know of his past, before he arrived here?" The pea gravel of the path crunched under their feet.

"If I remember correctly, and as I get older that becomes more of a challenge, Mr. Takagi was born and raised here in Kyoto. Like many of our priests, he attended Kokagakkan University in Ise. Before he came to Fushimi, he apprenticed at another Inari shrine in the Ise area. Since coming here, he moved up quickly through the ranks. He has tested to the rank of *meikai*, meaning that he could be a head priest at almost any Shinto shrine in the country. He has chosen to stay at Fushimi, though, the largest Inari shrine, which in some ways has blocked his path to the top. In fact"—Takamotsu paused in his walk and his speech and then resumed both—"you could say that I am actually blocking his path to the top."

Nomura thought that if what they suspected about Takagi was true, then Takamotsu was lucky he hadn't been taken out already.

The building they finally arrived at reminded Nomura of a college dormitory, bland and nondescript.

"Most of the priests who work and live here are housed in this building," explained Takamotsu. "Most share a room with another priest. Once they reach a certain rank, they are assigned a room of their own. There are between twenty to thirty priests and apprentices living here at any given time." He continued to a separate two-story building. "The head priest and the deputy priest, in this case myself and Mr. Takagi, live in this building. I live on the first floor and Mr. Takagi on the second. As you will see, the apartments are quite modest, although they afford us more privacy and some additional room, compared with the other priests." He seemed to be apologizing for the luxury of having his own room, however humble. "They have separate entrances. You need to climb the staircase to access Mr. Takagi's apartment."

The priest handed the key to Nomura, and the two detectives walked up the staircase while Takamotsu waited below.

"If it's all right with you, I have some business to attend to," said Takamotsu. "Please lock the door when you are finished and ask for me back at the desk. I don't think you'll have any problem finding your way back to the administration building—just follow the path." With that, the priest bowed, turned around, and headed back up to his office.

"Thank you," called Saito to the priest's disappearing back. Nomura unlocked the door. They both put on the same white gloves that they had worn that morning in Miss Tanaka's apartment.

They entered the apartment. As the priest had said, it was relatively small and modestly appointed. It was quite a bit different from the high-end, luxury apartment they visited earlier that day. The entire apartment had a floor of tatami mats, and the walls were traditional Japanese style: tan stucco with wood beams. There was a small single room that probably served as a dining/living area, complete with a square table with two cushions on the floor set in front of a small TV that looked to be at least ten years old. That room was attached to a very small kitchen with just enough room for one person to work without bumping their backside on the counters or drawers behind them. A small bathroom sat at one end of the living room with a bedroom right next to it. Saito started with the kitchen while Nomura headed toward the bedroom.

There was nothing particularly interesting in the kitchen. The refrigerator was tiny and mostly stocked with juices and a couple cans of beer. The cupboards contained several bags of rice crackers, dried seaweed, and various other snacks. The stove looked like it was only used to boil water for tea. There were several canisters of green and black teas on the counter. Saito supposed that the priests ate in a communal dining area and there was little need for Takagi to cook anything on his own. He made a mental note to ask the head priest about that when they got back to the office. He proceeded to the bathroom.

Nomura went through a latticed paper sliding door called a *shoji*, which separated the living room from the small but neatly kept bedroom. The room was sparse with a simple wooden dresser, a closet and a tall wooden wardrobe tucked away in the corner, an overhead light, and a wall calendar with the purple-and-white emblem of the Kyoto Songa, the local professional soccer team. Nomura slid open the doors to the built-in closet. Three sets of priest's robes, pure white, orange, and black, hung there, along with a navy-blue suit, three dress shirts, and two ties. Below the hanging clothes were several pairs of shoes: a pair of well-worn brown dress shoes, as well as *geta*, or wooden sandals, that went with the three sets of robes. There was also a pair of white sneakers.

The futon where the priest slept was folded up neatly and stacked on the top shelf. This was par for the course in most Japanese homes, where space was at a premium. Nomura remembered as a boy learning how to fold his futon into thirds and putting it away in the closet he shared with his two brothers. His wife taught his children to do it the exact same way, just like Japanese mothers had done for centuries. He leafed his way through the pockets of the suit jacket and the robes but found nothing. Wanting to be as thorough as possible, he pulled the futon down onto the tatami mat and unfolded it, carefully searching for anything that might be hidden in the folds. With the futon out of the closet, he looked around the shelving to see if he could find anything. He tapped the walls, looking for possible hidden access points, but found nothing. Confident that the closet held nothing sinister, he folded the futon and returned it to its space on the shelf.

The dresser produced similar findings, namely, nothing out of the ordinary: underwear, socks, T-shirts, a couple of belts, and some folded jeans and khaki pants. Nomura even removed the drawers to look behind and underneath but still found nothing.

Dejected at his failure to find anything that might help with the investigation and tie the priest to the crimes, he moved on to the large wardrobe in the corner. The door to the wardrobe was locked, although it was a rather simple, built-in lock, mostly designed to keep the doors tightly shut than to prevent a robbery. He called to Saito to join him.

When Saito arrived, Nomura asked him if he had his lock-picking tools with him.

Saito smiled and tapped his pants pocket. "I never leave home without them. Never know when they might come in handy."

"I thought as much. I've always found it interesting how your misplaced youth has benefited your detective work."

"I think you're exaggerating the extent of my youthful indiscretions. I never got into any trouble—I just had a knack for opening locks. Became somewhat of a hobby for me. Some kids collected horned beetles—I picked locks." Saito laughed as he pulled two small pieces of wire from his pocket.

"Sounds quite suspicious, Detective. I'm sure that a few minutes with a bright light in your face and some aggressive questioning might reveal something more nefarious than simply a boy's hobby." Nomura liked to tease Saito, who took his ribbing well. He was also glad to have Saito with him because he had relied on his skill in opening locks on more than one occasion. Mostly when they had a search warrant, but sometimes not.

Saito knelt in front of the wardrobe and went to work on the small, brass lock. It took him less than thirty seconds. He stood up and opened the doors and gave a "Ta-da!" as an exclamation of his success. Nomura couldn't help but smile at his partner's skill and flourish.

But the jovial mood quickly passed as they saw the contents of the wardrobe. Pinned to the back wall of the wardrobe was a detailed table of data across four sheets of A4 paper that had been taped together. The first column, entitled "targets," of the neatly handwritten table contained men's names, addresses, and in some cases phone numbers. The second column, entitled "parents," held the names of two individuals, paired, as well as the names of towns and prefectures. The third column was titled "grandparents" and again contained names, in most cases two people, but two of the six entries only contained the name of a single person. Two things caught Nomura's eyes immediately.

The first was the names of the individuals in the first column: Masaharu Fujiwara, Yoshimitsu Watanabe, Sanjuro Kanie, Tamotsu Sasaki, Akinori Kitasako, and Ichiro Sekiguchi. The first two were dead, of presumed suicides. The third was the owner of the bar who had attacked the fourth, who was in the hospital recovering from knife wounds. Each of them had check marks to the left of their names.

The second was in the last column, in every case, the name of the town was Izumo, Shimane prefecture.

"Damn, this is a hit list," muttered Saito.

"You're right about that," agreed Nomura. "And they're all directly tied to Izumo, just like Aiko Tokunaga predicted." He was again impressed by what she had been able to pull together. Her theory, however strange, looked to be gaining strength by the minute.

Saito pulled out his iPhone and took a picture of the chart. "I'm going to send this in to headquarters."

"Good. Have them find Kenji Kitasako and Ichiro Sekiguchi and make sure that they're OK. Tell them that if they are approached by an attractive young woman matching Hana's description, they are to contact us immediately, and in no case should they follow her home, take her to a hotel, apartment, anywhere."

"Will do," agreed Saito.

While Saito was sending his text, Nomura's attention turned to the rest of the wardrobe, in particular the set of small drawers at bottom. He knelt and opened the first drawer on the left, which contained various powders in small, plastic, sealed pouches. Other drawers held similar powders, what appeared to be dried tea leaves, some empty tea packets, and some white-silk-and-orange-stamped omamori. There were two larger drawers at the very bottom. They held paper envelopes of dried plants and flowers, with Latin names handwritten on the outside. There was also a small vial of a thick, milky substance. Nomura turned to Saito, who was finishing his message.

"Call CSI and have them get here immediately. They'll need to run analyses on these powders and envelopes and this liquid," he said. Saito nodded as he took the vial.

There was something wrapped in a dark-blue silk pouch leaning against the back wall. It was the size and shape of a flute. Nomura carefully opened the pouch and pulled out, to his surprise, what could only be a blowgun. Indeed, upon further inspection, the silk wrapping contained a pocket, inside of which were four tiny darts, exactly like the ones that Chieko Tokunaga had found sticking out of her ex-husband's neck.

Nomura slowly got to his feet.

Saito held the vial of the milky substance up to his eye for closer inspection. "I'm pretty sure this is the source of the bufotoxin that was on the tip of the dart that struck Dr. Wright. I did a little research on what the technicians found in their lab analysis. From what I could tell, this toxin can be extracted from a large toad, *Bufo marinus*, found in Southeast Asia, as well as here in Japan. Believe it or not, ninjas used to use this poison to dip their darts. It has a similar profile to digitalis poisoning and carries a high mortality rate.

"So, you're saying that this priest extracted this stuff from the gland of a toad and dipped his darts in it, like a ninja," said Nomura skeptically.

"Exactly. It's actually a very elegant means to kill someone. A person skilled using a blowgun can be deadly accurate from five to fifteen meters away. No sound, easy to conceal in a suit, or a priest's robes."

"Great, this case gets weirder by the minute. We've got people possessed by foxes and now poison ninja darts!" Nomura shrugged. "I'm waiting for the damn zombies and vampires to show up!

"I was hoping to find something that would link him to this mess, but I wasn't expecting to find this," he continued. "We have to figure out where Takagi is and how he's related to Hana Tanaka. This guy is clearly a sociopathic killer, and we need to find him ASAP!"

"Totally agree." Saito nodded. "A CSI team is on its way right now."

"Good," grunted Nomura. "Let's lock this place down and go talk to the Takamotsu again and see if he can help us find this lunatic. Tell CSI I want a full report on everything they find as soon as they can get it. First, let's get that milky substance tested and see if it matches the profile of the toxin that hit Dr. Wright. That needs to jump to the top of the priority list."

"Yep, will do," replied Saito.

They closed the door to the apartment, took off their white gloves, and headed back up the path to the main building. Saito suggested that they wait until the CSI team arrived before taking off, so they could make sure that no one got into the apartment and did anything funny with the contents of the wardrobe. Nomura agreed. They spent the next fifteen minutes asking Takamotsu for any information he had about Takagi. He wasn't able to share much more than he already had. Takagi was on a short sabbatical and wasn't due back at the temple for another week or so. He had never given Takamotsu any indication that he might be up to anything suspicious. The head priest could share Takagi's cell phone number and his email address, although Nomura imagined that he used several numbers and addresses for his private endeavors. Still, it was worth checking out. Saito called headquarters and ordered a summary of all cell phone activity on that number for the past thirty days.

The CSI team arrived in force, which caused a noticeable level of discomfort for the shrine-goers as well as the priests, who worked to maintain an appearance of normalcy. Nomura and Saito escorted them to the apartment and showed them the wardrobe before heading back to headquarters. They needed time to pull together what they had found. Nomura also wanted to talk with Aiko Tokunaga again. Her theory had proven much more accurate than he would ever have imagined. He smiled, thinking about how a seventy-six-year-old woman in Kawagoe had figured out what was going on hundreds of kilometers away when he and the Kyoto police department consistently came up short.

CHAPTER 52

Chieko's cell phone rang while she sat in her office. Her appointment schedule had been thrown off by her unexpected extended stay in Kyoto, and she was trying to reschedule those appointments for the following week. She wished she had an assistant who could handle these types of things, but at the moment, she couldn't afford one. She didn't recognize the number.

"Hello, this is Dr. Tokunaga."

"Yes, this is Shusaku Takagi from the Fushimi Inari Jinja. I'm sorry to bother you."

The hairs on the back of Chieko's neck bristled. This was one of the men she was convinced was at the center of Meiko's disappearance.

"Yes, Mr. Takagi, it's good to hear from you," she lied, trying to stay calm. "How can I help you?"

"I wouldn't have called unless I thought it was important."

"What is it?"

"It's about your daughter. I'm afraid that the police are involved, and in particular, a Detective Nomura. I believe there is a plot inside the department to try and frame your daughter for a number of apparent suicides that have occurred here in Kyoto."

She had no idea what he was he talking about. A plot by the police to frame Meiko? That didn't make any sense at all.

"How do you know that? Do you know where Meiko is?"

"I'd rather not talk about this in detail over the phone because I'm concerned that my prying into police affairs, to try and help your daughter, may have tagged me in an unfriendly light in their eyes. I think that I am being watched and that it's likely my phone is being tapped. I've probably said more than I should already. I know it's an imposition, but would it be possible for you and Dr. Wright to meet me at Fushimi Inari Jinja tomorrow at the end of the day?"

Chieko wasn't sure what to say. She and David had returned from Kyoto the previous evening. Though David seemed to have made a full recovery, the doctor had recommended taking it easy for the next week or so. Still, she was willing to do anything at this point to locate Meiko and bring her back safely. As much as she suspected the priest, the Kyoto police department hadn't been particularly helpful in finding Meiko either.

"All right. We'll meet you there. Just tell me where and when," she agreed. The priest provided the details for their meeting the next day, which was to take place at dusk.

Chieko called David right after she hung up with Takagi.

"Hi, Chieko." He sounded tired. Chieko thought he was probably still feeling the effects of poison or the treatment, maybe both.

"I just got off the phone with the priest from Fushimi Inari Jinja. You remember Mr. Takagi?"

"Yes, I remember him well. You were a big fan of his, if I'm not mistaken."

"Well, I don't disagree with his worldview as it relates to fox spirit possession, if that's what you mean." God, she hated how David could so easily put her on the defensive. It was a terrible gift that he was adept at using. "But that's not why I called. He says that he has some information about a police conspiracy to frame Meiko. It relates to Detective Nomura. He wasn't comfortable talking over the phone and wants us to meet him at the shrine tomorrow." It sounded like absolute BS, and she felt like an idiot agreeing to come, but what options did she have? She'd do anything to get Meiko back, even if it meant meeting up with one of the primary suspects.

"That sounds sort of fishy, doesn't it?" asked David. "I mean, he's one of the people who's likely tied up in this whole thing. What did you tell him?"

Yes, it did sound fishy, though she wouldn't admit that to David. "I didn't know what to say, so I said we would meet him." She hoped David didn't think of her as a complete fool. She hated how weak and helpless she sounded right now, especially in front of David.

"I would have done the same thing," he said, which came as a relief to Chieko. *Thank God! At least I'm not completely crazy. Or not alone in my craziness.* "After all, what are our choices?" continued David. "But if he's right, then we shouldn't contact the police about meeting tomorrow. It would defeat the purpose. But we know that they just warned us again about not keeping them in the loop. I just don't see a motive for the police other than to wrap up some cases. It seems like a stretch that they'd set this whole thing up. Besides, it doesn't explain Meiko's disappearance in the first place or why those men have pictures of her, as well as the tattoos."

"I know," agreed Chieko. "None of it makes sense. I don't know why the priest would create such an elaborate lie either. What could he get out of this?"

"You're siding with the priest over the police?" Chieko could hear the skepticism in David's question.

"I'm not siding with anyone," she replied. She knew he was right. It did sound like she was taking the priest at his word, even though his thesis sounded ridiculous. Was she so desperate to get her daughter back that she'd suspend logic? "I just know who has seemed to be on our side and who hasn't. Mr. Takagi has been nothing but helpful to us so far. The police haven't done anything except insinuate that Meiko is guilty."

"'Seemed to be' might be the key to that statement. Remember what the shaman told you about someone seeming to try to help us. What does Aiko think?"

"I haven't talked with her. I called you as soon as I hung up with the priest."

"I think it sounds pretty suspicious, but like you said, we don't have many choices left, at least not good ones. Give Aiko a call and get her thoughts. If she thinks we should go, then I'll meet you at the station."

"OK, that's a good idea." Chieko hated that she couldn't decide on the right path forward on her own, but she agreed with David that getting her mother's input would be helpful. "David, we're running out of time!" Tears welled in her eyes as she heard the words come out of her mouth.

"I know," said David in a supportive voice. "See what your mom says, and let's go from there."

CHAPTER 53

Takagi took a long drag on his cigarette and glanced at his watch. They should be here any minute. *They're not going to get away this time.* He should have taken care of them a lot earlier. He had no idea how persistent they would be. No worries—they would be out of the way soon enough. He waited for them next to the small orange torii gate that led down a narrow, winding dirt path through the more heavily forested outskirts of the compound. Trying to be as incognito as possible, he wore dark jeans, a black mock turtleneck, and a black baseball cap.

He saw them coming up the path, took a final drag on his cigarette, and then threw the butt down and stamped it out with his foot. *Lambs to the slaughter.* He wondered if this was how a Yakuza hit-man felt right before pulling off a job. It was nerve-racking and yet exhilarating. Putting on a broad smile, he waved to them because they didn't recognize him, which was exactly what he had been hoping. *So far so good.*

"Thank you for coming, and I apologize for asking you to come to such an obscure location." He greeted them cautiously, looking around to make sure they weren't being followed. "But recently I'm afraid that I have become a target of attention, and I wanted to stay away from the main shrine area."

"Who do you believe is targeting you?" asked Chieko. She sounded skeptical. He didn't blame her. *She's sharper than her ex-husband.* He thought about the story he had crafted. Confident that it would keep them occupied at least long enough to get them where he wanted. They might have fancy-sounding degrees, but they were no match for him.

"The police, among others." Answering Chieko's question, Takagi started walking, leading them deeper into the bamboo and cedar forest. "I can't go back to my room because they are watching me. I believe that they are at the center of a plot to frame both me and your daughter for the deaths of several men here in Kyoto."

"Why would they be suspicious of you?" asked David.

"I think it's because I've been asking questions and trying to help you find your daughter. It's pinged on their radar. They don't like people sticking their noses into police business, especially when there is a conspiracy involved." He continued to lead them down the path and could hear the faint sound of running water in the distance. *As long as we keep moving forward, we're fine.* "I'm not sure how aware you are of the level of corruption here in Kyoto between certain members of the police and organized crime. It's much deeper than it is in Tokyo or Osaka."

"But what would the police and the Yakuza want with Meiko?" asked Chieko.

"Let's just say that sometimes there are people who the Yakuza want to 'disappear' for various reasons. More often than not, they are victims of apparent suicides, and their deaths go unnoticed because suicide is not that uncommon here in Japan. People who lose their jobs, can't pay their bills, feel responsible for the misfortunes of those close to them often decide that it's more honorable to take their own lives and free their family of their debts."

"Yes, I'm aware of that," responded Chieko. "I still don't see what that has to do with either you or Meiko. You'll have to be clearer."

"Don't you see?" Takagi replied, trying not to raise his voice. "They are using Meiko as the reason these men committed suicide—a femme fatal, if you will. It doesn't hurt that she's a foreigner who seems to have lost her way, run away, or maybe even forgotten who she is. She's just a pawn they've found as an easy scapegoat."

"I'm still not following you," said Chieko, looking confused.

How come that doesn't surprise me? And she's the smarter of the two, for God's sake! I'm spoon-feeding you two idiots! Despite their advanced degrees, neither of them appeared that sharp to him. Well, it wouldn't be much longer anyway. He continued, trying to be as convincing as possible. "If the spouses and family members of these men were to find out that they were deeply in debt to the Yakuza or had been laundering money for them, then their suicides would seem more suspicious and the police would be forced to make trouble for them. But if they could blame an attractive young woman for their suicides, then the family, especially the spouses, would be much less likely to want to raise attention to that fact. It would be embarrassing. At the same time, they would want revenge against that woman. So, the police move in, identify a person like Meiko who fits the bill, and everything goes away quietly.

"There's a lot of cover-up money that passes between the Yakuza and corrupt policemen. It's in those policemen's best interest to keep attention focused away from both themselves and the Yakuza. Unfortunately, an innocent person like Meiko gets charged with being involved in their deaths. When you or your husband start looking for her, that's one thing—it's normal for the family to seek out a missing loved one. They can stall you, feed you false information, tell you they're doing everything they can. But when I started asking questions and seeing if I could find out anything about her, then it got a little too close to them, so now they have to find some way of dealing with me. I don't know what their plans are, and I'm not looking forward to finding out either."

The path wound precariously around several large rocks and onto a precipice overlooking a deep ravine that was at least a two-hundred-foot drop. They paused and peered into the rocky gorge and could not only hear but see the strongly rushing water of the stream below filled with runoff from the winter's snows. He needed to keep them calm and focused on his story rather than the location.

Now that he had them questioning everything they believed in, it was time to settle them down a bit. The gentle, caring Shinto priest persona always worked wonders. "I often come here to get away from the crowds that come to the shrine. It's very calming. In the springtime, the river is quite powerful. It makes you realize the wonder of nature all around us." Takagi motioned out toward the forested hills in the distance, the breeze gently wafting through the trees.

And this, my dear Sensei, is where the journey ends, at least for you. Standing less than a foot from Chieko, Takagi reached into his pocket for the small, but deadly sharp, switchblade he had brought with him. He visualized his next move. In one smooth and powerful movement, he would push Chieko over the edge, and then before David had a chance to realize what was happening, he would finish him off as well. He hoped that he could simply catch him off balance and push him over, but if he needed the knife, he had it at the ready. He wouldn't miss this time.

As he was about to make his move, a woman's voice called out from the forest, "Shusaku, stop! Chieko, get away from the priest! Now!"

CHAPTER 54

Chieko and David quickly stepped back from the priest, who was clearly caught off guard after hearing his first name called from a distance. The three of them turned toward where the voice came from, and at that instant, a defiant-looking Aiko emerged from the cedar forest, with Meiko at her side. The two women walked directly toward the priest, who seemed to be momentarily frozen in place.

"Shusaku Takagi, I know who you are, and I know what you are doing," Aiko stated forcefully as she continued walking toward the priest. "I never expected such disgraceful behavior from someone in my own family. Your father would be mortified at what you have done."

The priest regained his presence and smiled at the two women, while at the same time keeping an eye on David and Chieko as well.

"I have no idea what you are talking about. You must have me confused with someone else. We have never met in our lives." He turned his attention to Meiko. "Hana, I'm not sure what this woman has told you, but I can assure you they are lies. These people are dangerous. I only want to protect you."

Meiko glared at Takagi. "It won't work this time. I stopped wearing your omamori and stopped drinking your tea as well. The only one who is lying is you."

Takagi quickly reached into his sleeve and pulled out a stainless-steel dart gun, put it close to his mouth, and pointed it at David and Chieko.

"Stand back, all of you. I can put a dart in these two before you can move an inch. And I assure you, you won't wake up from this one, Wright Sensei." He spit the words out like venom.

Aiko and Meiko froze where they stood. Aiko knew that there was no way either she or Meiko could reach the priest before he shot the darts and killed David or Chieko and maybe both.

David held his hands up to show that he was not hiding anything.

"Mr. Takagi, I'm sure we can talk this through. We mean you no harm," he said, trying to stall for time.

"Shut up! I'm as tired of listening to your miserable Japanese almost as much as I'm sick and tired of your half-breed brat of a child. I knew that I should have killed you both when I had the chance. You've been nothing but flies in the ointment since I met you. But I'm not done, not by a long shot. There are more on my list who need to be taken care of." He turned slightly to his right to look at Aiko and Meiko while keeping aware of David and Chieko. "You're wrong about my father. He would be proud of what I've accomplished. He was the one who explained everything about what my family, our family, went through," he said, motioning to Aiko. "Those men deserved everything they got and more. You, of all people, should understand that." His eyes seemed to be on fire as rage burned inside.

He looked at Meiko with a satisfied grin. "Hana, you were very good at what you did. I'd even say that you enjoyed your part in our little game. Deep down, you knew what we were doing. You loved every minute of it. You can choose to live and continue to help me finish off what we started, or you can die with the rest of your family, right here, right now. It's up to you. But choose fast—we don't have all day."

Meiko looked at Aiko and then toward David and Chieko, who were both standing with their hands in the air. There didn't seem any way out of this mess.

CHAPTER 55

From somewhere in the woods behind David and Chieko, Meiko heard a strange male voice call out, "Drop the dart gun, Takagi." It was Detective Nomura, who appeared from behind a dense copse of cedars with a handgun focused on the priest.

From the opposite side of the woods, a second male voice called out, "I've got you covered from this side too, Takagi. Drop the dart gun!" It was Detective Saito, who appeared as a mirror image to his partner, Nomura.

Hearing the two detectives and realizing that he and Chieko were in a potential crossfire, David dropped to the ground and signaled for Chieko to do the same, which she did. Realizing the sensibility of this move, Aiko and Meiko both dropped to wet leaves, waiting for the next phase of the encounter to unfold. Meiko realized that if Takagi wanted to shoot any of them with the dart while they were lying less than fifteen feet away, he could do so easily. However, it would likely be his last move because the two detectives would be able to shoot him before he could load another dart.

The priest must have come to the same conclusion. He was surrounded, with little if any hope of escape. He kept the dart gun just outside of his lips, a deadly flute waiting to be played. He dropped to one knee and spun around to face Meiko and Aiko and let go a dart that sailed over both of their heads and lodged itself in Saito's shoulder. The detective fired his pistol, but the pain of the dart threw off his aim, and it whizzed past Takagi. Nomura's aim was true, and his shot hit Takagi in the chest, just below his right shoulder. The priest let out a discernable grunt and fell backward. David instinctively leaped to his feet and charged the fallen priest. Outweighing the priest by over fifty pounds, he wrested the dart gun out of his hand just as Nomura reached the two and placed his knee on Takagi's neck and pulled out a line of black plastic zip cuffs from his jacket pocket.

While Nomura was subduing a screaming Takagi, Aiko rushed to the side of Detective Saito, who was lying on his back, shaking. She removed his right arm from his jacket and unbuttoned his white shirt and fiercely ripped open the front of his shirt as she searched for the tiny dot where the dart had entered. There it was, a red pinprick from which a dark, milky liquid was seeping. She reached into the pocket of her jacket and pulled out a red box-cutting knife and quickly made an X over the dot. She laid the knife down and then carefully placed her lips over cut and started to suck on the wound and then spit out whatever she pulled into her mouth. She repeated this process at least twenty times.

Meanwhile, Chieko dialed the emergency line and explained that an officer was down and had been shot by a poisonous dart, most likely some type of bufotoxin. She referred them to Dr. Morioka at Kyoto General, who had treated David, and urged them to send paramedics immediately. She handed the phone to Nomura, who had by now handcuffed Takagi. Nomura confirmed everything Chieko had said and told the operator that Saito would die if he weren't treated quickly. He asked Takagi what type of poison was on the dart, but the priest refused to divulge his secrets.

Meiko appeared ready to pass out. Her head was swimming. This was all because of her. The man she had trusted for the past month had threatened to kill her and her family and had even shot a police officer with a poison dart. It was too much to take. Tears welled in her eyes as she tried to make sense of it all. Chieko approached her and put her arm around Meiko, who fell against her shoulder sobbing.

While Nomura walked Takagi out of the woods, David carried Saito like a giant baby. Saito was in and out of consciousness, and David kept talking to him, trying to keep him awake. They headed toward the main gate, which would be much more accessible to the paramedics and would hopefully save a few precious minutes. The three women followed, with Meiko in between Chieko and Aiko.

CHAPTER 56

KAWAGOE
APRIL 23RD

Aiko added some more of the thinly sliced *matsuzaka* beef to the cast-iron pan of mushrooms and onions that were slowly caramelizing in a bubbly sweet-and-salty sauce of sugar, mirin, and soy sauce. If there ever were a night for sukiyaki, then this was one of them. Sukiyaki was a dish often reserved for celebrations and family get-togethers. The past month had been stressful for everyone, but now that it was over, they could sip cold beers and feast on sautéed wagyu beef in the cozy confines of her home.

Chieko poured David another beer from one of the large bottles of Kirin on the table. The empty bottles were starting to pile up, but that was part of the fun of sitting around the table and eating sukiyaki: watching the pile of empties grow. They hadn't talked much on the train ride home. All of them were in some stage of shock, and they all had found it easier to sit and be quiet with their thoughts. Detective Nomura had called Chieko that morning and said that Detective Saito was in serious but stable condition. The doctors said that he was poisoned by the same bufotoxin in an even higher concentration than what Takagi had used to shoot David. Saito was fortunate, however, because Aiko's quick thinking had helped extract enough of the toxin to greatly improve his chances of survival. Had the detective been left untreated until he arrived at the hospital, the doctors felt that he would have died.

"Where did you learn to do that?" asked Chieko as she added more sliced onions to the pot. "I mean, seriously, who does that?" The onions sizzled as they hit the pan, and the hot skillet steamed with sweet, salty aromas rich in umami.

Aiko laughed, taking a long drink from her glass, only to have David refill it for her. "Believe it or not, I remember seeing someone do that on an episode of *Gunsmoke* when we were living in New York. That had to be almost fifty years ago!"

"Why did you cut an *X* on the wound?" asked David.

"I don't know, but that's what they did on the show, so it seemed reasonable. The puncture wound was so small that it would be difficult to actually draw anything out of it," replied Aiko, thoughtfully.

"More importantly," continued David, "how come you had a knife in your pocket?"

"Well, I knew that we might run into problems, and that was the only thing I could think to bring for protection," replied Aiko. They looked at her for a moment and then everyone burst into laughter, including Aiko. It was cathartic being back together as a family, especially after the intense, almost surreal, drama of the previous day.

As the sukiyaki gradually disappeared, along with most of the beer, Aiko brought out a large bottle of sake with some tiny, white, ceramic glasses. She filled each *guinomi*, and they toasted to Meiko's return.

"Mother, how did you figure all of this out? When did you realize that you were related to Takagi?" asked Chieko.

"I started getting this strange feeling when I read that the first suicide victim's family was from Izumo. Izumo is a rural place, and not many people in Japan have even been there, let alone come from there. So, that got my senses sort of tingling. I tried to look up as much information as I could on his family but wasn't able to pull up much."

David topped off Aiko's empty sake cup before refilling his own.

"Then the second victim's name came out, and he also was originally from Izumo. The hairs on the back of my neck started standing up, and I knew it wasn't just a coincidence. I tried doing some more research, but it was hard to find much about either of the families. Then, as the investigation went further, there were a couple of names I could add in: Detectives Nomura and Saito, Takagi, and the shaman, Shiho Urabe. At that point, I came up with an idea that I should have thought about earlier. I remembered that the son of one of your father's *kohai*, a junior colleague at the trading company, worked for the city of Kyoto. Your father and this man, Nakajima, used to go out drinking a lot, and I knew that he would be happy to help out, if he could. As expected, he was glad to help and put me in touch with his son, Jiro. Now, you can imagine that what I was asking for was a bit out of the ordinary, and I'm sure that Jiro could get into some trouble if his superiors found out about what he shared. But he was able to provide me with detailed family information about everyone I asked about."

Aiko turned to Meiko. "As you may or may not know, Japan keeps extensive genealogical records of all of its citizens. Everyone is born into what is referred to as a *koseki*, or family registry. Japanese law requires all Japanese households to report births, adoptions, deaths, marriages, divorces, paternity, and the like to their local authority, which compiles that information for all Japanese citizens within their jurisdiction. When a woman marries a man, she becomes a member of his koseki. In your parents' case, because David is not Japanese, he and Chieko created a new koseki, using Chieko's maiden name."

Aiko turned back to David and Chieko. "When I started working backward from those individuals, I found that in addition to the two victims, Shusaku Takagi, the priest, was also originally from Izumo. I knew at that point that the priest was a central figure in this entire strange tragedy. The thing that really got me was that Takagi's father was Yukio Takagi." She paused, turning to Chieko. "Does that name mean anything to you?"

Chieko thought for a moment and then shrugged. "Not really. Should it?"

"Perhaps not. I haven't been very forthcoming in sharing everything about my family with you. You know that when I was a young girl, our family was chased out of Izumo because they believed that my mother, Hana, and, by extension, me were possessed by the fox spirit. I was adopted by my mother's sister, and I grew up here in Kawagoe. But I had a younger brother who was very young, maybe three or four, when I was adopted. His name was Yukio Takagi, and he grew up in the Kansai region near Kyoto. He passed away several years ago, and unfortunately, I'm ashamed to admit that I did not keep up relations with him. I didn't even know where he was living. Yukio had two children, a girl named Machiko and a younger son name Shusaku, who ultimately became a priest."

"Grandma, are you saying that the priest is your nephew?" asked Meiko, skeptically.

"That's exactly what I'm saying." Aiko looked around at everyone's looks of utter disbelief. "His father must have instilled in him a deep hatred for all of the people who kicked his family out of Izumo and brought such hardships to his family. I'm sure that finding Meiko was an incredible bit of good fortune for him. I doubt he had any idea when you met that he was your cousin. But given his obsession with seeking revenge, and a little research into your family history, which would be easy to obtain on the internet, I have no doubt that it didn't take him long to realize who you were. Keep in mind that high-level priests can get access to a lot of information normal people can't. I'm sure he saw it as destiny. It was then that he started drugging you and controlling your mind. He even called you Hana, after my mother, the grandmother he never knew, who was driven out of Izumo."

Meiko listened intently, trying to make sense of everything. She looked confused and, as far as Aiko was concerned, was still not nearly her normal, bubbly self. She knew from experience that time was the ultimate healer, and the Meiko she knew and loved would be back with them in time. She would do everything she could to ensure that happened. But there was no need to rush things.

"So, all of the victims who were targeted were descendants of families who helped chase your parents out of Izumo?" asked Chieko.

"It would appear so. You have to understand that I don't remember many of the names of the families who were involved, and I undoubtedly was sheltered from a lot of the abuse that my parents, and especially my mother, received. I remember being taunted by children in the neighborhood, but I only have a vague recollection of their names, and mostly just their first names."

"Those were very painful experiences, especially for a young girl," replied Chieko with a look of genuine concern. "I'm sure that you have blocked out many of your memories from that period in your life."

"Probably so," agreed Aiko. She had never thought of it that way, but it made sense.

"So not only did he want to exact his revenge on these individuals but he wanted to do it in a way that would taunt them for their ancestors' actions related to fox possession. He must have been planning this for quite some time. It was just unfortunate that Meiko ended up being an unwitting pawn in his scheme," David said, pouring another round of sake.

"Do you honestly believe that it was just bad luck that he found Meiko?" inquired Aiko.

"Well, of course there were a lot of strange circumstances at play here. Are you suggesting that there is more to it than just coincidence?" asked David.

"Think about all that has happened. Meiko goes to Kyoto to visit the temples during cherry blossom season. Nothing strange about that—millions of tourists do it every year. But somehow, despite being healthy in every way, she stumbles and passes out after she sees a fox running down a path. Not a raccoon, or a dog, or a monkey, but a fox. It just so happens that she goes unconscious at the very same shrine where this priest works, and he, among the dozens of priests who work at this enormous shrine, is the one who finds her. It also ultimately turns out that she is his cousin. Not only is he her cousin, her grandmother is the sister of his father, part of the family who was so irreverently kicked out of Izumo, which is ultimately at the root of his need for revenge. How incredibly unlikely is that?" Aiko asked as she stood up. "I'm going to make some tea. I've had enough sake for one night."

"Mother, what are you getting at?" asked Chieko. "Certainly, there are a lot of coincidences at play here, but sometimes the stars align and things happen. There have been many instances of that throughout history." Chieko stood up to help Aiko with the teacups and to clear the sake bottle and cups from the table, despite David's half-hearted protests.

"I think what Aiko is insinuating is that the fox spirit, and maybe even Nogitsune, may have had something to do with this," commented David as he finished what remained of his sake. "Am I right?"

"Oh, for the love of God, David!" exclaimed Chieko as she set down the teacups. "I think you've definitely had enough alcohol for one evening. I thought that you were done with this whole fox spirit nonsense."

David held up his hands in mock protest. "I'm just speculating on what your mother might be proposing here. I remain a neutral, yet interested, observer in this matter."

Meiko smiled as she watched her parents interacting as if they were still married, or at least as if they still liked each other. After almost a month of not knowing who she was, it was comforting to be around her family—people she knew truly loved and cared for her, with no ulterior motives.

Aiko returned to the table with a large, electric carafe of water and a small teapot that she filled and let steep for a minute or so. Kotetsu stretched out next to her, and Aiko rubbed gently under his chin.

"I know that you think I'm just a superstitious old woman," she said, directing her comments toward Chieko. "I've seen too much to think this is just a coincidence. The shaman you talked to seemed convinced after seeing Meiko's photos that she was possessed by Nogitsune. She also said that Nogitsune always worked through a third party. In this case, that would be the priest. Who's to say that Nogitsune hasn't been biding her time for the last hundred years, which would be but an instant for a vengeful deity, waiting for the right moment to get her revenge? How do we know that similar things aren't happening all over Japan as we speak? There's a reason why Meiko has the exact same tattoo on her ankle as I do, even though those tattoos were made nearly seventy years apart. There's a reason why a stray fox ran down a path where Meiko was walking, at a shrine that honors the fox spirit and its master, Inari. If you remove your skeptical twenty-first-century filter for the moment, you can't help but think that something beyond our current understanding is at work here."

"But if this Nogitsune is so powerful, why would the priest have to drug and hypnotize Meiko in order to control her? Why couldn't Nogitsune just do all of that herself?" asked a skeptical Chieko.

"I don't know the specifics through which Nogitsune operates. Perhaps she uses whatever means are necessary to possess and control her victim. If that requires drugs or hypnosis, then so be it. She had a receptive and motivated accomplice in the priest. She may have influenced his thinking in how to come up with the drugs he used, the poisons he made to protect their plans, and even the means of hypnosis.

It's certainly not out of the realm of possibility to think that the priest, a man deeply rooted in the spirit world, would be very open to the influence of a deity, especially one who shared his desire for vengeance."

"Chieko, you have to admit that many people feel that they have heard the voice of God and have been motivated to do both wonderful and tragic things based on those revelations," added David.

"That's absolutely true. People hear voices all the time. Many of them are also psychotic in one way or another," agreed Chieko. "I'm not questioning whether people hear voices that they attribute to their god, but what you're saying goes well beyond that. You're giving credence to the notion that Nogitsune, and other fox spirits, actually exist. These are prerational and certainly prescientific rational for hard-to-explain events. It's nothing more than the classic 'god in the gaps' argument, an infinitely useful explanation to fill in the spaces where logic fails. The problem is that, useful though it may be, it doesn't make it true," responded Chieko.

"Chieko, at some point, we will just need to agree to disagree," said Aiko. "I firmly believe that there are forces at work that go well beyond our understanding of the physical world. You have been trained to either ignore or explain away those things. That's fine. But at some point, you need to admit that you are operating from a paradigm of your own that shapes not only your interpretation of events but the prism through which you see them. Your paradigm might be more advanced than mine, but we both have our own paradigms. At least I'm willing to admit that mine exists and that it is imperfect."

"Wow! Touché, Aiko. I couldn't have explained that better myself, and I'm pretty good at talking about paradigms," said David, clapping his hands in joy. "I believe that something well beyond coincidence was at work here. I don't know much about fox possession or Nogitsune, but I've seen too much from too many cultures to dismiss such beliefs as foolish superstitions. This whole episode will make a wonderful addition to my book."

Chieko laughed and shook her head. "I'm clearly out-numbered here. Mother, you are right: I do have my own paradigm for interpreting the world around us, and it's hard for me to admit that it isn't the best and most reasonable one out there. But, like you said, it is a paradigm nonetheless; it's not reality. I hate to admit it, but we're all not much better than the five blind men trying to describe the elephant. We're all just seeing bits and pieces and trying to make sense of it."

She turned to David. "And as for you, Professor. I knew that you would somehow find a way to capitalize on this entire fiasco. It will probably turn into one of your best-selling books."

"Hey," protested David, "it's what I do. Painters paint, pitchers pitch, and I write books about strange things that make people think about their beliefs. It would be an injus-tice to my loyal readers, and folklore scholars everywhere, if I didn't share my experience here." He turned to Meiko. "That is, as long as Meiko is fine with it. I would change the names and things like that, of course."

Meiko, who had been quiet most of the evening, shrugged. "It's fine with me, Dad. In fact, I'd be disappointed if you didn't write it up. After all, I'm not sure what exactly went on anyway. It's like I've been in some strange dream for the past month, and I'm not sure which parts are real and which are made up."

Chieko put her arm around Meiko's shoulders. "You've been through an incredibly stressful experience, in addition to consuming what is likely some hallucinogenic drug concoction every day for over a month. You're bound to feel confused and frightened. But you're back with us now, and we're not going to let you out of our sight for a long while. I've scheduled you to come in for a thorough examination the day after tomorrow. They'll do a full workup on you. I've also arranged some sessions with a colleague of mine who specializes in post-traumatic stress."

"By that time, hopefully we will have more information on exactly what that priest was giving you," added David. "By the way, Meiko, how was it that you were able to break the cycle, and how in the world did you meet up with Aiko? I never heard that part of the story."

"It all started with my blog. A lot of people responded to it, and I couldn't decide who was legitimate and who was just trying to use me. It's scary when you don't know who you are. I only had brief flashes of my memories, and I was never sure what was real or not." Meiko sipped her tea. She talked without looking at anyone, just staring at the table in front of her, as if in a trance.

"Then, Grandma started sending me photos and more information about me and my past. She sent pictures of us together when I was little, with Grandpa too. We communicated, and I told her about the priest, the omamori, and the tea. She told me that I needed to get rid of the omamori and to stop drinking whatever the priest was giving me. By that point, it had just become a ritual for me. I was drinking that tea morning, noon, and night. But once I stopped, it all started getting clearer, and things started making sense. But that was just before she came down and got me, right before we met up with you guys at the shrine." She paused and then started to gently sob.

"I don't know what I did to those men. I feel terrible, but I really don't remember much of anything. I think that I must have done some horrible things. I don't want to go to sleep because I'm afraid that I will have bad dreams and see their faces again and then maybe I won't wake up again, or I'll wake up and I won't know who I am. I'm so ashamed, and frightened."

"I know, I know, sweetheart," comforted Chieko, holding her tightly and rocking gently. "It's going to take time. You don't have anything to feel guilty about. You were a pawn in that monstrous priest's deranged game. I'll give you something to help you sleep through the night, nothing too strong. You'll need it for the next couple of nights."

"Aiko," exclaimed David, raising his teacup, "I have to offer a toast to you. If it weren't for your amateur detective skills, I'm not sure we ever would have found Meiko. We are all indebted to you. Kanpai!"

They all raised their cups and echoed David's toast in unison.

"It's probably time that we go to bed. We've all had a long couple of days," said Aiko as she got up from the table.

"I agree," said Chieko, standing up with Meiko. "I'll take Meiko to bed. She can sleep on the futon next to me."

"Good night, everyone, sleep tight," said David.

"*Oyasuminasai*," they all said and then headed off to their rooms.

CHAPTER 57
KYOTO

The shaman picked up her cell phone, which had just started ringing. She was sitting at the same table where she had met with David and Chieko. A stream of incense snaked its way upward filling the room with its pungent aroma.

"Yes," she replied calmly.

"Hello, this is Chieko Tokunaga, Meiko's mother."

"Of course, Tokunaga Sensei, have you found your daughter?" asked the shaman.

"Yes, we did. It turns out that one of the priests at Fushimi Inari Jinja was behind all of this," explained Chieko.

"I see," replied the shaman. "I'm not surprised that someone from Fushimi was serving as Nogitsune's tool. Is your daughter all right?"

"Well, obviously she's very distraught and confused about everything that's happened. She seems to be adjusting well, but we're going to do a complete psychological and physical workup on her, and I imagine that it will be several months before she's back to normal. Even then, she will live with this terrible experience for the rest of her life."

"I'm glad that you found her when you did. She's fortunate to have a strong support group around her," replied the shaman.

"Thank you," replied Chieko. "But I'm not sure what you meant about the priest serving as Nogitsune's tool. From what I know, he was obsessed with something that happened to his family over sixty years ago. He was clearly deranged and used drugs and hypnosis to control Meiko. I don't think Nogitsune had anything to do with it."

"Maybe not," agreed the shaman. "But can I ask if this priest had any relationship to anyone in your family, a cousin, grandparents, or anything like that?"

There was a pause before Chieko responded. "In fact, he was my mother's nephew. She didn't even know of his existence until a few days ago. His father and my mother were separated when they were very young children."

"Again, Tokunaga Sensei," said the shaman calmly, "I know that you look on my beliefs with extreme skepticism, and I don't blame you." Chieko started to interject, but the shaman continued. "But even a learned psychologist like yourself would have to agree that someone or something was guiding this man's actions and leading him to your daughter, a cousin he had never met before. The fact that he's a high priest at the largest Inari shrine in the world is certainly no coincidence."

"I agree that there are a lot of unanswered coincidences and strange connections here," replied Chieko. "I'm still not ready to attribute all of that to a malevolent spirit."

"I understand," replied the shaman, pouring another cup of tea from the small iron pot. "The important thing is that your daughter is back with you and out of the hands of that priest. Thank you for letting me know. You must have a lot of things on your mind right now, and you didn't have to make the call."

"You're welcome. I thought it was only right after how you helped my ex-husband and me."

"I wish I could have been of more assistance to you." The shaman paused before continuing. "I would recommend that you have the fox tattoo removed from your daughter soon."

The line went silent for a moment. "How did you know that Meiko has a fox tattoo?" asked Chieko.

"Oh, I was sure that she would have one. I told you that the first time we met," replied the shaman without hesitation.

"Yes, now I remember," sputtered Chieko. "That's a good idea. I can't imagine that she will want to have a permanent memory of this horrific experience with her forever." She also thought that her mother should have her tattoo removed as well.

"Indeed," agreed the shaman. "If there is any way I can be of assistance to you, please don't hesitate to contact me."

"I won't. Thank you again," said Chieko before ending the call.

The shaman set the phone on the table and sipped her tea slowly. It was only lukewarm and needed to be refreshed, but her mind was not on the tea. She closed her eyes and took a deep breath. *It's not the first time you've used a Shinto priest to assist you, is it Nogitsune? I'm sure it won't be the last either.*

She cupped her chin in her hand and stared vacantly out the small window toward the small garden just outside her house. There were a few stray cherry blossoms left on some of the trees, but most had fallen and covered the ground in soft, pink-white petals that had turned brown around the edges. At the center of the garden was a small granite shrine. At its base slept a stone statue of a baby fox curled up, it's tail wrapped around its head.

HISTORY OF

FOX POSSESSION IN JAPAN

Shinto is the oldest major religion in Japan and is unique to Japan. It is polytheistic, or druidic, in nature. The word *Shinto* means "way of the gods." Its followers believe in multiple gods, spirits, or divine powers typically associated with nature, such as wind, water, mountains, and rice. As mentioned in this story, Inari is believed to be the god of rice, fertility, sake, tea, and even prosperity. Japanese, as a language, doesn't differentiate between singular and plural; therefore, the word *kami* could indicate one god or many. It's ambiguous.

There is some disagreement among scholars regarding the origins of kitsune myths in Japan. Some contend that they go back to the fifth century BCE and were an indigenous Japanese concept. It's clear that Japanese regarded the fox positively as early as the fourth century CE. Japan, at that time, was an agrarian society, heavily focused on the cultivation of rice, which was introduced to Japan in the third century BCE from China and Korea. They viewed the fox as a beneficial animal because it helped keep down the rodent population and therefore protected both the rice fields as well as the harvested rice. It made a logical servant to a god focused on rice.

There are over eighty thousand Shinto shrines all over Japan, and almost three thousand of them are dedicated to the god Inari. Some Shinto shrines are large, such as the Meiji shrine in Tokyo or those in Nikko and Ise, while others are very small. Shinto is practiced by approximately 80 percent of Japanese, in some form, although very few identify themselves as Shintoists. In this story, I made it a point to refer to Shinto shrines versus Buddhist temples. The two are often difficult to distinguish from a distance, although the difference becomes apparent. It's akin to the difference between a Catholic church and a Jewish synagogue.

Inari shrines in Japan are filled with statues of foxes. It would be impossible to visit an Inari shrine and not see at least one fox statue. On the rear wall of almost every Inari shrine you will find a circular opening, about eight inches in diameter, one or two feet above the ground. It is often covered with a wooden plank that can be slid back and forth to open and close it. This opening is a foxhole, and if it is open, there will likely be offerings of tofu, rice with *azuki* (red) beans, or other food that foxes supposedly enjoy.

Inari Mountain, just outside of Kyoto, was the site of worship for centuries before the founding of the Fushimi Inari shrine in 711. This shrine is the parent shrine of all Inari shrines in Japan. It's a beautiful Shinto shrine, most famous for the thousands of bright vermillion torii that straddle a winding path up to the top of the mountain.

Most folklorists attribute the idea of the fox as seductress as something that came from China in the seventh and eighth centuries CE. In this belief system, there are two common classifications of kitsune. The *Zenko* (literally meaning "good fox") are benevolent, celestial foxes associated with the god Inari. Mischievous and malicious foxes are referred to as *Yako* or *Ninko* but are also called Nogitsune. These "wild foxes" do not serve Inari. In fact, these bad foxes are afraid of the good Inari foxes.

Kitsune are thought to be shapeshifters, possessing the ability to take on human form—after they turn one hundred years old. The most common forms assumed by the kitsune are beautiful women, young girls, and in some cases, elderly men. Some folklorists have pointed out that kitsune stories bear a striking resemblance to Old Man Coyote stories of Native Americans. Beliefs about the fox as a shapeshifter were so prevalent in medieval Japan, a woman alone, especially at dusk or at night, was assumed to be a fox. Interestingly, dogs can always see the true fox, whether that fox is in human form or not. For that reason, kitsune avoid and despise dogs.

Kitsunetsuki, or fox possession, always involves the possession of a young woman. There are no stories that I am aware of where a man is possessed by a fox spirit. Typically, the possessed woman tries to deceive, manipulate, and control the men around her. As in many other patriarchal societies, and especially in medieval times, women in Japan were often seen through the bane/benefactor duality. In other words, a woman was considered either a dangerous, manipulative femme fatale or a lady to be venerated and protected. As with shapeshifting foxes, if a fox possesses a woman, dogs will always see that possessed woman as a fox.

Girls who come from a "fox-possessed" family often find it hard to get married. In fact, just as in this story, entire families were ostracized by their communities after a member of the family was thought to be possessed. By the eleventh century, fox possession was considered a disease and continued to be so up until the early part of the twentieth century. Dementias and hallucinations were often ascribed to fox possession, just as they were ascribed to demonic possession in

Europe. Victims of kitsunetsuki often find themselves tired, exhausted, or ill for days or weeks after their rescue, often to the point of death.

I originally became interested in fox possession when I was studying at Waseda University in Tokyo, the same university where David was teaching. I was in the international division, and one of my professors had a PhD in anthropology, with a focus on folklore. He was American, but his wife was Japanese and came from one of the rural areas in the north of Japan. He said that she still had scars all the way down her back where they had placed burning hot stones when she was a teenager because they were convinced that she was possessed by an evil fox spirit. Consistent with demonic possession beliefs in other parts of the world, one of the ways of expelling the fox spirit was by creating pain for the flesh of the possessed individual. He told us this story in 1985, so this exorcism of sorts took place sometime during the early 1970s. I found it fascinating that such beliefs would continue so late into the twentieth century. He spent the better part of class sharing fox-related stories from around Japan.

I don't want the reader to think that there is currently widespread belief in the supernatural, shapeshifting, and spiritual-possessing nature of foxes. My wife is Japanese, and we have many Japanese friends. When I asked them about kitsunetsuki, when I started writing this book, none of them knew much about it. They knew what the word meant but weren't familiar with the specific folklore associated with foxes. Nonetheless, there is a rich tradition of fox-related folklore that has found itself into classical artworks, *noh* plays, and Japanese literature. As with most folklore anywhere in the world, this has more familiarity, and acceptance, in the countryside than in large cities like Tokyo or Kyoto.

I had two interesting experiences with foxes while writing this book. The first happened early on, during the time I was outlining the chapters and working through my very first draft. I was hitting golf balls at a driving range in Pittsburgh before playing an early-morning round at a course I've played at least twenty-five times. We had a very early tee time, so we were on the range before 7:00 a.m. There was still a little early morning mist and dew on the grass. It was a beautiful late-summer morning in Western Pennsylvania. As I was hitting balls, I noticed a strange animal slowly walking across the range, probably two hundred yards off. At first, I thought it was a racoon or a very young coyote. I pointed it out to my playing partner. He walked to our cart and took out his range finder, and we zoomed in on the animal. Being a native of Pittsburgh and more familiar with the local species, he quickly identified it as a fox. I looked through the finder, and sure enough, it was a small, reddish-brown fox. In my entire life, I'd never seen a fox outside of a zoo. I've never seen a fox on any golf course I've played, before or since. I told my playing partner about the book I was writing and how strange it was to spot a real fox. I didn't think much of it, but it was certainly a bit eerie.

The second experience happened in Tokyo after I had finished the second draft of the book. My wife and I were in Ginza waiting for our seat at Takechan, the same restaurant where David and Meiko ate in chapter four. Ginza has some of the most expensive real estate in the world, but it's also filled with some wonderful little shops, bars, and restaurants. It's a very nice place to walk around and kill time.

I didn't want to walk very far because they were likely to call our name shortly, and I was pretty sure that they would only call it once before moving on to someone else in the queue. Within two blocks of the restaurant, on the same street, was a tiny Inari shrine recessed into the wall of a building. I describe it in detail in chapter four. In all my time accompanying my wife back to her home country, almost yearly for thirty years, I had never run into such a little Inari shrine, complete with a small fox statue. The fact that it was so close to where I was going to eat, a place I'd never before been, felt like way more than just a coincidence. Who knows. The most likely explanation is that I was much more attuned to everything related to foxes while I was writing the book. That would certainly be Chieko's explanation.

ACKNOWLEDGMENTS

While writing itself is a solitary process, getting a book published requires the work of a host of dedicated and skilled professionals. I'd like to thank my editor, Diane O'Connell—no relation—who has worked closely with me for almost ten years. Her discerning eye and great insights have helped me understand, appreciate, and hopefully develop in the craft of writing. Kristin Thiel served as copy and line editor and her attention to detail and suggestions greatly helped in shaping the final version of this book. Vinnie Kinsella took charge of the interior design, and also helped me better understand the ins-and-outs of the publishing process. Kathi Dunn, as she did with my previous novel, came up with an engaging and elegant cover design. Finally, my greatest supporter and most respected critic remains my wife Mari. I wouldn't be the writer, and more importantly the person that I am, without her.

I hope that you enjoyed this book. As an author, I try and write books that I would like to read. If you liked it as well, then I ask you to go to Amazon and/or Goodreads and rate it. You can write a lot, a little, or nothing at all. But ratings drive book sales, and I would certainly appreciate your support.

If you're interested in learning a bit more about me or my other novels—there's only one right now, The Painter of Time—or what is in the works, then please visit my website: www.matthewoconnellauthor.com. Also, feel free to drop me an email and let me know what you think: drmatt92131@gmail.com. I will respond.

Thanks again!

Matt

Made in the USA
San Bernardino, CA
08 March 2019